Praise for the n

"Sherryl Woods writes e...
about family, friendship a...
reads!"
—#1 Ne... ...mes bestselling author
Debbie Macomber

"During the course of this gripping, emotionally
wrenching but satisfying tale, Woods deftly and
realistically handles such issues as survival guilt,
drug abuse as adolescent rebellion, and family dynamics
when a vital member is suddenly gone."
—*Booklist* on *Flamingo Diner*

"Woods is a master heartstring puller."
—*Publishers Weekly* on *Seaview Inn*

"Once again, Woods, with such authenticity, weaves a
tale of true love and the challenges that can knock up
against that love."
—*RT Book Reviews* on *Beach Lane*

"Woods...is noted for appealing character-driven stories
that are often infused with the flavor and fragrance of the
South."
—*Library Journal*

"A reunion story punctuated by family drama, Woods's
first novel in her new Ocean Breeze series is touching,
tense and tantalizing."
—*RT Book Reviews* on *Sand Castle Bay*

"A whimsical, sweet scenario...the digressions have their
own charm, and Woods never fails to come back to the
romantic point."
—*Publishers Weekly* on *Sweet Tea at Sunrise*

SHERRYL WOODS

Where Azaleas Bloom

mira

Recycling programs for this product may not exist in your area.

ISBN-13: 978-0-7783-8607-0

Where Azaleas Bloom

First published in 2012. This edition published in 2022.

Copyright © 2012 by Sherryl Woods

All rights reserved. No part of this book may be used or reproduced in any manner whatsoever without written permission except in the case of brief quotations embodied in critical articles and reviews.

This is a work of fiction. Names, characters, places and incidents are either the product of the author's imagination or are used fictitiously. Any resemblance to actual persons, living or dead, businesses, companies, events or locales is entirely coincidental.

For questions and comments about the quality of this book, please contact us at CustomerService@Harlequin.com.

Mira
22 Adelaide St. West, 41st Floor
Toronto, Ontario M5H 4E3, Canada
www.Harlequin.com

Printed in U.S.A.

Dear Friends,

So many people have been hit by hard economic times in recent years, but I've been particularly touched by women whose dire financial situation has been tied to a divorce. I wanted to write about one woman's determination to get her family back on solid ground… and the hero who's just as determined to stand by her. That theme, I thought, made a perfect Sweet Magnolias story, an example of the difficult periods in life when good friends can make all the difference.

Where Azaleas Bloom focuses on Lynn Morrow, neighbor to Carter and Raylene. So many of you have asked to read more about them and how they're doing since their marriage. It was a great way to put them front and center again, too. As books often do for me, this one took a surprising twist at the end—a twist that only adds to the complications faced by this struggling single mom.

I hope you'll be rooting for Lynn and her kids and that you'll fall just a little bit in love with Mitch Franklin, a man wise enough to let her find her own way, but strong enough to be there if she falters. Observant readers will remember that Mitch appeared in the very first Sweet Magnolias book, *Stealing Home*. He's the contractor who built The Corner Spa.

I hope you enjoy this wrap-up to the latest trilogy and that you enjoy the latest season of *Sweet Magnolias* on Netflix. There's plenty more to discover with *The Sweet Magnolias Cookbook*, in stores now.

All best,

Sherryl Woods

Where Azaleas Bloom

One

Lynn Morrow was at her wit's end. Her tiny desk tucked into a corner of the kitchen was piled high with bills and her checkbook balance was a stunningly low $24.35. Not since college had she seen such a scary balance.

The refrigerator held a half-empty carton of milk, five eggs and some rapidly wilting lettuce. There was a can of diced tomatoes in the cupboard, along with a box of spaghetti, a few spoonfuls of peanut butter left in a jar and maybe a bowlful of Cheerios in the bottom of the box. That, too, reminded her of college. But it was one thing to scrape by at nineteen, and quite another to try to do it in her forties with kids to care for.

"Mom, I'm starving," Jeremy announced when he walked in the door from school. It was the standard cry of her ten-year-old. "What can I have for a snack?"

Lexie, who was right on his heels, took one look at her mother, apparently interpreted her dire expression for the near-panic Lynn was feeling, and turned on her brother. "You don't need food. You need sensitivity training."

Tears sprang to Lynn's eyes as Jeremy bolted from the room. Lately, Alexis, who was only fourteen, had spent way too much time trying to protect her mother. Ever since the divorce proceedings had been initiated, Lynn had been struggling to make ends meet. She and Ed were still in court wrangling over everything from custody of the kids to support. The temporary order in place barely kept her and the kids above water and, by the end of the month, she was scraping bottom financially, even with the part-time job she'd managed to find at her neighbor Raylene's boutique on Serenity's Main Street.

One of these days she supposed she'd thank Ed for providing this unexpected life challenge, but she really, really wasn't there yet. She was spitting mad, not because he'd left, but because of the upheaval he'd left in his wake.

She'd worked hard to keep her worries from spilling over onto the kids, but Lexie was a smart girl. She'd quickly figured out what was going on. Sometimes her overnight transformation from carefree teen into world-weary adult nearly broke Lynn's heart. Lexie should be paying attention to her grades, maybe having her first crush on a boy, not trying to be her mother's savior.

Now, with her brother gone in an indignant huff, Lexie came over to give Lynn a hug. She seemed to know instinctively just when Lynn was in desperate need of one.

"Dad's late with the check again, isn't he? How bad is it?" Lexie asked.

Lynn tried to reassure her. "We're going to be fine, sweetie. I don't want you to worry about this."

"We're not going to be *fine*," Lexie retorted angrily. "How did Dad turn out to be such a huge jerk?"

Lynn wondered about the same thing, but somehow Ed had turned into a man she didn't even recognize any longer. He'd taken his midlife crisis to new heights. He was self-absorbed, self-indulgent and thoughtless.

His family might not have enough money to put food on the table, but she'd overheard a conversation two days ago when it was mentioned that he was off on some expensive golf vacation, his third in the past six months. The wife of one of his business associates apparently hadn't realized Lynn was nearby when she'd made her remarks about Ed's latest spending spree. Or perhaps she had, Lynn thought cynically.

"Don't talk about your father that way," she admonished Lexie now, albeit halfheartedly. She didn't want her children to start hating their father, but she wasn't quite prepared to sing his praises, either. Every single day felt like a balancing act between her own ragged emotions and her children's needs. No matter how upbeat she pretended to be, lately it seemed she wasn't fooling anyone.

Lexie's eyes filled with tears, though it was impossible to tell if she was reacting to Lynn's stern admonition or to her own panic. "It's really bad, isn't it?"

"Bad enough," Lynn admitted carefully. She gave Lexie's hand a squeeze. "But this is a temporary blip, sweetheart. It will get sorted out. I promise."

"Are we going to have to move?" Lexie asked, giving voice to what was obviously her greatest fear.

Lynn wasn't one to sugarcoat bad news, though she'd hoped to have a plan in place before revealing the sad truth. "More than likely," she said quietly.

Though she'd been counting on Helen Decatur-Whitney, who was fierce when it came to getting the best possible settlement for her clients, she also knew that even Helen couldn't work miracles. Still, she tried to reassure her daughter. "Hopefully, Helen will be able to work this out in court before it comes to that, but I won't lie to you—giving up the house is a real possibility."

"But I love it here," Lexie protested with a sniff. "It's a great house and my best friend lives right next door." Then, apparently seeing something in Lynn's face, she squared her shoulders. "But it'll be okay." She gave her mother a plaintive look that nearly shredded what was left of Lynn's heart. "Won't it?"

"As long as you, Jeremy and I are together, it will be okay," she vowed.

She would do everything in her power to see that it was. Right now, though, with unpaid bills and little money, she was feeling pretty darn powerless. For a woman who'd always felt confident and in control, that was a new sensation, one she didn't much like. Just one more thing to lay at Ed's feet when she was doling out blame.

Contractor Mitch Franklin had been working on a new addition for Raylene and Carter Rollins for a few weeks now. He'd started in late fall, taken only a brief break during the holidays, and was hoping to have every interior detail finished for them in time for the annual Memorial Day party the couple hosted for all their friends. Normally, winters in Serenity tended to be mild with only a few days when the weather was too bad for construction, but this year had been a nasty exception with bitter cold and more snow and ice storms than he could remember in a lifetime here in South Carolina. While the snow and ice seldom lasted, he was still further behind schedule than he liked.

With various other jobs he was finishing up—mostly interior work—Mitch was proud that he'd kept his crew working enough to put paychecks in their pockets. Now, though, the crunch was on to get this addition built. To keep costs in check he had his men working the usual number of hours, but he'd gotten into the habit of putting in a lot of overtime. He had a reputation for bringing his jobs in on time and he didn't want this to be an exception.

Of course, there were other things motivating him, as well. For one thing, Raylene was an amazing cook, who usually invited him to join the family for a meal if he was still hanging around at dinnertime. For another, his home felt way too empty without his wife, who'd been killed by a drunk driver a year ago. It had been bad enough with his two boys away at school, but with Amy gone, too, he could barely stand to be in his house even to sleep. The bed he'd shared with his wife for twenty-two years was way too cold and lonely.

His sons were exactly where they needed to be, in college and living their lives, but he was at loose ends way more than he liked. Raylene, Carter and Carter's younger sisters were filling a huge, gaping hole in Mitch's life. He suspected that Raylene understood that.

He looked up when Raylene wandered into the midst of what would eventually be a new family room with soaring windows and a spectacular stonework fireplace.

"Thought I told you not to come in here without a hard hat," he scolded pointlessly. To his everlasting dismay, she did whatever she liked. She'd been that way as far back as he could remember, though it seemed she'd gone a little crazy now that she'd recovered from her agoraphobia and was getting out of the house and around town again. Seemed to him that she'd gotten a little reckless.

"I can't help sneaking in every chance I get," she said, looking around, her expression filled with delight. "You're making such incredible progress, Mitch, and it really is going to be amazing. I usually don't like to rush the seasons, but I can hardly wait for Memorial Day to have everyone over."

Mitch wasn't used to people who threw parties at the drop of a hat, but he'd noticed that Raylene and her husband, Police Chief Carter Rollins, and their friends looked for any excuse to get together.

"You talking about that Sweet Magnolia crew you hang out with?" he asked. "Didn't you have them all poking around in here right before the holidays, some kind of celebration when that bullying situation at the high school was resolved?"

"What can I say? That seems like eons ago and we're a curious bunch. Maybe it's time I invite them over for another sneak peek. They couldn't really tell what was happening back then. Mostly it was a demolition mess with the new building materials piled everywhere. Just look at it now! You can already tell how fantastic it's going to be."

He frowned at her. "Promise me you won't have them poking around in here until I give the word that it's safe," he insisted, knowing he was probably wasting his breath. "Even if my guys are off the job, there are things people can trip over or send crashing down on someone's head. And the electrician still has some work left to do."

She laughed. "I was just teasing you. I know how you hate people tramping all over your work site, myself included."

"Then why do you do it? Just to annoy me?"

"Nope. I figure it's really *my* work site, so I get special privileges."

He shook his head. "Know who you sound like? Maddie Maddox. I swear that woman almost gave me a heart attack when we were doing the renovations for The Corner Spa." He glanced at Raylene. "You knew we did those, right?"

"Of course. Maddie recommended you."

"Well, she insisted on sitting right there, practically in

the middle of the chaos, the whole time we were working. Said she had things to get done. I have no idea how she could think, much less work with all that hammering and whatnot going on. It makes me a little crazy, and I'm used to it."

"When Maddie's motivated, I suspect there's not much that can deter her," Raylene said.

"She's a real pistol, all right," Mitch said, a grudging note of respect in his voice. "Truth is, I thought working for the three of them—her, Helen and Dana Sue—would be a nightmare. Whoever heard of three women agreeing on anything? Boy, was I wrong! Maddie knew what she wanted, and the other two left her to it. Never before knew Helen to let someone else take charge like that."

"They're a great team," Raylene agreed. "They inspire me, and they're the best friends in the world."

"Friends are important, all right," Mitch said. "I should have done a better job of keeping in touch with mine. With Amy gone and the boys away, I really regret that. I don't much like hanging out with my crew. It blurs the lines, if you know what I mean. Still, they've been there to back me up since Amy was killed. There are good people in this town."

"There are," Raylene agreed. "And it's never too late to restore old friendships or to make new ones. I cut Annie Townsend and Sarah McDonald out of my life for way too long, but look at us now. We're thick as thieves again. That's one of the best things about moving back home to Serenity." She grinned. "That and marrying Carter, of course."

"Of course," he said dryly, knowing perfectly well that those two couldn't seem to keep their hands to themselves.

She gave him a sly look. "You'd be a great catch for some woman, you know."

"Don't go getting any ideas about matchmaking, you hear? Enough of that goes on in this town. Grace Wharton has made my social life her personal mission. I can't walk in the door at Wharton's without her dragging one woman or another over to meet me."

"And not a one of them has interested you?"

"Not so far," he declared. "Can't see that changing, either." Unable to keep a nostalgic note from his voice, he added, "Once a man has a woman like Amy in his life, he's not likely to get that lucky again."

Clearly undeterred, Raylene said, "Well, I'm just saying you're a good-looking man. You have a few other appealing traits I've noticed, as well." Grinning impudently, she gave him a thoroughly disconcerting once-over.

Mitch felt his cheeks heat at the compliment and the blatant survey. He'd been happily married every one of the twenty-two years he'd had with Amy. Before they'd met, he'd had quite a roving eye, but he could honestly say that once he'd said *I do,* that had been it for him. She'd been his whole world.

At forty-three now, he knew there was every chance some woman would eventually come along, but right now he wasn't interested. The way he saw it, people grieved in their own ways, and his had been to bury himself in work even more so than he always had.

Raylene regarded him with amusement. "Okay, if I promise to stop bugging you about dating, will you stay for dinner? The girls asked for lasagna today. There's plenty."

Tempted as he was, Mitch asked worriedly, "What does Carter think about having me at his dinner table just about every night?"

"He thinks it means you'll finish this addition that much faster," she said. "Please, stay. You're part of the family now. And you know perfectly well that I love cooking for a crowd."

"And you know that I can't say no to your lasagna," he said, giving in a little too easily. "Thanks, Raylene."

When they eventually sat down at the large dining room table, he noticed that he wasn't the only guest. Lexie Morrow from next door seemed to be almost as much of a fixture at the table as he was. Tonight she, her brother and her mother were there.

Mitch couldn't help taking a frank survey of Lynn. Her complexion was even paler than usual, and there was no mistaking the worry in her eyes. He'd known her practically since grade school, had a brief, though intense, unrequited crush on her in seventh grade, but it had been all about Ed for her, even back then. Over the years they'd both moved on, and rarely saw each other except in passing.

"Everything okay, Lynn?" he asked quietly, leaning in close so the others at the table wouldn't overhear.

She smiled, but it looked forced to him. He remembered how her carefree laughter had once reminded him of the joyous sound of church bells pealing. He hadn't heard that sound in a long time. Looked to him as if she didn't have much to laugh about these days, not with the divorce he'd heard about still pending.

"Everything's fine," she said, but despite her effort, the lie didn't sound convincing.

Mitch glanced around the table and noted that both Lexie and Jeremy were eating as if they hadn't had a meal in days. Thinking again about the toll divorce could take, he wondered just how tough times were for Lynn. He'd heard plenty of rumors about her husband taking off every few weeks on various trips and wondered if that was having an impact on Lynn's finances. Just the thought of the man gallivanting around while his family suffered was enough to twist Mitch's stomach into knots. He told himself he'd have felt the same way even if he didn't have a few fond memories of the woman.

Then, again, maybe just because of those memories, he was seeing trouble where there was none. Wouldn't be the first time his imagination had run wild. He seemed to be the kind of man who was always looking for someone to help.

After dinner he lingered until the Morrows were ready to head home, then walked out with them. It was pitch-dark outside and there was no light burning at home.

"Why don't I walk up the path with you?" he suggested. "It's pretty dark out here."

"Oh, I just forgot to leave on the outside light," Lynn said, but the embarrassed nervousness in her voice suggested otherwise. "I think it's burned out anyway."

"Let me check it for you," Mitch offered.

"That's okay. I know I'm out of spare bulbs. They're on the shopping list, but I keep forgetting them."

He heard the claim for what it was, another face-saving lie.

"No problem. I always have extras in the truck." He walked over and grabbed one out of the back before she could object, then crossed the yard. "If you're going to be out at night, you'll need this," he said as he quickly removed the old bulb and screwed in the replacement. "Even in Serenity, it's important to take safety precautions."

"I know," Lynn said. Then, as if it were costing her considerable pride, she managed to mutter, "Thanks."

"Not a problem. If you ever need anything done around

here, let me know. For the next couple of months or so, I'll be at Raylene's every day. I'd be happy to help out. No charge, of course. Just a neighborly gesture between old friends."

Lynn gave him a wan smile. "I appreciate that, but we're managing okay."

Mitch understood pride all too well. He merely nodded. "Well, the offer's on the table, if anything comes up. Don't hesitate, okay?"

"Thanks. Good night, Mitch." She hesitated, then added, "I know I should have let you know when the accident happened, but I was real sorry to hear about Amy. Losing her must have been hard for you and your sons."

He nodded. "She was a good woman. Not a day goes by that I don't miss her. It's been a year now, and I still walk in the house some nights and call out to her." He shrugged. "They say that will pass."

She touched his arm briefly. "*They,* whoever they are, say a lot of things, but I think it's mostly because they don't want to say that loss of any kind really sucks."

"Yeah," he admitted, "it really does. Good night, Lynn."

The kids had gone inside right away and now she hurried after them. Mitch stood where he was, staring after her.

Something wasn't right here. Anyone could see that. But he understood the need to reclaim independence after a blow. He also knew that it was a woman's natural tendency to protect her kids at all costs. If Lynn needed help badly enough for their sake, she'd turn to anyone who offered a helping hand. And if she ever asked, he'd be right there. Somebody needed to fix the unmistakable sorrow and fear that never seemed to leave her eyes.

And he, more than he'd realized, needed a project. Maybe, he thought, they might actually need each other.

"Raylene's lasagna is the best," Jeremy murmured sleepily when Lynn went to check on him before bed. "How come you don't cook like that anymore?"

"There's not enough time in the day," Lynn told him.

"But Raylene works, too, and she does it," he persisted.

She knew her ten-year-old couldn't possibly understand how uncomfortable this entire conversation was making her, but it was hard to resist the desire to snap. "Tell me what you miss most and I'll make it for you soon," she promised.

"Steak and baked potatoes," he said at once. "That was Dad's favorite, too."

And way beyond their current budget, Lynn thought wearily. Somehow, though, she would make it happen.

"I'll see what I can do."

"Tomorrow?" he pressed excitedly.

"Not tomorrow, but soon," she said firmly, sighing at the unmistakable disappointment in his eyes. "Now go to sleep. You have school in the morning. Did you study for your history test?"

He gave her a shrug. "Enough."

Which meant, she feared, not at all. Why hadn't she sat down with him immediately after dinner and gone over the information with him the way she used to?

Because she'd been trying to figure out how to make that paltry $24.35 last another week, she thought angrily, while her soon-to-be ex was off dining on steak himself, no doubt.

"I'm getting you up a half hour early," she told Jeremy. "We'll go over the material together."

"Mom!" he muttered with a dramatic groan.

"And don't even think about faking a stomachache or a sore throat or an earache, you hear me?" She leaned down and gave him a noisy kiss that had him giggling, despite the required protest that he was too old for such displays of affection.

Leaving her son, she tapped on Lexie's door. "Still studying?"

To her dismay, Lexie looked up from the book she'd apparently been pretending to read, her cheeks streaked with tears. "I miss Daddy," she whispered. "I'm sorry, but I do."

Lynn sat down beside her on the bed and gathered her into her arms. "You don't ever have to be sorry about missing your father," she assured her.

"But it must make you sad when I say that," Lexie said knowingly. "I know how hard you're trying to make everything seem normal."

Lynn managed a smile for her daughter. She sometimes wondered if faking a smile would get easier with practice, but so far it hadn't.

"I think it's obvious that things aren't normal and no amount of pretending is going to change that." She tucked a finger under Lexie's chin. "Now look at me. You love your dad and, despite what's happened between the two of us, I know he loves you. I will never stand in the way of that."

"Then how come he hasn't been around for so long?"

Lynn sighed. "I wish I could explain your father's actions, but I can't. Maybe he's been extra busy at work."

"I tried his cell phone, but it went to voice mail, and Noelle in his office said he's away," Lexie said, proving that she'd gone as close to the source as she could get for answers. "She sounded kinda funny when I called, so I don't think it's on business. Do you know where he went?"

Lynn didn't want to explain about the golf trip to Lexie. Lexie was feeling unimportant enough as it was. Besides, Lynn didn't know for sure. Rumors were always rampant in Serenity. Only some of them proved to be true.

"Not really," she told her daughter, whose tears were finally drying up, though the stricken expression on her face was still there. "Why don't I see what I can find out tomorrow, so you'll know when he's due home. Will that help?"

Lexie nodded. "You know what I don't get? How can I still miss him so much, when I'm so mad at him?"

Lynn allowed herself a small and this time genuine smile at the very complex question. Hadn't she wondered the exact same thing herself more than once? As furious as she was at Ed most of the time these days, there were moments when the thought of never having his arms around her again made her want to weep.

"Relationships are complicated, sweetie. Love doesn't go away just because someone's done something to disappoint you. You know how mad I get when Jeremy drinks milk right out of the carton or when you leave damp towels all over the bathroom floor?" She tickled Lexie. "I still love you."

"Or what about when you tell me ten times to clean up my room?" Lexie asked, getting into the spirit of the teasing. "I get annoyed, but I still love *you*."

"Or when you deliberately disobey me no matter how many times I tell you you're not allowed to have a snack right before dinner?" Lynn said.

Unfortunately, that one caused Lexie's grin to fade. "Like there's anything here to have for a snack these days."

Once again, Lynn felt the weight of every bit of unanticipated fallout from the divorce. There were the huge things, like Ed not being around when the kids needed him or the mortgage payments being late again and again. And there were the seemingly trivial ones like this, no after-school snacks. Added together she felt as if she'd failed her kids. No matter how much she wanted to lay all the blame squarely at Ed's feet, she couldn't. She was their mom. She should be finding a way to provide for her children. Going to work for Raylene had been a start, but it obviously wasn't enough, not when Ed wasn't holding up his end of the bargain.

She vowed right then to take on a second job, even if it meant frying burgers at one of the new fast-food restaurants outside of town, anything to put an end to the dismay of seeing her children suffer because of decisions she and Ed had made.

"I'm sorry," Lexie whispered. "I shouldn't have said that. It was mean."

"It was the truth," Lynn said, then added with determination, "but not for long."

Lexie regarded her hopefully. "What are you going to do?"

"I'll find a better job, one with more hours. Or another part-time job," Lynn said.

"Maybe I could get some babysitting jobs," Lexie offered eagerly.

"I appreciate your wanting to do that, but I'd like you to be a little older before you take on that kind of responsibility," Lynn said. "Right now your job is to get great grades so you can get into whatever college you'd like to go to. I want you and Jeremy to have the most amazing futures you can possibly have, and you'll need college degrees for that."

"You always say that," Lexie protested, as yet unconcerned about the importance of winning a scholarship if she expected to get into a terrific school. She was focused on the here and now. "Lots of kids my age babysit. You let me stay with Jeremy."

"He's ten and he's your brother," Lynn reminded her. "It's not quite the same thing as taking care of a baby or a toddler."

"What if I took the babysitting certification class at the community center? Then could I?" She gave Lynn a pleading look. "Please. I want to help out."

"If you do that and pass the course, then we'll see. But this will be for your savings and your spending money, okay? It's not up to you to chip in for expenses around here."

Lexie threw her arms around Lynn. "Thank you, thank you, thank you! I'll sign up tomorrow. I already know lots of people who need babysitters. The minute I pass the class, I'm going to hand out flyers."

Lynn smiled at her enthusiasm, wishing she could muster up that same level of excitement for her own job hunt. "Okay, my little entrepreneur. For now get some sleep. Love you."

"Love you, Mom."

Lynn turned out the light on her way out the door, but the second she was gone, Lexie flipped it back on. Lynn smiled, knowing exactly what she was up to. She was texting Mandy the big news about taking that babysitting course. She was probably hoping to get her best friend to sign up, too.

Which Mandy would likely do, Lynn thought. Those two never did anything without the other one tagging along. It was just one more reason she intended to do everything she possibly could to stay right here in this house, so her daughter wouldn't be ripped away from the friend who'd provided the best support system a girl Lexie's age could possibly have.

Two

Mitch had gotten into the habit of stopping in at Wharton's for breakfast, something he'd never have considered when Amy was alive. She'd always made sure he left the house with a hearty meal to sustain him through the morning. Now Grace Wharton looked over him just as protectively, but her efforts always came with a heavy dose of meddling.

"You're working too much," she declared as she set a steaming cup of coffee down in front of him.

"And how would you know that?"

"You're in here practically before I can get the coffee brewed in the morning and I know for a fact you're over there hammering away at Raylene and Carter's till they kick you out at night. Now, since I know you wouldn't be looking twice at a married woman, what's the attraction? You wouldn't be thinking of trying to rekindle something with Lynn Morrow, now that she and Ed are divorcing, would you?"

Mitch blinked at the way she'd cut right to the heart of the matter before he'd even had a chance to consider such a thing himself. "What's to rekindle?" he asked, hoping to throw her off stride. Not that a full-speed train heading in her direction would cause Grace to falter once she was on a mission. "Lynn and I were never an item."

Since Wharton's wasn't yet busy because, as she'd noted, it was barely past dawn, Grace settled down opposite him in the booth and gave him one of her don't-fool-with-me looks. "You must think my memory's bad, Mitch. I can recall perfectly well the way you trailed around after her back in middle school with that lovesick expression written all over your face. If she came in here for a soda or a milk shake with her friends, you were never far behind with that adoring look about you."

He winced at the probably accurate description. "Was I that pitiful?"

"Not pitiful," she soothed. "Just a boy suffering from his first unrequited love, as near as I could tell."

"Well, if you knew it was unrequited, then you also know there's nothing to be rekindled. Besides, I rarely catch a glimpse of Lynn while I'm working over at Raylene's."

"Sometimes it doesn't take more than a glimpse to know when a possibility's intriguing," she said. "Seems to me she could use a steady man like you in her life. Ed Morrow wasn't exactly a prize, and if I didn't think much of him before, I think even less of him now." There was a weight behind her words that suggested she'd heard things that maybe others didn't know. There were, despite what everyone in town thought, things not even Grace would share with the world, not if she felt somebody stood to be hurt by the talk.

She looked Mitch directly in the eye. "And you already know what I think about it being time for you to move on."

He laughed. "Grace, you probably know a lot more

about romance than I ever did, but it seems to me that being steady almost never sends a woman's pulse scrambling."

"It does when she's been dealing with a man like Ed. And you know exactly what I mean, a man with a broken moral compass," Grace replied firmly. "Trust me on that. I hear things."

Mitch nodded. "More than you need to, I suspect," he said wryly. "And I'll keep your advice in mind should something change. Now, do you suppose I could get my eggs, ham and grits?"

"You'll get oatmeal on a chilly morning like this," she countered, then gave him a wink. "Then we'll see about the rest."

"How on earth do you keep customers coming in here if you boss 'em around like this?"

"What can I say? I have a charming personality," she said. "And I always have the best gossip in town."

That, to his dismay, was all too true. "Just as long as I'm not your hot topic for today, I'll put up with the oatmeal," he called after her.

"Why would I talk about you? So far, you haven't done a single outrageous thing," she called back, then added, "more's the pity."

Trying to imagine what would happen if he did break any of the hard and fast rules he'd lived by since Amy's death, Mitch prayed for the fortitude to keep it that way. As much as he loved Grace's sass and vinegar, he wasn't quite ready to be on the menu right along with the tuna melt.

Satisfied that she'd grilled Jeremy sufficiently to eke out a passing grade on his history test, Lynn sent him off to school, then walked into town. Outside Wharton's, she grabbed the local weekly, then went in for a cup of coffee she intended to nurse as long as possible. Grace gave frequent refills, so it was usually enough caffeine to get Lynn through the day.

"Well, well, look who's here," Grace said loudly as she entered.

Only then did Lynn notice Mitch sitting by himself in a booth just inside the door. He gave her what looked like a nervous smile, then gestured to the table. "Join me?" he asked with apparent sincerity.

"Are you sure? You look as if you've finished. Don't you need to be over at Raylene's soon?"

"The crew knows what to do if they get there before I do," he assured her. "Coffee?"

"Yes," she said eagerly even as Grace arrived with a cup and filled it to the brim, then refilled Mitch's, a smirk on her face.

Lynn watched her walk away. "Was she smirking?"

Mitch sighed. "She was. Trust me, you don't want to know why. How about something to eat? My treat."

"No, thanks," she said, though she couldn't help gazing longingly at a plate of French toast as Grace carried it by.

"When was the last time you had Grace's French toast?" Mitch asked with a knowing grin.

"A while," she admitted. "But seriously, I'm not hungry."

"Nobody looks at food the way you just did unless it's a real temptation," Mitch said, then called out to Grace. "An order of French toast, Grace, and put it on my tab."

"Done," she called back.

Lynn regarded him with dismay. "You really didn't have to do that."

"I wanted to. Having someone besides Grace to talk to while I finish my second cup of coffee is a real treat."

"I heard that," Grace said as she passed by. She gave Lynn a wink. "The man has the hots for me, and don't think I don't know it. So does Neville, but my husband claims he's past caring what I do as long as I quit bothering him."

Lynn laughed, noting the pained expression on Mitch's face. "You know she wouldn't tease you like that if she didn't adore you."

"I know." He leaned across the table and confided, "The woman scares the daylights out of me. If she has her way, she'll marry me off before the summer's over. You probably want to run for your life."

Once again, Lynn couldn't control a chuckle. "I think you're tougher than that."

He gave her a look then that she couldn't quite interpret.

"I used to think so, too," he said, his voice suddenly sober.

Before she could try to figure out what he'd meant by that, Grace put a plate of thick, golden French toast in front of her, along with a pitcher of warm maple syrup, butter and a shaker of cinnamon and sugar.

"I wasn't sure which way you liked it," Grace said. "Me, I like the syrup, but a lot of folks prefer the cinnamon."

"I like it drowning in butter and syrup," Lynn admitted. She spread butter over the slices, doused them in syrup, then tried the first mouthful. "Oh, my God," she murmured, drawing a smile from Mitch. "What?"

"I remember that look," he said. "You used to get the same expression on your face at Rosalina's when you'd take your first bite of pizza."

"As if I'd died and gone to heaven?" she said. "No doubt about it. When it comes to certain foods, it's as if they speak to some part of my soul."

"So, pizza and French toast do that?" he asked, clearly amused. "What else?"

"Chocolate decadence cake," she said readily. "Almost better than sex." The second the words left her mouth, she felt herself blushing furiously. "Sorry. I probably shouldn't have said that."

He laughed. "I don't see why not, if it's true. I'll have to remember your very high opinion of those things. Now tell me what you're doing in here so early."

She tapped the newspaper she'd set on the table. "Looking for another job."

Mitch frowned. "I thought you were working for Raylene."

"Only part-time. I need more hours."

"But what about the kids?" he asked, then waved off the question. "Sorry, none of my business. I guess I just assumed Ed would be paying support."

"He is," she said quickly.

Mitch held her gaze. "But? I know I heard a *but* in your voice just then."

"Nothing. It doesn't matter."

"Is he late with a check or something?"

Lynn squirmed. "Mitch, I'm really not comfortable talking about this." She didn't want everyone in town speculating about Ed and the way he was behaving. Not that they weren't already, but she didn't want to confirm or add to the talk.

Mitch clearly wasn't going to back down, though. His expression filled with concern, he pressed, "I thought we were old friends. If there's a problem, maybe I can help."

"It's sweet of you to offer, it really is, but this will work out," she insisted. "And it's not going to kill me to work a few more hours every week. It won't hurt the kids, either," she added defensively.

"I know you're a great mother, Lynn," he replied patiently. "I wasn't suggesting otherwise. I see enough of Jeremy and Lexie over at Raylene's to see how well they're turning out, and I know they have you to thank for that."

She drank in his praise. She'd heard far too little of it from her soon-to-be ex-husband. "Thank you for saying that. They're great kids. I worry myself sick sometimes about how the divorce is affecting them. Lexie's growing up too fast, that's for sure. She's a sensitive girl and no matter how hard I try to keep my problems from her, she picks up on everything."

"She looks just fine to me," Mitch consoled her. "You should hear her and Mandy over at Raylene's. I can hear them giggling over the sound of all the hammering and, even more impressive, over that music they play. She sounds like a happy, healthy teenager to me."

"I wish I'd heard that," Lynn said wistfully. "She and Mandy don't hang out at our house much these days."

"Could be she feels guilty about having fun when she knows you're sad," Mitch said, surprising her with his insightfulness. "Kids are like that. Those first months after Amy died, mine did plenty of tiptoeing around whenever they came home on visits. Surprised the heck out of me. I didn't think either one of those boys had a sensitive bone in their bodies, but they were raised by Amy, so of course they did."

She saw the faraway look in his eyes and responded to that. "There's no mistaking how much you loved her, Mitch," she said gently. As hard as the divorce proceedings were, she knew it was nothing like losing someone you loved so deeply with such finality.

"Always will, I imagine," he said. "But every day does get a little easier."

He seemed to snap himself back to the moment. "Now I'd better get over to Raylene's or she'll be wondering what happened to me. She always has some kind of checklist for me before she goes off to work." He leaned closer and confided, "Don't tell her, but I stuff 'em in my pocket and never look at 'em again."

"Is that because you really don't give a hoot about what she wants or because you have a photographic memory?" Lynn asked.

He shrugged. "Maybe a little of both. I know I'll get to all of it eventually. I haven't been in this business my entire life without knowing what needs to be done and when. See you around, Lynn. Thanks for the company."

"Thanks for the breakfast," she said, then watched as he walked away. She was still following him with her gaze when Grace appeared just as he was climbing into his shiny new four-by-four parked out front. She couldn't help wondering if a man who took such good care of his truck would be equally thoughtful when it came to caring for a woman.

"That man does look good in a pair of jeans," Grace said with a dramatic sigh. She pinned Lynn with a look. "Just in case you hadn't noticed."

"Hard not to notice," Lynn replied, then gave Grace a chiding look. "But don't go getting any ideas in your head, you hear me? I'm not looking for a man, and he says he's not looking for anyone, either."

"And sometimes people lie to themselves because it feels safer," Grace retorted.

She sashayed off, leaving Lynn alone with the discouragingly paltry list of classified ads. Contemplating Mitch's sexy butt in a pair of jeans was a whole lot more fascinating than the few menial jobs available in Serenity.

But, she told herself staunchly as she forced her gaze back to the paper, ogling a man wouldn't put food on the table. And that was what she needed today, not the fleeting and dangerous satisfaction of feeling her pulse race for the first time in a very long time.

Lynn was down to her last possibility, a cashier's job at a mini-mart in a dicey section of town. Even in a tranquil community like Serenity, there were places to be avoided. Unfortunately, she was too desperate to take that into consideration.

To her chagrin, she was being interviewed by a girl half her age. She'd probably barely met the twenty-one-year-old age requirement specified in the ad.

"You willing to work nights?" Karena asked, snapping gum as she spoke, her expression bored.

"What are the hours exactly?" Lynn asked, inwardly cringing at the thought of leaving the kids at home alone in the evening.

"Eleven at night to seven in the morning," Karena replied.

Dismayed, Lynn shook her head at once. That was out of the question. "Sorry. I have kids at home. I can't do that."

"Well, that's all we have." Karena stood up, ending the interview.

"Thanks, anyway," Lynn managed to say. "Sorry to have wasted your time, but the ad didn't mention that it was a night job."

When she got back to her car, she rested her head against the steering wheel and fought the tears that were never far away these days. She tried hard not to give in to them, but sometimes she simply couldn't hold back all the pain and frustration. A few minutes later, a tap on her window had her sitting upright, her heart racing.

"Mitch!" she exclaimed. "You scared me half to death."

He gestured for her to roll down the window. When she'd complied, he regarded her with what looked like real distress. "Please tell me you were not even thinking about applying for a job here," he said, heat in his voice.

She frowned at his tone. "I did apply, but the only thing available is overnight. Obviously, I can't do that."

"You shouldn't be working here at any hour. It's dangerous."

"If the clientele's so rough, what are you doing here?"

"I was on my way to my plumbing supplier's and saw the HELP WANTED sign in the window and your car in the parking lot. After our conversation earlier, I stopped to check it out, make sure you weren't about to do anything crazy."

"There's nothing crazy about needing a job."

"Of course not, but not here, Lynn," he said flatly.

Annoyed by his attitude, she retorted, "I already told you I couldn't take it because of the hours. What business is this of yours, anyway?"

"Just one friend looking out for another," he said, clearly not fazed by her attitude. "Do you know the reason they need a new night clerk? The last one was shot a week ago during a robbery."

Lynn started trembling uncontrollably. "Good God," she murmured. "I had no idea."

"It was in the paper, the same one you were reading this morning."

"I just checked out the ads."

"Well, I imagine if I hadn't come along to tell you,

Carter would have stepped in. He has more problems around this area than anywhere else in town." He hesitated, clearly waging some sort of internal debate with himself. "If you're this desperate for a job, work for me," he said with unmistakable reluctance.

She almost laughed, but the expression on his face said he was serious. Not happy, but definitely serious. "You? Doing what? The last do-it-yourself job I tried to tackle at the house was such a disaster, it had to be redone by a professional."

He had the audacity to smile at that. "I wasn't suggesting putting you on one of my construction crews. I could use the help with paperwork."

She studied him skeptically. "Don't you already have someone?"

"Nah. In the winter I can usually keep up with the billing and payroll myself, but with spring coming on and more jobs, it's harder for me to manage all that and the paperwork, too."

"I doubt I'd be much better at that than I was at wallpapering the kitchen," she told him candidly.

"It's an easy system," he assured her. "I can teach you in an hour."

"You have an office?"

"No, that's the beauty of it. You can work at home. I'll just bring my laptop and a printer to your place and leave 'em. How about we give it a trial run, see how it goes? If you're comfortable with it, we'll take it from there."

Lynn felt a faint frisson of hope. "And you swear you're not making up work just to give me a job?"

"Cross my heart," he said with a grin, sketching an exaggerated cross on his chest. "You can start tomorrow. I'll bring the laptop by in the morning and show you the basics.

There are half a dozen bills that need to go out, and maybe you'll be up to speed to do payroll by the end of the week."

"If all this is as simple as you make it sound, how many hours are you thinking?"

"Just part-time, maybe twenty. You'd be able to keep the job at Raylene's, too. Would that be enough to help?"

"It would be a godsend," she told him, especially the part about working at home. "But only if you're sure. You didn't look all that certain when you first mentioned it. Were you already having second thoughts before the words were even out of your mouth?"

"Not at all," he said, sounding more convincing. "I'm sure about this, Lynn."

"And you'll fire me if I'm lousy?"

"I don't think you're going to be lousy, but if you are, something tells me I won't have to do a thing. You'll quit, either out of frustration or mind-numbing boredom."

She looked into his eyes, a gray-blue shade she'd never noticed before and filled with kindness. "I seem to spend a lot of time thanking you lately, but I have to say it again."

"Don't," he said. "You'll be solving a problem for me."

She smiled. "I guess we'll see about that, won't we?"

"I'll be over first thing in the morning, then, as soon as the kids have left for school. Is that okay?"

She nodded. "That'll be perfect. I don't have to be at Raylene's shop until ten. I'll be home just after two and can jump right back into whatever you need me to do."

"Then that's what we'll do," he said. "And I'll stop by before I head home at the end of the day, in case you have any questions. Or you can just run next door if something crops up that you don't understand."

"This really is a blessing, Mitch. Thank you."

"No more thanks, understood? This is a business arrangement, okay? I need help. You're looking for a job. It works out well for both of us."

She shook her head. "Sorry. I can't promise you I won't keep thanking you. I have the funniest feeling you're my guardian angel."

The remark seemed to fluster him. "Sweetheart, I can assure you I'm no angel. You can ask anyone in town about that."

Lynn shook her head, not buying it. "I think you're wrong about that, Mitch. I've never heard a single bad word ever said about you."

"Then you never spoke to Nettie Rogers, who swears I trampled her azaleas when I was rebuilding her screened-in porch. And then there's Sissy Adams, who accused me of changing the sunny shade of yellow paint she chose to mustard just to annoy her, never mind that the woman is flat-out color blind. I could have painted her walls bright orange and I swear she wouldn't have been able to tell that from neon pink."

Lynn laughed. "You're exaggerating, but those aren't exactly the sort of sins I was thinking about."

He grinned at her, a surprising twinkle in his eyes. "Now sins are an entirely different kettle of fish," he said. "I think we'd best save those for another day, or you'll quit this job before you've even started. Now head on out of here. I want to see you safely on the road before I drive away."

"See you in the morning, then," Lynn said, turning on the engine and putting the car in gear. She was about to open her mouth to utter another thank-you, but the expression on Mitch's face stopped her. He looked as if he were just daring her to say the forbidden words again.

Lynn waited until she was out of sight before murmuring one more time, "Thank you, Mitch. You *are* my guardian angel, no matter what you say."

Who knew that a guardian angel could come in the guise of a guy in blue jeans with red hair, twinkling gray-blue eyes and one very sexy butt?

Three

Despite the relief she felt at having a job lined up, Lynn's stomach remained tied up in knots as she drove toward the center of town. She hadn't forgotten her promise to Lexie to find out where Ed was and when he was due back. She had her own valid reasons for wanting to know those things, as well. She knew that trying to wrangle information out of the very loyal and discreet Noelle over the phone would be a waste of time, but face-to-face, Ed's secretary would have a lot more trouble holding out.

The success of Ed's insurance business was ostentatiously showcased in the large brick building he'd built just off Main Street. Personally, Lynn had always thought it was pretentious, but he'd insisted it was good for business, especially the insurance business, to look impressive and solid.

Lynn parked in the large lot out back and went in through the closest entrance, drawing startled glances from several of Ed's colleagues who hadn't laid eyes on her since she and Ed had split up. Assuming they'd taken his side and not wanting to put any of them on the spot, she nodded politely and kept right on walking to his large suite of offices in the front.

"Hi, Noelle," she said.

Ed's secretary uttered a small gasp, but recovered quickly. "Mrs. Morrow, how are you?"

"Just fine, Noelle. And you?"

"Doing all right. What can I do for you? Ed's not here."

"So I've gathered. Any idea where I can reach him or when he'll be back?"

"As I told Lexie when she called, I'm not entirely sure."

"On either point?" Lynn asked skeptically. "I can't recall a single time when Ed has ever been out of touch with you."

"Well, of course, I speak to him if there's an emergency," Noelle said, looking increasingly uncomfortable. For all her loyalty to her boss, she was also a sympathetic woman and a single mother herself. Lynn thought she probably understood the situation all too well.

"Then how about sharing with me how you go about contacting him?" Lynn requested. "Please, Noelle. You spoke to Lexie. You know how much she misses her father. And there are things I need to discuss with him that can't wait."

"He'll be back soon," Noelle said, holding firm.

"How soon?"

"Next week at the latest, maybe sooner."

Lynn shook her head. "Not good enough. I want to speak to him today."

Noelle regarded her with what appeared to be genuine sympathy. "I really wish I could help you, but I need this job. I can't violate his confidence. He'd fire me." She gave Lynn an earnest look. "You know he would."

Lynn sighed. Unfortunately, she knew that all too well. Even before she'd walked into the building, she'd known she was going to be putting Noelle in an impossible position. The last thing she wanted to do was to get another single mom fired.

She was struck by a sudden thought. Ed always kept petty cash in his office in a secret compartment at the back of one of his drawers. Since he'd failed to send his support check, she figured she was entitled to get that money however she could.

"Would you mind if I left a note on his desk?" she asked Noelle.

"No problem," Noelle said, looking relieved that Lynn wasn't going to keep pressing her.

"Thanks. I'll just be a minute." She walked into the office she'd worked so hard to decorate for him, choosing colors that were warm and inviting and furnishings that were tasteful and, at Ed's insistence, far more expensive than they'd needed to be.

She sat in his ergonomic leather chair behind the oversize mahogany desk and opened the bottom drawer. Reaching into the compartment hidden behind a stack of company stationery, she plucked out two hundred-dollar bills and guiltily stuffed them into her purse.

To make good on the request that had gotten her into the room, she removed a piece of stationery and jotted a quick note asking Ed to call her immediately on his return, folded it and shoved it into an envelope, then tucked it into a corner of the pristine blotter centered on his desk.

"All done," she told Noelle, exiting quickly. "I left the note on his desk. Please make sure he reads it, okay? As soon as he sees my handwriting he'll toss it in the trash, otherwise."

"I'll do my best," Noelle promised, then regarded Lynn apologetically. "I'm sorry I couldn't be more help."

"You helped enough," Lynn assured her.

Back in her car, she found herself trembling for the second time that day. No matter how strongly she felt that she was owed much more than that two hundred dollars, she couldn't help thinking that she'd turned into a thief. That's what this divorce was doing to her.

Then she thought of her kids and squared her shoulders. She'd done what she had to do and if anyone should be ashamed of their behavior these days, it was Ed. And she'd tell him exactly that if he had the audacity to make an issue of this.

Even with the promise of another paycheck soon and the money she'd stolen from petty cash in her purse, Lynn couldn't bring herself to go on a spending splurge at the grocery store. Who knew what other crises might arise before Ed finally paid up the way he was supposed to?

She left the store with two small sacks of groceries and a heavy heart. This would barely get them through the weekend, and then what? A couple of hundred dollars seemed like a fortune, but it wouldn't last long. It would barely cover the electric bill, much less make any dent in the overdue mortgage.

After putting the few pitiful purchases into the refrigerator and pantry, she knew she had to do something more to address the situation. Not even another paycheck was going to solve things, not with interest and late fees adding up on their bills. Reluctantly, she picked up the phone and called Helen.

"The support check hasn't come again," she told the attorney. "I just spent practically the last dime I have on enough groceries to get us through the next couple of days." She drew in a deep breath, then confessed, "I actually resorted to taking money from petty cash in Ed's office. I know it's theft, but what was I supposed to do, Helen? Let my kids starve?"

Helen uttered an epithet that would have blistered Ed's ears had she said it in court. "Look, I can't very well condone stealing, but let's pretend you never told me about that. Believe me, I get how desperate you must have been to resort to that."

"It's not going to make a dent in the bills," Lynn said in frustration. "But it will cover groceries for a couple of weeks and one or two other things, if I pinch every penny."

"I'll stop by with a check before the day's out," Helen promised her. "And before you say no, believe me, I will get it back from Ed, even if I have to take it out of his sorry hide!"

Lynn smiled. "I want to be there for that," she said. "Just anticipating it will be the one huge bright spot in my life."

"What about those bills you mentioned?" Helen asked. "Are you managing? Is Ed covering what he's supposed to be covering—the mortgage payment, the utilities?"

Lynn drew in a deep breath, then told her, "I just got a notice from the bank. They haven't received the last two house payments. They're threatening to foreclose. The electric company has given me two weeks to pay or they'll disconnect service."

"That scum!" Helen said fiercely. "Does he really want to take the roof from over your heads?"

"I don't think he cares about anything but himself these days," Lynn said. "I've managed to find a part-time job at Raylene's shop, but in this economy the pay's terrible. And today, Mitch Franklin hired me part-time to handle his billing and payroll, but even with both jobs, there's no way I can keep up. And the kids need clothes and supplies for school. I can't bear the looks in their eyes when I tell them there's no money for something they need, never mind for a few extras like seeing a movie with their friends. Forget putting gas in the car. Until today when I went looking for a second job, I hadn't driven anywhere in weeks."

Once she'd started, she couldn't seem to stop herself from pouring out all the frustrations and fears she'd kept bottled up. Helen listened without comment, then said with quiet reassurance, "We're going to fix this, Lynn. I promise you that."

"Before I'm homeless?" Lynn asked wryly.

"Absolutely," Helen said. "I'll speak to the bank. If need be, I'll get the court to intervene while we straighten this out."

Lynn breathed a sigh of relief. She could bear just about anything, she thought, except the thought of being on the streets with no place to go. Her parents had died several years ago. Her sisters lived in other states. If they knew how bad things were, they'd try to help, but she simply couldn't bring herself to endure the humiliation of asking them. She'd been saving that for a truly desperate last resort.

"I'll be by in an hour or two with that check," Helen promised her. "You'll still have time to get to the bank to cash it. In the meantime, I'll call Jimmy Bob West and put the fear of God into him about his client's behavior. Once I get to your place, we'll take a look at those bills and see what we can work out, okay?"

"Thank you, Helen. I honestly don't know what I'd do without you in my corner. If it were just me, I could walk away. Start over, even from the very bottom. But I owe the kids better than that."

"You're a strong woman, Lynn. Try to remember that.

You'll do whatever it takes to keep your family healthy and safe. I just wish you'd told me about this sooner. Maybe I could have done something before things deteriorated so badly."

"I was taught that asking for help was a sign of weakness," Lynn said. "I kept thinking I could figure things out or that Ed would shape up."

"Turning to friends, and especially to your attorney, is not a weakness," Helen replied emphatically. "Remember that. I'll see you soon."

"Thanks," Lynn said, her spirits marginally improved.

But then, as if to mock her, when she went to wash her hands in the downstairs bathroom, the cold-water knob came off in her hand.

"This is just the bloody last straw," she muttered, sitting down on the toilet and letting the tears come. She wasn't sure which was flowing harder, her tears or the water leaking in the sink.

"This is not solving anything," she muttered, making an attempt to find the shut-off valve, only to discover it was stuck. She thought of Mitch. She doubted he'd had any idea what he was letting himself in for by offering to help her out. These days it seemed the disasters in her life were way too plentiful. Still, he *had* offered and he was right next door.

She splashed water on her swollen eyes, ran a brush through her hair, then hurried to Raylene's. At her knock, Raylene opened the door at once. She frowned when she saw Lynn.

"Are you okay? You've been crying. What can I do to help?"

"Just a frustrating day," Lynn told her. "Is Mitch here? Do you suppose I could borrow him for a minute? I have an impending plumbing disaster and I'm at a loss. He offered to help out if I ever needed anything."

"Of course he will," Raylene said. "I'll get him and send him right over."

"Thanks."

Raylene started away, then came back. "Lynn, if you ever need anything at all, you know Carter and I will be happy to pitch in. Mandy adores Lexie, and we love having her over here anytime she wants to come. You and Jeremy are always welcome, too. I imagine it's been tough since Ed left. I put that much together when you came to me for a job."

"We're managing," Lynn said tightly, wondering if Helen had filled Raylene in on how bad things were, if Raylene had only given her a job out of pity. She immediately stopped herself from even considering such a possibility. Helen's ethical standards were too high for her to be blabbing about her clients' woes.

And after all Raylene had been through—her first husband's abuse, a bout with agoraphobia and a final confrontation with her ex after his release from jail—Raylene was quick to lend a hand to everyone these days. She said it thrilled her to finally be able to repay some of the kindness extended to her when she'd been psychologically trapped in her own home for so long.

Lynn forced a smile. "Thanks for offering, though. You've already done plenty for us."

"We're always happy to help. I mean that."

Lynn nodded. "I know you do." For the second time that day, she'd been reminded that she did have friends, people who would be there for her if only she asked.

"Okay, then," Raylene said, then left to get Mitch as Lynn walked back home.

When Mitch appeared at her house and immediately set to work on repairing the knob, she couldn't help noticing how quietly competent he was. He was also a man of few words. She liked that he didn't ask a lot of questions about how she'd managed to break the stupid thing in the first place. Ed would have turned the whole incident into a flurry of accusations about her incompetence.

When the job was done, Mitch washed his hands, then smiled at her. "Good as new," he declared. "Or as good as a twenty-year-old fixture is likely to be. You might think about replacing it one of these days."

"I'll put it on the list," she said.

He gave her a chiding look. "Is this one of those long lists that no one ever gets to?"

"Pretty much."

"I could get one for you at cost and replace it in no time," he offered.

Lynn shook her head. "That's okay. This one will have to hold up a while longer."

"Okay, then," he said, not pressing. When they got to the kitchen, he hesitated. "Other than that knob coming off in your hand, has something else happened since I saw you earlier? You look even more stressed."

"How flattering."

He winced. "Sorry. I'm not up on polite chitchat. If I want to know something, I figure the best way to find out is to ask. The kids are okay?"

She smiled at his determined attempt to try to pry information out of her. "They'll be home from school any minute. I'm sure you'll see Lexie next door and can determine for yourself how she's doing."

He looked vaguely chagrined. "Okay. Message received. I didn't mean to pry. Sorry if I struck a nerve."

"I'm the one who's sorry, Mitch. It's just been a tough day," she said. "You were right. I am stressed out."

"Take a break and put your feet up," he advised. "I'll be over in the morning."

"See you then."

He started to leave, then turned back. "Hey, I don't suppose you could convince Lexie that it would be politically correct to play the local country station at full volume, rather than that crazy stuff she and Mandy like?"

"I haven't had any luck around here," she said. "That would be my preference, too. The country music Travis and Sarah play on the radio station here in town is much more my taste."

"Mine, too. I think I've lived a lot of those lyrics."

"Haven't we all?" she agreed. Lately, she had a hunch her experiences could provide lyrics for an entire CD of love-gone-wrong songs. Maybe *that* should be her new calling.

Mitch stood there awkwardly for a moment longer, then shrugged. "I'd better get back over there. If I'm gone too long, my crew's liable to put up a wall where no wall was intended to be."

She laughed. "Something tells me you have them trained better than that. It looks amazing from over here. I can't wait to see how it turns out."

"You'll have to let me give you a tour one of these days. Raylene has a hard hat she can loan you, assuming she can find the thing. Near as I can tell she enjoys making my heart stop by coming into the addition without it."

"I'd like that," Lynn said. "We always talked about building an addition to this place, but we never got around to it. Now it will never happen."

She waved off the revealing comment as soon as it was

out of her mouth. "Spilt milk," she muttered. "Thanks, again, for helping out with the plumbing crisis, Mitch. You're a lifesaver."

"Anytime. I told you that."

She watched him walk away, fascinated yet again by the way his faded, well-worn jeans curved quite nicely over an incredibly sexy posterior. As soon as the outrageous, totally inappropriate thought crossed her mind, she slapped her hand over her mouth as if she'd said it aloud.

What had gotten into her today? She was completely flipping out over finances, she'd stolen money from her husband's office and she was still thinking about how appealing Mitch looked in a pair of jeans? Crazy. The last thing she needed in her life these days was another complication. And Mitch Franklin, sweet and sexy as he might be, would most definitely be a complication.

Starting tomorrow morning she was going to have to be on full alert to make sure she kept these wayward thoughts of hers in check or working for the man was going to be incredibly awkward. Even as she reminded herself of that, she wondered if just maybe that was why he'd hesitated before offering her the job. Was he as aware of her as she suddenly was of him? Or had he just noticed that she'd developed this insane appreciation for his backside?

Either way, she reminded herself sternly, tomorrow morning needed to be all about business. She would keep her eyes on the computer screen and far, far away from Mitch or any particularly intriguing part of his anatomy.

When Mitch got back to Raylene's, his crew had gone for the day and she immediately gave him a speculative look. "You were gone a long time. Problems making the repair?"

He frowned, bothered by what he thought was a hint of censure in her voice. "You don't mind that I went over there, do you?"

She immediately looked chagrined. "Of course not. I actually meant to tease you. I thought maybe fixing the sink or whatever was broken was the least of what was going on."

Mitch regarded her with a narrowed gaze. "Don't you start! I get enough meddling from Grace."

"So, Grace has seen you with Lynn, too?"

"I am not having this conversation with you," he said flatly.

"Not even if I tell you that we're having roasted chicken for dinner with mashed potatoes and gravy?" she taunted. "I made it just for you."

"Bring me a plate while I work," he said firmly. "I need to catch up on a few things before I leave."

Raylene shook her head, a glint of amusement in her eyes. "You eat at the table like a civilized person or you don't eat. That's what I tell the girls and it applies to you, too."

"I could just leave now," he retorted. "I'm not on the clock."

"You could, but I know roasted chicken is your favorite. Would you deny yourself that just to avoid a few innocent questions?"

"There is absolutely nothing innocent about any of your questions, Raylene. You could give those *60 Minutes* reporters a run for their money."

"Then you must know it won't do any good for you to try to dodge me," she said cheerfully. "See you at the table in a half hour."

For a man who'd been bemoaning the loss of the most

important woman in his life and the ensuing loneliness, he suddenly had a surplus of bossy, know-it-all women around him. Once he was back home tonight, he was going to have to think about exactly how he felt about that.

"I may have some idea about what's been happening to that money Ed's supposed to be paying," Helen told Lynn when she stopped by with a check.

As soon as the words left her mouth, she glanced around guiltily. "Are the kids here?"

Lynn shook her head. "Lexie's next door and Jeremy's down the street playing with friends in the park."

"Good. I wouldn't want them to overhear this."

"What's happening?"

"Jimmy Bob is supposed to be taking care of those payments, right?"

Lynn nodded. "That's what Ed told me."

"Well, Jimmy Bob's nowhere to be found at the moment."

Lynn regarded her with surprise. "You mean he's vanished?"

"Vanished, gone on vacation, who knows? All I know is the office was closed up tight when I stopped by, and there was a sign on the door that said the law practice was closed indefinitely. I called my investigator and asked him to see what he could find out."

"I know you're not crazy about the way Jimmy Bob practices law, but isn't this odd, even for him?" Lynn asked.

Helen nodded. "He's pulled quite a few stunts over the years, but I've never known him to disappear in the middle of a case. We have another court date next week. Unless he gets a postponement, which so far I've had no indication that he's asked for, the judge is going to expect him to appear. Ed, too."

"Maybe they've both run off on this fun-filled golf trip I hear Ed is on."

Helen shrugged. "Could be, but that doesn't feel right, either. His secretary should be there fielding calls at least. He doesn't even have an answering machine turned on."

"Maybe he just figured if he was on vacation, she might as well be, too," Lynn speculated. "That happens, doesn't it? Small offices just shut down and everyone goes on vacation at the same time?"

"Not in my profession, with court dates always changing and emergencies cropping up with clients," Helen insisted. "Of course, Jimmy Bob doesn't always operate the way a real professional should."

She waved off the discussion. "There's no point in trying to figure out what Jimmy Bob is up to. We'll know soon enough. In the meantime, the check should tide you over, and I've scheduled an appointment with the bank manager tomorrow. I'll let you know what sort of temporary terms I'm able to negotiate. I don't think they'll be unreasonable until we get this mess straightened out."

"Thank you, Helen. I honestly don't know what I'd do without you. I think I knew when we were still in high school that you were going to be this mega-successful attorney for the underdog. Remember when you defended Jane Thompson before the student court for cheating? Nobody thought you stood a chance of getting her off."

"She was innocent," Helen said, smiling.

"Really?" Lynn said skeptically. "She wasn't caught redhanded passing a note in the middle of an exam?"

"She was caught red-handed with a note," Helen admitted. "But, in fact, it was Jimmy Bob West who'd shoved it into her hand when he saw the teacher heading their way. He was scum even back then."

"Didn't he try to convince you to go into practice with him a few years ago?" Lynn asked. "I'd like to have been there when you gave him an answer."

Helen chuckled. "I just told him that, regretfully, I'd rather eat dirt than work with him, or words to that effect."

"I suspect they were a lot more colorful," Lynn said.

"A lot more," Helen conceded. "But Jimmy Bob, being the man he is, didn't take the slightest offense. He still asks from time to time."

She gave Lynn a hug. "Hang in there, okay? And call me immediately the next time there's a problem. Meantime, I'll be in touch about that court date and whatever we find out about Jimmy Bob's whereabouts."

"Have a good evening," Lynn told her. She waved the check in the air. "I'm going to relax for the first time in days."

At the very least, she was going to be able to sleep tonight.

Four

Flo Decatur was sitting on the sofa reading a book to her granddaughter, Sarah Beth, when Helen came in from work looking beat.

"Mommy!" Sarah Beth cried joyfully, running to throw her arms around Helen. "Gramma's reading my favorite story."

"Of course she is," Helen said. "You have Gramma wound around your little finger."

Sarah Beth's face puckered up with a frown. "What does that mean?"

"It means I love you," Flo interpreted. "Even more than chocolate ice cream with hot fudge on top."

Her granddaughter's eyes widened. "More than gooey chocolate cake like Daddy makes?"

"Even more than that," Flo confirmed.

Sarah Beth turned to her mother. "Can we have ice cream and cake for dinner?"

Helen laughed, then gave Flo a feigned frown. "Thanks a lot. Now peas and carrots won't cut it."

"Peas and carrots never cut it with you, either," Flo said realistically, then followed her into the kitchen. "Why don't

you go take a shower and change into something comfortable, while I put whatever Erik sent home from Sullivan's
on the table? I'll see that Sarah Beth's fed, too. You look
as if you could use a few minutes to relax and unwind."

She was surprised when Helen gave her an impulsive
hug. "You have no idea how wonderful that sounds." Helen
gave her pint-size imp of a daughter a pointed look. "And
try to keep Miss Sarah Beth here out of the cake until after
she's eaten dinner."

"I've got it covered," Flo assured her, then winked at
Sarah Beth.

Flo had come to treasure these regular dinners with her
daughter and granddaughter. Though she was happily settled into her own apartment now and had an active social
life, she missed the time she'd spent in this house while
she'd been recovering from a broken hip. She was captur-
ing so many new family memories, the kind that had been
few and far between when she'd been struggling to make
ends meet as a single mom back when Helen had been
Sarah Beth's age. She liked to think that she and Helen
were actually friends now, and not just mother and daughter with a contentious relationship.

She also enjoyed the meals her son-in-law sent home
from Sullivan's. That restaurant of Dana Sue's where he
was the sous-chef had better food than anything Flo had
ever put on her table at home, and she'd at one time been
considered the best when it came to her church's potluck
suppers.

Tonight Erik had sent home two fried catfish dinners
for her and Helen, some chicken tenders and mashed potatoes for Sarah Beth, along with some of that gooey mol-
ten chocolate cake that was Sarah Beth's favorite. Flo's,
too, for that matter.

Flo poured a glass of milk for her granddaughter, then made cocktails for herself and Helen. She sat with Sarah Beth while she ate, then sent her off to her room to play before bedtime. "But give Mommy some peace and quiet, okay?"

"Uh-huh," Sarah Beth said, then scampered off, dragging a tattered stuffed tiger with her.

By then, Helen was back, looking refreshed, though worry was still etched on her forehead.

"Bad day?" Flo asked, always interested in the legal cases her daughter was involved in. They'd realized a while back that Helen's interest in law probably went back to all the TV shows like *Divorce Court* and *The People's Court* that Flo used to keep on while she did the baskets of ironing that brought in a few extra dollars each week.

"You have no idea," Helen said, taking a sip of her drink, then closing her eyes with a sigh of satisfaction. "I needed this."

"One of these days I'll make you a batch of margaritas," Flo said, grinning. "I know they're a personal favorite of yours. You must have gotten that from me. Made a batch for the first time in years not long ago."

Helen regarded her with amusement. "Do you really want to remind me of the Senior Magnolias fiasco at Liz's?"

Flo chuckled. "Yep, that was the night and I refuse to apologize for it. Frances needed a distraction from the diagnosis the doctor had given her."

"Even so, I hope you learned a lesson when the neighbors called the police," Helen said with mock sternness.

Her mother just grinned. "Afraid not. Best time we've had in years, at least as best we can remember."

Helen sobered. "How's Frances really doing these days? She seemed pretty sharp at the bullying rally a couple of weeks ago."

"She's fighting this cognitive impairment thing or whatever it is with the same determination she's faced everything else in her life. I think stirring up a ruckus that day was good for her." She winked. "So were the margaritas. You should know firsthand the healing effect one of those and a night with friends can have."

"The operative word being *one,*" Helen chided, but she was smiling.

"Yes, well, we might have gone a little overboard," Flo conceded. "We're old. Allowances should be made."

Her daughter laughed at that. "I imagine people have been making allowances for the three of you for years. I'll bet you all created chaos in this town back in the day," Helen said, regarding her mom with something Flo thought might have been a hint of approval.

"Well, I can't speak for Frances and Liz, since they have a good ten years or more on me, but I certainly did," Flo said. "I imagine we have a few more commotions left in us."

But even as she spoke, she frowned. "Despite what I just said about Frances giving this her best fight, I'm not at all sure she'll be able to live alone much longer. Maybe it's not Alzheimer's yet, maybe it won't be, but there's been a worrisome change in her. Liz and I have been nudging her to face that, but she's not ready to deal with going into assisted living just yet. It's a hard thing for anyone to think about being dependent on other people, but especially for someone like Frances, who's always been the one to help others."

"I'm sorry."

Flo sighed. "So am I. One thing I hate about getting older is seeing so many of my friends lose their vitality. It seems once we start on that downhill slide, there's no turning back. That's why I intend to live every second I'm able to the absolute fullest."

"Other than your broken hip, you've been lucky," Helen reminded her. "The doctor says you have the heart of a healthy woman twenty years younger."

"I've been blessed, no question about it," Flo agreed. "And I'm so grateful to be back here in Serenity where I get to spend time with you and Sarah Beth. Florida was nice and I'll always be grateful to you for setting me up in that nice condo down there, but home is better."

"I'm glad you're here, too," Helen said.

Flo gave her a knowing look. "You didn't feel that way when I said I wanted to move back from Boca Raton."

"No," Helen agreed. "I thought it was a mistake, but I was wrong."

Flo chuckled at the pained expression on her daughter's face. "Hurts spitting out an admission like that, doesn't it?"

"You have no idea," Helen said, grinning. "Fortunately, thanks to Erik calling me on every single mistake I make, I'm learning to accept that I'm as human as everyone else."

"You do know your husband is one in a million, don't you?"

"I do, and I thank God for him every day," Helen said.

Flo nodded in satisfaction. "That's good, then. Now, why don't you tell me what went wrong with your day?"

"Just one of those nasty divorce cases that makes me question why it's illegal to chase down some of these deadbeat men with a shotgun."

Flo hesitated. "I know you can't give me details about your cases, but this wouldn't have anything to do with Ed and Lynn Morrow, would it?"

Helen regarded her with surprise. "Why would you ask that?" she said in a way that to Flo's ears was answer enough.

"I know you took her case. I also know that Sarah and Travis are worried sick about Lynn. They used to live next door, you know, in Sarah's parents' house. Raylene's there now, and she mentioned a few things to Sarah. I guess Raylene gave Lynn a part-time job, and she's been trying to have Lynn and the kids over for dinner a couple of times a week, but they all seem to think things are pretty bad."

"How did all this information get from Raylene and Sarah to you?" Helen asked curiously.

"Liz, of course. Living in the guest cottage behind Sarah and Travis, she sees them all the time. They've become like family. Sarah confides in her."

"And Liz naturally mentioned it to you," Helen concluded. "The Serenity grapevine at its best."

"It's not always a bad thing," Flo reminded her. "I know it can hurt being the talk of the town, but sometimes it lets people know when folks need help. I can't abide idle gossip, but this is different. At least, that's how it seems to me."

"I suppose you're right."

She regarded her daughter intently. "So, just how bad are things? Is there anything I can do? I've been in that position, a single mom with nowhere to turn. If I can help, I'd like to. Liz feels the same way, but we're at a loss about what we could do without offending Lynn's pride."

Helen looked at Flo with amazement.

"Is that incredulous look on your face about your not believing I have a compassionate bone in my body or because you're stunned by my insight?" Flo asked wryly.

"I guess I'm just surprised that you'd want to get involved when neither of you knows Lynn that well. It's very thoughtful of both of you, but you're right. I don't think Lynn's open to a lot of outside help right now. Admitting there are problems, even to me, is hard for her."

"Are you going to be able to fix this for her?"

"I hope so," Helen said. "I'm just afraid it's going to take longer than I anticipated."

"Well, if you need backup, you can count on Liz and me. Frances, too, more than likely, if she's feeling up to it." Flo regarded her daughter with a grin. "At our ages, we don't mind stirring up a little trouble, if need be. Might be fun to land myself in jail for a worthy cause."

Helen looked vaguely alarmed. "What sort of trouble are you contemplating?"

"Picketing outside of Ed's office came to mind," Flo said eagerly. "Folks expect their insurance people to behave responsibly. A little public humiliation might go a long way toward making him shape up and do the right thing by his family."

Helen's expression lit up momentarily, but then she shook her head. "Much as I love that idea, I think we'll stick to a legal approach for now, Mom. But believe me, if I can't get him to change his ways in a big fat hurry, the three of you are welcome to take him on."

Flo nodded. "Just say the word. I'm pretty good at making up protest signs, if I do say so myself. They turned out real good for that antibullying rally, and the ones Liz dreamed up in support of Laura Reed at the school were downright inspired. All those civil rights demonstrations Liz carried out years ago taught her a thing or two about effective protests."

"I can't deny that the three of you played a big part in rallying public sentiment," Helen said. "Let's see how this plays out in court next week before we take the next step, okay?"

"Whatever you want," Flo said, then stood up. "I hate to leave you with the dishes, but I need to run."

Helen regarded her with a startled expression. "It's still early. Don't you want to stay and help me tuck in Sarah Beth?"

Flo took a deep breath, then blurted, "Actually, I have a date." She held her breath, waiting for Helen's reaction. It was pretty much what she'd expected—her daughter looked as if Flo had spoken in a foreign language.

"A date? Since when? Who?"

"Oh, I'll tell you all about him next time I'm over," Flo said breezily. "I don't want to keep him waiting. We're going over to Columbia dancing."

"At this hour?"

"You just said yourself that it's still early. And I'm a night owl."

Helen frowned. "Since when? You didn't used to be."

"Because I had to be up and out the door for work at the crack of dawn," Flo explained patiently. "Now I can stay up as late as I like." She pressed a kiss to her daughter's cheek. "Love you. Tell Sarah Beth good-night for me."

She grabbed her purse and hurried out before Helen could gather enough of her wits to do the kind of cross-examination that Flo knew was coming sooner or later. To Flo's way of thinking, later was better.

For all her open-mindedness about most things, when it came to her mother's social life, Helen was downright stuffy. She had been ever since Flo had carelessly mentioned leaving a box of condoms in the nightstand beside her bed as they were driving away from Boca Raton. The poor girl had nearly had a heart attack right there on I-95! Flo hoped to avoid causing that reaction a second time.

Lynn dressed with extra care in the morning. She told herself it was simply because she always tried to look nice when she was working for Raylene in her upscale boutique.

She knew, though, that the pink blush on her cheeks and the mascara she was applying had more to do with Mitch stopping by than it did with impressing Raylene's customers.

She was in the kitchen with a pot of coffee brewed when Mitch tapped on the back door.

"Come in. It's open," she called out.

He walked into the kitchen, frowning. "Do you leave that door unlocked all the time?"

"Only when I'm expecting someone to pop in from right next door," she said.

"Well, it's a bad idea," he grumbled, clearly not placated.

"Duly noted," she said, amused by just how far his protectiveness seemed to go.

His gaze narrowed suspiciously. "You're not really paying a bit of attention to me, are you?" he asked.

"Honestly? Not so much."

"I'm beginning to think you and Raylene are going to be the death of me. She refuses to wear a hard hat in a construction zone. You leave the door open for anyone to just walk in. I was taught to look out for women."

"And I was taught to look out for myself," she replied.

"Then do it," he said with frustration.

She regarded him with a tolerant expression. "Coffee?"

"Are you trying to change the subject?"

"Yes," she said, already pouring the coffee into a mug. "Otherwise, I fear our working relationship is going to get off to a very bad start. Besides, you seem to be caffeine-deprived. That would explain the cranky mood."

Mitch shook his head and sighed. "You're probably right." He set the laptop on the table. "Is this okay for now?"

"Sure. I'll make room for it on my desk later."

"I have the printer in the truck."

"Looks as if the laptop will work with mine," she said. "Let's hold off on that till we know."

"Okay, but I'm bringing you supplies tomorrow—paper, ink cartridges, whatever you need."

"Fair enough."

He took a sip of coffee, then opened the laptop and turned it on. "Pull up a chair and sit here next to me," he said.

Lynn dragged a chair closer and peered at the screen, trying not to notice the heat radiating from his body or the solid masculine strength suggested by all that muscle. She gave herself a mental shake. She hadn't spent this much time noticing a man's body in a long time. Now surely wasn't the time to start.

"You paying attention?" Mitch asked, amusement suddenly threading through his voice.

She blinked over at him. "Of course. Why?"

"You seemed a little distracted, that's all."

She waved a little notebook and pen in his direction. "See. Ready to take notes."

"Written anything yet?"

"So far you haven't even opened the program."

He grinned. "Fair enough. It's password-protected, okay?" He told her the password, which she wrote down. Then he walked her step by step through the billing system and the payroll program. "Make sense so far?"

Lynn nodded. "So far, but then I haven't actually had to use it yet."

He pulled several pieces of paper from his back pocket. "Notes for the billing," he explained. "You'll find the customers, their addresses and their account numbers in the system. Mostly people pay about fifty percent upfront, the remainder when the job's completed. If there's an interim bill for fixtures, that's sent out when the expense is incurred. My fee is usually paid once everybody has signed off on the punch list that indicates all the details are done to the customer's satisfaction."

"So those notes of yours indicate exactly what sort of bill I'm sending out, right?"

He winced. "Well, in theory they should. Since I usually know what they're for, I might not have written it down on these pages. Why don't I do that before you get home this afternoon, make sure you have everything you need?"

"Then I'll just fiddle around with the system until I leave for Raylene's this morning, see if I understand how it works."

"Sounds good to me. Any questions?"

"None so far, but I imagine I'll have plenty for you by this afternoon."

"Okay, then. I'll get out of your hair. See you later, Lynn."

Suddenly he seemed anxious to leave, which suited her since she didn't understand why being close to him got to her the way it did.

"See you," she said, determinedly focusing on the computer screen and not on Mitch.

She knew he hesitated before leaving, but eventually he walked away, closing the back door securely behind him. Locking it, too, if she wasn't mistaken. Even though the gesture exasperated her just a little, she couldn't seem to stop smiling.

The woman was going to be trouble, Mitch thought as he walked back to Raylene's. Oh, not when it came to the work. He had every confidence she would pick up on that with ease. No, it was this attraction simmering between them. It had always been there, for him, anyway, but thanks to Grace's interference, he was forced to acknowledge that on some level it had never died the way he'd thought it surely had.

As for Lynn, well, he couldn't say with certainty what she was feeling beyond gratitude, but there'd been a moment there when he'd had the feeling she was as attuned to him as he was to her.

His cell phone rang just before he headed into the back door at Raylene's. Caller ID told him it was his older son.

"Hey, Nate. What's up?"

"Just checking in, Dad. What's up with you?"

"Working, the same as always."

"You still building that addition for the police chief and his wife? How's it going?"

"It's coming along. Did you really call just to check on my job progress, or do you need money?"

"Dad, you give me and Luke plenty of money. Can't I just call to see what you're up to?"

"Always glad to hear from you," Mitch confirmed. "But you'll pardon me if experience has just taught me that it's usually a financial shortfall that earns me a call at this hour of the morning."

"Well, I'm solvent," Nate assured him. He hesitated, then said, "Actually, I was thinking of coming home for the weekend. Is that okay?"

"You know it is," Mitch said eagerly. "You don't even have to ask."

"Um," Nate began, suddenly sounding nervous, "would it be okay if I brought someone with me?"

Mitch stopped in his tracks. "Since you've hauled half a dozen friends home with no notice, I'm guessing this is a female sort of someone."

"Yeah. Her name's Jo, short for Josephine, if you can believe it. Does anyone name their girls that anymore?"

"Obviously, some parents do," Mitch said. "I'll look forward to meeting her."

"Okay, so here's the deal. I need to know if you're gonna freak out if she stays in my room."

Mitch sucked in a deep breath and lifted his eyes heavenward. "How about a little help here, Amy?" he murmured, trying to think how she would handle this. He knew as well as anyone that a twenty-one-year-old was likely to be sleeping with anyone he was dating seriously. And he had to assume this was serious if Nate wanted to bring the girl home. And yet he wasn't sure he was quite ready to sanction such behavior under his roof.

"Sorry, pal. Not acceptable."

"But, Dad," Nate began.

"Your mom always had firm rules about this sort of thing," Mitch reminded him. "You knew them when you went away to college. What you do at school is up to you, but in our house guests stay in the guest rooms."

"It's not like she's a guest exactly," Nate said. "I wanted to tell you this when we got there, but I guess I'd better do it now. We're engaged."

Mitch felt the sudden, unexpected sting of tears in his eyes. More than ever, he wished Amy were alive for this moment. She'd know what to say, how to react. He, however, had to force his enthusiasm. Nate was so darn young. His life hadn't even started yet.

"Engaged, huh?" he said, trying to inject an upbeat note into his voice. "Congratulations, son. I mean that. I wish your mom were here. She'd be so excited for you."

"I know," Nate said quietly. "It's kinda hard knowing

she'll never get to meet Jo, give her a stamp of approval, if you know what I mean."

Mitch smiled. "I know exactly what you mean." Amy had always been careful about sharing her opinion of the girls their sons had dated, but they'd known anyway. She'd been terrible about hiding her feelings. And those feelings had clearly influenced both Nate and Luke. The lousy choices had never lasted long, even though she'd kept her mouth clamped firmly shut.

"So, now that you know about the engagement, can she stay in my room?" Nate asked.

Mitch was still struggling with the idea of his son being ready to make such a huge commitment. The sleeping arrangements seemed minor all of a sudden.

"How about we talk about that when you get here?" He wanted to see for himself just how committed the two of them seemed to be. Or maybe he was just trying to postpone the inevitable—admitting that his son had grown up on him.

"Okay, Dad," Nate said, conceding the point. "See you tomorrow night."

"Drive carefully."

"Always," Nate replied.

There'd been a time when Nate might have rolled his eyes at the admonition. Luke, too. But since Amy's tragic accident, none of them took anything for granted when it came to driving. Mitch knew one thing with one hundred percent certainty—neither of his sons would ever drive drunk. And even sober, they'd drive responsibly and defensively. He hated the way they'd had to learn that lesson, but he had to admit he was glad they'd taken it to heart.

Now he just had to pray that Nate had taken to heart everything Amy and Mitch had taught him about the responsibility that went along with love and marriage.

Five

"I heard she might have to apply for food stamps," a woman shopper at Raylene's boutique said. Her entrance set off the bell that would have let Lynn know she was there. Her voice, unfortunately, was plenty loud enough to carry to Lynn in the back room, stopping her in her tracks. Lynn knew she should make her presence known, but instead, flushed with embarrassment, she waited to see what might be said next.

"You're kidding!" her companion responded. "Isn't Ed playing golf at Pinehurst or someplace like that this week?"

Lynn felt a chill. There was no doubt at all that they were speculating about her and the financial mess she was in. How was she supposed to go out there now and wait on them? Unfortunately, Raylene had just left for the bank and Adelia was off today. She had no choice.

She drew herself up, plastered a smile on her face and walked out front as if she hadn't just overheard the two women talking about her. Worse, as soon as she saw them, she recognized them.

"Good morning, Alicia. How are you? And you, too, Kelly Ann?"

Both women, who'd been in school with her and now had kids about the same ages as Lexie and Jeremy, blushed furiously.

Alicia recovered first. "Lynn, I had no idea you were working here," she said.

"Apparently not," Lynn said wryly. Unable to stop herself, she felt compelled to add, "Unless, of course, you set out to embarrass me."

As soon as she'd uttered the bold comment, Lynn formulated an apology, but to her astonishment, Kelly Ann walked over to her and gave her an impulsive and apparently sincere hug.

"Don't you dare think a thing like that," Kelly Ann admonished. "If anyone in this town ought to be embarrassed, it's that no-account husband of yours." She said it with unmistakable and obviously heartfelt disdain.

Lynn regarded her with gratitude. "I appreciate the sentiment, but please, if you hear people talking about what's going on with us, try to quiet them down. I don't want the kids to hear this kind of gossip. The situation is tough enough on them as it is."

"We'll put a stop to it," Alicia promised, obviously eager to make amends for her careless comments. "I just wasn't thinking. You know me. If I know something, I tend to blab it. I'll watch it from here on out. I know how I'd feel if it were me people were talking about and my kids overheard it."

"When did you start working here, hon?" Kelly Ann asked, thankfully changing the subject.

"Just a couple of months ago, part-time. Raylene has Adelia Hernandez working full-time. I fill in on weekends or when either of them is off during the week."

"Does Raylene have you on commission?" As soon as

she'd asked, Kelly Ann turned pale. "Is that too personal? I was only asking because I thought maybe we could make up for being so thoughtless before."

Lynn nodded. "Salary, plus commission," she confirmed.

"Well, then, Alicia, we need to whip out our credit cards and get busy," Kelly Ann said cheerily.

Lynn, who hadn't bought so much as a cheap T-shirt for herself since the separation, watched in awe as the two women quickly spent more money than she made in a month.

Kelly Ann stood back and surveyed their purchases with satisfaction as Lynn put everything into bags. She gave Lynn a wide grin.

"That ought to make up just a little bit for us coming in here and being so insensitive," she said.

"I appreciate the sales," Lynn said. For once it didn't seem to matter whether the purchases were made out of guilt or pity. She simply focused on what a nice boost they'd be to her paycheck.

"Do you have a regular schedule?" Kelly Ann asked. "If you do, we'll make sure to come in when you're working."

"No. I'm usually here three days a week, but I'm never sure which days those might be. It depends on when Raylene or Adelia need to be off," Lynn said. Even though she was picking up more hours from Mitch, she added, "And if you happen to hear of anyone else looking for someone part-time or full-time, let me know."

"We surely will," Alicia promised.

Kelly Ann gave Lynn another hug before they left. Lynn stared after them. While it grated to recall how the encounter had begun, she felt better about how it had ended. It had been a revelation, in fact.

Maybe people in town really would take her side over Ed's. She'd wondered about that. He was the son of a beloved insurance executive whose company handled policies for most everyone in town. Ed was now the big shot in charge, a position that commanded a lot of respect. She'd been so intent on running their home and being involved in a few things at school that her own circle of friends had grown smaller.

Just thinking about the possibility that she could have moral support while this awful mess played out buoyed her spirits. It was possible that the deliberate attempts to isolate herself to avoid the judgments she thought people might be making had been unnecessary. It was time to hold her chin up and start facing people.

When Raylene returned from the bank, she looked at the receipt book and whistled. "Nice sales!"

Lynn chuckled. "Guilt sales," she said, then explained what had happened.

Raylene shook her head. "I'm glad it turned out okay and you'll make a nice commission, but I hope those two learned a lesson."

"I doubt it," Lynn said with a shrug. "You grew up in this town, same as me. People talk. It's not going to change."

Raylene sighed. "I suppose, but I don't have to like it, especially when I see one of my friends hurt by their thoughtlessness."

"I'm not hurt, not really," Lynn said. "In fact, it was eye-opening. I assumed everyone was going to take Ed's side, so I've been avoiding people. He's the big wheel in town. He prides himself on knowing everybody and taking real good care of them."

"He's not taking such good care of you, though, is he?" Raylene said knowingly. "That will matter to people, Lynn. Family counts in this town, and the way a man treats his family says a lot about his own moral character. It wouldn't surprise me a bit to see him lose business over the way he's handling this divorce. Carter was saying just last night that once the insurance policy for the police department is up in a few months, he wants to negotiate with another company."

"You're kidding," Lynn said, astounded. "Because of me and the kids?"

"Because a man who screws up his personal life can't be trusted with other people's business," Raylene said. "And that's just about a direct quote. Of course, Carter is one of those stand-up guys with a strict moral code, which makes him a fantastic police chief but a little tough for those of us with flaws. You remember how we met, the day Sarah's little boy ran off while I was supposed to be watching him? Carter didn't think much of me then."

Lynn recalled the terrifying incident all too well. "Give the man a break. He didn't understand about the agoraphobia at that point. And he did apologize for his judgmental attitude after Travis filled him in."

"He did," Raylene said, smiling. "And proved he had plenty of redeeming qualities."

"The man adores you," Lynn said. "Flaws and all, assuming you have any. He certainly stuck right by you while you were fighting the agoraphobia and couldn't leave the house. I think we all marveled at that."

"He was a saint, no question about it. And he's been a rock for his sisters since their parents died, but he has his judgmental moments. Of course, when it comes to dealing with Ed, I happen to agree with his decision. I'm moving all my policies the first chance I get, too."

Lynn gave her a wry look. "Much as I love the idea of retribution, you do realize that if Ed's business goes under, my situation will get even worse."

Raylene stared at her with dismay. "Well, fudge! I hadn't thought of that."

"Believe me, I have," Lynn said. "I have nightmares about it. One second I want the man to wind up a pauper, the next I realize he could drag me and the kids down with him."

Raylene's expression turned thoughtful. "Okay, then, we need to find you another job, something better than what I can offer you for now. You're smart. You've been running a household for years, without a lot of help from Ed, I imagine. You have skills that can be used in the workforce. We just have to focus on creating the perfect résumé."

"I did snag another part-time job just yesterday," Lynn admitted.

Raylene's eyes lit up. "Really? Tell me."

"Mitch hired me to handle his billing and payroll. I just started learning his system this morning. We're going to go over a few more things later this afternoon when I get home from here."

A grin spread across Raylene's face. Lynn suspected that the twinkle in her eyes had nothing at all to do with Lynn having found more work.

"Mitch, huh?" Raylene said, clearly fascinated. "How'd that happen?"

Lynn didn't want to mention her foolish decision to check out a clerk's job in a dangerous section of town, so she said simply, "He knew I was looking for something part-time and mentioned that he could use some help. The best part is I get to work from home."

Raylene's grin spread. "The best part, huh? I'd have thought that would be spending more time with Mitch. The man is a serious hunk."

"So Grace has mentioned," Lynn said wryly. "That seems to be the consensus in certain circles."

"And you hadn't noticed?"

"I've known Mitch since grade school. He's an old friend, that's all."

"Maybe that's what he was in school, when you were gaga over Ed, but circumstances have changed," Raylene reminded her. "You could do a lot worse. And don't forget I've seen the way he looks at you when you're both at the house for dinner."

"That's concern, nothing more. He's worried about the toll the divorce is taking on me and the kids. That's the kind of man he is."

"And there's something wrong with being thoughtful and compassionate?"

"Of course not, but it's not exactly the basis for some big romance, the way you're hinting."

Raylene laughed. "Honey, I'm not even hinting. I'm telling you flat-out you need to take another look at the man before someone else comes along and snaps him up. He's been immune to most of the passes I know have been directed his way, but you can't count on that resistance to last forever."

"Come on, Raylene," Lynn protested. "How can I even think about him that way? He's still grieving for Amy, and my divorce isn't even final. For all I know, we could wind up losing the house and having to move to be closer to one of my sisters. Why start something that doesn't have a chance?"

Raylene gave her a chiding look. "I am way too familiar with that defeatist attitude. I kept trying to let Carter off the hook. I worked really hard not to fall in love with him, because I thought my situation would never change and I refused to have him tied down to a woman who couldn't even leave the house. The thing was, he didn't want to give up. He fought for what we had. I think you and Mitch could have that same kind of staying power."

"Based on the way he's looked at me at dinner?" Lynn said skeptically. "You're still lost in some romantic fog. Not every situation has a fairy-tale ending."

"I'm just saying you shouldn't give up without a fight. Assuming you're even the tiniest bit attracted to him, that is," she said, regarding Lynn slyly. "Are you?"

Lynn hesitated, then said, "Okay, I am the tiniest bit attracted." She held two fingers maybe an inch apart. "This much, anyway."

Raylene laughed. "Couples have started with a lot less. Come to dinner tonight. Mitch usually stays, as you know. Let me get the lay of the land."

"No way," Lynn said, shuddering at the thought. "I do not want to sit there with you studying us like we're specimens under a microscope. It would be too embarrassing."

"Are you saying that you'll never join us for dinner again?" Raylene asked with a frown. "The last thing I meant to do was scare you off."

"You didn't. Not entirely anyway. I just don't think I can pretend it's simply another casual dinner after all this talk of attraction and looks and such. Maybe in a couple of weeks, but not tonight."

Raylene relented and backed off. "If you change your

mind or Mitch talks you into it, the offer's open. You're always welcome."

"What makes you think Mitch will even attempt to talk me into it? When would he do that?"

"You did say he's coming over when you get home from work, right? I imagine I can plant the idea in his head before then," Raylene said with confidence. "I promise I'll be more subtle about it than I was with you."

"Have you caught some kind of matchmaking fever? I hear it's been going around in Serenity."

"What can I say? It's a community curse," Raylene said unrepentantly. "Now go on home and freshen up so you'll be stunning when Mitch drops by. You've done more than your share of selling in here this morning. You'll have a nice fat commission in your check this week."

"I am not setting out to impress Mitch," Lynn said with what she hoped sounded like suitable indignation.

"Of course you're not," Raylene said innocently. "I'm just thinking a little eyeliner to go with that mascara you put on this morning, a touch of gloss on your lips and maybe another swipe of that blush."

Lynn groaned. "Was I that obvious?"

Raylene laughed. "Not to Mitch, I'm sure. He probably just noticed you looked more beautiful than ever. Only women pay attention to the little, telltale details like extra makeup."

"I am so humiliated," Lynn said. "I feel like a teenager who got caught drawing hearts and initials on the front of her school notebook. And I know exactly how that felt, because it happened way too often when my crush on Ed first developed. I do not want to be that lovesick girl ever again."

"How about a strong woman going after what she

wants?" Raylene asked. "I think that would demonstrate a whole new level of maturity and intelligence."

"Or make me look more foolish than ever," Lynn said direly.

Raylene gave her a sympathetic look. "From what I've seen when you're around Mitch, I don't think you need to worry about that a bit."

But even her friend's words of encouragement didn't quite calm the very bad case of nerves Lynn was suddenly feeling as she headed for home and an unavoidable encounter with the man who'd been at the center of their conversation.

Mitch had been so distracted all day by his son's unexpected announcement, even the guys had called him on it. When he was in his truck and heading for home before remembering he was supposed to stop over at Lynn's, he knew his worry over Nate's decision ran even deeper than he'd realized.

He considered calling Lynn to postpone till tomorrow, but he didn't want her worrying that he'd changed his mind about the job. He turned the truck around and headed back to her house, parking in her driveway this time, not Raylene's.

When Lynn answered the front door and spotted his truck, she studied him with confusion. "Weren't you just next door working?"

He nodded. "Sorry. I took off, then remembered I was supposed to come over to check on how you were making out with the computer systems. I turned around and came back."

She frowned at the admission. "Was there someplace else you needed to be? This can wait."

"To be perfectly honest, I'd be glad for the company," he told her. "I can't promise you, though, that my mind's going to be on work."

Lynn looked vaguely alarmed by that. "Why?"

"Are you sure you want me laying my problems on you? You seem to have plenty going on in your life these days."

"Which is why listening to you would be a real break," she assured him. "Come on in and tell me."

"I had a call from my son Nate this morning," Mitch explained as he followed her inside. "He announced that he's engaged and wants to bring the girl home this weekend. I didn't even know he was seriously dating anyone."

"Wow! That must have come as a shock."

"You have no idea."

She gestured toward the sofa. "Why don't you have a seat in here for a minute? Can I get you something to drink? I have iced tea and water. I'm afraid that's it. There might be a can of frozen lemonade left in the freezer. I could make that."

"Iced tea would be great."

"Sweetened or not?"

"Straight's good," he said, following her into the kitchen, startling her when she turned suddenly and found him right behind her.

"I thought you were going to wait in the living room."

He shrugged. "I like the feel of this kitchen. If it's all right, let's just stay in here." Besides, he was less likely to act on impulse and give in to the ridiculous urge he had to kiss her if they were separated by her kitchen table.

"Sure, here's fine," she said, putting ice into two large glasses, then adding the tea from an old-fashioned glass pitcher like the ones his mom used to have with fruit painted on the glass. She'd always served orange juice in hers.

"So, you really weren't expecting Nate's big news?" she said, when she'd taken a seat opposite him.

He shook his head. "I honestly don't know what he's thinking. He's still a kid."

"How old?"

"Twenty-one."

She fought a smile. "And how old were you when you and Amy got married?"

Mitch frowned at the question. "Twenty, but that's not the point."

"Really?"

"I was old at twenty. I'd already been working construction for a couple of years. I knew what I wanted out of life. Nate's changed his major three times. I'm not even a hundred percent sure what his degree will be in. I'm not criticizing him for that. He's hardly the first kid to get out of college and not be sure he wants to work in the field he majored in, but shouldn't he figure that out, maybe even be earning some money before he takes a huge step and gets married?"

"Maybe they're not planning to get married right away," Lynn suggested. "Did he mention the timetable?"

"No," Mitch confessed, taking hope for the first time since morning.

"Or how old his fiancée is? Maybe she's even younger than he is and wants to finish college. They could be planning on a long engagement."

"Or he could have told me this just so I'd let the girl sleep in his room," Mitch added dryly, reaching a conclusion he should have formed early on. "I'd just blown that idea out of the water right before he made his big announcement."

Lynn looked startled. "You don't think he'd lie just to get your approval for sleeping with her, do you?"

Mitch considered the question, which he thought was fair, but eventually shook his head. "Nah. Nate's not like that. He's always been pretty open with us, or at least with his mother. He figured out early on that we appreciated honesty more than evasions."

"A lesson more kids should learn," Lynn said. "I constantly tell Jeremy and Lexie that the truth will get them in a lot less trouble than a lie. They're still working on believing that, since I punish them either way."

Mitch chuckled. "Yeah, that's a hard one for kids to figure out. Maybe you need to tell them in advance, here's what's going to happen if you tell me the truth and this is the much harsher punishment if I catch you in a lie. Sometimes it takes that kind of clarity to get through to them."

"Good plan, but they usually don't think they're going to get caught in the lie."

"But they always do, don't they? They'll catch on eventually. My boys did." He met her gaze. "And I don't want you to get the wrong idea. Nate and Luke are terrific young men. Amy saw to that."

"I imagine you were a big influence, too," Lynn told him. "How could you not be? You're an admirable man."

Mitch couldn't help being flattered and a little startled by her open declaration. "You sound as if you mean that."

"I do. I told you before that I've never heard a bad word about you around town, but I've seen it for myself recently. You've taken me under your wing, given me a job." She flushed as if she felt she'd said too much. "And speaking of that, we should probably get to work. I'm sure you're anxious to get home and have dinner. You didn't plan on staying to have dinner at Raylene's tonight, did you?"

He shook his head. "Nah, I figured they deserved a night off from having me underfoot. I wasn't such good company anyway."

"Your company's just fine," Lynn said.

Mitch hesitated. "But I am starving," he said. "How about I order some food from Rosalina's? We can eat while we go over these bills."

She looked as if she were about to refuse, so he held her gaze. "You have anything against pepperoni or jalapeños on your pizza?"

Her eyes widened. "Jalapeños?"

"Trust me. It's worth staying awake half the night for that combination. You'll never want a plain old cheese pizza again."

"If you say so."

"Is that a yes? I can give Rosalina's a call?"

"Sure, why not?" she said.

"I'll order a salad, too. We can pretend we're being healthy. How about soda? You want a bottle of soda to go with that?" he asked, already hitting speed dial on his cell phone.

"You have their number programmed into your phone?" she teased.

"And the entire menu memorized," he said unrepentantly. "Now, about that soda?"

"Sure. Diet soda, if that's okay."

"Suits me." He placed the order, then sat back and took a good long look at the woman seated across the table. She looked different somehow.

"Why are you staring at me like that?" she asked, squirming uncomfortably.

"You look different."

"Different how?"

"More rested, I guess. Did you take a nap this afternoon?"

She shook her head, but there was an odd smile tugging at her lips.

"Well, your eyes are brighter. It looks good."

To his surprise, she actually laughed the way he'd remembered. "What?" he demanded.

"It's eye makeup. Raylene swore to me that men never noticed things like that, so I put some on for the first time in ages."

Mitch could see it, then, the thin stroke of liner on her lids, the hint of pale blue shadow, the darkened lashes.

"Was that for my benefit?" he asked, oddly pleased to think it might be.

She blushed furiously at the question. "Maybe it was just a test. Maybe I was trying to prove her wrong, to show her that some men are observant."

He grinned at the deliberate evasion. So she wasn't totally immune, after all. Now he just needed to figure out what he wanted to do with that information.

Six

When Lynn saw the enormous amount of food Mitch had ordered, she blinked. "Were you planning on feeding an army?"

"What can I say? I like pizza and salad, and leftovers are always good, right? The kids will gobble this right up."

She saw the ploy for what it was, a face-saving way to put a little extra food on her table. Before she could call him on it, he frowned at her.

"Do not make a fuss over this, Lynnie," he said, resorting to the nickname only he had ever dared to use. "It's pizza. I'm not having steaks and champagne delivered, along with boxes of fresh produce."

"You should take the leftovers home with you," she insisted with a touch of defiance. She wasn't about to tolerate his pity.

"Nate's coming home this weekend. We'll be going out to eat, more than likely."

"But did you ever know a college kid who couldn't eat his weight in pizza?" she countered just as stubbornly.

"How about we wait and see how many leftovers there are?" he suggested. "I have a big appetite. And the kids might turn up and want their share."

"The Jolly Green Giant doesn't have a big enough appetite to go through this much food," she insisted. "And the kids are eating with friends."

"You realize while we're debating this, the pizza's getting cold," he said, reaching for a slice.

She started to argue some more, but finally relented. It was clearly futile, at least for now. "Okay," she said, then warned, "but the discussion's not over."

He grinned. "We'll see about that."

Regarding him with frustration, she asked, "Do you have to win *every* argument?"

"Only when I'm right," he said. "And, just so you know, I've never been afraid to admit when I'm wrong, either."

"Now *that* I can hardly wait to see," Lynn told him, taking her first bite of pizza and nearly choking at the heat that burst in her mouth. It was true that the slice had cooled, but the jalapeños hadn't.

"Come on, wimp. It's not that hot," Mitch teased as she began picking off the jalapeños.

"Are you kidding me? I could heat the house from the fire in these things."

"So, no more jalapeños for you," he said, looking disappointed.

"No, no, I left one piece on here," she said, pointing out a tiny sliver. "Just enough for a hint of spice."

Mitch studied her for a minute. "Is that the way you want to live your life these days, Lynn? Being safe, with barely enough spice to keep things interesting?"

She thought she detected a hint of criticism in there, but it was a legitimate question. "For now, yes," she told him. "For the kids' sake I have to be cautious. Things are topsy-turvy enough around here without my rushing into things."

He nodded. "Fair enough."

"Isn't that the pot calling the kettle black? I thought you weren't looking for anything more right now, either," she said, puzzled by his reaction.

"I wasn't," he said, then added more firmly, "I'm not."

"But?"

"I seem to be a lot more open to the possibilities than I was a few days ago." He looked into her eyes. "And just so you know, I'm probably no crazier about that than you are."

Lynn was rattled by his candor. She couldn't think of a single thing to say in response.

They continued eating in silence. To her surprise, it didn't feel the least bit strained. It felt…comfortable.

"Maybe we should pretend we never had this conversation," she suggested eventually. "We could just go on working together, be friends, no complications."

"A nice theory," he agreed, still holding her gaze. "I just think maybe it's too late."

"It's not too late," she said a little urgently. "It can't be. That's all I can handle, Mitch. Seriously."

He smiled at her reaction. "No need to panic. We're not impulsive kids. We don't have to rush into anything. I just figured you deserved to know where my head is."

"Are you sure your head has anything to do with it?"

A grin broke across his face at the question, and then his booming laugh filled the kitchen. "Now that, my friend, is something I imagine I'll be puzzling over for most of the night."

Lynn couldn't bear seeing him out on that limb all by himself for another second. She finally allowed herself to relax and grinned back at him. "Since we're being honest, me, too."

Mitch's expression sobered at once. "Now that is the best news I've heard in a very long while."

He sounded so sure of that, Lynn thought, while she thought maybe it was the scariest bit of news ever.

When her doorbell rang the next morning a little after nine, Lynn glanced up gratefully from the computer. What had seemed so simple last night with Mitch's coaxing was proving completely bewildering this morning.

When she opened the front door, though, and found Raylene on her doorstep with a coffee cake and a smug expression, she had second thoughts.

"I thought maybe you'd have time for a cup of coffee before I leave for the store," Raylene said, then added hurriedly, "The coffee cake stays, even if you want me to leave."

Since the aroma of the apparently still-warm cinnamon pecan coffee cake was too tempting to ignore, Lynn stepped aside. "Come on in. I just made a fresh pot of coffee. I figure I'm going to need it if I'm going to figure out this billing system of Mitch's."

Raylene looked momentarily chagrined. "You were working. I'm sorry."

"It's fine. I'm not on a rigid timetable. I think Mitch finally realized there's going to be a learning curve with me. I'll get the bills out today, but his payroll system is going to take a lot longer. He'll pick up the computer later and deal with that himself this week."

Raylene joined her in the kitchen. "A knife? Forks? Plates?" she asked, glancing around.

Lynn realized then that this was one of the few times in the years they'd known each other that Raylene had been in her kitchen. She pointed to the drawers and cabinet. "I'll get napkins."

"I'll cut the coffee cake while you pour the coffee."

As soon as they were settled at the table, Lynn gave her friend—and boss, she reminded herself—an amused look over the rim of her cup. "I assume there's a price for this neighborly gesture."

Raylene looked momentarily taken aback, then chuckled. "Okay, I want information. I know Mitch was here till late last night. Lexie called Mandy the second she got home to report that. As if I needed confirmation," she scoffed. "His truck was right there in the driveway in plain view. I saw Tony from Rosalina's deliver food, too."

"Very observant," Lynn noted, more entertained than annoyed.

"I'm the best asset the neighborhood crime watch has," Raylene said. "It comes from all that time I spent hunkered down inside the house. Not much gets past me."

"And here I thought it was just my social life you were finding fascinating," Lynn teased.

"Well, seeing that you have one is a definite bonus," Raylene admitted. "So how'd it go? Any progress?"

"As I said, I understand the billing system," Lynn replied, being deliberately obtuse.

"That is so not what I was asking," Raylene said, her exasperation plain. "Come on. Spill. Were there sparks?"

Lynn thought of the way Mitch had looked at her a few times the night before, the way her pulse had scrambled under the scrutiny. "Maybe one or two," she admitted. "And that is absolutely all I'm saying."

Raylene grinned. "Good enough," she said. "At least for now. By the way, I didn't come over this morning just to pry information out of you. I wanted to invite you over next week. We're having a Sweet Magnolias get-together on Tuesday. It used to be we had them spur of the moment, but it's getting harder and harder to coordinate everyone's schedule, so now we plan."

Lynn regarded her with surprise. "You're having one of those infamous margarita nights and you want me to come?" Though the Sweet Magnolias were not a formal organization, there was a certain exclusivity to being invited to join the group of longtime friends.

"We do," Raylene confirmed. "I know you probably have your own friends, but I also know that when life's offering challenges, you can never have too many women on your side. Will you come?"

Lynn thought about how much she'd been longing for the kind of support system she knew Raylene had. Now, thanks to her neighbor, it was being offered. "I'd love to come, if you're sure the others won't mind an interloper."

"First, you have to stop thinking of yourself as any sort of outsider or interloper," Raylene scolded. "And this wasn't even my idea. Sarah and Helen both suggested it, and the whole group agreed we want you there."

"That's very kind of everyone. What can I bring?" she asked automatically, because she knew all the women contributed something. It would be a stretch to provide much, but she couldn't go empty-handed.

"Just your presence will do this time," Raylene said. "We rotate who brings the various things, and this time it's all taken care of. Your turn will come, though, never fear."

"I can't tell you how much I'm looking forward to this," Lynn confessed.

"Let's see if you still feel that way after the traditional Sweet Magnolias inquisition," Raylene taunted. "These women make my intrusive questions look like child's play."

Lynn stared at her. "You're kidding!"

"Not so much," Raylene said, standing up, evidently satisfied at planting the prospect of more questions in Lynn's head. "Now I'd better be off to work. With the success you and Adelia are having making these gigantic sales, I'm starting to feel like a slacker. Today's my day to catch up. And, also thanks to you two, I need to order more spring inventory or our racks will be bare."

"I'm glad you stopped by," Lynn said, meaning it.

She'd forgotten what it was like to have a real friend. And now, thanks to Raylene, she had not only one, but several more on the horizon. Even if their questions were likely to make her squirm.

Mitch left Raylene's at four on Friday, determined to run the vacuum at home and take a serious stab at straightening up the house. He'd had a housekeeper come in a few times, but she'd constantly moved things around. Not knowing where his paperwork might turn up had driven him crazy, so he'd let her go after a couple of months.

Since he wasn't entirely sure what time Nate and this fiancée of his would arrive, he'd gone to the grocery store and filled the refrigerator with a few of his son's favorites. He'd bought a rotisserie chicken, some prepared potato salad, coleslaw and a cherry pie, in case they wanted dinner. Nothing would be as good as what Amy would have made, but he'd discovered that the store's offerings weren't half bad.

It was nearly eight by the time he heard his son's car in the driveway. Mitch walked outside to greet the couple, pulling Nate into a bear hug, then turning to meet the young woman with him. He had to fight to keep his mouth from dropping open. She looked no more than sixteen. Surely Nate was smarter than that, though. If not, they needed to have a serious talk in a big hurry. And he could forget about sharing a bedroom with this innocent-looking young thing!

"Dad, this is Jo. She'll be graduating this May, too. She's getting a master's in chemistry."

Mitch blinked, trying to wrap his mind around that.

Nate grinned, clearly having expected exactly that reaction. "She doesn't look twenty-three, does she?"

"She certainly doesn't," Mitch said, breathing a sigh of relief. "Chemistry, huh. That's a tough field."

"I'm going for an engineering degree after this," she told him. "My dad's a chemical engineer, too, and I've been hanging around his lab since I could climb up onto a stool next to him."

"I'm impressed," Mitch said candidly. He gave his son a long look. "Is she motivating you to think about some postgraduate work?"

Nate shook his head. "Nah. I think one brain in the family will be plenty."

Mitch let the comment pass. This wasn't the time to chide his son for his seeming lack of direction.

"Well, let's get your things inside and get you settled. Then you can tell me all about your plans," Mitch said. "There's food, if you're hungry. And I thought tomorrow we might go to Sullivan's." He turned to Jo. "That's the best restaurant in town. It has a great reputation around the state."

"I know," she said. "Nate's told me all about it and I read some of the reviews online. I'd love to go there."

"But not tomorrow," Nate said. "Sorry, Dad. Some of my buddies from high school are coming home this weekend. Luke said he'd drive over in the morning, too. I want to get the gang together at Rosalina's so they can meet Jo.

Maybe we can go to Sullivan's for Sunday brunch before we head back to school."

Mitch nodded. "Works for me. You say your brother's coming home?"

"He told me he was. He didn't call?"

"Of course not."

"Typical," Nate said.

Inside the house, Nate gave him a questioning look. Mitch knew exactly what he was wondering. "Your room," he said, though getting the words out without a hint of regret was a struggle.

Nate clapped a hand on his back as he headed toward the steps. "Thanks, Dad."

With the couple upstairs, Mitch stood in front of the mantel staring at his favorite family picture. Though there had been many through the years taken in a photography studio, this one, taken on a trip to the beach with everyone windblown, sunburned and laughing, was his favorite.

"Oh, Amy, guide me through this," he murmured, looking into her eyes.

He sensed, rather than heard, Nate come up beside him. "Do you think Mom would approve?" he asked hesitantly.

Mitch turned to him. "I know she would," he said with conviction. Even he had seen the way the two of them had looked at each other. It was a lot like the way he and Amy were looking at each other over their children's heads in the picture. Whatever reservations he might have were almost beside the point in the face of all that undisguised joy.

In the morning Mitch left Nate and Jo asleep at the house and headed over to Raylene's. He only intended to hand out paychecks, make sure the work was progressing well, then head back home, but instead he found himself gravitating to Lynn's.

He knocked on the back door, tested the knob, then shook his head when it opened immediately.

"Lynn, are you here?" he called out.

"I'll be right there," she replied. "There's coffee if you want some. Help yourself."

He poured himself a cup, then waited, resisting the urge to wander into the living room. He'd noticed on his last visit that there was a virtual shrine to Ed set up on top of an old upright piano. He knew the pictures had probably been kept out for the sake of Jeremy and Lexie, but he'd wanted to smash them so they wouldn't be in Lynn's face. Who knew, though? Maybe she wanted them there as much as the kids did. Maybe she wasn't as over the man as he wanted to believe she was.

He'd just settled at the kitchen table—a much more welcoming environment to his way of thinking—when Lexie came in. She was still in her pajamas or what he assumed passed for pajamas these days. Looked a lot like what he saw some girls wearing at the mall, too. The loose pants and a tank top seemed to be go-anywhere attire, though he imagined there was some distinction that eluded him.

"How come you're over here?" Lexie asked curiously as she poured some cereal into a bowl.

Mitch noticed that she was careful not to fill the bowl or to add much more than a splash of milk. Given the amount of food she managed to consume over at Raylene's, he knew it wasn't because she was dieting excessively. The thought of her having to restrict every mouthful she took in her own home to make sure there was enough left for her mom and brother made him want to go down to that fancy brick mausoleum Ed had built and slug the man squarely in the jaw.

"I just stopped by to see how your mom's doing with those bills she was going to send for me," he told Lexie as she sat across from him and started eating. "You knew she was working for me part-time, right?"

"Is that why you were here the other night, too?" she asked, looking him straight in the eye. "Mandy thinks it's because you've got a thing for my mom."

Mitch nearly choked on a sip of coffee. She and her best friend were speculating over his motives? What sort of romantic ideas had he unleashed in those two? And how was he supposed to respond?

He settled for at least a half truth. "Your mom and I have been friends for a long time. We've known each other most of our lives."

Lexie's eyes lit up. "Did you ever date?" she inquired, her curiosity obviously fanned.

Only in his dreams, Mitch thought, suddenly trying to contain his amusement at the determined cross-examination. "No."

"Did you want to?" she persisted. "I mean, I know my mom fell for my dad when they were pretty young, but what about you? Did you want to ask her out?"

"I considered it," he said. Knowing full well that she'd turn him down had deterred him. No adolescent kid risked certain rejection.

"Why didn't you?"

"As you said, your mom was crazy about your dad. We all knew it."

Lexie gave him a look that was entirely too world-weary for a girl her age. "She's not anymore."

Thank heaven Lynn came into the kitchen before he

had to think of a response to that. She studied her daughter with a narrowed gaze.

"What was that about?"

"Just trying to figure things out," Lexie said cheerfully. "Gotta run. Mandy and I are going to the library, and then we have that babysitting certification class. We might go shopping or have lunch after that."

"You need money?" Lynn asked.

Lexie immediately shook her head. "Mandy's got it," she called over her shoulder as she took off for her room.

Mitch saw the defeated look on Lynn's face before she could cover it. "She's an intuitive kid," he said.

"To me that's another way of saying she's growing up entirely too fast. Do you know she's turned down an allowance from me ever since Ed left? Now she's taking this babysitting class, hoping I'll let her take a few jobs."

"All kids need a little spending money of their own."

"They do," Lynn agreed. "That's not why she wants it. She wants to help with the bills around here." She shook her head. "I've already told her that's not her responsibility. Any money she makes will go into savings or she can spend it on herself."

"It's clear that she's very protective of you. You should have heard her just now."

Lynn regarded him with alarm. "What did she say?"

"Settle down," he said. "She asked a few questions, that's all. Dropped a few hints."

"About what?"

"My intentions. Your availability," he told her, grinning now that the uncomfortable moments were behind him.

Lynn groaned. "She didn't! Are you kidding me?"

"She did."

"I am so, so sorry."

"Don't be. I'm glad to know that somebody else has your back."

Lynn looked thoroughly disconcerted by the conversation, so Mitch let it drop. "Actually, I stopped by to see if you'd had any problems with the billing. I'm sorry I didn't get by here yesterday."

"It took a while, but they all got done. I dropped them in the mail late yesterday afternoon. Now, as long as nobody comes over here screaming about being overcharged because I put a decimal point in the wrong place, I think I have that under control." She finally turned away from the sink and faced him. "So, how did it go last night? With Nate and the fiancée? Are you still worried?"

"Not half as much as I was. She looks like she ought to be in high school, but she's twenty-three and getting a master's in May, then studying to be a chemical engineer."

"Wow!"

Mitch chuckled. "I know. Intimidates the heck out of me, but, surprisingly, Nate just thinks she's amazing. He's content to have her be the brains in the family, likely even the major breadwinner, as far as I can tell." He frowned. "Should I be worried about that, do you think? Should he be showing more ambition?"

"I imagine every couple figures out the kind of relationship balance that works for them. Look at Helen and Erik. She's a high-powered attorney with a statewide reputation and he's a chef in a small-town restaurant. He doesn't seem to be the least bit threatened by that."

"Need I remind you that that restaurant has an outstanding reputation all over the state?" Mitch said. "I doubt Dana Sue would appreciate any hint that it's some local dive."

Lynn winced. "I didn't mean it that way. I was just making a point. And to continue with that, Cal doesn't seem to notice that Maddie's ten years older than he is. There are all sorts of things that make couples seem unlikely to outsiders, but that work perfectly for them."

Mitch nodded. "I suppose in a way that was even true for Amy and me. I was a blue-collar guy all the way and she was a debutante. Did you know that?"

Lynn shook her head. "I never would have guessed. The few times I met her, she seemed totally down-to-earth." She shrugged. "Then, again, so's Raylene, and she was a debutante, too."

"With Amy sometimes I wondered how our paths even crossed, but fate stepped in and there she was one day when I was over at Sullivan's Island with my folks. Her blue-blood Charleston family nearly had a coronary when we said we wanted to get married. They insisted that she had to go to college, and if it was what she still wanted after graduation, they promised to go along with it. Then she got pregnant with Nate, and that was that. They couldn't get us down the aisle fast enough. I think they finally reconciled themselves to having me in the family when Luke was born, and Amy and I were still together and happy."

"My folks never approved of Ed," Lynn confided. "I think they saw him in a way I didn't until we started this divorce process. My father always thought he was shallow and self-involved. Most of the time my mom managed to get him to keep his opinion to himself, but both of them slipped up enough that I knew exactly how they felt."

Her smile was rueful. "Of course, I wouldn't listen, because what do parents know? Some days I wish I had listened, but then I wouldn't have Lexie and Jeremy. They're worth whatever pain I'm going through now. And I can't help thinking the one good thing about having lost my parents a few years ago is that they don't have to see the way he's behaving now. And I don't have to hear so many I-told-you-so comments."

"What about his folks? I know they're still right here in town. Have they stepped up at all?"

A hint of temper sparked in her eyes. "And suggest for even an instant that their precious son might be in the wrong? Not a chance," she said heatedly, then flushed. "Sorry. They're good people, but they have a blind spot where Ed's concerned. Heaven knows what he's told them about the divorce, but I'm sure they think I'm the one in the wrong."

"Maybe you need to set them straight before they say something in front of the kids," he suggested.

"Too late," Lynn said. "Lexie already refuses to go over there because her grandmother said something about me that upset her. She refuses to tell me what was said. It's taken everything in me not to go charging over there to warn them they'll never see either of my kids again if they don't watch what they say around them."

"Maybe you should," he told her, angry on her behalf.

She shook her head. "I don't want to escalate things. As far as I know, there was only the one slip. I'm sure when Lexie stopped going over, they got the message. For all their flaws, they adore the kids. I know they have to be missing her."

Mitch would have been content to stay right here for a second cup of coffee, but he knew he was getting entirely too comfortable being with Lynn. The other night they'd established the need to take it slow, for both their sakes. He had to honor that.

"I should get over and check on my crew." He hesitated, debating with himself, then decided to ask. "I'm taking the kids to Sullivan's for brunch tomorrow. Luke's coming home, so he'll be there, too. Would you, Lexie and Jeremy like to come along?"

The invitation clearly flustered her. "Thanks, but I think that's a bad idea."

Mitch frowned. "What's bad about it?"

"You're going out for a family celebration. I think your boys would take it the wrong way if I came along with my kids. It might raise questions that not even we know how to answer at this point."

Mitch reluctantly concurred. Her wisdom, inconvenient though it might feel, was another thing he saw to admire about her. "You're probably right. Another time, then, okay?"

She smiled. "We'll see."

Knowing it was useless to press for more when her mind was clearly made up, he stood. "See you on Monday, then."

"See you," she said. "I'm glad you have your family home this weekend and that things are good with Nate."

"Thanks." He headed for the back door. As he opened it, he turned and regarded her with the stern expression he usually reserved to get through to his sons. "And lock the darn door, you hear me?"

Lynn's laugh rang out. While the sound pleased him, it also signaled that she wasn't taking his admonition one bit seriously. For the second time in recent days, he shook his head and turned the lock himself. He wondered just how long it would take her to flip it back.

Seven

When they were seated around a table at Sullivan's on Sunday, Mitch surveyed his family and felt a familiar stirring of sorrow. Amy should have been here for this. He had a hunch his invitation to Lynn the day before had, in part, been an attempt to fill the void that would be left by his late wife's absence. He knew, though, that Lynn had been wise to decline. It wasn't the time to introduce someone new into his sons' lives, especially when things with Lynn were far from certain.

"Dad, you okay?" Luke asked, leaning closer and regarding him with concern.

Mitch was still surprised when his younger son showed so much insight. Nate was more like him in a lot of ways with his carefree exuberance, but Luke was pure Amy, filled with compassion and taking everything to heart.

"Just wishing your mom were here for this," he told Luke.

"I know. I think she'd love Jo, though, don't you?"

Mitch nodded. "I do."

"Hey, Dad, how about a bottle of champagne?" Nate asked.

"Sure, why not?" he said, beckoning their waitress.

When she returned with the requested bottle and glasses, Mitch declined. "I'm good with sparkling water."

The waitress poured three glasses, though she gave Luke a considering look before filling his. Mitch, however, moved the glass aside. "He'll have sparkling water, too."

"But I'll be twenty-one in a couple of months," Luke protested.

"Then in two months, we'll have champagne and toast you," Mitch said. "I don't want Dana Sue losing her liquor license because her waitress looked the other way and served you."

Since he noticed that Nate had been watching him curiously ever since he'd declined the drink for himself, Mitch decided to forgo the rest of the lecture about underage drinking. Instead, he raised his glass in a toast.

"To Nate and Jo," he began. "I hope you have many wonderful years together and, Nate, I especially hope that the two of you are blessed with as much happiness as your mom and I had."

"Hear, hear," Luke echoed, lifting his own glass of sparkling water. "To Nate and Jo. I'm not losing a brother. I'm gaining a really smart and probably successful sister."

"Could I make a toast?" Jo asked softly, her expression uncertain.

"Of course," Mitch said. "This is your celebration, after all."

"To Amy," she said, her gaze resting on each of them in turn. "From everything Nate has told me, she must have been an incredible woman. I truly wish I'd had the chance to know her."

"To Amy," Mitch said, his voice choked by her sweetly sentimental tribute to a woman she'd never even met, but respected just the same. It told him a lot about his son, too, that Nate had talked about his mother so glowingly.

"To Mom," Nate and Luke echoed. Nate leaned over and kissed his fiancée. "Thank you."

"I just wanted to acknowledge that she's very much with us today," Jo said, proving once more what an amazing girl Nate had found.

Since there was a drive ahead for both Nate and Luke, they wrapped up the meal quickly after just one drink. Mitch knew Nate would go for a run to work off that single glass of champagne before getting behind the wheel, and Luke likely would go with him. The two had an ongoing challenge to see if they could best each other in every sport. Once it had been baseball and football. They'd even had a go at tennis. These days it was running. Nate had always been the stronger athlete, but Luke was quickly catching up to him. He'd entered his first triathlon, scheduled for later this spring, and had been taunting his brother about it for weeks now.

As they headed out of Sullivan's, Mitch was surprised when Luke and Jo walked on ahead, leaving Nate behind to walk with him. "Why didn't you touch the champagne, Dad? Is it because of what happened to Mom?"

Mitch was surprised that it was Nate who'd picked up on it. "Not entirely," he said.

"There's no beer in the house, either."

Mitch gave him an annoyed look. "You taking inventory?"

"No, I went to grab one after my run yesterday and I noticed, that's all. You always kept the fridge stocked."

"And now I don't," Mitch said flatly.

"If it's not because of the drunk driver, then what's going on?" Nate persisted.

Mitch studied his son with annoyance. "You're not going to let this go, are you?"

Nate shook his head. "Look, right after the accident, Luke and I noticed you were drinking a little more than usual. Was it a lot more?"

Mitch sighed. Of course they'd noticed. He hadn't done much to hide the difficulty he was having dealing with his grief and the sorry way he'd chosen to drown it. "For a couple of months, yes," he admitted. "Eventually I realized I was getting too dependent on alcohol to take away the pain, so I stopped. It's no big deal."

"Did it bother you that I wanted to order champagne at lunch?"

He smiled at the worry in his son's eyes. "Not at all. It was a celebration. It deserved a toast. And I could have had a glass of champagne if I'd wanted one, but I've lost my taste for alcohol. I think it's best left that way." He hadn't wanted to disrespect Amy's memory by turning into a drunk, and he'd seen for himself the danger of that happening the more he'd wallowed in the pain of losing her. The irony, not lost on him, was that even an alcoholic haze hadn't helped with the grief. Not really. He'd still had to feel it down to his soul to start getting past it.

Nate regarded him sympathetically. "I wish I'd come home more often right after the accident. I just couldn't. It hurt to be in the house without Mom there."

"Believe me, I know."

"And that's what I'm saying," Nate said earnestly. "I should have seen how much harder it was for you. I'm sorry for being so selfish and clueless."

"Stop that this minute," Mitch chided. "You're neither selfish nor clueless. You were doing exactly what you should have been doing—going to school, living your life, meeting a terrific girl."

Nate clearly wasn't ready to let it go. "Luke knew. He came home more than I did."

Mitch grinned. "Because he was broke more than you were. Don't paint your brother as a saint. Not that I wasn't glad to have him home, no matter what the reason." He deliberately sought to change the subject. "By the way, have you and Jo talked about where you'll live once you're married?"

Nate gave him a long look, but then moved on. "It depends on where she goes to school next year. She's been accepted at Stanford."

Mitch's step faltered at the news. "Stanford, huh? That's incredible."

"But a long way from home," Nate said, sounding unhappy. "I'm hoping she'll choose someplace closer to here, but it's up to her."

"Don't try to influence her," Mitch cautioned. "It's an important decision and she should make the one that's right for her."

"She says we're a team now and that the decisions have to be right for both of us."

Mitch continued to be impressed with Jo's maturity. "Well, then, I know you'll work it out."

As they reached the house, Nate touched his arm, stopping him. "Just one more thing, okay? If you need us here—me or Luke or both of us—you just have to call."

"I'll remember that," Mitch said, touched yet again by the sensitivity Amy had ingrained in their sons.

In a way it reminded him that she would always be with them. It also reminded him that with her generous spirit and warm heart, she would be the first to tell him to move on with his life, to find happiness.

Maybe that was with Lynn. Maybe not. But he was finally ready, he thought, to find out.

"You've been avoiding me," Helen declared, catching Erik in the kitchen at Sullivan's on Sunday when he couldn't escape.

"I see you every day," her husband reminded her. "We sleep in the same bed at night."

"But I can't cross-examine you at night, because just when I open my mouth with a question, you find some clever way to distract me. Call me crazy, but I think it's deliberate."

"Maybe I just can't keep my hands off you," he suggested, a twinkle in his eyes.

Helen rolled her eyes in response. Flattery wasn't going to get him off the hook. "*And* every time I bring up my mother, you find some excuse to take off."

"You're exaggerating," he said, though there was a hint of a smile on his lips.

That blasted smile of his exasperated her as much as his obvious avoidance of a conversation he clearly didn't want to have.

"Step away from the food processor," she ordered in a tone that was usually effective in intimidating witnesses in the courtroom. When he'd reluctantly done as she'd asked, she said, "Now tell me what you know about my mom dating."

He actually managed to feign a surprised look. "Flo's dating?" he asked, his tone almost believable. Almost, but not quite.

"Oh, don't even try that with me," she said, waving off his blatant attempt at feigning innocence. "I know she tells you all sorts of things she's never mentioned to me. You're her hero who can do no wrong. I'm her daughter. She won't say a thing to me about something like this because she's afraid I'll disapprove."

"You do have a history of being pretty stuffy when it comes to her having a social life," he suggested gently.

"That doesn't mean she should hide it from me. Now tell me who she's dating. Or is it a whole lot of men? That might be better," she said, considering it. "She'd never sleep with a lot of men." She shuddered at the thought of her mother sleeping with *any* man.

Erik shook his head. "And you wonder why she keeps secrets from you. Listen to yourself."

"It's just weird, that's all. She's past seventy. Should she be having a sex life at that age?"

Erik chuckled, but quickly tried to hide it. "If she wants one, I'd say the answer has to be yes."

Helen barely resisted the urge to stamp her foot. "I knew you'd take her side."

"Because it's her life. She's entitled to live it however she wants to. Weren't you the one who was always telling me how many sacrifices she made to get enough money to send you to college and then law school? You moved her down to Boca Raton and bought her a condo so she could finally have the kind of life you thought she deserved."

"I was thinking about her swimming and relaxing in the sun, playing cards with her friends, going shopping. Dating and sex never once crossed my mind."

"Because that was something else she sacrificed during those years when you were her whole focus," he suggested.

Helen frowned at his reasonable attitude. "What if it were your mother? Would you be sounding so blasé about it?"

"I'm pretty sure my mother and father are still getting it on like bunnies," Erik said with increasing amusement.

Helen poked him in the ribs. "You do not believe that."

"I do. My dad looks pretty darn happy whenever I see him."

"Why are you not taking me seriously?"

"I do take you seriously. And I know you're all worked up out of concern for your mother and not because you're a prude, right?"

"Right," she said, albeit not entirely truthfully. "Do you really not know anything about what's going on?"

"Nothing I can share," he said. "Talk to Flo. At least pretend to be interested, rather than getting on your high horse and ripping into her."

"I do not get on a high horse and rip into my mother," she protested. At Erik's raised eyebrow, she sighed. "Okay, sometimes I do. I'll try not to this time."

"I'm sure she'll appreciate that. Now, is it okay if I go back to making dessert for the many customers who might be expecting something delicious on the menu?"

"If you must," she conceded. "You have flour on your cheek, by the way." She stood on tiptoe and pressed a kiss to the spot. "Right there." She grinned. "And a little here."

"For a woman who's all worked up over her mother having a few innocent dates, you surely do seem intent on getting me riled up where anyone could walk in on us."

"It's a contradiction, isn't it?" she said cheerfully. "See you tonight. We'll finish what I tried to start."

He grinned. "Looking forward to it."

Helen left Sullivan's humming. She might not have gotten everything she wanted from her husband, but she surely did have the promise of an interesting evening ahead.

Flo woke up to the smell of coffee brewing. She tried to recall a single other moment in her life when a man had been that considerate. Helen's daddy surely hadn't been. He'd been a good man, but in his view certain tasks were women's work. And in those years, she hadn't had enough gumption to call him on it.

None of the other men who'd passed through her life had had much to recommend them, either, not even in the short-term. Now there was Donnie, who'd surprised the heck out of her by being not only an incredible dancer, but about as thoughtful as anyone could possibly be.

She sighed, stretched and was about to go in search of that coffee when he came into her bedroom carrying a cookie sheet with a napkin on it, a plate filled with food, coffee and a rose he'd obviously nabbed from the bush in front of her apartment building. It took a lot to rattle her, but the gesture brought tears to her eyes.

"Why'd you do this?" she couldn't help asking, even as she took her first sip of coffee. It was black and strong, just the way she liked it.

"Because you're a woman who deserves to be pampered," he said. "I know there hasn't been much of that in your life, but now you have me."

"Do I?" she whispered. "Have you, I mean?"

"Darlin', what do you think's been goin' on these past months? I've been courtin' you the best way I know how."

"Donnie, you're going to turn my head with talk like that."

"That's the idea," he said, looking deep into her eyes. "Flo, do you not have any idea what a treasure you are?"

She honestly couldn't say that she did. "A treasure?" she echoed doubtfully.

"You're an amazing mother. You raised Helen to be an incredible woman, and you did it with no help from anyone. I've seen the way that granddaughter of yours looks at you. She adores you. You're the best friend Frances and Liz could ask for." He grinned. "And you do one heckuva two-step!"

"I just hope that last one doesn't land me in the hospital with another broken hip," she said, trying to lighten the moment from the unexpected emotional intensity of his words.

"Not with me there to hold you," he promised. "I won't let you stumble, much less fall."

"Donnie, how is it that some woman didn't snap you up years ago?"

He winked at her. "I was just waiting for you."

"I don't believe that for one single minute. I've seen the way all the women my age hang around the post office hoping to catch your eye."

He laughed. "You're exaggerating."

"No, I'm not, which makes me wonder, why me?"

His expression turned thoughtful as he considered her question, rather than brushing it off as many men would have.

"Because you weren't trying, I suppose," he said eventually. "I've always been drawn to a challenge. My first wife ran a pretty good race before she let me catch her. Since she died, I've never been interested in easy." He shrugged, his expression even more serious. "Or maybe I was never ready for anything before now."

Flo reached for his hand. "I'm glad you were ready when I came along."

"Me, too." He hesitated, then added, "And that's the thing, Flo. I'm wondering when you're going to tell your daughter about us. As much of a kick as I get out of all these secret dates of ours, I want things out in the open. I'm proud to be with you. It worries me that you don't feel the same way about me."

Flo's mood instantly deflated. "Don't ever think such a thing. I do care about you. That's exactly why I'm keeping quiet. I know my Helen. She won't approve," she said flatly.

Donnie frowned. "Why not? I'm a couple years younger, so what? Why wouldn't she approve of me?"

"It's more than a couple of years," she corrected. "It's twelve, but your age isn't the problem. *You're* not the problem. It's me, or I should say it's the situation. Helen has a little trouble thinking of me like this."

Donnie looked perplexed. *"This?"*

"Being intimate with someone," she explained. "It freaks her out."

His eyes widened. "You're kidding. Helen's a worldly woman. Surely she knows people our age still have active libidos."

Flo allowed herself a smile. "She may know it intellectually. She may even accept it when it comes to other seniors, but not her mama."

"Well, it's not exactly like she has a real say," he said, then frowned. "Or does she?"

"Of course not. I just didn't want to stir that particular pot till I had a real reason to."

"But Erik knows?" he asked. "Isn't that tricky for him?"

Flo sighed. "It's put him in an impossible situation," she agreed. In fact, between that and Donnie's reaction just now, she knew it was time to open this particular can of beans with her daughter. If only she'd seen something besides complete shock in Helen's eyes the other night when she'd so much as mentioned having a date, she thought with real regret. Then maybe the prospect of telling Helen she was involved in an increasingly serious relationship wouldn't terrify her so.

"I'll tell her," she said, though she couldn't seem to make herself sound excited about it.

"Want me with you when you do?" he asked. "She's less likely to overreact with me right there."

Flo laughed at his optimism. "If you believe that, you don't know Helen. She'll just use the opportunity to cut off your... Well, let's just say it's a bad idea."

Donnie looked a little taken aback by that. "Seriously?"

She nodded. "I'm not expecting it to go well."

In fact, she had a feeling it was going to take a real effort to keep Helen from trying to have her committed. Or maybe the real worry should be giving her surprisingly stuffy daughter a heart attack.

On Tuesday morning Lynn heard a key turn and then the opening of the front door. Since the kids were already at school, it could only be one person—her soon-to-be ex-husband.

Annoyed by his presumption, she bolted into the living room and stopped him in his tracks. Hands on hips, she stood right in his path and looked him in the eye. "Hand it over."

Ed looked genuinely taken aback by her attitude. "Hand what over?"

"The key. You have no right to be walking in here anymore."

"It's my house," he protested, his eyes flashing with unmistakable temper.

"Not until the court changes something," she retorted, then leveled a look directly into his eyes. "Then again, it may belong to the bank soon, and we'll both be out of luck."

"What is that supposed to mean?"

"Your sleazy attorney hasn't been paying the mortgage—that's what it means."

Ed's eyes widened with shock. "That can't be."

"He's missed two payments. I have the bank notice to prove it." She shook her head. "Why you trusted that man to handle the divorce for you and to deal with these bills is beyond me. Everybody in town knows Jimmy Bob has questionable ethics."

"It's not as if there are a lot of alternatives," he said, then added defensively, "Besides, I've known Jimmy Bob forever."

"Then you really should have known better."

"Lynn, I swear to you, I've given him the money right on schedule."

"Then you might want to take that up with him," she said, adding, "if you can find him."

"Now what are you talking about?"

"Helen went looking for Jimmy Bob herself last week. His office is closed, and he seemed to have taken off for parts unknown."

Ed looked so genuinely stunned by that news, Lynn almost took pity on him.

"That's why you were in such a dither to get in touch with me," he concluded, as if a lightbulb had finally come on to illuminate a perplexing problem. "I came over here to tell you never to come to the office again. Noelle said you were really upset. She just about took my head off when I got back this morning." He shook his head. "Women sure do stick together. I thought that woman would walk through fire for me."

Lynn hid a smile that would only get Noelle in more hot water. She couldn't have been prouder of her, though.

"Something you might want to remember, since so many of your clients are women," she reminded him instead.

He looked momentarily taken aback by that, but he could hardly deny that there was validity to her warning. Rather than acknowledging such a thing, though, he went back on the attack.

"I know you took money from petty cash, too," he accused. "That's business money. What the hell were you thinking?"

"That I might want to buy groceries for our children," she said, not bothering to deny the accusation. There might not have been any proof, but she thought it might give him second thoughts to realize just how desperate the situation he'd left her in had been.

"You get support payments," he countered. "How are you squandering that money?"

"I *was* getting support payments," she corrected. "Those stopped, too, apparently around the same time Jimmy Bob went missing. Are you beginning to see a pattern here?"

"Jimmy Bob wouldn't steal from a client," he said emphatically, though there was a hint of doubt in his eyes. "Especially me. As I said, we go way back."

Lynn shrugged. "All I know for a fact is that the mortgage hasn't been paid and I haven't had support checks."

"I'll get to the bottom of it," he said tightly. "And I'll have a check sent over for the support money."

"Send it to Helen. She gave me a loan the other day."

"You told her about this?" he asked, looking alarmed. Obviously, he was smart enough to know what Helen could do with something like this in court.

"What else was I supposed to do? She's my lawyer. You were off who knows where, and I had exactly twenty-four dollars and change in the bank."

"You know she's going to make a ruckus about this," he said wearily. "Dammit, Lynn, what were you thinking?"

She didn't bother responding to that. She'd already explained.

He sighed heavily, then drew himself up. "How are the kids?"

"Scared," she told him candidly. "Lexie's a wreck because she knows things are bad around here. She wants to get babysitting jobs so she can help out."

"Good for her. She needs to develop a sense of responsibility," he said, missing the point entirely.

"She's fourteen, Ed. A sense of responsibility is important, but she should not be worrying about her family being homeless if she doesn't chip in a few dollars." She skewered him with a look. "Not when her father is going out of town on golf vacations every other minute."

"So you're saying she hates me now," he said, clearly feeling put upon. "Thanks for that."

"If she hates you, it's your doing, not mine, but I don't think you have to worry about that."

"Really?"

"You're her dad. She adores you," she said. "But she's feeling very conflicted about that. She's already cut your parents out of her life, and nothing I've said has changed her mind about that. If I were you, I'd spend some time with her, reassure her and Jeremy that you still give two figs about the two of them, even if you don't care about me."

He wilted a bit more under her stare. "I do care about you," he corrected softly. "I may not be in love with you anymore, but I do still care. And I never meant for things to get this messed up. I honestly wish it hadn't turned out this way, Lynn. You didn't deserve this. Neither did the kids."

She could see the genuine regret in his eyes. "I believe

you mean that, but you made this choice, Ed. I wish to heaven I could figure why you weren't willing to work on our marriage. Sure, we had problems. No relationship is perfect, but if you'd explained how unhappy you were, maybe I could have changed, maybe even fixed things."

He shook his head. "This couldn't have been fixed," he said flatly.

"Wasn't it at least worth trying?"

"That's all I did for all those years," he said. "I tried."

Lynn regarded him with a perplexed expression. "Being married to me was hard for you from the beginning?"

"I'm sorry, but yes. You wanted so much. You gave so much. I never knew what to do with all that."

Lynn couldn't imagine how giving a husband all your love could be such a trial, but it hardly mattered. "That's beside the point now," she said, resigned to accepting his view of things. "This is where we are, and we have to figure out how to make it work with the least collateral damage to the kids."

"I agree, and I'll get all these financial things straightened out. I promise."

There was real sincerity and at least a hint of a genuine apology in his voice, but Lynn had grown cynical about his promises. She'd believe this one when it was kept, and not a moment sooner.

Eight

When Lynn walked next door on Tuesday evening for the Sweet Magnolias margarita gathering, she was relieved to find that Helen had arrived ahead of her. Though Helen seemed to be engrossed in supervising younger women in the fine art of making margaritas, Lynn was able to pull her aside.

"Did Ed get a check to you today to reimburse you for that loan?" Lynn asked.

Helen nodded. "Surprised the heck out of me, to be honest. How'd you know?"

"He stopped by the house to scold me for upsetting his secretary and for stealing from petty cash," Lynn said, fighting a grin. "I guess I stirred up more of a hornet's nest than I'd realized. Noelle apparently gave him quite an earful."

"Good for her," Helen enthused.

"I know. Yea, sisterhood!" Lynn said. "And when I told Ed why I'd done it, I think I could have knocked him over with a feather."

"No doubt," Helen said. "He was still looking chagrined

when I saw him. He delivered the check personally and assured me it would never happen again."

"Did you believe him?"

Helen shrugged.

"Me, neither," Lynn said. "Oh, he looked shocked by what Jimmy Bob did, disappearing the way he has and not making payments, but having him as the fall guy is probably very convenient. We only have Ed's word that he actually gave that money to Jimmy Bob in the first place."

"My thoughts, as well," Helen said.

"Any leads on Jimmy Bob's whereabouts?"

"Unfortunately, no. And we go to court on Friday for another hearing. I have no idea what to expect. Could be a last-minute postponement or an absent lawyer. I can tell you the judge won't be happy if Jimmy Bob just fails to show up. Hal Cantor hates having his time wasted, especially by an attorney who should know better."

"That could work in our favor, couldn't it?" Lynn asked hopefully.

"In the long run, possibly, but short-term he'll have no choice but to grant Ed a continuance. He won't allow him to continue without legal representation. I'd like to get this settled once and for all so you can get your life back on an even keel."

"No one wants that more than I do," Lynn said fervently.

Helen glanced around, clearly looking to make sure they were still alone. "Can I ask you something? Do you know why Ed wants this divorce so badly?"

Lynn frowned at what seemed to be an obvious question. "He doesn't love me anymore. He's made that plain. Earlier he all but told me I'd expected too much from him from the beginning."

"Is there another woman?"

Lynn hesitated, then shook her head. "Not that I know of. To be blunt, our sex life never exactly burned up the sheets, so it's not as if it suddenly cooled down. And even if I were the stereotypical clueless wife, don't you think someone else in town would have dropped a hint by now? Grace usually finds out everything."

"Could be whoever he's seeing isn't local," Helen speculated. "He has been going out of town a lot, supposedly on golfing trips, right?"

"That's what I've heard," Lynn said. "It kinda surprised me, because Ed wasn't into golf at all when we got married. He only took it up because of business. A lot of clients like going to the club to play. I think the day Ed joined that country club was the proudest day of his life, barring none. Not even our wedding day or the birth of our kids ever seemed to mean as much to him. He equated getting in with success. Not that it was any big surprise, since his father was a founding member."

Helen nodded, her expression thoughtful.

"What are you thinking?" Lynn asked, puzzled by this whole line of questioning.

"Nothing, really," Helen insisted. "You know how nature abhors a vacuum. My mind's the same way. When I'm missing a piece of a puzzle, I can't help trying to find things that might fit."

Lynn had no idea what to make of that, but before she could pursue it, the front door opened and more guests poured in, including Flo Decatur. Helen took one look at her mother, muttered an excuse to Lynn and marched purposefully in Flo's direction. Two seconds later, Flo's eyes were flashing sparks and she'd latched onto her daughter's arm and dragged her outside.

"Uh-oh," Maddie Maddox murmured in Lynn's ear. "Somebody's in trouble."

Lynn chuckled. "Really? Helen? What could she possibly have done to tick off Flo?"

"I'm not sure, but I think it might have something to do with Helen figuring out that her mother has a boyfriend. I imagine Helen objects." She grinned. "What I wouldn't give to be a fly on the wall for that conversation. Two stubborn, immovable women on a collision course."

Lynn gave her a conspiratorial look and suggested in jest, "We could open the windows. It's a nice night."

Maddie gave her a long look, then burst out laughing. "You're going to be the perfect addition to this crowd." She winked. "Let's do it."

Lynn instantly regretted the impulsive suggestion. "I was kidding."

"I know, but it's a great idea," Maddie said. "It's a little stuffy in here, don't you think?" She turned to Dana Sue and Raylene for support. "Sweetie," she said, directing her words to Raylene. "Let's open some windows. Do you mind?"

"Of course not," Raylene said. "I'll help. Lynn, could you get the ones in the dining room? I think we'll settle down in there as soon as everyone's here and has a drink in hand. I'll be so glad to have the addition finished, so we can spread out, but for now the dining room will have to do."

At Maddie's obviously disappointed expression, Dana Sue regarded her curiously. "What?"

"Helen," Maddie muttered. "On the porch with Flo."

Dana Sue's eyes immediately lit up. "You wanted to eavesdrop, didn't you?"

"Well, of course I did," Maddie admitted without even a second of cursory hesitation. "Don't you?"

"I would love to know what set Flo off," Dana Sue conceded. "But I can wait. The second they come back inside, we'll give them each a margarita and pry the juicy details right out of them."

A slow grin spread across Maddie's face. "That'll work."

Lynn shook her head, amused by the workings of their minds. "I think I'll go open those windows for Raylene."

"And I'll go help with the margaritas," Maddie said. "The sooner we get this party started, the sooner we'll find out what's going on."

Feeling a stirring of intense loyalty, Lynn wondered if she shouldn't warn Helen about all the speculation going on. Then, again, Helen, Maddie and Dana Sue had been friends forever. Helen had to know they were going to pump her for information the second she showed her face. And, she thought, Helen was one tough cookie. If she didn't want them to know anything, she certainly knew perfectly well how to keep her mouth firmly shut. She'd probably kept more confidences in this town over the years than any other resident, even when her tongue had been loosened by a couple of margaritas!

"You're dating Donald Leighton!" Helen's incredulous words carried all the way into the living room, bringing conversation in there to a halt.

"Oh, my," Frances murmured. "Flo finally told her."

"About time," Liz said. "I have no idea why she was so secretive in the first place. In this town Helen was bound to find out sooner or later."

Frances gestured in the direction of the porch. "Did you not hear Helen's reaction just now? That's exactly why Flo didn't want to say a word. Maybe I should go out there and try to calm them down before things get any more heated."

Maddie stood up. "That's okay. I'll go."

She had the tone of a martyr in her voice, Lynn noticed, but she seemed awfully eager to be the one to intervene. Dana Sue immediately latched onto her hand and pulled her right back down on the sofa.

"Stay out of it," Dana Sue instructed. "They need to work this out for themselves. They're two adults and, more important, they're mother and daughter."

Lynn chuckled at Maddie's obvious disappointment, but she did stay where she was.

"So," Sarah McDonald said in a deliberately upbeat tone, "Flo has a boyfriend. I think that's fantastic."

"She's happier than I've ever seen her," Liz confided. "Donnie treats her like a queen. Why, she told me he brought her breakfast in bed just the other day."

Maddie groaned. "Oh, my. I hope she doesn't mention that to Helen."

"Why not?" Liz demanded. "I think it was sweet."

"It *was* sweet," Maddie confirmed. "Helen won't be focusing on the gesture, though."

Liz looked perplexed for a minute, then chuckled. "Ah, it's her being in bed that will trouble Helen."

"And all that implies," Frances said, looking amused. "I thought you young women were more evolved than that. I can't say I want to have a man in my life these days, but if Flo does, I say more power to her!"

Lynn noticed that Maddie's expression had turned thoughtful. Apparently, Dana Sue noticed it, too.

"You wondering how you'd react if your mother suddenly took up with a man?" Dana Sue inquired, clearly amused.

Maddie nodded. "She's beautiful. She's still a vital woman. And she certainly has opportunities to meet plenty of men at these art shows of hers. I wonder why she hasn't looked at another man since my dad died."

"Maybe she has," Dana Sue teased. "Maybe she's just more discreet than Flo."

Maddie scowled at her. "I did not need to hear that."

Dana Sue shrugged unrepentantly. "I was just saying…"

"Well, don't."

"Or maybe your father was her soul mate," Lynn suggested hesitantly, thinking of Mitch and Amy. Maybe some people were meant to have only one significant love of their life. If you lost a partner like that, would you ever really be emotionally ready to move on?

"You're not thinking about Paula now," Raylene said to Lynn after assessing her expression for a minute. Raylene's eyes were sparkling with merriment when she accused, "You're thinking about Mitch."

The revealing remark caught everyone's attention at once, and every single Sweet Magnolia in the room instantly shifted her focus to Lynn.

"You're seeing Mitch Franklin?" Maddie asked, then slowly nodded. "I can see that. He's a terrific guy. Good for you."

"We're not dating," Lynn protested. "We've seen each other a few times here and there. I'm doing a little part-time work for him, that's all. And how did this get to be about me? Let's go back to discussing Flo."

Raylene shook her head. "It was always going to get around to being about you. I warned you about that."

Lynn sighed, resigned to a few more intrusive, if well-meant comments.

"You think he's still hung up on Amy, don't you?" Maddie guessed. "He was deeply in love with her, that's for sure. But I don't think he's the kind of man who'll pine forever. And don't they say that a man who's been in a happy relationship usually yearns for another one, at least eventually, because he knows just how good married life can be?"

"A nice spin," Lynn said. "But given my problems these days, I'm not sure any man with half a brain would take me on."

"A knight in shining armor would," Raylene corrected. "And that's who Mitch is. As Maddie said, he's a genuinely good guy—one of the few."

"Other than our husbands," Annie Townsend said loyally. "We all landed the cream of the Serenity crop."

Lynn noticed that Laura Reed, who was about to marry local pediatrician J. C. Fullerton, looked increasingly troubled by the conversation.

"Laura, is something wrong?" Lynn asked.

"I'm trying to decide whether or not to mention something," Laura told them.

"Something about Mitch?" Raylene asked.

Laura nodded. "You know before J.C. and I got together a few months ago, I wasn't really dating all that much. Sometimes I'd go out for a drink on Friday nights with some of the other single teachers. There was a time there, it must have been not too long after Amy died, when Mitch was always at the bar, drinking alone and drinking way too much."

Lynn stilled at the news, her heart thumping unsteadily. "Mitch drinks a lot?" she asked with real trepidation.

"I've never seen him touch so much as a beer," Raylene said, frowning at Laura. "That can't be right."

"I'm just saying it's what I saw," Laura said defensively. "And it was more than once. I haven't been back there in quite a while, so maybe that's in the past. That's why I wasn't sure whether to mention it."

"No, you should have," Lynn said stiffly. "It's something I needed to know."

What Laura couldn't possibly have known was that Lynn had way too much experience with alcoholics. Her dad had been one. He'd been a mean drunk, too.

She thought back to the horror of those days. Sure, it had been more verbal abuse than physical or, she liked to believe, her mother would have walked out the door and taken Lynn and her sisters with her. In Lynn's opinion she should have gone anyway, just the way Sarah McDonald had gotten away from her first husband. Walter Price hadn't been a drunk, but he'd been verbally abusive. He'd shaped up and was now married again, but it had taken the shock of Sarah's leaving to force him to change. Nothing had ever sobered up Lynn's dad. He'd died of liver complications a few years back. Ironically and sadly, her mother had died before him.

Still, Lynn couldn't be around a man who was drinking heavily without a knot forming in her stomach. She told herself it was good that she'd found this out now, before she'd allowed herself to get any more involved with Mitch. Though she'd personally seen no indication that he had a drinking problem, with two impressionable kids in the house, it wasn't a risk she was willing to take.

Working for him was one thing, but anything else? No, she decided regretfully, it simply couldn't be.

Flo regarded her daughter with real disappointment. "How did I raise a woman who could be so judgmental?" she asked wearily after she and Helen had gone round and round about what Helen termed her inappropriate behavior.

"I'm not being judgmental," Helen insisted. "I'm just worried about your making a complete fool of yourself."

"By dating a man who treats me with respect and genuine affection?"

"Don is at least ten years younger than you."

"Twelve, if you must know, but what's your point?"

"It can't possibly last, Mom. He'll break your heart."

"And you don't think I know a thing or two about broken hearts? Most of the men who stole my heart for a minute or two over the years weren't worth spit compared to Donnie." She gave Helen a defiant look. "And I'm sorry if this makes you uncomfortable or embarrasses you in some way, but it's my life. I intend to live it any way I choose."

"I swear to God," Helen began, but she didn't finish the thought.

Flo almost smiled at that. "You'll what? Have me committed?"

Helen sighed heavily. "Okay, I know that's crazy. There's not a judge around who'll buy that you're not in your right mind, even if I happen to think you've lost it."

Flo gave a nod of satisfaction. "Glad to know you have limits and that you recognize that much about me." She hesitated, then said, "I have a proposition, if you'd like to hear it."

Though she still looked agitated, Helen gestured for her to go on.

"You and Erik have dinner with us one night," Flo suggested. "We'll go to Rosalina's."

"You want to go on a double date with me?" Helen asked incredulously.

"And Erik," Flo stressed, knowing that he'd be the voice of reason if Helen got herself all worked up and wasn't behaving politely.

"Oh, sure, because you have him wound around your finger," Helen said.

Flo smiled at her frustration. "That's one reason, for sure. I was also thinking you might enjoy a night out with your husband. I'll even pay for a sitter, so you won't have a worry on your mind."

"I'd rather you stay home and sit with Sarah Beth," Helen muttered.

Flo dared to laugh at that. "It would defeat the purpose of this double date, don't you think? Come on. What do you have to lose, except maybe being forced to admit you're wrong about me and Donnie?"

"I hate being wrong."

"I know you do," Flo soothed. "I'll make it easy on you. I promise not to say I told you so even once."

A smile finally tugged at Helen's lips. "You'll never be able to pull that off."

"I can," Flo insisted. "Cross my heart."

Helen studied her, then finally shook her head. "I suppose it will be worth it just to see you try to keep from rubbing it in. First, though, I have to admit I'm wrong. There's no guarantee that'll happen."

"It'll happen," Flo said confidently. "I have faith in Donnie, but I have even more faith in your being fair and just. That is why you went into law, isn't it, to make sure trials are fair and impartial?"

Helen gave her a long look, then chuckled. "I swear every now and then I get a glimpse of just where I learned to manipulate a witness into saying what I want."

"Thank you, Mama," Flo coached.

"Thank you, Mama," Helen said dutifully, though she didn't look entirely happy about it.

Still, though, she'd come a long way since the beginning

of their contentious conversation. Flo was content with the progress they'd made. She just had to keep reminding herself that some victories required baby steps.

Mitch frowned at the way Lynn was avoiding making eye contact when he stopped by on Wednesday to go over the payroll instructions one more time.

"Something wrong?" he asked eventually.

"No. Why?"

"You haven't once looked at me since I walked into the house," he said.

"Because I'm focused on this blasted computer screen," she claimed. "You want me to get the payroll done before your crew quits on you, right?"

He wasn't buying it, but prolonging the discussion was unlikely to get him anywhere.

"I saw Ed the other day," he mentioned casually, wondering if that was behind her stiff behavior. "He's back from his trip."

"I know," she said tersely.

"You've seen him?"

She did turn to him then. "Why do you care about this?"

"Just trying to figure out this mood you're in. I thought Ed's return might have something to do with it."

"I am not in a mood," she retorted, her eyes flashing with indignation.

Mitch thought that fiery reaction was a whole lot better than the indifference she'd been radiating earlier. "Sorry, I think you are."

"You don't know me that well."

"I do," he said mildly.

She regarded him with obvious frustration. "Mitch, we've barely seen each other since high school."

"Until the past couple of weeks," he said agreeably. "I've seen enough to know you haven't changed that dramatically from the sweet, even-tempered girl I knew."

"That's what you think," she muttered. "Getting a divorce has a way of changing things."

"So this is about Ed."

"No, it's about my having a job to do and your not helping me to get it done," she said impatiently. "I have another job to get to in…" She glanced at her watch. "Twenty minutes. Could you please explain this one more time and do it in ten minutes, preferably in English, rather than tech mumbo jumbo?"

He smiled. "Why don't we just tackle it again when you get home and aren't in such a rush?" He stood up, then impulsively bent down and brushed a kiss across her forehead. "Maybe your mood will be improved by then, too."

He was almost to the back door when a wad of paper sailed past his head. The next one struck him in the back. He laughed.

"Very mature, Lynnie," he called over his shoulder.

"Just be glad I didn't get my cast-iron skillet."

He was beginning to realize that she really was annoyed with him, either for some transgression she had yet to mention or because she thought he was being presumptuous for calling her on her attitude. He turned around and walked back into the kitchen, pulled a chair closer, then straddled it from behind, resting his arms on the back.

"Okay, what's this about?" he asked, too close for her to avoid making eye contact without being any more revealing than she already had been.

"Mitch, please, just go on over to Raylene's so I can get to work. It takes me ten minutes to walk to the boutique."

"I'll drive you. Let's settle this, and then we'll go."

"There's nothing to settle," she said stubbornly.

"I beg to differ."

"Beg to differ all you want to, but I'm telling you there's nothing going on."

"You don't suddenly have a problem with me?"

"No," she said, but she managed to avoid his gaze when she said it.

"You do," he concluded, then sighed. "Tell me."

"Mitch, really. I don't have time for this."

Reluctantly, he stood up. "Let's go then. Grab your purse. I'll drop you off on my way to Ronnie's hardware store. I have supplies coming in this morning."

"I can walk."

"I know you are perfectly capable of walking," he said, barely holding on to his temper. "But I am willing to save you a couple of minutes and give you a ride, since I'm going just a few doors down from the boutique. Do you really want to fight about this, too?"

Apparently, her common sense finally kicked in, because she gave him a chagrined look. "Thank you."

"Anytime," he said, managing to contain a smile since the thanks had clearly cost her.

They made the drive in a couple of minutes. The silence in his truck was deafening. After he'd stopped in front of the boutique to let her out, he reached over and touched her arm as she exited. "We'll finish this later."

Dismay flashed in her eyes, followed by resignation. "Is that an edict from my boss?"

"Nope, just a promise from a concerned friend," he said mildly. "Have a good day, Lynnie."

She hesitated, then said, "Yeah, you, too."

Mitch watched until she'd gone inside, then drove down the block and parked in front of the hardware store. He stayed right where he was after he'd cut the engine, trying to puzzle out what might be going on with Lynn, but if there were clues, he'd missed them.

One thing he'd learned during his marriage, though, was that some puzzles shouldn't be left unresolved. They tended to get more complicated and difficult as time passed.

"Tonight, Lynn," he murmured determinedly. "I'll get to the bottom of whatever's going on tonight."

Stubborn as she obviously was, he didn't think she could keep the problem to herself forever.

Nine

"I was awful," Lynn told Raylene during a break between customers at the boutique. "There he was being all worried and concerned that I was upset, and I was being standoffish and mean."

"Standoffish under the circumstances I can see," Raylene said. "But mean? I can't imagine it. Not you. You're the most thoughtful person I know."

"No, that would be Mitch. The man has been nothing but kind to me. He's given me a job, for goodness' sake, and what do I do? At the first hint that he might have a drinking problem, I treat him like a pariah. And the truth is, I've never even seen him touch a drink. All I have to go on is what Laura said she saw."

Raylene nodded. "I was shocked by that, too. It doesn't fit with the man I know, either. Still, it's not something she'd make up."

"I know that," Lynn said in frustration. "That's why I found it so disturbing. Laura doesn't gossip, and she was clearly uncomfortable telling us about this."

"Do you want my advice?"

Lynn nodded. She needed another perspective. "Absolutely."

"You recall that when I met Carter he jumped to a lot of conclusions about my being careless and irresponsible because Sarah's little boy had run away while I was supposed to be watching him. Until Travis explained to him about my agoraphobia, Carter made some pretty terrible judgments about the kind of person I am. He still says that taught him a valuable lesson about never jumping to conclusions without facts."

"I remember that day, and the way Carter reacted when he brought Tommy back," Lynn said. "He definitely made a rush to judgment."

"If you can see that, then don't do the same thing. Give Mitch a chance to set the record straight."

"Ask him if he drinks?" Lynn said, dismayed by the thought of asking such an intrusive question when she'd personally seen no evidence to suggest that he had a problem. "I can't do that. How could I possibly explain why I was asking? If it's not true, it would totally humiliate him to think people in town are saying otherwise."

"Then here's what I personally think is the better alternative," Raylene said. "You concentrate on what you know to be true about Mitch—that he's thoughtful and dependable and kind. Trust what you know until he actually does something to shake your faith in him."

"I know you're right, but I'm scared," Lynn said.

"Of what?"

"Falling for him, *then* finding out he's not the man I thought he was."

Raylene looked unreasonably delighted by her response. "Then you *are* in danger of falling for him? Fantastic!"

"Is it fantastic?" Lynn wondered.

"I think so," Raylene confirmed. "Look, I understand your desire to protect yourself and the kids from getting hurt, but I honestly don't see it happening, not with the Mitch I know. Trust your gut."

Lynn gave her a wry look. "My gut told me Ed was the perfect man for me. It's not terribly reliable."

"I think you're wrong about that. One mistake—"

"A *huge* mistake," Lynn corrected.

"Okay, I'll give you that one," Raylene conceded. "But I'd hate to see you give up on something special happening with Mitch for no reason."

But was it for no reason? Lynn wondered. It would be difficult for Laura Reed to misinterpret what she'd seen with her own eyes. And she wasn't the kind of woman who'd spread rumors if she hadn't been genuinely worried by what she'd observed.

Raylene was right, though. The situation called for caution or confrontation. Since confrontation, especially without firsthand evidence, went against her basic instincts, caution was the only answer.

"Are you seeing Mitch tonight?" Raylene asked.

"Unless he thought about this morning and decided not to waste his time on a woman who was being impossible," she said.

"I doubt Mitch could ever look at time spent with you as a waste," Raylene said. "You'll see him. Now let's look on these racks and find something fabulous for you to wear."

Lynn immediately shook her head. "I can't afford fabulous."

"You can if it's on the sale rack and we take off your employee discount. I'll practically have to pay you to wear it. Besides, for me, a well-dressed employee is a walking advertisement."

"But we're just going to do payroll at my place," Lynn protested, even though her attention kept straying to the sales rack. When she'd been straightening it earlier, there had been one dress that had caught her eye—something in a cheerful lime green that would be terrific for summer.

"Not once he sees you in the perfect dress, I'll bet," Raylene said, handing her a simple linen dress in peach that Lynn hadn't even noticed.

"Are you sure?" Lynn asked. "I like the lime green."

"Trust me," Raylene insisted. "The lime green will be overpowering. This peach will make your skin glow." She grinned. "I'm predicting there's a fancy dinner in your future. And if he asks, don't you dare say no."

Somewhat reassured by the conversation with Raylene and stunned by the way she looked in the dress that Raylene had plucked from the rack, Lynn left the store at midafternoon with a whole new attitude.

"Bring it on," she murmured as she walked home. But even as she uttered the brave words, a part of her couldn't help worrying that she was in way over her head.

Mitch stood beside his truck watching Lynn walk down the block. He'd been alternately glancing at his watch and down the street around the time he knew she usually left Raylene's shop. In fact, lately, he seemed to be paying a little too much attention to her comings and goings. He waited until she was closer before calling out a greeting.

To his surprise, after the way she'd been acting earlier today, a genuine smile lit her face.

"Well, now, that's a sight for sore eyes," he declared, grinning back at her.

"What?"

"That smile of yours. It's been a while since I've seen it. You definitely weren't too happy with me this morning."

"You were right. I had something on my mind," she finally acknowledged. "Sorry."

"No need to be sorry. Is the problem resolved now?"

"Not entirely, but I got my perspective back. Actually I had a good day in general," she said. "Ed called. He says he's making progress on getting a few financial issues straightened out. I made several good sales today. I even bought myself a new dress." She held up the boutique's shiny bag triumphantly. "To be honest, I feel hopeful for the first time in a very long time."

Though he probably should have settled for the evening they'd planned working on the payroll, Mitch made a quick decision. "Feel like telling me about it over dinner? Nothing fancy. Just Rosalina's. I'm afraid I've just about worn out my welcome with Raylene and Carter. I need to get out in the world again."

"Raylene and Carter love having you stay for dinner," Lynn contradicted. "She's told me how much they enjoy your company."

"Carter's just tolerating it," he insisted. "He's counting on that addition moving along a little faster if I keep longer hours."

"You've said that before, but I honestly don't think it's all about that," Lynn said. "I think he likes having you around when he has to work the late shifts at the police department. Neither he nor Raylene have entirely forgotten about that business with Raylene's ex-husband. He might be back in jail now, but it's left them jumpy."

Mitch nodded. "That was a nasty business, all right. So, Lynn, how about it? Pizza at Rosalina's. We can bring the kids along if you like. You can wear your new dress."

For some reason he couldn't fathom, she chuckled. "What?"

"Raylene predicted I'd be having dinner out tonight. She all but insisted I buy this dress just in case."

"Well, bless Raylene," he said. "The woman does have amazing insight from time to time. So, is that a yes?"

She studied him with a worried frown. "Are you sure about all this, Mitch? Do you really want the kids along, too?"

Though he'd prefer a more intimate evening with her, he knew it was still too soon for that. The kids would add the buffer they both needed to keep these fresh, unexplored emotions in check.

"I'd be glad to have the company," he said candidly, deliberately making it sound as if they'd be doing him a favor. "I've never enjoyed eating out alone."

She hesitated another minute, clearly wrestling between desire and caution. "The kids won't drive you crazy?"

He laughed. "Not if I give them a bunch of quarters for the video games, they won't. That always worked like a charm with Nate and Luke."

"That definitely ought to keep Jeremy and Lexie occupied," she agreed, smiling. "Okay, then. It sounds great. Should we meet you there?"

He knew that car of hers hadn't left the driveway much lately and suspected he knew why. The price of gasoline could play havoc with a tight budget. And even though Rosalina's wasn't at the other end of the world, he didn't want her wasting any obviously precious gas to get there.

"No, just give me a half hour to run home, shower and change, and I'll pick you guys up." He'd also need that time to run inside and leave a note for Raylene, letting her know he wouldn't be hanging around tonight. This unexpected opportunity was way too good to pass up.

He smiled to himself. Not that she'd be one bit surprised. Apparently, she knew the two of them better than they knew themselves.

Lynn noticed heads turning when they arrived at Rosalina's. There was a rise in volume, too, as speculative comments were exchanged. Though she loved Serenity, had spent her teens learning to appreciate its close-knit ways, she'd never gotten used to this. Just like so many other times since she and Ed had separated, she felt as if her smile was frozen in place and her cheeks were hot with embarrassment. Thankfully, Jeremy and Lexie appeared oblivious, already heading off to the area that contained a variety of video and arcade games.

"Pay no attention to the gossip," Mitch said quietly, leaning down so that his breath fanned against her cheek.

"Hard to ignore the stares," she replied, "and the whispers."

He winked at her. "Ever stop to think that it may be because no one's seen me out with a woman since Amy died?"

She gave him a startled look, then chuckled. "No, that never once crossed my mind. How self-absorbed is that?"

"Just human nature, darlin'. When we have things going on in our lives that are uncomfortable, we always think everyone else can't wait to talk about us." He chuckled. "Sadly, in Serenity, it's more than likely true."

Lynn finally allowed herself to relax, surprised by the discovery that Mitch's understanding not only of the situation but of her reaction to it had settled her nerves.

After they were seated in a corner booth, she glanced at the menu, uncertain what to order. She was so hungry these days, she would gladly have sampled a little of everything on it.

"How about two large pizzas?" Mitch suggested. "That way there will be leftovers to take home."

"Sounds good to me," she said, thinking of how eagerly the kids would eat more than their share, just as they had when they'd discovered the leftovers after Mitch had had pizza delivered to the house a few nights ago.

"And salad?"

"For me and Lexie, yes. None for Jeremy. He won't touch it, no matter how miserable I make his life."

"My boys were the same way until Cal Maddox was coaching them for baseball and insisted they eat their vegetables, right along with the meat and other protein the football coach encouraged them to eat," Mitch said. "They finally got the message about nutrition fueling their bodies. Does Jeremy play any sports?"

"Not yet. He hasn't seemed interested in the various teams in town and I haven't encouraged him to try out. His dad wasn't a big athlete, so Ed hasn't tried to influence him, either."

"Seems to me team sports are good for boys," Mitch said. "But only if they're interested. Nate and Luke couldn't wait to play. They're still competitive, though they're not involved in organized sports at college." He set aside the menu. "Now, tell me, what would you like to drink? Soda? Beer?"

She hesitated, considering her reply carefully. Was this the perfect time to test the situation? "I'd love a beer if you're having one."

"Not me," Mitch said easily. "But you go ahead if you want one."

And there was her answer, she thought with regret. Or

was it? She regarded him curiously. "You declined as if there's a story there," she said carefully. "Is there?"

"Beer provided a little too much comfort right after Amy died," he told her openly and without even a hint of embarrassment.

"Oh," she murmured, not sure what to say. He'd made the admission with such complete candor that she was momentarily taken aback. "So you don't drink anymore?"

He shook his head. "I woke up one day to the horrifying realization that I wasn't one bit better than the drunk driver who killed my wife. Only difference was, I had sense enough not to get behind the wheel. Haven't touched alcohol since then."

Lynn wondered if it was even possible to quit just like that. Her dad certainly hadn't been able to. Then, again, had he ever even tried?

"You must be incredibly strong to just turn your back on it like that," she said. "Did you join Alcoholics Anonymous or some other kind of support group?"

"No, though I would have in a heartbeat if I hadn't been able to do it on my own." He gave her a serious look. "I don't think I'm an alcoholic, Lynn, not by any means. Before Amy died, I'd have a beer or two in the evening from time to time, but even that wasn't something I did regularly. When I saw that I was relying on it to dull the pain after she died, though, I realized that I could be on a slippery slope."

He shrugged as if it were of only passing consequence. "It's not something I miss or struggle with. Except for those couple of months, booze was never a big part of my life."

She should have been reassured by his words, by his conviction that it wasn't a real issue for him, but history had taught her to be wary just the same. The fact that he'd confirmed what Laura had seen disturbed her, no matter how hard she tried to fight it. She just couldn't imagine that one day drinking had been a problem and, just like that, now it wasn't. Could it be that easy?

"So, do you still want that beer?" he asked. "It won't bother me a bit."

She shook her head. "No, soda's fine."

He frowned. "Don't change your mind because of me."

"I'm not. It's no big deal," she insisted.

Mitch placed their order, then met her gaze, held it just a second longer than usual. "Now, why don't you tell me what made this such a good day?"

"Besides this chance to get out for dinner?" she said.

"You were happy long before I suggested this."

She thought back over the morning, her conversation with Raylene and then the sales she'd made to cap off the day. "I had a few good sales," she told him, focusing on that. "I think I told you that earlier. I'm still not in the same class as Adelia Hernandez, who could sell ice in the North Pole, but I'm getting better at closing the deal. At first if someone appeared uncertain, I let it go. I didn't want to be pushy. Now I've learned to point out why they can't live without that particular blouse or dress or suit."

"The way Raylene talked you into buying this dress?" he teased. "Whatever she said to convince you, she was right. The peach color makes your skin glow."

"That's exactly what Raylene said," Lynn said. "Did she coach you?"

"Nope, just calling it like I see it." His expression turned serious. "You're a beautiful woman, Lynn. You always were."

"Always?" she said skeptically. "I seem to recall that the first time you set eyes on me, right after we moved to town, Taylor Vincent had just shoved me into a mud puddle and I was a mess."

He laughed. "But a beautiful mess," he insisted.

She hadn't thought about that incident in years, but suddenly realized just how telling that moment had been. "You slugged Taylor Vincent," she said, suddenly remembering the scene vividly. She'd been shocked that someone she hardly knew had stood up for her. "Even then, you were ready to slay dragons for me."

"Taylor Vincent was a bully," he declared, then added a little sheepishly, "He'd made you cry. Even way back then I couldn't stand to see a girl cry."

"He ruined my new coat. I was so proud of that coat."

"It was red with a black velvet collar," Mitch recalled.

Startled by his memory, she gaped at him. "You remember that?"

"I told you you'd made an impression," he said.

"My mom had made that coat for me. I was only supposed to wear it for special occasions, but I wanted to show it off at school. Even though we had it dry-cleaned and it was good as new, it was never the same for me after that." She smiled at him. "You were my hero that day."

"And then you fell for Ed," he said.

Her smile faded. "And then I fell for Ed," she said, unable to keep a note of regret from her voice. Almost immediately, though, she felt the need to defend her feelings, if not Ed. "He wasn't always as inconsiderate and selfish as he's been recently."

Mitch didn't look as if he believed her, but he shrugged. "He must have had some good qualities for you to be so crazy about him for all those years."

"And because of him, I have two incredible kids," she said. "I just wish I weren't so sure everyone in town probably believes that I must have done something awful for a paragon like Ed to leave me."

"Did you? Do something awful, I mean?"

"Absolutely not. I was shocked when he said he wanted a divorce. Our marriage wasn't some great American love story, but it seemed okay. Keep in mind that I didn't have a lot to compare it to. My parents had a rocky time of it. By comparison, Ed and I had something quiet and steady. It was… I don't know, a relief, maybe. It was comfortable. I was content. I thought he was, too."

"That's what I thought," Mitch said. "As far back as I can remember, you did nothing but love that man. I never quite understood what you saw in him, but then you'd broken my heart, so maybe I was a touch biased."

"I broke your heart?" she said, shocked by the unexpected admission.

"In seventh grade," he confirmed. "I finally worked up the gumption to suggest we have a soda at Wharton's after school and you turned me down flat. Said you were meeting Ed, though I seem to recall even then that he was taking you for granted. He never even showed up that afternoon. It killed me watching you sit there with your friends looking so disappointed."

Lynn thought back to those relatively innocent days. Mitch was right—Ed had taken her for granted. It was a pattern that had never been broken. Why hadn't she seen that before? Was it because, as she'd just said, it was such a relief to have a life without the constant fighting and upheaval she'd experienced growing up?

"Why didn't you tell me your opinion of Ed?" she asked Mitch. "Maybe I'd have listened to you. We were friends. I trusted you."

"Did you not just hear me say you'd broken my heart? Besides, I was only thirteen and fighting acne. What did I know about relationships and how they were supposed to work? You were the first girl I'd had nerve enough to ask out."

She regarded him with belated regret. "I'm sorry I hurt you. At that age kids are so incredibly thoughtless and careless about feelings, aren't they?" She sighed. "I hope Lexie makes it through these teen years and her first serious crush without getting her heart broken."

"Unfortunately, that's not something parents can control," Mitch said. "Amy did her best to protect our sons from heartbreak. She tried to warn them away from girls she knew were destined to hurt them. And she taught them to do the right and honorable thing when it came to the girls they dated, but I know they've made their share of mistakes, probably hurt girls as often as they've been hurt."

Mitch leveled a look into her eyes. "Can I ask you something?"

"Sure."

"Would you take Ed back if he wanted to reconcile?"

Lynn understood why he wanted to know. Why pursue her, if her heart still belonged to another man? She wished she had an unequivocal answer she could give him.

"I don't think so," she said slowly, trying to be as honest about this as he'd been earlier about the drinking. "I've seen him in a new light recently and he's not the man I thought he was." And thinking of the sparks that simmered when Mitch was around, she was starting to realize that the chemistry between her and Ed had been lacking, too.

"But?" Mitch coaxed.

"There are Lexie and Jeremy to consider. They need their dad."

"They can have their father around without your welcoming him back in your life," Mitch said reasonably. "I guess what I'm trying to get at is whether *you* want to reconcile. Not because of your kids. For you."

"If you'd asked me a week or two ago when things were really a mess, the answer would have been easier," she said. "I was furious and disillusioned."

"But now he's back in town and all's right with the world?" Mitch asked, a hint of reproach in his voice.

Lynn gave him a sharp look. "Hardly. I don't want to be with a man who so clearly doesn't want to be with me. That hasn't changed. I guess in the end it's a moot point. Reconciliation isn't in the cards."

Mitch didn't look as if he found that reassuring. Even she could see that she'd left his very direct question unanswered. She still hadn't said what *she* wanted.

And the truth was that she didn't know. She wanted the security of her marriage back, the stability that came with knowing who she was and what her role was—wife and mother. But that view of herself had apparently been based on a lie or at least a misconception. How had she not seen how much was wrong at the very core of her relationship with her husband?

Finally, she was starting to figure out who she might become in this new, upside-down world. In time, she knew that would be a good thing, but for now it was scary. Uncertainty had never been her favorite thing. Life with an unpredictable alcoholic had taught her that. She couldn't help wondering if she'd chosen Ed for precisely that reason, because with his future in his father's insurance business already carved out, he'd offered the security and stability she'd always longed for. The fireworks she'd read about in romance novels or heard about from her friends hadn't seemed to matter.

She forced a smile. "I think we've gotten way too serious all of a sudden."

He looked as if he thought maybe they were finally getting real, but eventually he nodded. "And here comes our food. I'll go get the kids."

Once Lexie and Jeremy came back to the table, the conversation centered on sports and school. Though Jeremy didn't play, he loved going to the high school games, tagging along with Lexie and her friends whenever they'd let him.

Lynn noted how relaxed Mitch was with her kids. She couldn't help comparing that to Ed, who'd seemed uncomfortable carrying on a conversation with them even before the separation and now barely paid any attention to them at all. Mitch seemed genuinely interested in everything they had to say.

She was surprised when Jeremy asked about the construction next door.

"Would it be okay if I came over sometime to see what you're doing?" he asked shyly. "I know it's supposed to be off-limits. Raylene said so. Mom, too."

Mitch reached over and ruffled his hair. "Absolutely, as long as I'm there. I'll find a hard hat for you and show you around."

"Could I help?" Jeremy asked excitedly. "I like to build stuff. I mean I've just done it with Lego, not real wood or anything like that, but it must be way cool to look at a piece of paper and then put a whole house together."

"It is definitely way cool," Mitch confirmed. "I'd be happy to teach you a few things."

"No saws," Lynn said at once. "No nail guns. And—"

Jeremy groaned, his cheeks pink with embarrassment. "Mom!"

She glanced at Mitch, caught him grinning. "You see where I'm going with this, right?"

"Got it," he confirmed. "I'll get him back to your place in the same condition you send him over."

"That'll do," she said, satisfied that she could take him at his word.

And when, she thought in amazement, was the last time she'd felt that kind of confidence in any man? Despite all the doubts that had been stirred up tonight when it came to Mitch and his drinking, she realized with complete and total confidence that she could trust him, not just with her children but maybe even with her heart.

As soon as that thought came to her, though, she put on her mental brakes. One step at a time, she warned herself. One day at a time. It was a way of life she'd come to appreciate, if not embrace.

Clearly, it seemed, Mitch had as well for his own reasons. How could she not respect a man who saw himself clearly enough to anticipate a problem and then set out to correct it? That sort of self-awareness was rare. So was the strength of character needed to make changes.

Tonight Mitch had gone a long way toward allaying her fears, but it wouldn't hurt to keep at least a part of her heart safe a little longer.

Ten

Flo was a nervous wreck. How on earth could a woman get to be in her seventies and still get flustered over a date, especially when it was a date with a man she'd been seeing for months? She felt as if she were back in high school, a time that should have long since faded from memory.

Of course, the issue wasn't so much having dinner with Donnie, but being joined for the meal by Erik and Helen. When Donnie had left her apartment this morning, he hadn't been the least bit rattled by the prospect of being cross-examined by her daughter, who'd made a career of dissecting witnesses.

"You're naive if you think she's not going to try to trip you up," she'd told him.

He regarded her with amusement. "About what? I have nothing to hide. And my intentions as far as you're concerned are honorable."

"Honorable?" Flo had scoffed. "Not in Helen's book. They'd only be honorable if you put a ring on my finger, and we've agreed we don't want to get married."

"If it would ease things between you and Helen, I'd be happy to reevaluate that," he'd said, stunning her.

"Do not go there," she'd ordered. "Not when I'm already a basket case. We agreed, and that's that."

"Stubborn woman," he'd accused right before kissing her.

"You know I'm right about this," she'd called after him.

And she was. They didn't need marriage at their age. This arrangement they had was perfectly comfortable. It suited them having their own space to escape to. At least it suited her. Didn't it suit Donnie, after all, she worried? What if he'd changed his mind and she'd cut him off? She groaned. Now there was one more thing to fret over.

She called Liz, looking for a distraction. "You busy?"

"I thought I'd head over to the community center and play cards," she said. "Want to come?"

"I'll be there," Flo said eagerly. "Have you spoken to Frances?"

"She says she's tired and wants to rest at home."

Flo didn't like the sound of that. She was a little surprised that Liz had accepted such an answer. "That doesn't sound right," she told Liz. "I think I'll stop by on my way to the community center."

"Not without me, you won't," Liz said. "To be honest, I've been debating with myself about going over there ever since I spoke to her. I don't want to start treating her as if she's incapable of making a decision for herself."

"That's not what we're doing," Flo insisted. "She's our friend. We know the situation. Of course we're going to be concerned when something seems a little off-kilter. With her family still in the dark about this cognitive disorder, it's up to us to pay close attention. We agreed on that, Frances included."

"Right," Liz said. "You'll pick me up? I hate to ask Travis to drop me off over there."

"Give me ten minutes," Flo said. "I have to put my face on."

"And you can do that and still be here in ten minutes?" Liz teased.

"At this stage, mascara and lipstick will get me out the door looking presentable. Everything else is pretty much a waste of time. These wrinkles of mine can't be covered up. Your skin's still smooth as a baby's bottom. One of these days I'm going to figure out what you did to accomplish that. You must have slipped off to Columbia or Charleston for a face-lift sometime or another."

Liz laughed. "Clean living," she countered. "Never smoked. Don't drink much. And the blessing of good genes."

"Well, it's too late for me to claim any of that," Flo said. "See you shortly."

Twenty minutes later they arrived at Frances's apartment. After pounding on the door, Frances finally opened it looking half-asleep and disheveled.

"What on earth are the two of you doing here?" she demanded. She frowned at Liz. "I told you I was going back to bed."

"And I got worried when I heard that," Flo told her unrepentantly. "Sue me."

A smile tugged at Frances's lips. "Not if you have Helen on your side in court. I suppose, since you're here, you might as well come on in. I'll put on a pot of tea. Maybe that will get my blood stirring."

Liz and Flo followed her into the kitchen.

"Are you feeling okay?" Flo asked worriedly.

"Other than being exhausted because I stayed up half the night watching a marathon of Fred Astaire movies, I'm fine." She sighed. "That man was one very smooth dancer."

"Even better than my Donnie," Flo agreed.

Liz shook her head impatiently. "That's it? That's why you're so tired, because you were awake watching movies till dawn? Why didn't you just say that when I called?"

Frances gave her a defiant look, as she poured boiling water into a teapot she'd already filled with Earl Grey tea. "It never occurred to me I had to fill you in on my every activity. If you want to live vicariously, Flo's life is much more exciting than mine."

Liz looked momentarily taken aback, then chuckled. "No, I suppose you don't have to report what you're doing, though it might have been nice if you'd invited me over. I'm a big Fred Astaire fan myself."

"Next time I will," Frances promised, the tension gone from her voice.

Flo looked from one friend to the other, grateful to have them in her life. "Since we're all here, I could use some advice."

Liz grinned. "Is this about that double date you're having soon with Helen and Erik?" She shook her head. "What were you thinking?"

"That it may be insane to need it at this stage of my life, but I'd like my daughter's approval," Flo said. "Helen and I have been closer since I came back from Florida. I don't want my dating Donnie to change that."

"Do you really think she has any right to have a say?" Frances asked.

Liz gave her a chiding look. "No more than my kids had a right to decide I needed to move out of my own home. I could have put my foot down. There isn't a judge in this region who would have declared me incompetent," she said feistily.

"Not if they were in *their* right minds," Flo agreed, smiling at the idea of it.

"But," Liz continued, "out of respect for their feelings and their concerns, we found this compromise. The guest-house on my old property is the perfect size for me, to be honest, and having Travis and Sarah right there in my old house to look out for me is a comfort to all of us."

Frances looked at her skeptically. "And you think that's the same as Helen butting into Flo's social life?"

Liz nodded. "Helen's concerned, just the way my kids are."

"No," Flo contradicted. "Helen's embarrassed, though why she feels that way is beyond me. I'm hardly the first senior citizen to date."

"I don't think it's the dating that makes her crazy," Frances said. "It's the image of your sharing a bed with Donnie."

"Well, she just has to get over that," Flo said emphatically.

"And you think having a dinner together will ease her mind?" Frances asked.

"I think when she sees how well Donnie treats me and what a thoughtful man he is, yes," Flo said.

"And if she's not reassured?" Liz asked. "What then, Flo?"

Flo sighed. "To be honest, I haven't let myself think that far ahead. Donnie's bright idea would be to get married."

Frances's eyes lit up. "Then do it."

Flo frowned. "Just to please my daughter? No, absolutely not."

Liz gave her a penetrating look. "Are you saying it wouldn't please you? Do you care about Donnie?"

"Of course, I do. But, seriously, what's the sense of getting married at my age? Besides, it's been so long since I lived with a man, I'm not sure I'd be able to tolerate all the changes I'd have to make." She shook her head. "No, things are just the way they're supposed to be. Donnie and I agreed."

"Did you really?" Frances asked. "Or did you state your case and ignore his? You did say he'd suggested marriage, right?"

"Oh, he didn't mean that," Flo scoffed. "It was just a way to pacify my daughter."

"I'm not so sure about that," Liz said. "Donnie's a whole lot younger than any of us, so I don't know him all that well beyond saying good morning and how are you at the post office. Seems to me, though, that he'd never have mentioned getting married if he didn't want to. He doesn't have the same negative recollections of it that you do."

"That's true," Frances confirmed. "I used to see him with his wife at church and they always looked happy as could be."

"That was then," Flo insisted, more rattled than she wanted to admit by their impressions of the situation. "Let's just focus on my date, okay? How am I going to make sure Helen behaves?"

"Tell her not to come," Liz said. "That's the only way I can see."

"Maybe I need to have a talk with Erik," Flo suggested.

"And put him in the middle?" Frances said. "Don't do it. It'll only make matters worse."

"She's right," Liz said. "If you won't call this off, then you're just going to have to say a prayer and hope for the best."

That, unfortunately, was not the reassurance Flo had been hoping for from her friends. Even more unfortunately, they were probably right about disaster looming on the horizon.

* * *

Lynn had finally triumphed over Mitch's payroll system. She'd finished the checks at midnight. They were all sitting on the kitchen counter now just waiting for him to stop by and sign them before distributing them to his crews. At his insistence and after some debate about his being overly generous, she'd even cut her own check for the agreed-upon amount.

Yesterday, with the money Helen had loaned her in the bank and the promise of more later today from Mitch and Raylene, she'd done the first serious grocery shopping she'd done in months. This morning she'd gotten up at dawn to bake a coffee cake to share with Mitch when he stopped by. She'd brewed a pot of coffee, too. For the first time in ages, she'd felt like her old self.

There was a familiar tap on the kitchen door and the knob jiggled. She smiled when Mitch couldn't open the door. His second knock actually sounded impatient. She hurried over and unlocked the door, then grinned at him.

"See, I can be trained," she said.

"I'm proud of you," he said, then sniffed the air appreciatively. "It smells great in here. Have you been baking already this morning?"

"A cinnamon pecan coffee cake," she said. "Raylene gave me her recipe."

"What's the occasion? You have a meeting this morning?"

"No," she said, then admitted, "I thought maybe you'd have time for a cup of coffee."

"I'll make time," he said eagerly. "Does that coffee cake come with it?"

"Of course." She cut him a generous slice and set it on the table, then poured the coffee and brought it over.

"Any problems getting those checks finished?" he asked.

"Nope. I finally got the hang of it," she said proudly. "I don't think I've disgraced myself or given anyone more money than they're entitled to. They're all on the counter awaiting your signature. I'd advise you to double-check them, though, at least this time."

"I trust you."

"It's not me you need to worry about exactly. It's my math and computer skills. I'll feel better if you took a close look."

"Will do, then. You're a real godsend, Lynnie. I hope you realize that."

"Is that because I provided coffee and cake?"

"No, because you took over a task I have no time to do these days. I just want you to know I appreciate it. Now tell me what you've been up to. I've been trying to wrap up a job across town the past couple of days. We hit a glitch with a permit, so I've been down at Town Hall trying to get that straightened out."

"I wondered why I hadn't seen you next door," she said, then could have kicked herself.

He grinned. "You missed me?"

"I like knowing you're nearby in case there's a crisis I can't handle, that's all," she insisted.

"You missed me," he repeated, looking entirely too happy about it.

"Okay, maybe a little bit," she conceded. "Don't let it go to your head."

"If I do, I know you'll bring me straight back down to earth," he told her.

He looked as if he had something more on his mind, but the front doorbell rang.

"I'll be right back," Lynn promised.

When she saw Ed on the stoop, she sighed. "I wasn't expecting you."

"What? You want me to call ahead now, too? Isn't it enough that I turned over my key and can't walk in?"

"Sorry. I don't want to fight with you. I'm just surprised. That's all."

"I thought we could talk about the kids. Things have been kind of rough lately, especially with Lexie. I'd like to improve them."

Before she could stop him, he headed for the kitchen then halted abruptly.

"Mitch," he said tightly. "What are you doing here?"

"He's here to pick up the payroll checks I finished for him last night," Lynn said defensively.

Mitch gave her a lingering look that held a hint of disappointment, but he took her hint and stood up. "I'll just grab 'em and go," he said. "I signed yours and left it on the counter, Lynnie."

"Thanks."

"I'll call you later."

She nodded. Relief washed over her when he'd gone. Not that he hadn't had more right to be here than Ed did, but she'd known it would get awkward. Even now, Ed was obviously feeling territorial, and he wasn't the sort of man who'd hide it well.

She turned back to find him pouring his own cup of coffee and leaning back against the counter.

"So," he said, studying her speculatively, "you and Mitch? I'd never have guessed it. Then again, he did have a thing for you years ago."

"You don't know what you're talking about," she claimed, though she could feel the heat climbing into her cheeks. "If you want to talk about Jeremy and Alexis, let's talk. Otherwise, you can go."

"I thought I'd take them over to the beach this weekend. They used to love going to Sullivan's Island."

"It was one of their favorite family outings," she agreed.

"When I mentioned it, Jeremy was all for it, but Lexie refused to go."

"Really? She didn't say a word to me about it."

"You need to talk to her, straighten out this attitude she has toward me."

Lynn stared at him incredulously. "If she has an attitude, who do you think brought it on? Not me, Ed. That's all on you and your parents. It's up to you to fix it. You might start by warning your mother not to bad-mouth me in front of them. Lexie, especially, is very protective of me these days."

"Which you've no doubt encouraged," he said.

She stared at him in amazement. "Are you really that clueless? I could praise you to the heavens, but she would still see that I was struggling to put food on the table, that I couldn't sleep trying to figure out which bills I could pay with the few dollars left in the bank."

"You should have kept all that from her," he said stubbornly.

"It's hard to keep it a secret when there's no food in the refrigerator or the cupboards. Do you have any idea how many times we've had dinner at Carter and Raylene's?"

"Why is that a big deal?"

"They included us because they knew the situation was dire over here. Mandy picked up on that from Lexie. Raylene figured it out for herself when I came to her looking for a job."

"So now half the town considers me some kind of deadbeat?" Ed demanded. "Thanks for that."

"You can thank Jimmy Bob for that," she corrected. "Has your attorney turned up? Will he be in court tomorrow?"

Ed finally squirmed uncomfortably. "He filed for a continuance. Hal Cantor granted it. Hasn't Helen told you?"

Lynn's gaze narrowed. "When did this happen?"

"Late yesterday. Jimmy Bob's still out of town."

"Doing something more important than showing up in court for his client?"

"He's tied up, that's all I know."

"And you believe him? Maybe he's taking an extended vacation with the money he was supposed to be paying me in child support or our bank for the mortgage."

"I told you I'd taken care of that," Ed said stiffly. "It won't happen again. I'll pay closer attention or I'll handle it myself."

"Look, how you handle it is none of my concern as long as you don't leave me and the kids without food on the table or a roof over our heads. Understood?"

"Crystal clear," he said. "Now, about Lexie."

"Talk to her yourself," she repeated. "Despite everything that's happened recently, she adores you. I'm sure with all your charm you can think of the right words to get through to her."

"When did you get so cold?"

"I'm not cold. I'm learning to stand up for myself," she said, then actually smiled. "Thanks for that, by the way. It's something I should have learned to do years ago."

"Does this new attitude have something to do with Mitch Franklin?" Ed speculated. "How much is he hanging around here?"

"I told you I've been working part-time for him."

"And were you working for him when you and the kids were with him at Rosalina's?" he inquired, seemingly delighted when the question brought a blush to her cheeks. "Didn't think I'd hear about that, did you? You should have known better. Three people had called me before you ever left the restaurant."

"Nice to know your spy network is thorough," she said. "But what I do these days or whom I see is absolutely none of your business. I don't ask what you're up to."

"It's my business if they're hanging around my kids."

"Do you have some kind of problem with Mitch?" she asked.

"I just don't like walking into my house and finding him with my wife at eight o'clock in the morning. Was he here all night?"

Lynn stood up, trying not to let him see that she was trembling over his outrageous insinuations. "Get out, Ed. And don't come back here without making arrangements ahead of time."

For an instant he looked taken aback by her fury, but then his expression turned smug. "So, that's the way things are," he said. "I thought you were smarter than to fool around right under my nose."

"Get out now," she said. "I mean it."

Thankfully he didn't argue. The second he was gone, she sat down hard and picked up the phone. She dialed Helen's number, though the first two times she got it wrong because she was shaking so badly.

"What's the matter?" Helen asked as soon as she heard Lynn's voice. "Are you crying?"

"Trying not to," she said. "Ed was just here."

"I'll be right over."

"You don't have to come," Lynn said, but she was talking to dead air.

Not ten minutes later, she heard a car squeal to a stop out front and Helen burst into the house through the door Ed had obviously left unlocked.

"What happened?" she said, her hands gripping Lynn's shoulders. "Are you okay? Did he hurt you?"

Lynn shook her head, even as she burst into tears. After an awkward beat, Helen gathered her close.

"Oh, sweetie, nothing can be that bad. Don't shed a single tear over that man."

Lynn finally calmed down enough to draw in a deep breath. She took the tissue Helen handed her and dabbed away her tears.

"I'm sorry. I didn't realize how furious and upset I was until I saw you. Then I kinda came unglued."

"Do you have coffee?"

Lynn managed a small smile. "Given the morning I've had and the parade of people stopping in, it's a good thing I thought to make a big pot."

At the kitchen table, she filled Helen in on Ed's visit and his hints about her relationship with Mitch.

"Could he make something out of that?" she asked worriedly. "Mitch has been so kind to me. I don't want him to get dragged into the middle of my divorce because of that."

"I wouldn't put anything past Ed or Jimmy Bob, but you've done nothing wrong, Lynn. Nothing! You need to remember that."

"Ed says the court date has been pushed back again."

"Unfortunately, yes. I just found out this morning. I gather that happened right at the end of the day yesterday. Hal Cantor's office was very apologetic when they called this morning. His clerk said he's fit to be tied about all these delays and excuses from Jimmy Bob."

"Is there a way to stop this?"

"First I have to find Jimmy Bob," Helen said. "The investigator told me last night he has a lead. He thinks he's in the Cayman Islands."

"Why on earth would he go there?"

"He's on an extended vacation, or he's hiding out from something or someone. The investigator's going down to check it out."

Lynn stared at her with alarm. "I can't afford to pay expenses for a trip like that."

"Not to worry. Ed will cover it if I find that they've dreamed this up as a way to avoid bringing the case before the judge. If not, I will. I'd love to be the one to catch Jimmy Bob with his fingers in some cookie jar where they don't belong."

Lynn was a little surprised by the venom in Helen's voice. "You really don't like him, do you?"

"I like him fine," Helen corrected. "I just don't trust him, and I think he's a disgrace to the profession." She studied Lynn. "You okay now?"

"Better, thanks."

"Then I'd better get back to my office. I had three clients in the waiting room when I ran out. Barb's probably ready to string me up by now. She hates it when my schedule gets thrown off, especially when I'm the one responsible for ruining her orderly plan for the day."

"Apologize to her for me," Lynn said.

"No apology necessary. And it gives me a chance to remind her once in a while that it's still my office and I'm the boss. She forgets that from time to time."

"Thanks for coming over."

"Anytime, you know that. I'm not just your attorney, I'm your friend."

Tears stung Lynn's eyes once more, but she managed to keep them in check until Helen had gone. Then she allowed them to flow freely.

Eleven

The minute Jeremy came home from school, he raced past Lynn and headed straight upstairs with barely a greeting. Minutes later, he'd changed his clothes and was about to head right back out when Lynn snagged the back of his shirt.

"Hey, you, don't you want a snack?" she asked.

"There are snacks?" he asked, the question all too telling about the way things had been recently.

Lynn nodded. "I baked cookies."

Her son's expression immediately brightened. "Chocolate chip?"

"Of course."

He pumped his fist in the air. "All right!" Ignoring the milk she'd poured, he grabbed a handful of the still-warm cookies and started once again for the door.

"Don't you want to sit here and drink some milk with those?" she asked. All afternoon she'd been craving a return to the old days when the kids would share their day with her over a snack.

"Can't," he mumbled, his mouth full.

"Why not? Where are you off to in such a hurry?"

"Next door. Remember, Mitch said I could help."

"Does he know you're coming over this afternoon?"

"Uh-huh. I told him when I was there yesterday."

Lynn frowned. "You were there yesterday?"

"And the day before. Don't freak out, Mom. He said it was okay."

"I'm just wondering why you didn't mention it to me. I thought you'd gone over to your friend Ray's house."

He shrugged. "It's boring over there. All he wants to do is play video games. This is more fun."

Lynn resolved to make sure Mitch was as thrilled about it as Jeremy obviously was. "Don't make a pest of yourself, okay?"

"No way," he promised, darting off.

She shook her head as the screen door slammed shut behind him. Two minutes later, her phone rang.

"I hear your son neglected to mention that he's been coming over here after school," Mitch said. "You okay with that?"

"I am, if you are," she said. "But, Mitch, don't feel obligated to let him stay if he's in your way."

"Actually, he's a good helper. I might have you cut a paycheck for him this week."

"Absolutely not," she said, certain he'd be doing it only to put a few more dollars into her pocket.

"I'm just saying he works hard. He should be rewarded. A child is never too young to understand the value of a strong work ethic."

"I can't disagree with you about that." She hesitated, then said, "Are you free for dinner? Jeremy's been asking for steak and baked potatoes, and I finally had enough in the budget to get them yesterday. I thought we could barbecue on the back deck."

Nerves stirred at his silence.

"It's fine if you have plans or if you don't want to," she said hurriedly. "It's no big deal."

"I'm just wondering if it's a great idea, given the way Ed reacted to finding me over there this morning. I got the distinct impression he wasn't pleased."

"He doesn't have a say," Lynn said heatedly, then sighed. "But, to be honest, I wanted to talk to you about that. Maybe after dinner?"

"Okay, sure," he said at last. "Do you know how to work that fancy grill I've seen out on your deck?"

"Turning it on scares me to death," she said. "I'm always convinced the gas will explode in a huge ball of flame."

"Then leave it till I get there," he suggested. "Grilling's about the only form of cooking at which I excel."

"I'm happy to leave it to you," she said, relieved by his offer.

"Six-thirty okay? I'd like to go home and shower before I come by."

"That's perfect," she said. "See you then."

That gave her only slightly more than two hours to toss a salad, bake the potatoes and panic over whether she'd just made a terrible mistake.

When he'd finished his call to Lynn, Mitch found Jeremy sitting on the floor raptly watching Terry Jenkins cutting the trim for the windows.

"How does he know how to make the corners fit together?" Jeremy asked Mitch.

"Come over here with me," Mitch said, taking him over to his worktable. He sketched out the angles needed for the cuts, then demonstrated how to mark them on the wood. "Then the machine does the rest."

"It looks easy," Jeremy said. "Is it?"

"Once you get the hang of it," Mitch told him. "Want to try?"

Jeremy's eyes lit up. "Can I?" Then his excitement faded. "That's a saw, isn't it? Mom said no saws."

"I think her biggest worry is that you'd try to do something without supervision, but you're not going to do that, right?"

"Never," Jeremy promised, sketching a cross on his chest. "Promise."

"Then I think we're okay. Hey, Terry, how many more pieces do you need for that frame?"

Terry glanced at Jeremy, clearly guessing Mitch's intention. "You gonna take over for me?" he asked the boy.

Jeremy nodded excitedly.

"How about I help you out this time?" Terry suggested, positioning himself behind Jeremy. "You see the line I've marked?"

"Uh-huh," Jeremy said, his brow knit in concentration.

"Then you put your hands here, and here," he said, covering Jeremy's little hands with his work-roughened ones as Mitch stood by, grinning. Terry was a master carpenter with grandchildren of his own. Mitch knew he'd done exactly this with them on many work sites over the years, introducing them to his craft with gentle guidance. He'd taught Mitch much of what he knew as well, taking him under his wing when Mitch had started hanging around the work sites with one of Terry's sons.

Satisfied that the boy was in good hands, he walked back over to check the specs for the fieldstone he needed to order for the fireplace. He'd barely glanced at the paper when he heard Jeremy's whoop of exhilaration.

"I did it!" he shouted, then came running back to Mitch.

"See, look. Terry says it's just right, that he can use it on the window. I made something that's gonna be in Raylene and Carter's house, like forever!"

"Good job," Mitch enthused. "Since it's almost time to shut down for the day, how about sweeping up around here? You up for that?"

"Sure," Jeremy said as if Mitch had offered him an equally exciting task, rather than what his men considered necessary drudgery.

He grinned as he watched Jeremy tackle the task with extra exuberance. When Terry joined him, he gave Mitch a knowing look.

"Kid's cute," Terry said.

"And eager to learn," Mitch replied.

"His mom's not bad-looking, either."

Mitch frowned at his longtime employee. "Do you have a point you're trying to make?"

"Just saying I've seen you over there a time or two lately."

"So?" Mitch said defensively.

"Settle down," Terry said. "I'm not criticizing. If you ask me, it's about time you had a little fun in your life again. It's what Amy would want for you." He smiled. "And Lynn, she's good people."

"Okay," Mitch said slowly, sensing there was more on his old friend's mind.

"Ed's another kettle of fish. He's not going to be happy about your poaching on his turf."

Mitch had realized the same thing this morning, but he couldn't help defending himself—and Lynn—to Terry. "The divorce is practically final."

"*Practically*'s not final," Terry cautioned. "A lot of people in town respect Ed, though I'm not entirely sure why.

Some folks are conservative in their thinking. You don't want to get them to talking about Lynn, do you?"

"Of course not," Mitch said. "It's not as if we're running around flaunting some big romance. We've been out once with the kids, that's it."

Terry's deep laugh rumbled in his chest. "Yeah, that dinner at Rosalina's hit the grapevine before the two of you got your sodas." He looked directly into Mitch's eyes. "Word of advice from a man who's lived his life in this town?"

Mitch nodded reluctantly.

"It's not what you do in plain view that's gonna get you into trouble."

"Meaning?"

"Your truck in her driveway late at night or early in the morning. That's going to stir talk, the kind you don't want. Park right here at Raylene's. She won't care and you've got a legitimate reason for being here."

As much as it annoyed Mitch to be told he needed to be sneaking in and out of Lynn's, especially when he'd barely stolen so much as a kiss, he could see Terry's point.

"Will do," he said. "Thanks."

Terry nodded toward Jeremy. "Take your helper there on home. I'll finish up in here."

"Thanks, again," Mitch said. "I'll do that."

And he resolved that when he came back for dinner at Lynn's tonight, he'd walk.

Lynn listened to Jeremy's report on his afternoon helping out on the construction site with a mix of delight and annoyance. She loved seeing her son so excited, but hadn't she made herself clear to Mitch what he was and wasn't allowed to do?

The minute Mitch returned from his quick trip home

to shower and change, she frowned at him. "A miter saw? You let my ten-year-old use a miter saw?"

Jeremy winced. "Sorry I blabbed," he whispered to Mitch, then scampered from the kitchen to the safety of the back deck.

"Did he mention that Terry was right there with him?"

"You mean the same Terry who lost the tip of his finger on the job a couple of years ago?" she said wryly.

Mitch had forgotten all about that. "He's the one," he confirmed. "Taught him a valuable lesson, so he's extra careful now."

"I'm not quite ready for Jeremy to be learning those kind of valuable lessons," she said, standing in front of him, hands on hips.

Before she guessed his intentions, Mitch leaned in and kissed her. She thought she heard him murmur, "God, you're cute," just before his lips settled on hers.

He never once touched her beyond the contact of their lips, but the kiss took her breath away just the same. She sighed when he eventually pulled away.

"You are not going to win an argument by kissing me," she told him when he stepped back. Needing to cool off, she took a minute to stick her head in the fridge as she grabbed the lemonade she'd made earlier. When she emerged, he was smiling.

"Were we arguing?" he inquired innocently. "I thought you were ranting a little and I was just listening."

She blinked at that, then sputtered, "Now that's just plain old condescending, Mitch Franklin. I was trying to get through to you that I need to know my son is going to be safe over there or I'll have to keep him at home."

His expression sobered at once. "Jeremy will always be

safe with me," he said quietly. "He's your son, Lynn. I'd never put him at risk."

"Then we're clear?"

"We're clear."

"No more saws," she said flatly. "I told you that the other night. It's one thing for Jeremy to ignore my rules. It's entirely another for you to do it."

"To his credit, Jeremy reminded me of the rules."

She seemed surprised by that. "He did?"

"Yep, first thing out of his mouth."

"Then what were you thinking?"

"That when a kid shows a real interest in something, that interest should be encouraged, as long as it can be done safely and with strict supervision."

"So you'd let him jump out of a plane, if he sounded excited about it?" she inquired, trying to determine just how far that philosophy of his might go.

"With the right equipment and a certified instructor, who knows? Maybe."

"That's insane."

"Okay, he's probably a little young to be jumping out of planes," Mitch conceded. "But can't you see my point? Kids shouldn't be discouraged from trying new things, as long as their safety's not at risk. Once adults put a damper on a kid's enthusiasm for things and set too many limits for them, it's death to their imaginations."

Lynn sighed. She could see that Mitch was probably the ideal father for boys, one who'd give them the freedom to test their limits. She wondered if that same freedom would extend to girls.

"Did you ever wish you had a daughter?" she asked as she handed him a glass of icy lemonade, then took a sip of her own.

He seemed startled by the question. "Sure, but we decided two kids were plenty. Is there some reason you're asking?"

"Just wondering how you'd react if your fourteen-year-old daughter expressed a genuine interest in, say, going to a boy-girl party."

He frowned. "Would the parents be there? Do I know them? How late?"

She chuckled. "There you go. I knew I could find something that would freak you out the same way the thought of that saw freaks me out."

Mitch chuckled. "Okay, you got me. I live by a double standard. I'm an old-fashioned guy who still believes in protecting the women he cares about, no matter what age they might be." Suddenly his expression sobered. "Which brings me to something I wanted to talk to you about."

"Can it wait till we've eaten?" she asked, pulling a platter of steaks from the refrigerator. "These should probably go on the grill now."

He hesitated, then nodded. "I'm on it." He took the platter and went outside.

Lexie came into the kitchen just as he left, smiling. "He's here a lot. I think Mandy's right. He has the hots for you."

"You and Mandy talk too much," Lynn said. "Take the salad outside."

Lexie accepted the bowl and the dressing. "Won't change what I know," she said, though she dutifully did as she'd been told.

When Lynn started to go outside a few minutes later with the foil-wrapped baked potatoes that she'd precooked in the oven, Jeremy was helping Mitch with the steaks and Lexie was entertaining him with a story about something that had happened in her French class. One of the other students had suddenly started speaking Spanish, momentarily confusing everyone, including the teacher.

"Mrs. Riley looked as if she ought to understand what Melinda was saying, but she didn't have a clue," Lexie said. "Then it finally dawned on her that Melinda's bilingual in Spanish and had just slipped up."

Lynn stood just inside and smiled at the sound of Mitch's laughter swirling in the air with her son's and daughter's. She hadn't heard such happy sounds around here in a long time.

"How are those steaks coming along?" she called out as she joined them.

"If anyone wants them rare, they're done," Mitch said.

"Medium," Lynn declared.

"Mine, too," Lexie added.

Jeremy looked to Mitch, who'd already taken his off the flames and set it on the platter. "Rare, like Mitch's!" he chimed in.

Mitch smiled down at him. "You sure about that, buddy?"

"That's what you're having, right?" Jeremy asked.

"I sure am."

"Then it's the way I want mine," her son insisted.

As touched as she was by the scene, Lynn couldn't help worrying that her son was rapidly developing a case of hero worship. But looking at the smile on his face and the adoration in his eyes, somehow she couldn't make herself regret bringing Mitch into their lives.

After dinner, Lexie and Jeremy cleaned up, leaving Mitch alone on the deck with Lynn. He couldn't recall when he'd had a nicer evening, he thought as the sun disappeared below the horizon. He'd known all night, though, that something was on Lynn's mind. He had his own concerns to share, as well. It wasn't a conversation he was much looking forward to.

"You first," he suggested eventually.

She gave him a startled look, as if she'd forgotten that she'd told him earlier that she wanted to discuss something with him.

"Is this about Ed's visit this morning?" he prompted.

She sighed. "Yes. To be honest, for a little while tonight, I'd pushed that completely out of my head."

"How worked up was he when he left here? I tried to keep an ear out in case things got too heated."

"Oh, he didn't yell, but he did try to make something out of your being here."

"Is that why Helen came rushing over right after he left?" he asked, knowing that he was giving away his attentiveness to everything going on in her life.

She lifted a brow at the revelation, then nodded. "You saw that?"

"Hard to miss when she squealed into the driveway like she was making a turn on the track at Daytona."

"She overreacted just a little when I called her," Lynn said.

Mitch frowned. "Since when does Helen overreact? Exactly how badly did Ed upset you?"

"He didn't. I mean I'm not worried for me. It's you I'm concerned about. I'm afraid he might try to drag you into the middle of our problems. You don't deserve to get caught up in my drama."

"There's nothing Ed can do to me," Mitch assured her.

She gave him a world-weary look. "If you believe that, then you don't know him very well."

"I know enough," Mitch insisted.

"He can make your life uncomfortable in a lot of different ways," Lynn countered. "It's an easy thing to spread gossip in this town. You know that, Mitch. I don't want your reputation hurt because he's looking to make trouble for you."

Mitch stood up, then hunkered down in front of her, forcing her to look into his eyes. "Lynn, you do know we haven't done anything wrong."

"I know that."

"And I like spending time with you. I think you feel the same way."

"I do, but—"

"No buts," he said flatly. He thought then of Terry's earlier warning. "Unless you'd rather I stay away. Is that what you want? Will it make it easier for you if people aren't talking and keeping Ed all stirred up?"

She looked away. "Maybe," she conceded, but then her gaze met his. "But that's not what I want, Mitch. I enjoy spending time with you. It's been…" She looked as if she were searching for the right word. "Restful, I guess, though that may not sound terribly flattering. Until the past couple of weeks, I'd forgotten what it was like not to be tense and on edge all the time. I'd come close to forgetting how to laugh. So had the kids."

He nodded, pleased, even though she hadn't mentioned the sparks that kept him up nights. "Good to know," he said. "Then here's what I'm thinking. We'll get together when we want to, but we won't go parading around town. I don't like the idea of hiding out, but for now, maybe it's for the best. The last thing I want is for Ed to have some kind of ammunition he thinks he can use against you." He paused, then said, "Or would you rather take a break?

You're in charge here, Lynnie. Whatever you need, we'll make it work."

She suddenly blinked back tears. "You're so blasted considerate."

He smiled, even though her tears were almost the undoing of him. "And that's a bad thing?"

"No, it just makes me wonder all the more why I didn't choose you all those years ago."

"I'd like to think that's only because I took myself out of the running way back when I was thirteen. Who knows what might have happened if I'd been brave enough to stand my ground." He grinned. "My bad."

"Or maybe the timing now is exactly right," she said.

He smiled at the hint of wistfulness in her voice. "Maybe so."

He, for one, could hardly wait to find out.

Flo felt as if she'd been holding her breath for the entire two hours she and Donnie had been sitting in Rosalina's with Helen and Erik. Erik and Donnie had done their best to keep the conversation flowing, but Helen looked as if she'd been sucking on lemons.

"Helen, did you know Donnie has just about every episode of *Law & Order* on tape?" Flo asked, hoping to spark a common interest between the two.

"Really?" Helen said, though without much enthusiasm.

"I'm a big fan of Sam Waterston," Donnie said. "I started watching the series from day one. It seems real authentic to me."

"Helen thinks so, too, don't you?" Flo said, giving her daughter a sharp look that commanded that she at least try.

"Actually, it is one of the best legal shows I've seen,"

Helen said. She hesitated, then asked, "Are you and my mother serious about each other?"

"Helen!" Flo protested, even as Erik nudged his wife and gave her a warning look.

"What?" Helen demanded. "It's a reasonable question."

"It is," Donnie said, not showing any hint that he was losing his composure. "I've had more fun since I started seeing your mother than I'd had since I lost my wife. I'm one of those people who believes you can't have enough laughter in your life." He held Helen's gaze. "Your mother keeps me laughing. She has something to say about just about everything and it usually strikes a chord with me." He winked at Flo. "Not that we don't disagree about a few things."

"Such as?" Helen asked, seizing on that.

"Whether or not we should get married," Donnie said with annoying candor.

"Donald Leighton!" Flo protested. "This is not the time."

Helen's eyes had lit up, though. "Tell me more," she encouraged Donnie.

"I think when two people care about each other the way we do and are as well-suited as we are, it makes sense to get married. Why be alone at this stage of our lives?"

"An interesting point of view," Helen said. "Mom? You don't agree?"

"I do not," Flo said irritably.

Despite the sudden tension, Donnie looked thoroughly amused. "And there you have it. So far, she's winning, but I hold out high hopes I can change her mind one of these days."

"You're losing ground right this second," Flo grumbled.

Thankfully, Erik stepped in. "How about dessert at our

place? I brought home an apple pie I baked today. You'll be able to say good-night to Sarah Beth, Flo."

She regarded her son-in-law fondly. "You know I can't say no to that." She gave Donnie and her daughter a warning look. "But if the subject of marriage comes up again, don't rule out my stuffing some of that pie down someone's throat."

Erik choked back a laugh at her threat, so Flo gave him a scowl. "I mean it."

"I know you do," Erik said. "I'm just trying to imagine the likelihood of Helen listening to you."

"I can take a hint," Helen protested.

"That was no hint," Flo retorted. "It was a direct warning."

Helen looked from Erik to her, then back again to her husband. "Okay, I'll behave. I promise."

"Now why would you want to go and do that," Donnie asked, clearly willing to stir the pot, either for the sake of some excitement or because he sensed he finally had an ally who could win this battle for him.

Flo frowned at him. "What is wrong with you? I just neutralized her."

"Hey, she's on my side," he said. "I may not want her neutralized."

For the first time all evening, Helen seemed visibly impressed with Donnie. "I like you, Donnie Leighton."

He sat up a little straighter and shot a triumphant look at Flo. "There you go. You wanted a stamp of approval. Now you've got it."

Helen looked surprised by his comment. "You wanted my approval?" she asked Flo.

"Well, of course I did," Flo replied impatiently. "What did you think this uncomfortable meal was supposed to be about?"

"Oh, I don't know. Maybe your getting on my last nerve," Helen said.

Flo looked at her, then laughed. "No, sweetie, that was just a perk."

Twelve

Mitch was just wrapping up for the day at Raylene's when he looked up and saw Carter stepping into the new addition.

"Come to see how the work's progressing?" Mitch asked, joining him.

"Nah, Raylene and I sneak in here just about every night to see what you've accomplished. It's looking real good, Mitch. You do incredible work."

"Thanks. I'm glad you're pleased." He studied the police chief, who was wearing his uniform tonight. That must mean he was working the streets, something he still insisted on doing, rotating shifts with his men. "Something on your mind?"

"You haven't been at dinner for a few nights now," Carter said, looking oddly uncomfortable for a man wearing a holstered gun at his hip.

"I figured you'd seen enough of me at your dinner table."

Carter winced. "I was afraid you were going to say something like that. Mitch, I hope I didn't plant that idea in your head. You're always welcome here. I want you to know that, and if I said something to make you think otherwise, I'm sorry."

"For a man who's supposed to keep his eyes and ears on everything going on in this town, I'm astonished you haven't heard."

"Heard what?"

"I've been going over to Lynn's for dinner for the past week or so."

Carter blinked. "Lynn's? Right next door?"

"Yep."

His gaze narrowed. "And my wife knows that?"

"Your wife's among those who practically pushed me into Lynn's arms. Not that I've been in her arms," he added hurriedly. "I'm just saying…"

"I get it, Mitch. You don't have to explain yourself to me. I'm not like Raylene. I'm perfectly comfortable without details."

"I just didn't want you getting the wrong idea."

"Because of Ed," Carter guessed. He shook his head. "How did it come to be that so many people in this town trust that man? He's hiding something. I have no idea what it is, but when a man won't look me in the eye the way you're doing right now, I get suspicious."

"As a comparative newcomer to town, you don't have the same perspective other folks do," Mitch suggested. "I imagine you see a lot of things the rest of us have turned a blind eye to. Because Ed's daddy ran that business honestly and with genuine concern for the best interests of his clients, I think everyone just assumed Ed would do the same. To some extent, I suppose he has, but he's definitely not his father."

"I've only run across Jack once or twice, but he seems like a stand-up guy."

"He is," Mitch confirmed. "As for the business continuing to do well, a good measure of that success is because nobody came along to open up a competing insurance agency. People in Serenity don't like going to outsiders in neighboring towns with their personal business. They like their doctors, lawyers and their insurance agents to be people they know. They feel more comfortable when they know not only them, but their whole family history."

"And no one yet has noticed that this particular emperor, so to speak, has no clothes, just like the one in the fairy tale?" Carter asked.

"Lately there's been some talk," Mitch said. "A few people don't like the way Ed's treated Lynn and his kids. I actually think a few have even wondered why Jack didn't step in. If the bank had foreclosed on their house the way it was rumored, I think Ed would have been doomed."

Carter looked startled. "Lynn's situation had gotten that bad?"

Mitch nodded. "She never admitted it to me, but I think so, yes. And I know for a fact that she was having trouble putting food on the table."

"Raylene picked up on that much, too. What about now?" Carter asked, clearly concerned. "Is it better over there? Anything I can do?"

"Lynn says things are okay, but I doubt her pride would allow her to say otherwise," Mitch said. "Whatever was going on, though, she does seem to have a little cash again. Of course, she's working for both Raylene and me, so maybe that's been enough to help her get by. For all I know, Ed could still be a deadbeat. There's a part of me that wishes that were true so the court could come down on him and nail his sorry hide to a wall."

"Not that you care, right?" Carter said, clearly amused by his vehemence.

"The guy's been a thorn in my side for years," Mitch said.

"How so?"

"Old story," Mitch confided with a shrug. "He got the girl."

Carter's eyes widened. "Really? You and Lynn had a thing? When?"

"I wouldn't exactly call it a thing," Mitch said, wishing he hadn't brought it up. "I was thirteen and thought she was about the best thing since the invention of baseball. She never gave me a second look because of Ed Morrow." He shrugged. "I thought I got over it. Seems like I didn't."

"Then this thing now, it could be serious?"

"Way too soon to know something like that," Mitch insisted. "I enjoy her company. I like her kids. We'll see where that leads us. First, though, she needs to have her divorce finalized and to be free of that man once and for all. She needs to be steady on her own two feet, so she can make a decision that's really right for her, rather than turning to me out of necessity or misguided gratitude."

Carter nodded. "But you already know what you want, don't you?"

Mitch shrugged. "I can't deny it. I had a soft spot for her all those years ago. Apparently, I still do."

"Good luck, then. I'd offer to put in a good word for you, but I imagine Raylene already has the booster thing under control."

Mitch rolled his eyes. "Your wife's a meddler, that's for sure. If Grace Wharton ever retires from that business, Raylene is definitely the top candidate in Serenity to take over for her."

"You might not want to mention that to Raylene," Carter warned. "She'll be so excited by the compliment, she's likely to head over to Wharton's and try to muzzle Grace so she can have that role all to herself right now. Since

Raylene came out of her shell and out of the house, she seems to be discovering all sorts of hidden talents in herself. I'm not one to discourage her, but this is one I'd like to see her keep under wraps."

Mitch laughed. "Good luck with that."

"I know," Carter said with a rueful shake of his head. "It's a lost cause. See you around, Mitch. You and Lynn should come to dinner one night this week. Raylene likes having a full house at mealtime."

"Maybe we'll do that," Mitch agreed.

Then, again, he wasn't sure he wanted to encourage the meddling that would start with the appetizers and last right on through dessert.

Lynn was fixing dinner when Lexie sat down at the kitchen table, her expression pensive.

"Something going on?" Lynn asked.

"Dad's ticked off at me," she confessed.

Lynn turned the burner under the stew to simmer, then joined her daughter at the table. "Why is that?"

"Because I wouldn't go to Sullivan's Island with him and Jeremy."

"What makes you think he's ticked off about that?" she asked, though she wasn't surprised that Ed had made no effort to mend fences. Instead, he'd apparently taken his displeasure out on Lexie when she'd held firm on her refusal to go.

"He told me I was behaving like a spoiled brat," Lexie said. "That I should be grateful to have a dad who wanted to take me someplace great for a weekend getaway." She gave Lynn a plaintive look. "It wasn't about that at all."

"I know," Lynn said. "Maybe you should look at it from

his point of view for a minute, though. Your dad was trying. He wanted to do something special with you and Jeremy."

"Mom, I know what a weekend in Sullivan's Island costs," Lexie said impatiently. "I looked the hotel up on-line. How can he spend that kind of money on me and Jeremy when we didn't even have enough for groceries?"

"I think that situation has been resolved," Lynn told her. "It was just a misunderstanding."

"How does a man just ignore the fact that his family is about to lose their house?" Lexie retorted. "That's huge, Mom. It can't be some silly little misunderstanding."

Lynn sighed and told herself she had to say the right thing, even if it choked her to try to defend Ed. "Your dad's attorney made a mistake. As soon as your dad found out about it, he fixed things. All of that is really between me and your father. I don't want it to change your relationship with him. He loves you, Lexie, and I know you love him."

"It's all just so mixed up," Lexie said. "Can I tell you something else?"

"Of course."

"After Dad left, I prayed every night that he'd change his mind and come back."

Lynn allowed herself a smile. "That's not unusual. Most kids want their parents to reconcile. Every kid dreams of having the perfect family."

"I'm not finished," Lexie said. "My point is that now I don't feel that way. I like Mitch. You laugh when he's around. And he really listens to me and Jeremy, not like Dad, who makes a big pretense of caring when he wants to impress people, especially Grandma and Grandpa."

Lynn found it astonishing that her daughter had pegged Ed so accurately. Still, though, she tried to come to his defense. "Not everyone shows their love in the same way, sweetheart. It's harder for your dad. Mitch is really comfortable around kids. Your dad was an only child. He spent all his time around adults."

Lexie rolled her eyes. "Mom, he must have been a kid once. He went to school. Didn't he ever have friends?"

"Obviously, but it's not the same thing relating to a peer as a kid and then relating to a child when you're the adult."

"What you're really saying is that he had terrible examples at parenting. Grandma and Grandpa aren't exactly the warm and fuzzy type. Well, Grandpa's not bad, but Grandma…" She shook her head. "What's with her, anyway?"

Again, Lexie had nailed a problem Lynn had only belatedly recognized. "They try. So does your dad. That trip was meant to show you how hard he's trying. I'm sure it hurt his feelings when you refused to go. Believe it or not, parents have feelings, too."

"I guess," Lexie said. She regarded Lynn worriedly. "Are you saying I should have gone?"

"No, sweetheart. It was always up to you, but it never hurts to think about what consequences your actions might have on someone else's feelings."

Lexie regarded her with dismay, though whether it was over her actions or her fear of Lynn's disapproval was impossible to tell.

"Does that mean I should apologize to Dad?" Lexie asked, sounding resigned.

"Something to consider," Lynn told her.

"I'll think about it," Lexie promised, then gave Lynn a defiant look. "But I'm not going back to Grandma and Grandpa's. I don't care who that hurts. Grandma needs to apologize to me for what she said about you. It was mean."

"I appreciate your wanting to defend me, sweetie, but even that is my battle, not yours."

"They said it to *me*," Lexie corrected stubbornly. "That makes it my battle. Nobody gets to talk that way about my mom."

"You could tell your grandmother how you feel. Maybe she would apologize if she understood how it hurt you."

"No way."

"It's up to you, but not everyone is lucky enough to have their grandparents in their lives. I don't want you to regret cutting them out of yours."

"Believe me, I'm not going to regret anything," Lexie insisted.

Lynn thought there would come a time when she would, but right this second wasn't the moment to push. Trying to mend fences between Lexie and Ed was probably enough adult pressure for one day.

"When's your next court date?" Mitch asked as he and Lynn sat on the back deck at the end of the evening.

She promptly made a face. "Hard to say. It's supposed to be on Monday, but Jimmy Bob West is still missing. Helen's investigator trailed him to the Cayman Islands of all places, but by the time he got down there, Jimmy Bob was nowhere to be found."

"Shouldn't the judge insist that Ed get another attorney? You shouldn't be left in limbo forever."

"Helen thinks that could happen if there's another request for a postponement. I gather Hal Cantor is no happier than we are about all these delays and excuses."

"Hal's a good guy, and he's no pushover. I've done a couple of jobs for him and got to know him pretty well.

If he thinks Ed isn't acting in good faith, Ed could get on Hal's bad side in a big hurry."

"That would suit me just fine."

He turned to look at her, noting the color in her cheeks that hadn't been there just a few weeks ago. She looked good, almost back to her old self. If only those lines of tension he saw around her eyes would ease, but he knew better than to expect miracles. Those would only go away when the stress of the divorce was behind her.

"I noticed Lexie seemed quieter than usual tonight," he said. "She okay?"

She smiled. "How could you possibly have noticed that with Jeremy chattering away a mile a minute? He is so excited about going out for baseball this summer, thanks to your encouragement. I was stunned when he asked me about it."

"Do you mind that I made the suggestion?"

"Of course not. I'd have made it myself if he'd shown even the slightest interest. How on earth did you talk him into it?"

"I didn't do much, to be honest. We had the opening day Braves game on the radio next door. Ty Townsend was pitching, so the guys were talking about him, how he's a local, that kind of stuff. Jeremy's ears perked up. I guess he hadn't realized we had a local sports celebrity from right here in town."

"But he's met Ty," Lynn said. "He and Annie are over at Raylene's a lot."

"I guess he just hadn't made the connection."

"I suppose those of us who know Ty don't make a big production about him being a superstar pitcher. To us he's just someone we've all known forever."

"That's as it should be," Mitch said. "Gives him a haven away from all the paparazzi and sports reporters."

"How did it go from Jeremy asking about Ty to his wanting to play ball himself?" Lynn asked.

"First, he asked me if I'd ever played baseball. I told him I had way back in high school, but not even half as well as Ty. Then he asked me if I'd liked it anyway."

Lynn frowned. "That seems like an odd question."

Mitch nodded. "I thought so, too. Seems he's always been picked last when they played at school, so he started pretending he didn't care, that baseball was just a dumb game."

Lynn's eyes widened. "You're kidding. He never said a word about that."

"Probably embarrassed," Mitch said. "Anyway, I told him that at his age, the game should be about having fun, and that if he wanted to play, he should try, that it was the only way he'd ever get better." He hesitated. "Did he mention that I'm going to help out coaching the team?"

"Really?" she said, looking surprised. "That didn't come up at all."

He gave her a lingering look. "Does that worry you? Not that he didn't say anything, but that I'm going to be spending more time with him?"

"Why on earth would I be worried about that? You're great with him."

"It could be tricky," he told her candidly. "You and me, we're moving along at a snail's pace here." When she started to speak, he held up a hand. "Not that I'm complaining. We're doing what's best for now. But it does worry me some that Jeremy could get too attached."

Lynn sighed. "I have thought of that," she acknowledged. "But he's been so happy, I convinced myself there couldn't be any harm in a little hero worship."

Mitch smiled at her characterization of it. He liked the idea of being somebody's hero. Even better would be to become hers. "Just so you know, even if things never work out for us beyond being friends the way we are now, I won't turn my back on Jeremy. Lexie, either, for that matter. I'll find a way to be around as much as they need me."

When she didn't respond, he glanced over and realized that she was fighting tears. "What?" he asked. "I meant that in a good way. I just wanted to reassure you."

"I know you did," she said, swiping impatiently at the dampness on her cheeks until he handed her a napkin that was handy. "You are just so incredibly sweet and thoughtful sometimes it makes me want to cry."

"Well, maybe you could put a lid on the waterworks," he teased. "Next thing you know you'll have me bawling, too."

She laughed, just as he'd intended.

"I don't see that happening," she said.

"Hey, I'm as sentimental as the next guy. I cried in the delivery room when both of my boys were born."

That seemed to bring on a fresh batch of tears, for reasons he couldn't begin to fathom. "What now? What did I say?"

"Ed refused to come into the delivery room. He said it was no place for a man."

Mitch couldn't hide his surprise. "You know my opinion of Ed has never been very high, but it's pretty much shot to blazes right now. I try real hard not to judge other people, but that's just flat-out wrong unless you didn't want him in there."

"When Lexie was on the way, I begged him to change his mind," she admitted. "He refused. I tried again with

Jeremy, but it was clear I wasn't going to have any better luck convincing him then, either."

"Well, he missed out on one of the most amazing moments a couple can ever share," Mitch declared. "I pity him."

"He's missed out on a lot from that day on," Lynn said. "Lexie's pulling away from him these days, and I think it won't be long before Jeremy does, too."

Mitch frowned at that. "Not because I'm in the picture, I hope. I don't want to push my way in and try to take his place. For whatever flaws the man might have, he is their father."

"It's not about you, though I do think Lexie's every bit as enamored of you as Jeremy is. Ed's burned some bridges with her and is showing no inclination to fix things. As for Jeremy, he's still blissfully unaware of most of his father's shortcomings, but that won't last forever."

Though it went against his grain to ask, he forced himself to say, "Anything I can do?"

"It's not up to you to fix this. Ed has to."

"I could say something to him," Mitch offered, though as soon as he tried to envision how Ed would react to such an overture, he shook his head. "Never mind. Bad idea. If I were in his shoes, I'd just slug me."

Lynn laughed. "That's probably not Ed's style, but you're right. He wouldn't take it well. Thanks for offering, though."

They fell into a companionable silence then. Mitch stared out at the large backyard that was in definite need of some care. The grass looked sadly overgrown and neglected and the landscaping was nonexistent.

"You ever thought about putting in a garden back here?" he asked, knowing it might be an expense she could ill afford. Still, there were a few things that could be done inexpensively to create a real oasis in the large space. "Raylene could probably give you some tips. She has a real nice one."

"Her yard is gorgeous," Lynn agreed with unmistakable envy. "And I always thought that would be our next big project around here, but right now, with things the way they are, there's not a lot to spend on something that isn't a necessity."

"What would you do if money were no object?" he asked, curious to hear her vision.

"You know your client who has all those azaleas?" She smiled. "The ones she accused you of destroying?"

"Of course."

"I'd like something like that, azaleas of every color imaginable all around in a big circle, maybe, with a birdbath or even a fountain in the middle. Or maybe some fancy birdhouse. Spring's my favorite season, and I think it would be so beautiful back here, then, with all the shades of purple, fuchsia and white in full bloom." She closed her eyes, a smile on her lips. "I can practically see it. I visited some formal gardens once just like that at the National Arboretum. I never knew there could be so many varieties. I was the only one on our class trip who wanted to go there, so one of the teachers took me, while everyone else went to the Washington Monument."

"I remember that trip," he said, then slanted a look her way. "You sure you didn't beg off from the monument thing because you were scared of heights?"

She looked startled for an instant, then chuckled. "No, I didn't, but you're right, going all the way up would have scared the daylights out of me. How did you know that?"

"Because even out here on this deck, you never go close to the railing."

"You noticed that?"

"I notice everything about you," he reminded her quietly.

"And you don't think I'm a terrible sissy?" she asked. "We're not even that high off the ground back here."

"Oh, I imagine you could break a few bones if you tumbled off the deck," he said, "But you have nothing to worry about, Lynnie."

"Oh?"

His gaze captured hers, held. "For as long as you let me, I plan to be around to catch you."

Thirteen

Lynn was alone in the boutique when Wilma Morrow, Ed's mother, walked through the door, took one look at her and paled.

"You! What on earth are you doing here?" she said as if she'd found Lynn in a brothel or some equally disreputable place.

"Working," Lynn responded, keeping her tone polite. "May I help you?"

Wilma's gaze narrowed. "This is totally inappropriate," she muttered. "How could you do something like this? Did you take this job to deliberately humiliate my son?"

Lynn stared at her incredulously, her determination to remember that she was dealing with a customer, *not* her mother-in-law, instantly out the window. "You'll need to explain that to me," she said evenly. "This is a respectable job."

Wilma waved a perfectly manicured hand dismissively. "Well, of course it is, but that's not the point. Morrow women are well-provided-for by their husbands. Any suggestion otherwise is food for gossip in this town. You ought to be home taking care of your children."

Lynn kept her gaze steady and managed to keep her voice even, though she was shaking inside with outrage. "I'm working to take care of my children, something your son wasn't doing."

Wilma looked momentarily shaken. "That can't be right. Ed would never neglect his family. That's not how he was raised."

"Perhaps not, but those are the facts."

"Explain yourself," Wilma ordered.

"Sorry, if you want to know more you'll have to speak to your son," Lynn said, deciding it would serve no purpose to reveal the truth beyond what she'd already said. Besides, it might be satisfying to know that Ed was having to explain himself to his shrew of a mother. Just thinking about it made it easier to smile as she said, "Now, if I can show you something, I'll be happy to. Otherwise, I have new stock I need to price and put on the racks."

Wilma blinked rapidly. "You're dismissing me?"

"Not at all," Lynn said sweetly. "Feel free to stay as long as you like and look around."

She was about to turn her back and return to the task she'd been doing when she heard Wilma's huff of disapproval.

"It's little wonder that Lexie behaves the way she does with you as her mother. The child has absolutely no manners, something she obviously learned from you."

Lynn drew in a deep breath in an attempt to calm herself, but the effort was wasted. By the time she faced her mother-in-law, she was fuming. "My daughter is one of the most incredibly polite teenagers I know. If she was rude to you, perhaps you should consider what you did to cause it."

"Excuse me?" Wilma said, drawing herself up indignantly for the second time.

"Not sure what I'm talking about?" Lynn queried. "Let me explain. You said something completely inappropriate to *my* daughter about *me*. She took offense. Because it was so hurtful, she's flatly refused to tell me what you said, but until you apologize, it's unlikely she'll be coming over for any visits. And, just to clarify, that's her decision, not mine. Personally, I think it's important that she have her grandparents in her life, but I won't try to influence her."

Even though Wilma looked vaguely shaken, she evidently wasn't quite ready to concede the battle. "Children should be taught to respect their elders."

"And that's exactly what I've taught mine, but Lexie is no longer a child. She's a young woman who's learned that respect should be earned. You disappointed her, Wilma. What puzzles me is whether you even understand that whatever you said was wrong."

"I only spoke the truth."

"The truth, or your view of it? You're entitled to your opinion of me. For better or worse, I'm an adult. I can take it. Lexie's my daughter. She loves me, and you clearly feel absolutely no remorse about trying to drive a wedge between us. How would you feel if I had done that with Ed, if I'd spoken so negatively of you that he'd felt compelled to take sides?"

She regarded Wilma with pity. "Do you want to know what's ironic? Despite everything that's happened recently, despite everything your son has done or everything you've said behind my back, I have yet to speak disrespectfully about you to anyone."

Wilma stared at her for what felt like an eternity, patches of bright red in her cheeks. For a moment it looked as if she were going to respond, but instead she whirled around and walked out.

"Brava!" Raylene said, applauding as she came out of the back room.

Lynn turned toward her in dismay. "You heard? I'm so sorry. I know she was a customer, but she made me so furious, I just couldn't bite my tongue a second more."

"You lasted a lot longer than I would have under the same circumstances."

"We lost a sale, though."

"Doubtful," Raylene said. "She pops in here from time to time and I believe she bought a scarf on sale once, but generally she mutters about the quality not being up to her standards. She's a vicious old woman, Lynn. I'm not sure how Jack Morrow has tolerated her all these years."

Lynn was momentarily startled by Raylene's assessment. Then she confided, "I've wondered the same thing. I always thought I had to be missing her good qualities."

"Maybe she had them once. I surely haven't seen evidence of her good nature since I moved back here. She reminds me of a lot of wealthy old biddies who are so self-important they think they can get away with saying and doing anything."

"I still feel bad about speaking that way to a customer," Lynn said. "But thanks for backing me up."

"Always," Raylene said. "By the way, I left you a note earlier. Did you see it? I meant to tell you the second you came in that Helen had called, but I was running late for my appointment."

Lynn shook her head. "Did she say what it was about?"

"Not to me. She just said you should call first chance you get. Why don't you take a break and do that now? It looks as if this is going to be a quiet day. I can manage for a while. Go have a cup of coffee at Wharton's, if you like. You can bring one back for me. The one I had earlier at Sullivan's with Karen Cruz wore off a long time ago."

"Thanks. Maybe I'll run by Helen's office, then grab that coffee and bring it back," Lynn said, eager to find out what was going on.

"Take your time."

Ten minutes later she was at Helen's office, though she winced when she saw the packed reception area.

"I'm sorry," she told Barb. "She left me a message and I thought I'd run over in case she was free for a second." She glanced around. "Obviously, she's backed up. I'll just call her later."

"Nonsense," Barb said, lowering her voice. "I'll slip you right in as soon as her current appointment is over. I know she's anxious to speak to you. Just don't take too long or I'll have a rebellion on my hands."

"Thanks, Barb," Lynn said, just as a man she didn't recognize left Helen's office.

"Now," Barb said as if she were the starter at a race.

Lynn hurried back. Helen grinned when she spotted her.

"I know you weren't on the calendar," Helen said. "You must be Barb's way of protesting the fact that I overscheduled myself this morning. I added a few clients without mentioning them to her. She prides herself on never having a waiting room full of people, because she ensures that my schedule runs like clockwork. Then I go and muck it up by adding people she doesn't know about, taking too long with some clients. You're just a reminder that two can play at that game."

"I probably should have just called you back," Lynn said regretfully.

"No, this is better. I won't get to calls until late this afternoon at this rate. I wanted you to know that my investigator found Jimmy Bob. He admitted that Ed encouraged this little extended vacation of his."

Lynn stared at her incredulously. "Why on earth would Ed do such a thing?" It also said quite a lot about his acting skills that he'd convinced her he was shocked by Jimmy Bob's absence.

Helen shook her head. "That's not clear yet. There's something definitely strange going on with Ed, though. Has he given you any indication that he's interested in a reconciliation? Sometimes that's behind a delaying tactic by one party or the other."

"Absolutely not," Lynn said. "He hasn't so much as hinted that he wants me back." She thought about his reaction to finding Mitch at the house, but discounted that as a momentary pang of possessiveness, or even spitefulness, nothing more.

"Then maybe it really is about the money," Helen speculated. "He knows that what he's paying you now is probably a pittance compared to the final judgment. Could be he's had some financial problems. That would explain those missed payments, even though he blamed them on Jimmy Bob."

"What did Jimmy Bob have to say about that?" Lynn asked.

"Not much. He claimed it was an oversight in his rush to leave town."

Lynn shook her head. "None of this makes a bit of sense. And if Ed is having financial problems, what about those trips he's been taking? And what about Jimmy Bob? He must be losing business by being away so long. Is Ed somehow compensating him for that?"

Helen gave her an approving look. "All very reasonable questions. As soon as Jimmy Bob gets back here, I intend to ask him. There's something odd going on with those two. I can't quite put my finger on it, but the thought of the two of them in cahoots makes my skin crawl."

"When is Jimmy Bob due back?"

"Tomorrow afternoon. He's flying back with my investigator. I gather he spoke to Hal Cantor to try for another postponement, but Hal strongly encouraged him to be in court on schedule. Jimmy Bob might be sleazy, but he's not dumb. He knows when a judge is out of patience."

"Then our court date on Monday should hold?"

"Looks that way to me," Helen confirmed. "I'm thinking we should ask for a financial records disclosure. It may be the only way to figure out exactly what's going on here. Those missed payments are sufficient grounds for it. You okay with that?"

Lynn hesitated. "That's only going to delay things, isn't it?"

Helen nodded. "I know you're anxious to end this, Lynn, but I think this is essential to protect your interests."

Lynn nodded her consent. "I trust your judgment."

"I'll see you in court first thing Monday morning, then. If anything else comes up, I'll let you know."

"You should probably know that I had a little set-to with Ed's mother this morning. She accused me of working at Raylene's purely to humiliate her son."

Helen looked incredulous. "What?"

"She seemed to think it might suggest he couldn't provide for me."

"Really?" Helen said, looking surprisingly pleased. "That makes me all the more certain that we're on the right track with this financial angle. Otherwise, why would she be so sensitive to what impression you might be giving people?"

"I hadn't thought of that," Lynn said. "I just thought she was being her usual overly critical self."

Helen smiled. "That could be, too. I'm just cynical. I've found there's usually a reason people overreact."

Lynn stood up. "I'd better get out of here before there's a riot in your waiting room. Thanks for seeing me."

"You can thank Barb for that," Helen said. "On your way out, tell her I've learned my lesson. She's in charge of the schedule from here on out."

Lynn regarded her with disbelief. "Really?"

"No, but it'll soothe her ruffled feathers for a day or two, till I do it again."

Flo and Liz had been at the community center for a half hour waiting for Frances to play cards.

"This isn't right," Flo said eventually. "Frances is never this late."

Liz nodded, her expression filled with worry. "Then you're thinking what I'm thinking. We need to go over there again."

Reluctantly, Flo nodded. "She's going to be furious if she just overslept or something," she said, even as she reached for her purse. "But, yes, I think we'd better go. I'd rather be safe than sorry."

As they got into Flo's car, Liz regarded her with dismay. "I hate this. Watching Frances start to slip away like this is breaking my heart. I was so sure when the doctor said it was only a mild cognitive disorder and the medications seemed to be helping that we'd have the old Frances for a good long time."

"I know. Me, too," Flo said. "I was so proud of her when she stood up and spoke at the rally against bullying. That was Frances at her finest."

Liz smiled. "I'm sure her tough words brought back a lot of memories to all those folks she once taught and lectured on good behavior."

It was only a few minutes to the small apartment complex where Frances had moved when she'd retired from teaching. Widowed and with her children living out of town, she'd wanted someplace small that she could manage on her own. Now, it seemed, even the apartment might be too much for her if she continued on this downward spiral.

"I wish we'd been able to convince her to look at those retirement communities," Liz said as they sat out front. She turned to Flo. "Do you think we should have pushed harder when she kept putting us off?"

"She wasn't ready," Flo said. "And we've been keeping a close eye on her, just the way we promised."

"But it may be time for her to tell her family what's going on," Liz said. "She seems increasingly forgetful lately. I think she's kept this from them long enough."

"And if she refuses?" Flo asked. "Are we going to tell them? We can see the decline, but it's not as if she's done anything truly dangerous."

Liz gave her a wry look. "Are we supposed to wait until she burns down the apartment or wanders off someplace? They're her children and, much as I'd hate to override her wishes and be the one to tell them, they should know."

Though it filled her with dismay, Flo reluctantly agreed. "I am not looking forward to any of this one bit."

"Neither am I," Liz said briskly. "But we're her friends and it's up to us to be candid with her."

When they got to the apartment, though, there was no response to their knocks. The neighbor across the hall stuck her head out.

"I saw Frances leave about an hour ago. I'm not sure where she was going, but she headed toward town."

"Thanks," Flo said, then turned to Liz. "Now what?"

"Now we go into town and look for her," Liz said determinedly. "If we don't find her at any of the likely places, I suppose we'll have to speak to Carter."

Flo was horrified by the idea of involving the police, but she knew Liz was right. Without being sure that Frances was safe, they couldn't take chances.

"Where to first?" she asked, anxious to find their friend before going to the police became necessary.

"Wharton's," Liz suggested at once.

When they got there, though, Grace said Frances hadn't been in.

"Is everything okay?" Grace asked worriedly. "She hasn't wandered off, has she?"

In an attempt to protect Frances from gossip, Flo shook her head. "Just a little mixup on where we're supposed to meet, that's all."

Grace didn't look as if she entirely bought the explanation, but she nodded. "If she comes in, I'll tell her you're looking for her."

"Now what?" Flo asked when she and Liz were back in the car.

"The Corner Spa?" Liz suggested. "Maybe she mixed up which day it was and thought the seniors exercise class was this morning."

When they were parked in front of the spa, Flo took a look at Liz's pale complexion and said, "Why don't I run in here and check? You wait in the car. There's no need for two of us to exhaust ourselves."

Liz nodded gratefully. "Thanks, Flo."

Flo went inside and looked around. Elliott Cruz, who

taught the seniors class, was working with one of his private clients. Flo walked over and beckoned to him.

"Has Frances been by here?"

Elliott, who knew her situation, frowned. "No, why?"

"She didn't show up at the senior center to play cards, she's not at home and Liz and I can't find her."

"You checked Wharton's?"

She nodded.

"Let me call Karen. Maybe she stopped by Sullivan's to see her." He made the call on his cell phone, then shook his head. "Karen hasn't seen her." His frown deepened. "I don't like this."

"Neither do Liz and I. She's waiting for me. I'd better get back outside. Will you call me if you see Frances or have any ideas about where else we ought to look?"

"Absolutely," he said. "I have a break in a half hour. If you need help, I can look around town, too."

"That would be great," Flo said.

She was across the gym, when she heard him calling her. She stopped until he joined her. "Try the school," he said. "She could have gotten mixed up and gone by to see the kids. She picks Daisy and Mack up for us from time to time."

Flo nodded. "That'll be my next stop then. Thanks."

When she and Liz pulled up in front of the elementary school, sure enough there was Frances sitting on a bench out front in the sunshine. She looked up in surprise when they approached.

"What are the two of you doing here?"

"You were supposed to meet us at the senior center to play cards," Liz said gently, as she sat down beside her.

Frances regarded them blankly. "I was? Why would I schedule that when I had a class to teach?"

Flo exchanged a look of alarm with Liz. "A class?" she said carefully. "You've retired, Frances."

Frances gave her an impatient look. "I know that. One of the teachers asked me to come in for career day. They like to bring in retirees to talk about teaching, rather than using the teachers who are currently in the classroom. I suppose they think we're more likely to make it sound glamorous."

Relief washed over Flo. "You're here for career day."

"Well, of course. I haven't lost all my wits just yet."

"Thank goodness," Liz said fervently. "You have no idea what we were imagining when we couldn't find you."

"I'm sorry I forgot about playing cards. When Myra Simpson called to ask me to speak to her class, I just said yes without thinking. I so rarely have anything on my calendar these days that can't be put off, it never even occurred to me to check."

"Have you already given your talk?"

Frances nodded. "I was quite a hit, if I do say so myself. There's nothing like a roomful of inquisitive youngsters to keep a person on her toes. I was just sitting out here enjoying this lovely April sunshine before walking back home."

"Well, I, for one, am completely worn-out," Liz said. "I think this calls for a special occasion lunch at Sullivan's. My treat."

Frances's eyes brightened. "Perhaps I need to scare you more often."

"Don't you dare," Liz said. "At my age, I can't afford to have that many more years scared off my life. I swear I lost at least five this morning alone."

"I'm sorry," Frances apologized again. "I'll write things on my calendar from now on."

Flo gave her a long look. "I doubt writing them down

is the real issue. You need to look at the stupid thing once in a while."

Frances chuckled. "Okay, that, too."

As they all climbed into Flo's car, Liz declared, "I'm ordering a glass of wine. I don't care what anybody says."

"Why would anybody say anything?" Flo asked. "I intend to join you."

"Don't even think about leaving me out," Frances chimed in from the backseat. "Or perhaps I'll have a margarita."

"No!" Flo and Liz said practically in unison.

"The last time we had margaritas without supervision, we nearly ended up in the pokey," Liz reminded her, laughing. "I vowed never to have another one except at those Sweet Magnolias gatherings."

"Ditto," Flo said. "I heard enough about my behavior that night from Helen to last a lifetime. I need to stay on her good side till she's reconciled to me and Donnie being a couple."

"So you're done with margaritas from now till eternity?" Liz teased.

"No," Flo protested. "She's coming around."

"Seriously?" Frances asked doubtfully.

"I swear it," Flo said. "Of course, the worrisome thing now is that she and Donnie seem to be in cahoots pushing for a wedding."

"Whoo-ee!" Frances said. "I sure wish I'd been a fly on the wall when that conversation took place."

Flo gave her a warning look. "You're supposed to be on my side."

"I am," Frances assured her. "Which is what makes this such fun. It's been a long time since I've seen you so flustered. Makes me wonder why that is. I'm thinking it's because you're running out of arguments against marriage."

"Not a chance," Flo insisted. "I still have the best one of all."

"What's that?" Frances asked.

"I don't want to," Flo said emphatically. "Try arguing with that."

"You know who you sound like," Frances teased. "That sweet little granddaughter of yours when she's throwing a tantrum."

Flo stared at her. "Because I have a firm conviction?"

"Because you're being stubborn," Frances countered.

Flo looked to Liz. "Do you agree?"

Liz hesitated for barely a second, then grinned. "Sounds that way to me," she said. "Reminds me of the expression that you're cutting off your nose to spite your face. You're crazy about Donnie. He's obviously nuts about you. Seems to me you're saying no just because Helen's in favor of the idea."

"I was against it before she ever got involved," Flo insisted. "You can ask Donnie, if you don't believe me."

"If you say so," Liz said.

"I do," Flo said irritably, suddenly wondering if maybe she wouldn't have that margarita, after all.

Fourteen

"You working at Raylene's tomorrow?" Mitch asked Lynn after dinner. He'd come to look forward to these evenings on her deck with a glass of lemonade or sweet tea and pleasant conversation. Tonight the lemonade was just a little tart and ice-cold.

She grinned at him. "Do you really need to ask? I thought you'd memorized my schedule by now."

He winced. "I pay attention, that's all," he said guiltily, then tried to regroup by adding, "Which means I know that sometimes the schedule changes if Raylene or Adelia need to be somewhere."

Though she was still smiling, she asked, "Is there some particular reason you wanted to know about tomorrow?"

"Just making conversation," he fibbed. "I had no idea it would turn into such a big deal."

Now she looked guilty. "Sorry. I'm just teasing you. It's been a while since anyone really cared about my plans for the day. Ed was always oblivious unless I forgot to pick up his dry cleaning. Yes, I'm working in the morning. I should be home around two-thirty."

Satisfied, he nodded. "Good to know."

Lynn studied him. "Look, I know it's not my imagination that you're acting kinda funny. If something's going on, you need to tell me what it is," she commanded in a tone that probably terrified the truth out of her kids.

Mitch gave her the most innocent look he could muster. "I swear I was just making conversation."

Her expression remained skeptical. "So that's your story and you're sticking to it?"

"Yes, ma'am," he said, hoping there wasn't a telltale twinkle in his eye.

She shook her head. "You're no better at fibbing than my children."

Actually, Mitch considered that a compliment since he was a big proponent of telling the truth, but under the circumstances it wasn't a line of conversation he wanted to pursue. Instead, he said casually, "Nice night, isn't it? You can feel summer in the air."

"You mean the heat and humidity?" Lynn said wryly. "They're right on schedule."

She took a long, slow drink of her lemonade, sighing with such pleasure that Mitch regretted he couldn't haul her off to bed and coax that same sound from deep in her throat.

"I wish it were possible to air-condition a deck," she said.

Mitch seized on the comment like a lifeline, anxious to get his mind out of dangerous territory. If there was one thing he knew and could discuss endlessly, it was construction possibilities. "You can, but you'd have to enclose it," he told her.

"And that would pretty much defeat the purpose of having an outdoor space, wouldn't it?" Lynn said, clearly unconvinced.

"Pretty much," he agreed, glancing around. "Of course, you could add a roof, turn this into a screened-in porch, then make glass panels to insert during the really hot months and put in one of those portable air-conditioning units." He grinned at her. "Ask any contractor. There's a solution to just about everything for the right price."

Lynn gave him an amused look. "I think maybe it would be simpler and certainly less expensive to adapt to the heat."

He laughed. "That's another alternative," he agreed. "Or I could get a big palm frond and fan you like some Roman slave."

To his surprise, she looked instantly intrigued by that notion.

"You'd do that?"

"If it would make you happy," he said solemnly. "I've told you before, I like seeing you smile." In fact, lately that had become his mission in life. He wondered if he wasn't becoming a little obsessive about it.

She smiled at him, "You keep talking like that, Mitch Franklin, you'll turn my head."

"I'm hoping," he responded.

She looked away nervously, a sure sign that she wasn't yet where he was with this relationship of theirs. Increasingly, though, he felt confident that she was at least heading in the same direction.

"When are the boys due home from college?" she asked, determinedly changing the subject to a more neutral one.

"A couple of weeks," he said, letting her get away with it. "They have finals the first couple of weeks in May, I think, and that's it."

"Do they have plans for the summer?"

"Luke's going to work for me. He's not crazy about the

work, but he likes the paycheck and he tolerates my bossing him around. Nate hasn't said yet, but I think he may stay near school after graduation to be close to his fiancée. He mentioned that Jo's taking one more class over the summer to wrap up her master's. He has a part-time job in a restaurant and they'll put him on full-time, if he wants it."

"But you'd rather have him home," she guessed.

"Can't deny it," Mitch admitted. "If his fiancée does go out West and he goes with her, this could be the last summer he'd be around. Maybe the last time ever."

He shrugged, feigning an indifference he was far from feeling. He knew it was time for his sons to grow up and leave the nest for their own lives, but he didn't have to like it. "But it's not about what I want," he added, a realization that grated on him just the same.

She gave him a sympathetic look. "Letting go must be incredibly hard."

"It's a killer," he agreed. "Just sending him off to college tore Amy up. I was so busy consoling her, I didn't notice how empty the house felt, even with Luke still at home then. Now, with all of them gone, I rattle around at loose ends. I'm always glad for a little company and commotion."

"Can I ask you something?" she said, regarding him intently. "Are you hanging out here just because you're lonely?"

Mitch nearly choked on his sip of lemonade. "Why on earth would you ask a thing like that? Haven't I made it plain enough how I feel about you?"

"Sure. I mean I know we're friends. And I know you thought you were imposing on Raylene and Carter by hanging out there for dinner. I thought maybe this turned into a comfortable alternative. There's nothing wrong with it, if that's what's going on," she said hurriedly. "I'm glad for the company, too. Even though I have Jeremy and Lexie at home, it's nice to have an adult to talk to at the end of the day like this."

Mitch didn't know whether to laugh or cry at her interpretation of what was happening. He could think of only one way to set her straight. After a moment's hesitation, he stood up and moved in front of her.

"Come here," he said quietly, leaning against the railing to give her space so she could make up her mind about whether to comply with his request.

She blinked at the intensity in his voice. "Why?"

He smiled at her sudden nervousness. "Just do it, Lynnie. Stand up."

Slowly, she got to her feet, her eyes locked with his.

"A little closer," he said, wanting her to take this next step fully conscious of what was about to happen.

"Another step," he coaxed.

When she was within an arm's reach, he touched her cheek, felt her tremble. He rubbed the pad of his thumb over her bottom lip, never once looking away. She swallowed hard, but she didn't move. In fact, she swayed toward him ever so slightly.

It had been a long time since Mitch had kissed any woman other than his wife, longer still since he'd wanted to. Now he thought maybe he might die if he didn't get to taste Lynnie's lips.

"I've wanted to do this since we were thirteen years old," he said, his voice ragged as he took the next step, then bent to place his mouth over hers.

Her lips were soft as silk and bore the faintest hint of tart citrus and sweet sugar from the lemonade. All his senses, denied this sort of closeness for way too long, sparked to life as he kissed her, first gently, then more hungrily.

Her hands fluttered briefly at her sides, then came to rest on his shoulders, then slid behind his neck, holding him close. Her response encouraged him to deepen the kiss until they were both breathing hard and he, at least, was feeling a little reckless. That white-hot flash of desire told him it was time to back off. A kiss, he'd promised himself more than once, was the most he could allow himself until the divorce was final, until she was emotionally steady and knew without a doubt what she wanted. *Who* she wanted. He prayed she'd choose him.

In the meantime, though, what a kiss it had been, he thought, smiling as he released her. "Are my intentions any clearer now?" he asked.

She sighed, slowly opening her eyes, her expression vaguely dazed. "Crystal clear," she whispered a little breathlessly.

"And that's okay with you?"

"Uh-huh," she murmured, still looking shaken.

Mitch smiled. "Good to know."

A slow smile broke across her face. "Definitely good to know."

"I think maybe I should go now," he said, since his blood was still thrumming through his veins with a little too much anticipation for things that weren't in the cards just yet.

"Already?" she asked, her disappointment plain.

"Wouldn't want to wear out my welcome," he told her.

"Not a chance of that," she murmured, her fingers touching her lips as he turned and walked away.

Mitch couldn't help the satisfaction that stole through him or the tune he whistled as he headed back over to Raylene's to get his truck.

Unfortunately, he found Raylene standing right beside his four-by-four, hands on hips, a worried frown on her face.

"Are you playing games with her, Mitch Franklin?" she inquired, sounding as indignant as any mother hen.

"No idea what you're talking about," he said, hoping he was doing a better job fibbing now than he had been earlier with Lynn.

"The kissing right out there for anyone to see," she explained.

"We weren't in the middle of the town green," he replied irritably, since there was no point in denying it had happened.

"But I saw," Raylene explained patiently. "And anyone else in the neighborhood who happened to be out on their decks tonight probably saw. You don't think word of a thing like that will spread by morning? How do you suppose Ed's going to react?"

"Blast it all!" Mitch muttered under his breath. For a few brief, amazing moments he'd mostly forgotten about Ed and why it was important for him to keep his feelings for Lynn under wraps a while longer. Lynn had just made that remark about him coming around to spend time with her because it was comfortable, and the next thing he knew, he'd been determined to prove there was a lot more than comfortable on his mind.

"Exactly," Raylene said, looking pleased that he'd caught on so quickly to her concern. "You know I'm not criticizing you for getting involved with her, right? I'm all for it. I'm just worried that Ed will find some way to use this in court."

"You're not the first to warn me about that," Mitch said, thinking of Terry. "And most of the time I've been real careful, but something happened tonight. I guess I lost my head."

"You sure it wasn't your heart?" Raylene inquired.

"Nah," he said. "I lost that to her a long time ago. But, trust me, I hear what you're saying. I'll be more discreet from here on out."

She nodded. "All I'm suggesting," she said, then winked. "Looked pretty hot from over here, by the way."

Mitch frowned at her, trying to hide his amusement. "You are not getting details from me, Raylene. Go back inside. Call your husband. Let him whisper a few sweet nothings in your ear. You'll forget all about me and Lynn."

He could only hope that all the other nearby neighbors who'd witnessed the kiss would forget as readily.

Lynn suspected she probably still had a glow in her cheeks when she arrived at work in the morning. She knew she couldn't seem to stop smiling. Raylene gave her a knowing look.

"Interesting night?" Raylene inquired.

Lynn regarded her suspiciously. "What do you know?"

"I saw the kiss," her friend admitted. "Looked like a doozy. Was it?"

"I'm not talking about this," Lynn said emphatically, even though she was still a little stunned by the wonder of it. She'd had no idea a kiss could generate that much heat, which said a lot about her marriage, if she stopped to think about it.

"Darn," Raylene grumbled. "Mitch wouldn't say a word, either."

Now Lynn knew she was blushing. "You actually asked Mitch about the kiss?"

"Well, sure," Raylene said unrepentantly. "Right after I

warned him that maybe he should be more discreet before Ed gets wind that things between you two are heating up."

"This is none of Ed's business," she said defensively.

"Well, of course it's not," Raylene agreed. "That doesn't mean Jimmy Bob wouldn't love to have some ammunition to use against you in court. Character assassination is one of his favorite weapons. That's all I'm saying."

Lynn winced. She knew Raylene was right. In fact, she spent the rest of the morning worrying about the kiss, concluding that there could be no more of it, maybe even no more contact with Mitch at all until after these drawn-out divorce proceedings eventually ended. She should probably tell him that when she saw him this afternoon.

But when she arrived at home, there was a local landscaper's truck in her driveway and a flurry of activity in her backyard. She walked around the side of the house, then stood there, her mouth agape.

Azaleas, still in full bloom, had turned what had been a drab, neglected yard into exactly the sort of garden she'd imagined. As she walked along a newly placed flagstone path, set amid freshly laid sod, she heard water gurgling and spotted a fountain flowing into a small pond.

Tears came to her eyes as she turned in circles, drinking in the amazing transformation. It was the little slice of paradise she'd dreamed of.

Only one person knew what she'd envisioned, only one man was sweet enough to create it for her. She'd turned to race next door, when Mitch slipped up behind her.

"What do you think?" he asked, sounding more nervous than she'd ever heard him.

She turned to face him and, despite all her best intentions, kissed him hard on the mouth in full view of the workmen who were putting the finishing touches on the landscaping.

Mitch chuckled. "I gather you like it."

"It's the most amazing thing anyone has ever done for me," she told him, her heart full of joy. "Why, Mitch?"

He touched a finger to the upturned corner of her mouth. "To see this," he said. "This smile of yours makes me want to slay all those dragons you once talked about."

"This is why you were so concerned with my schedule for today," she realized.

"I wanted to be sure they'd have time to finish it before you got home," he said. "I wanted you to see the full effect. If there's anything you want changed, just say the word."

"Nothing," she assured him. "It's perfect." She looked into his eyes. "You're perfect."

"Hardly," he said, clearly embarrassed. "I thought maybe you'd want to put a few benches along the path or maybe one of those freestanding swings, so two people could sit out here in the evening. I couldn't decide what you might like. We can go looking one of these days."

Lynn shook her head. "Mitch, this is enough, just the way it is. Too much, in fact. I know what this kind of landscaping must cost."

"Not when you're such good friends with a contractor who has a relationship with this particular nursery. They owed me a few favors for the big jobs I've brought them over the years. Don't start fretting over the cost, you hear me?"

"Thank you," she said softly, accepting the sweet gesture gracefully. "I can't tell you how beautiful it is and how thoughtful you are for doing it. I remember when Carter put in a garden for Raylene because she couldn't go outside. I was so envious, and not just of the beautiful garden, either. I thought it was the sweetest gesture a man had ever made. Now you've gone and done the same thing for me."

Mitch frowned. "I didn't realize Carter had done something similar."

Lynn detected a hint of disappointment in his eyes. "Don't you dare think that makes this less incredible. I am going to cook such a meal for you tonight! What's your favorite pie? I'll even bake a pie. Or a cake. You tell me."

"I wouldn't say no to a cherry pie," he told her, smiling once more. "But all I really need is this…" He touched her cheek again. "The look on your face and the sparkle in your eyes, those are thanks enough."

To her astonishment, after living with a man who paid little heed to her needs or desires, Mitch honestly seemed to mean it. What an amazing revelation! And, in that moment, she fell just a little bit in love.

After basking in the sensation of being cherished that Mitch's gesture had stirred, Lynn wasn't prepared for the animosity and tension she sensed when she walked into the courtroom on Monday.

She was about to join Helen when Ed latched onto her arm and pulled her aside, his expression angry.

"My mother!" he said. "You had to have a confrontation with my mother in the middle of a public place. What were you thinking?"

"I was thinking she was being rude and impossible," Lynn told him, refusing to feel guilty about the scene. "And there was no one else in the store at the time." At least not until Raylene had made her presence known at the end.

"Well, believe me, she was not one bit happy about your attitude."

Lynn smiled at that. "Ditto. Hers wasn't a barrel of laughs, either."

Ed sighed. "No, I'm sure it wasn't. What did you tell her? She was all over me about missing those support payments. Why would you say anything about that to her of all people?"

"Because she thought I was only working to humiliate you. I explained that it was a necessity, but left it to you to fill in the blanks. I didn't want to be the one to completely disillusion her."

Ed swiped a hand though his thick hair. It looked as if he'd been doing that a lot this morning since not a single strand was in place the way it usually was.

"This is turning into such a mess," he said, sounding genuinely miserable. "I know I'm the one who wanted to end our marriage, but I thought we could do it with some dignity."

"So did I," Lynn said. "It's obviously too late for that now."

"Helen's gonna make a big deal about those missed payments, isn't she?"

"Of course," Lynn said. "Did you think it wouldn't come up?"

"I was hoping, especially since I fixed everything."

"Not quite everything," Lynn said. "It's still not clear why you encouraged Jimmy Bob to postpone all these court dates. I know you, Ed. You're up to something. Was he down in the Cayman Islands hiding your assets?"

He looked stunned by her stab-in-the-dark question, but he also looked nervous, which made her wonder if she hadn't inadvertently hit the nail on the head. Maybe his acting skills weren't up to one more lie.

"You might want to work on your answer to that one,"

she warned him. "I think it's going to come up, and just now your expression was a dead giveaway."

She brushed past him, took the seat next to Helen, then filled her in on the conversation. Helen's eyes widened. "Seriously? You think that's what he was up to?"

"I can't swear it, of course, since he didn't open up and confess, but he sure looked guilty as sin to me."

"Well, isn't that interesting," Helen murmured, jotting down a few notes.

To Lynn's astonishment, it took less than a half hour for Helen to get the judge's approval for the full financial disclosure she'd requested. He faced Jimmy Bob with a scowl.

"And I want her to have every single thing," he warned. "I don't want so much as a piggy bank to go unaccounted for, understood?"

"Yes, sir," Jimmy Bob said, looking a little queasy.

Not wanting to be around for Ed's reaction, Lynn bolted from the courtroom while Ed was still giving Jimmy Bob a blistering earful. Helen caught up with her outside.

"I don't know what's in the cookie jar," Helen said, looking pleased by the morning's events. "But we definitely caught the two of them with their hands in it. As soon as the records turn up, I'll want to sit down with you and see what you think might be missing. I have a hunch that, despite Hal's warning, we won't be seeing everything, especially whatever Ed might have socked away in the Cayman Islands. All we'll really be able to go on is whether things locally look incomplete. Will you be able to spot any gaps?"

"Maybe," Lynn said. "I have some idea of what the business brings in and what our joint account and other savings accounts used to have in them, but I'm sure there was plenty that Ed kept from me, especially when it comes to the business."

Helen's expression turned thoughtful. "Might be interesting to bring Jack in and get his take on that."

"You want to call his father as our witness? Is that really necessary?"

"He'd be the expert on the company, wouldn't he? If something's off, he'll spot it right away."

"But he'll never admit it to us," Lynn predicted.

"I imagine his retirement money is coming out of that company. If there are glaring discrepancies in the bottom line, it'll be in his own best interest to speak up."

"Against Ed?" Lynn said doubtfully. "Wilma would shoot him."

"Or maybe it would strip off those rose-colored glasses she wears when it comes to her son. I guess we'll see."

Lynn felt a wave of nausea just thinking about it. "All this is making me a little queasy. I'm not used to thinking like this."

"That's why you have me," Helen told her. "I'm very good at unearthing dirty little secrets and using them to my clients' advantage."

"Couldn't we just sit down and negotiate a fair settlement?" Lynn asked plaintively.

"That's always my first choice," Helen said. "And then they got sneaky, missed those payments and that told me there was no way they were going to play fair. I know this goes against your grain, Lynn, but the only way to deal with that is to fight back just as dirty."

"If you say so," Lynn said. But she wasn't terribly happy about it.

Mitch saw Lynn come back from the courthouse, her shoulders slumped, her expression dejected. He arrived at her back door seconds later.

"You okay?" he asked when she opened the door.

"Mitch, now really isn't the time," she said wearily.

"I gather it didn't go well."

"Oh, Helen won what she wanted, but it's going to get so ugly. I can feel it. If it's this hard on me, what's it going to do to Jeremy and Lexie? Lexie's relationship with her dad is strained enough as it is. Or what if they both start hating me for backing their father into a corner?"

"That's just not going to happen," Mitch told her. "Those kids adore you. And I know you'll protect them from as much of this as you possibly can." He studied her intently. "What's really worrying you?"

"I just told you," she insisted, but Mitch was already shaking his head.

"It's about more than that," he said with conviction.

"Okay, yes," she admitted with obvious reluctance. "There's a chance that Ed has been hiding money in the Cayman Islands. Right now, we don't know if that's true or, if it is, whether it's his personal assets or company funds. If it's our assets he's trying to keep from me, that's bad enough, but company money? Can you imagine the scandal of that? I'll never be able to protect the kids if charges of some kind are filed against their dad."

Mitch was stunned. He might not like the man, but that seemed extreme, even for Ed. "Do you really think Ed's capable of stealing from the company that his father built?"

"I honestly don't know what's going on with him these days," Lynn said wearily. "I just know he's not the man I married."

"Is there another woman? One he's trying to impress?"

Lynn shook her head. "Helen asked me that a while ago. I honestly don't think so. It's not as if I ever even caught him looking a little too long at another woman. He may not have been as attentive as I might have liked, but he wasn't having an affair. I'm sure of it."

"He's been going out of town a lot lately, hasn't he? It ought to be easy enough for Helen to find out if he was alone on those trips."

Lynn shuddered, clearly uncomfortable with even the idea of such an investigation. "Does it really matter now? Whatever he's doing these days is beside the point. Why make this any uglier than it already is? And if I start slinging mud about an affair now, that's a sure-fire way to get you dragged into this."

She was probably right about that, Mitch thought. He immediately backed off, reminding himself that this wasn't his fight. Lynn needed to handle it as she saw fit. "It's entirely up to you. I'm just saying it's another angle to check out if you need one."

"I know," she said. "Let's just hope it doesn't come to that."

Fifteen

Mitch took his cue from Lynn when she said she wasn't up for dinner. She even turned down his offer to grab takeout from Sullivan's so she wouldn't have to cook.

"Another night, okay? I'm wiped out," she said.

It went against his nature to leave her alone when she was obviously so distressed, but what choice did he have? If she needed to process what had happened in court on her own, he could hardly fault her for that.

"How about this? I could take Jeremy and Lexie out for pizza, give you some time alone. Would that help?"

Lynn smiled at him. "I know they'd love it, but do you really want to let yourself in for an evening of video games and nonstop chatter about school?"

"I wouldn't mind a bit," he said. "They're next door right now. Maybe Mandy would want to go along, too."

"If they're up for it and Raylene agrees, it's fine with me." She gave him another of those weary, halfhearted smiles. "Thank you."

"Not a problem. I'll call to let you know what's decided over there. If you change your mind in the meantime, just let me know."

All three of the kids immediately seized on the offer. Raylene added her approval of Mandy going along, so they piled into Mitch's truck and headed for Rosalina's.

As soon as they'd been seated, Jeremy raced off to play the games, but Lexie and Mandy stayed put. The girls exchanged a look and then Mandy looked him in the eye.

"Are you dating Mrs. Morrow?" she inquired directly. "I mean, like, for real?"

Uh-oh, Mitch thought. He hadn't considered the possibility of having two teenage meddlers on his hands. For the first time in months, he suddenly craved a drink.

"We enjoy each other's company," he said carefully. "We've known each other a very long time." He looked at Lexie. "Does that bother you?"

"No way," she said at once. "Jeremy and I are totally okay with it. Mom's been so much happier since you've been around."

"Do you think you'll get married?" Mandy asked, clearly having been designated to drive the conversation forward into ever more sensitive territory.

"We haven't talked about that," Mitch said. "It's way too soon. And this is a totally inappropriate conversation for us to be having." At least he thought it was. In the world of teenage girls these days, maybe it wasn't.

"But you *have* thought about it, right?" Mandy pressed, ignoring his comment completely. "This isn't, like, some kinda game. I hear men like to play games. Carter's warned me and Carrie about that."

Mitch sighed. "Maybe some men. Not me," he assured both girls, though his attention was on Lexie when he said it. "It's not a game for me. That's a promise."

He deliberately glanced at the menu he'd been clutching in an increasingly white-knuckled grip. "Maybe we should talk about what kind of pizza you all want. Have you decided? Or would you rather have something else?"

Mandy looked disappointed by the change of subject, but Lexie seized on it almost as eagerly as Mitch had. "Pizza, for sure," she said at once. "Jeremy will want pepperoni. Veggie for me, though."

"Veggie's good for me, too," Mandy agreed.

Just then, Mitch heard Jeremy's voice climb to an excited squeal that could be heard over the usual background noise of the always packed family restaurant.

"Dad, what are you doing here? Can you have dinner with us?"

Mitch frowned as Ed glanced around the room. Ed spotted Lexie before he realized who she was with. His eyes immediately narrowed as he took in Mitch's presence at the table.

"Where's your mother?" he demanded loudly of Jeremy, immediately looking as if he were spoiling for a fight.

Lexie reacted to his tone at once by jumping up and crossing the room.

Mitch couldn't hear what she said, but whatever it was, it didn't soothe Ed's ruffled feathers. Though he wasn't anxious for a confrontation, Mitch joined them.

"Ed, how are you?" he asked, trying to keep things between them civil for the sake of Lexie and Jeremy. Jeremy looked perplexed by his father's anger, but Lexie was clearly upset. She looked about two seconds away from bursting into tears.

"I was fine until a few minutes ago," Ed said, oblivious to his daughter's state of mind. "Lexie, Jeremy, go on over to that table over there," he added, gesturing to the opposite side of the room.

"But, Dad," Jeremy protested. "We're eating dinner with Mitch."

"No, you're not," Ed said. "You heard me. Now, go."

Now near tears himself, Jeremy scampered off, but Lexie stood her ground. "We came to dinner with Mitch," she said staunchly. "I'm eating with him and Mandy."

Ed looked as if he wanted to escalate the scene another notch or two, so Mitch felt compelled to step in. "Lexie, it's okay. I'm sure your dad would like to spend some time with you."

"But what about Mandy?" she protested. "She has permission to be here with you, not with my dad."

Mitch looked at Ed. "Is it okay with you, if Mandy joins you?" he asked, daring the other man to deny the request.

Even though he looked momentarily flustered, Ed finally nodded. "Of course. I'll get them all home."

"Then I'll tell Mandy to give her mom a call," Mitch said. "If it's okay with Raylene, she'll be right over."

"I'm coming with you," Lexie said, giving her father a defiant look before marching off to speak to Mandy.

Thankfully, Ed let her go, apparently satisfied with his victory. Still, he turned to Mitch.

"I don't want you hanging out with my kids," he said, keeping his voice low for once.

Mitch wanted to level the guy where he stood, but there were so many things wrong with that idea he convinced himself to ignore the urge.

"I'm not going to stand here and argue with you," Mitch said, his fists clenching at his sides. "This isn't the time or the place. It'll just upset Jeremy and Lexie and you've already caused them enough distress for one night. I don't know what your problem is with me, other than the fact that I've been spending some time with Lynn, but I'm gonna try real hard to make allowances because this has been a stressful day for both of you." He looked into Ed's eyes. "Don't push me, though."

"You're threatening me?" Ed demanded with a narrowed gaze.

"Just a caution," Mitch said mildly. "I don't like the way you've treated Lynn. Push me too hard and I'll turn the tables on you."

Ed laughed, though it seemed forced. "Just how are you going to do that?" he asked derisively.

"You don't want to find out what I'm capable of," Mitch said. "You may have that big old brick building in the middle of town, but I'm the one with friends. I haven't been systematically burning bridges the way you have recently. Believe me, I'm not the only one who's been bothered by your shabby treatment of your family."

For the first time, Ed looked vaguely shaken. "Just stay away from my kids," he ordered one last time, then walked away.

Mitch went back to his table where the girls were waiting.

"I am so, so sorry," Lexie said, her expression miserable. "I don't know what got into him."

"You don't need to apologize for your father, not to me," Mitch assured her, managing a smile. He turned to Mandy. "Did your mom give the okay for you to have dinner with them?"

Mandy nodded, but said, "I'd rather stay and eat with you."

Mitch spotted the quick flash of hurt in Lexie's eyes.

"Me, too," Lexie said to both of them. "But it's not like I have any say."

Mitch could see how torn Mandy was, so he made it easy for her. "Stick with Lexie, okay? I'm just going to pay for our drinks, then grab a couple of things to go."

"Will you take them to our house?" Lexie asked hopefully. "Mom's probably starving by now."

"Not tonight," he said.

Lexie sighed. "Because of Dad. He'll be dropping us off."

"I just think it's for the best," he told her. "Now, run along and have a good time with your father." Lexie looked so unhappy that he felt compelled to add, "You know he loves you, and I know you love him. Cut him some slack, okay?"

"You're the best," she said, her eyes shining. For a minute she looked as if she was going to throw her arms around him in an impulsive hug, but then she clearly thought better of it. "See you, Mitch."

"See you, kiddo."

He waited until he was in the truck before calling Lynn. "I just thought you ought to know that Ed showed up at Rosalina's, flexed his muscles a bit and the kids are having dinner with him."

"What?" she said incredulously. "Please tell me he didn't cause a scene."

"Close enough, but it was okay. The kids aren't that happy, but they're fine. I didn't feel it would serve any purpose to put up a fight. He was clearly feeling territorial. I imagine he'll have them home in an hour or so."

"Mitch, I am so sorry about this."

"You're not responsible for his behavior, but it is yet another warning sign that he's not overjoyed about you and me seeing each other or me being involved in Lexie and Jeremy's lives."

"I don't give a rat's behind if he's overjoyed or not," she said fiercely.

Mitch smiled at her show of attitude. "Well, I don't much care, either, but let's think about this. You're in the middle of a divorce, Lynnie. Why complicate it?"

"What are you saying—that we should stop seeing each other? I thought we'd decided against that. I know we're not in some heavy relationship, but I like where we are."

"So do I, but maybe it's time to rethink our decision, or at least to be a lot more careful about what we do and where we're seen. I don't want to make trouble for you, and Ed's clearly itching for a fight."

"You're probably right," she conceded with a resigned sigh. "But I don't like it."

"Neither do I."

"Then let's talk about it some more tomorrow. I'll have the paychecks ready in the morning. I'll make sure the coffee's on, okay?"

He smiled. "And the coffee cake?"

"Already in the oven," she admitted. "Baking relaxes me."

"Maybe I should tell you all my favorites," he teased. "That would keep you relaxed for a good long while."

"Bring a list in the morning," she said.

He smiled at her eagerness. "Night, Lynnie."

"Good night, Mitch."

"Call me if you need me."

"Oh?" she said.

She laced that lone word with enough innuendo to heat his blood. "You know what I meant," he said. "If Ed starts trouble."

"Oh, that," she said, sounding disappointed. "I can handle Ed."

Mitch wished he were as sure of that as she was.

Lynn was waiting when Ed walked into the house with the expressionless and way-too-serious kids. Both of them dropped quick kisses on her cheek then all but ran upstairs.

By the time Lynn heard their respective doors slam, she

was on her feet. "You will never contradict a decision of mine that way again," she said, standing practically toe-to-toe with her soon-to-be ex in a way that would never have occurred to her when they'd been married. "When the children are with me, they'll spend time with whomever I choose. You embarrassed them and tried to pick a fight with Mitch for no good reason."

Ed smirked at that. "So he came running straight to you? I should have known that's what the little whiner would do."

She stared at him incredulously. "Ed, what on earth has happened to you? I've never known you to be this mean and narrow-minded before. What's really going on?"

He seemed to be nonplussed by her questions, or maybe it was the real concern in her voice that threw him.

He gave her a long look, then sighed and sat down heavily on the edge of the sofa. "I swear to God, Lynn, I have no idea. I walked into Rosalina's, spotted my kids with Mitch and saw red. It's bad enough that he's after you, but I don't want him taking my kids, too."

"Mitch isn't trying to take anything from you," Lynn said reasonably. "You threw me away, remember? And the kids love you. They happen to like Mitch, too, but he's not their dad and he's not pretending to be. What's with this territorial nonsense?"

She studied him intently, wondering if Helen had been right. "Ed, are you regretting walking out on me?"

He regarded her with unmistakable misery. "In a way, sure. I know what I've lost." He gave her a pleading look. "But it's not as if I had an alternative."

"I don't understand," Lynn said, completely perplexed by his claim.

"I know you don't. I wish I could explain, but I can't. I just can't."

"Well, can you at least try to keep in mind how your kids feel about you and try not to do anything more to alienate them?"

"Yeah, I can try. I'm truly sorry if I upset them tonight. Just so you know, I did apologize."

"To Mitch, too?"

His lips curved slightly. "I'm afraid I'm not that evolved yet."

Despite her tension, Lynn smiled, as well. "Keep working at it. I'm sure you'll get there eventually."

She walked him to the door. "I hope you can work through whatever's going on with you. I really do."

"The fact that you really mean that after everything I've done…" He shook his head. "It means a lot."

She believed his words, but she'd also grown cynical enough in recent months to know that all the sincerity in the world wouldn't stop him from doing whatever crazy thing he had planned to make the divorce as difficult as possible.

Flo had only been to Donnie's house a few times. For whatever reasons, they'd both felt more comfortable in her apartment. Maybe the house still held too many memories of his late wife, even after all these years. She wasn't one to question him about it.

Tonight, though, he'd insisted they have dinner at his place. When she arrived, she found flowers on the table right along with what appeared to be his best china and even real sterling silver. There were candles lit, as well.

"What on earth?" she muttered when she saw the care he'd taken to make the evening special. "Donnie, it's beautiful."

"I wanted to show you how much I appreciate you," he said. "It's hard to do that when we're always at your place."

"Breakfast in bed sends a real good message," she reminded him, then smiled. "But this does take it to a whole new level. So, who cooked?"

He chuckled. "I did," he insisted. "Mostly, anyway. I did ask Erik for one of those chocolate cakes you love so much for dessert. He sent it over with some chocolate-dipped strawberries and champagne for later."

Flo felt her heart start beating a little harder. She had a dizzy sensation in her head as it dawned on her where this was heading.

"Donnie, no," she said softly.

"It's just dinner," he insisted.

"No, it's not. I can read the handwriting on the wall as well as anybody. You have something else up your sleeve."

"So what if I do?" he asked with a touch of defiance. "It's not as if we haven't been talking about the future for a while now."

"But you know how I feel. Flowers, candlelight, even that delicious cake, they're not going to get me to change my mind," she said stubbornly.

"How about we have dinner before we get into this and ruin a perfectly good meal?" he said.

She could see how much it meant to him, how much effort he'd put into the evening. "As long as you understand that it's not going to change the way I feel," she said.

He nodded. "Fair enough."

His response surprised her. "That's it? You're giving in that easily?"

He smiled at her exasperation. "I'll never give in. I've just decided to take a step back, give you time to settle down. I learned a lot from those horses I used to ride on my daddy's farm. Persuasion—and a little sugar—usually work a whole lot better than trying to muscle things in the direction I want them to go."

"You're comparing me to a nervous horse now?" she asked indignantly.

He laughed. "Flo, sometimes you make loving you so much harder than it needs to be."

The sweet sincerity and hint of frustration behind his words touched her more than any of his other gestures. Until this instant, she wasn't sure she'd truly believed any man could love her as Donnie professed to. Yet he seemed to see her clearly and loved her anyway.

"Let's eat," she said briskly, not ready to concede just yet that he might have won the battle, if not the whole darn war. "All this discussion has given me an appetite."

Clearly amused, he said, "You do know the discussion is just getting started, right?"

"I do."

"Okay, then. Let's eat. We have the whole night to figure out the rest."

Flo imagined they'd find some way to put that time to good use, and, if she had her way, there'd be very little talking involved.

Lynn had just hung up the phone after speaking to Mitch, who'd asked to postpone their get-together until tonight, when it rang again.

"I'm in serious need of a margarita night," Helen said right off. "My place tonight, okay?"

The tension in her attorney's voice alarmed Lynn. "Has something happened? Have you found out something bad about Ed's finances?"

"Sorry," Helen said. "This isn't about the divorce. I

should have said that right off the bat. It's about my mother. She called me ten minutes ago and says she has an announcement."

"She and Donnie are getting married?" Lynn guessed, trying not to allow her own delight at the news to creep into her voice. It was obvious Helen was less than thrilled.

"That would be my guess. She's taking me to lunch at Sullivan's. Since she has never once invited me to have lunch with her, much less in a fancy restaurant, she must have something huge on her mind."

"So margarita night is being planned in anticipation of your having a really bad day, not because it's already started?" Lynn said, amused. "Are the Senior Magnolias coming tonight?"

"Not if I can help it," Helen said grimly. "But if I know my meddling friend Maddie, they'll turn up. She'll think the best way to smooth things over between me and my mother is by putting us in the same place with a pitcher of margaritas. Anyway, you can be here, right?"

"Wouldn't miss it," Lynn said. This dance between Helen and her mom promised to provide more lively entertainment than she'd had in weeks. It would mean postponing her conversation with Mitch yet again, but maybe that was for the best. He didn't seem any more eager to hash things out than she was.

Thinking about what had happened the night before between Ed and Mitch, she said, "Before you go, I should tell you about something." She described the scene at Rosalina's. "Ed clearly has a problem with Mitch for some reason. Mitch has offered to back off, and he's probably right, but it's not what I want. We were going to talk about it tonight."

"Oh, dear, I didn't mean to disrupt your plans. Would

you rather spend the evening with Mitch and settle this now?" Helen asked at once. "It's okay if you would."

Lynn considered the offer. "No. I think maybe it's good that the Sweet Magnolias are getting together. It'll give me more time to think this through. Any advice?"

"How do you feel about Mitch?"

"I like him," Lynn said, then smiled as she thought of that one blazing kiss they'd shared. It had been a revelation. It truly had. "A lot."

"Then the answer's easy. Don't let anything get between you, not even Ed or his misguided possessiveness."

"But I don't want him to drag Mitch into the divorce," Lynn said.

"Let me worry about that," Helen said. "Another week or so and I'll all but guarantee we can neutralize anything he wants to try."

Lynn was startled by the conviction she heard in Helen's voice. "Is that because you're already on the trail of something?"

"No, it's gut instinct and my track record," Helen said confidently. "I haven't let a client down yet. And that is not just my massive ego talking, by the way. I have testimonials."

Lynn chuckled. "I don't doubt it for a minute. Thanks. See you tonight."

Now she just had to call Mitch and postpone their talk, making him believe it was all about showing up for a friend and not about putting off a tricky, potentially uncomfortable conversation.

Mitch heard the nervousness in Lynn's voice when she canceled their plans for the evening. Though her excuse had seemed genuine, he couldn't help wondering if maybe

Ed had gotten to her the night before, planting either doubts or fear in her head.

He was wondering if he shouldn't go next door and find out when Carter walked into the new addition, grabbing a hard hat at the last second.

"I figure you're at loose ends tonight, same as me," Carter said. "All the women are going over to Helen's for some Sweet Magnolias thing."

Mitch held up his cell phone. "Just heard about it," he confirmed.

"How'd you like to go out with me, Travis, Tom and some of the other men for a little basketball and a few beers?"

"Seriously? I haven't been on a basketball court since high school."

"That hardly matters. Cal, Tom and Travis are pretty competitive, but the rest of us just try not to make fools of ourselves or land in the hospital."

Mitch chuckled. "How's that usually work for you?"

"Only one split lip requiring stitches, a sprained ankle and a few minor cuts and bruises so far. Luckily, J. C. Fullerton plays, so he's been patching us up like the big old babies we are. That's one good thing about having a pediatrician in the gang."

Mitch considered the offer. He'd been thinking for a while now that he needed some real friends in his life. Here was his chance. The prospect of a few beers at the end of the evening gave him pause, but, as he'd told Lynn, it wasn't as if drinking were a serious problem. He'd just been wise enough to see that it could become one.

"Sure. Count me in," he told Carter.

"Want me to stop by and pick you up on my way to the park?"

"That'd be great," he said, already thinking that there

couldn't possibly be a better designated driver than the police chief.

Carter nodded. "See you in an hour, then."

Mitch gave him a wave, then went to check on a problem that Terry had alerted him to before he'd left the site. He smiled at the way his mood had turned around. He might not be spending the evening with Lynn, as he'd hoped, but as alternatives went, this could be good. He could work off a little steam and some of that aggressiveness he'd had to rein in the night before during his confrontation with Ed. Maybe, just maybe, he'd be able to hold off on slugging the jerk for a while longer.

Sixteen

Lynn was pretty sure she'd never seen Helen look as rattled as she did when Lynn arrived at her house for the Sweet Magnolias get-together.

"You okay?" she asked.

Helen shook her head. "But I can only talk about this once, so do you mind if we wait until everyone else arrives?"

"Of course not," Lynn said, though she was dying of curiosity. She put two pies onto the kitchen counter. "I brought along some dessert. I seem to have gone into some kind of baking frenzy now that I have groceries in the house again. The kids are in heaven, but I'll be big as a blimp if I keep it up."

Helen gave her a weary smile. "You have a very long way to go before you reach blimp status." She studied Lynn. "Any more thoughts about the Mitch situation?"

Lynn sighed and shook her head. "No, and it's making me crazy. He's so blasted thoughtful and kind. Did you hear that he created an entire azalea garden in my backyard? I was telling him how I envisioned landscaping back there if I ever got the chance and the next thing I knew, he'd had it done while I was at work. How sweet is that?" she asked.

To her surprise, rather than being impressed, Helen frowned. "Has Ed seen it?"

Lynn winced. "Oh, sweet heaven," she murmured. "He's going to freak out, isn't he?"

"If past experience is anything to judge by, more than likely," Helen agreed, then squared her shoulders and said forcefully, "But let him. Lynn, don't you dare allow me to put a damper on your excitement. It was an incredibly sweet gesture. You should just enjoy it and let me worry about the rest. I didn't mean to spoil it for you." She managed a halfhearted smile. "It's just this mood I'm in. I seem to be seeing the dark side of everything today."

"Was lunch with your mom that bad?" Lynn asked worriedly.

"You have no idea."

Before Helen could explain, the others started arriving, laden with more food and excited chatter. Lynn noticed that only Flo looked subdued as she walked in and went straight to a seat between Frances and Liz in the living room. The three women immediately put their heads together, chatting animatedly.

Lynn noted the frown on Helen's face when she spotted them.

"I know they're in there conspiring to make me feel like an idiot," Helen muttered.

Maddie overheard her. "Why would they do that?"

"Because I *am* an idiot, or at least I'm behaving like one," Helen admitted, looking faintly chagrined. "I need to shape up before Erik gets wind of how I'm reacting to this latest turn of events. He has no patience with me when I get like this, carrying on about my mother as if I were the parent, with any right at all to disapprove of her choices."

Maddie grinned. "I thought Erik must have endless patience just to live with you."

Helen scowled at her. "Not even a tiny bit amusing."

"So when are we going to hear the big news?" Dana Sue inquired, joining them.

Helen nodded toward her mother. "Ask her. It's her big announcement." She picked up a margarita glass and drained it, then tapped on it with a knife. "So, Mom, why don't you tell everyone what's going on?"

Flo gave her a lingering look that spoke volumes about her own displeasure. "Sure I will, honey bun," she said.

She had an unmistakable hint of sarcasm in her voice that made Lynn grin as she heard it. Mother-daughter dynamics were always complicated, it seemed. She'd heard that exact same tone in Lexie's voice a time or two.

"Donnie and I have made an important decision," Flo began. "It's one of which Helen clearly disapproves, but we're happy about it." She gave her daughter a defiant look as she announced, "We're moving in together."

It seemed as if every head in the room swiveled to take in Helen's reaction, but she kept her face astonishingly neutral. Only a tic at the corner of her eye gave away her annoyance.

Frances broke the strained silence. "Good for you," she enthused, as Liz gave Flo a heartfelt hug.

There were a few subdued whoops of approval from the other women, then, but Lynn noticed that Dana Sue and Maddie continued watching Helen worriedly.

"I don't know why you couldn't just give in and marry the man," Helen said, obviously unable to keep her opinion to herself another second. "I know that's what he wanted. Now you're going to make a complete spectacle of yourself. The whole town will be talking. You'll be a disgrace."

"Helen Decatur, you should be ashamed of yourself," Frances said in a tone that almost every single person in the room could probably remember hearing at one time or another in her classroom. "This is your mother you're talking to. You should respect her decision. I know she's given it a lot of thought, and this is clearly what's right for her."

Helen looked only momentarily taken aback. "You really approve of this? I figured you were faking it to try to calm me down."

"It's not up to me to approve or disapprove, now is it? You, either."

"It's okay, Frances," Flo said quietly. "The battle is between Helen and me. We'll work it out."

Frances wasn't finished, though. Keeping her focus on Helen, she added, "Life's short. It's not meant to be wasted on letting resentments simmer with the people we love." She gave Flo a little nudge in Helen's direction. "Go and fix this right this minute."

Flo gave her a resigned look, but she did cross the room. After a momentary hesitance, Helen finally followed her in the direction of the kitchen.

"I predict they'll either come out smiling or one of them will wind up dead," Maddie said, only partially in jest.

Dana Sue poked her in the ribs. "Do not say things like that. Maybe we should propose a toast."

Maddie frowned. "To what exactly?"

"Flo and Donnie?" Dana Sue suggested.

"Shouldn't Flo be here when we do that?" Liz asked.

"Of course," Dana Sue said, looking chagrined. "Let's just drink." She grabbed the pitcher of margaritas off the coffee table. "Who wants more?"

As Dana Sue served the drinks, Raylene came up beside Lynn. "Feeling better now that the focus isn't on you?"

Lynn laughed. "You have no idea. I do feel a little sorry for Flo and Helen, though. I can see both sides. I know Helen is actually far more worried about her mom than she is about what people will think."

Raylene nodded. "I think so, too, but those two apparently have communication issues that go way back." She rolled her eyes. "Boy, can I relate."

"You and your mom?" Lynn asked.

"We don't speak at all these days," Raylene confirmed with a shrug. "I'm finally reconciled to that."

Lynn nodded. "Sometimes I wish my mom had lived long enough for us to work out our differences, but maybe it's just wishful thinking to imagine that we would have. She made choices I don't think I could ever understand."

Raylene put an arm around her shoulders and gave her a squeeze. "At least we don't have the same kind of problems with our girls. You and Lexie get along really well, and my relationship with Carrie and Mandy is amazingly tranquil despite all the complexities of my being married to their big brother. Since he's been their guardian since their parents died, that puts me in the position of acting like an unofficial mom. It could have been incredibly awkward, but they're such great girls, it's turned out to be one of the best parts of being married to Carter." Her grin turned wicked. "Not *the* best part, of course."

Lynn laughed. "Here's to well-adjusted teenagers," she said.

If she could get Lexie—and Jeremy, for that matter—through this divorce without them being traumatized, well, what more could she possibly want?

"Helen, what exactly upsets you about my living with Donnie?" Flo asked reasonably when she and her daughter were alone in the kitchen.

"It's just not right," Helen said tightly.

"Is this some kind of lecture on morality?" Flo asked, wondering if she should point out that Helen was pregnant with Sarah Beth before she and Erik even considered getting married. In fact, if she'd heard the story right, even their friendship had been contentious, so the baby *and* the marriage had come as a surprise to a lot of people.

"Hardly," Helen said wryly. "Believe me, I know I'm in no position to make those kind of judgments."

"Then what is it?" Flo persisted, though she thought she knew. "Is it because the thought of my having sex makes you a little crazy? I recall the look on your face when you were driving me back from Florida and I mentioned those condoms in my nightstand. I thought for a minute you were going to drive us into a ditch."

Helen winced. "Mom, really!"

Flo chuckled at the reaction. "So that's it. I thought so. Sweetheart, don't you think if Donnie and I got married, we'd be having sex?"

"I really don't want to think about it at all," Helen said, her cheeks turning bright pink.

"Then don't. Won't it be easier for you to pretend we're nothing more than casual roommates if we just move in together? Tell yourself it's all about saving money on a mortgage and other expenses. You can even imagine we're sleeping in separate rooms, if that would help."

Helen regarded Flo in silence, then chuckled, her sense of humor finally kicking in. "Not even my imagination can stretch credulity that far, though it would be nice if it could. I'd like to go back to thinking about you as my mother, not as a woman who's entitled to find a relationship of her own."

"This from a woman who's been standing up in defense of women for years?" Flo chided.

"Believe me, I get how ridiculous I'm being. If this were Frances or Liz, I'd say more power to 'em. But it's you."

"Donnie makes me happy," Flo said quietly. "Shouldn't that count more than anything?"

Helen sighed heavily, then took Flo in her arms. "It does count, which is why I will suck it up for your sake and his, wish you both well and try really, really hard to envision that platonic roommate scenario you painted."

Flo laughed. "So no more talk about my disgracing myself or you?"

"None," Helen promised. "I really do want you to be happy, and if being with Donnie is what you want, I'll get used to it. And, just so you know, none of this has a thing in the world to do with Donnie Leighton. I'd have freaked out no matter who the man in your life turned out to be. Donnie's a good guy."

"I know that. He's the best one to come along since your daddy died."

Helen gave her a startled look. "Is that why you never dated much? Because you couldn't get over Daddy?"

"I suppose, though goodness knows your daddy had more than his share of flaws. I never wore rose-colored glasses about that," Flo said thoughtfully. "But the truth is, I was so busy trying to keep a roof over our heads, food on the table and a little money put aside for your education that dating was the last thing on my mind. I think that's why I've been so concerned about Lynn. Seemed to me she might be in the same position."

"She came close," Helen admitted. "But I think things are more stable now."

"And she's seeing that wonderful Mitch Franklin,"

Flo said. "Other than Elliott Cruz at the spa, I'm not sure there's another man in Serenity who looks quite as good in a pair of jeans."

"Mom!"

"Well, I notice those things," Flo said, refusing to apologize. "I might not have had much time to date, but I wasn't dead. And those faded Levi's that Donnie wears when we go to hear a little country music and do some dancing?" She picked up a napkin and fanned herself. "He's another one who was born to wear denim."

Helen merely shook her head, but there was a twinkle in her eyes.

Flo tucked her arm through her daughter's. "Think when we go back in there you can fake being at least a little bit happy for me?"

Helen turned and caught her in yet another impulsive hug, a surprise given her caution with overt displays of affection. The gesture was all the more meaningful because of it.

"I won't have to fake it, Mom. I swear I won't," she assured Flo.

Tears stung Flo's eyes. "Okay, then. You do know that even when I'm living with Donnie, you, Erik and Sarah Beth will still be as important to me as anything on this earth, right?"

"I know," Helen said with a sniff.

Flo pulled back and saw the surprising sheen of tears in her very strong daughter's eyes. "Don't you start crying," she ordered. "I'm already blubbering enough for both of us. Now we'd best get back in there before somebody calls Carter to come see if we've managed to kill each other."

"No worries on that score," Helen said, raising her voice

just a little. "I imagine when we open the door, we'll find Maddie and Dana Sue listening on the other side of it."

Helen gave the door a quick push, and sure enough her best friends stumbled back. Helen turned to Flo. "Told you so."

"They love you," Flo said.

Helen nodded, fresh tears spilling down her cheeks. "Yeah, I suppose they do."

"You *know* we do," Maddie corrected.

Flo saw the worry in Maddie's and Dana Sue's eyes fade, quickly replaced by affection. Looking at them, she thanked God that the three of them had had each other's backs through thick and thin. She hadn't realized how valuable those friendships were until she'd formed such a tight bond with Frances and Liz.

"How about another margarita?" she inquired. "I'm suddenly feeling a little parched."

"How about a virgin margarita?" Helen countered, pouring her what amounted to a glass of frozen limeade. "I thought we'd concluded that one was your limit."

"Spoilsport," Flo grumbled, but she accepted the drink gratefully, winking at Frances and Liz. "After all, I want to be as sober as can be when my daughter toasts my new living arrangement."

Helen gave her a startled look, then laughed. "To Mom and Donnie," she said, lifting her own very strong drink. "And to the guest room in which I am absolutely certain she will be sleeping!"

Hoots of laughter greeted the toast.

"I'm serious," Helen said, turning to Flo. "Right, Mom?"

"You just keep right on thinking that, sweetheart. I'll be sure to toss a nightie on the guest room bed when you come over." She winked at Frances and Liz. "I won't be needing it anyway."

* * *

Mitch had always thought he'd kept himself in pretty good shape, but compared to baseball coach Cal Maddox and some of these other guys, he'd obviously been deluding himself. He spent most of the evening on the basketball court doubled over, sucking air.

"I thought you said these guys weren't that competitive," he complained to Carter after taking an elbow to the ribs when he'd tried to block a shot.

"Well, they don't start out the evening that way," Carter said. "But there's something about the prospect of losing that spurs their motivation as the game goes on." He studied Mitch as they drank bottled water on the sidelines during a break. "You okay?"

"If you're asking if I'm going to live, the answer's yes. Will I ever be the same? That, I'm not so sure about. I think when my son's home from college, I'm going to get out here and practice some before I tangle with you guys again."

"You've scored three times," Carter pointed out. "That's more than some of the others have done."

"Pure luck," Mitch insisted.

"Luck, my aunt Fanny," Ronnie grumbled, joining them. "You're the first guy who's played who could get around me that fast." He took a long slug of water. "I swear to God, I think I may be getting too old for this."

Ty Townsend, who'd managed a one-night trip home before the Braves opened their next home stand in Atlanta, slapped his father-in-law on the back. "You were too old for this when I was ten."

Ronnie responded to the taunt with a sour look. "Smart-mouth kid."

Ty grinned unrepentantly. "You gonna tell Annie on me?"

"Nope," Ronnie said. "I'm gonna tell my wife. Dana Sue

has knives and several cast-iron skillets in that kitchen of hers at Sullivan's. Word on the street is that she's pretty adept with both."

Ty laughed. "I know that's true. I remember when she chased you off with a skillet before you guys got divorced. That scene was the talk of the town for weeks."

"Not a happy memory," Ronnie said, sobering. "Thank goodness, she put it behind us before we remarried. Okay, who's ready to get back on that court?"

"Not me," Carter said. "I'm ready for a drink. Since I'm driving tonight and the police chief to boot, it'll have to be soda for me, but I'll buy the first round of beers for the rest of you."

"No need to buy," Ronnie said. "I stocked the fridge earlier. Let's head on over to my house."

A few minutes later, they were all gathered on Ronnie's deck, beers in hand. Mitch took a sip of his and sighed. There was nothing better on a warm night, especially after a hard workout. Much as he loved that lemonade and iced tea he'd been drinking at Lynn's, this was better.

When Ronnie offered a second round, though, he declined. "I have an early morning," he said, determined to be at Lynn's first thing for that conversation they'd postponed twice already.

To his relief, Ronnie didn't push and, better yet, Mitch felt no real temptation to have that second drink. Hopefully, that meant that whatever pattern he'd fallen into after Amy's death had been a reaction to grief and nothing more. Not that he planned to test that theory by indulging very often. A beer after a game like tonight, or maybe while watching a pro or college game on TV—what was the harm in that?

* * *

When Raylene pulled into her driveway at home, she shook her head. "Looks like we wound up our evening earlier than the guys did," she said to Lynn.

Lynn gave her a curious look. "The guys were having a night out, too?"

"They were planning to play basketball in the park then stop over at Ronnie and Dana Sue's for a few beers after. I'm surprised you didn't know. Carter was planning to invite Mitch along."

"Really?" Lynn said, her pulse picking up at the mention of those beers. "Mitch didn't mention it."

Surely he wouldn't go along with the guys and have a beer, or even more, not after the conversation they'd had about his drinking. Hadn't he learned his lesson, after all? She knew that for alcoholics temptation was always just around the corner.

"You feel like coming in for coffee?" Raylene asked.

"No, I should get home and make sure the kids have their homework done for school tomorrow. I imagine Lexie's spent most of the evening on the phone with Mandy."

"I think you can count on that," Raylene said. "Okay, then, I'll see you at work tomorrow." She hesitated, then said, "Hey, do you think you could open for me in the morning? I'd like to stop by Sullivan's and spend a little time with Karen. She wasn't at Helen's tonight. I figure she was working, but I haven't seen a lot of her recently. I want to make sure everything's going okay."

Lynn gave her a startled look. "Are you sure? I mean about having me open. I've never done it before."

"All you need to worry about is unlocking the door,"

Raylene assured her. "If you'll give me a minute, I'll run inside and get you the money for the cash register. I bring it home, rather than leaving it there. One less thing to worry about if there's ever a break-in."

"Okay, then. If you're comfortable with it, I'll be happy to open," Lynn said.

"Great. And I won't be that late. I just don't want to rush, if Karen needs to talk."

Lynn waited while Raylene ran into the house, then returned with the cash for her.

"Thanks for doing this."

"No problem. I'll get there bright and early."

"Ten on the nose will do. I don't like to be late, but the truth is we're never busy much before midmorning."

Lynn nodded. "I'll call your cell if there's anything I can't figure out."

At home she got the kids' homework checked, then sent them off to bed. She got herself ready for bed, but even after she'd crawled under the covers, she couldn't seem to turn off her mind. It kept going back to Raylene's offhand comment about the men going out for beers. And no matter how she tried to convince herself that she was making way too much out of an innocent remark, she couldn't seem to untangle the knot of dread that had formed in the pit of her stomach.

It was after nine by the time Mitch finally finished checking his various job sites around the city and reached Raylene's. He parked in her driveway, had a quick word with Terry and the rest of his crew, then went next door.

Lynn answered, looking harried.

"Everything okay?" he asked at once.

"I'm supposed to open today for Raylene, my hair

dryer broke and every pair of hose I put on had runs." She frowned. "Why are you here? After we canceled yesterday, I left those paychecks with Terry. Didn't he give them to you?"

"Of course he did. We have some unfinished business, though."

She gestured toward her damp hair. "This is the only unfinished business I have time for this morning, Mitch. Can whatever's on your mind wait?"

Something in her voice alerted him that her mood wasn't all about a broken hair dryer and some ruined hose.

"Until?" he said quietly.

She frowned. "What?"

"When is it you think you'll be ready to have that conversation?"

"Later," she said. "I have to go."

"Lynn," he protested, only to have the door closed in his face. He stared at it incredulously.

His first instinct was to knock again and keep right on knocking until she opened it and talked to him. Common sense, though, told him she was in no mood for a rational conversation right now. Maybe she was mad at him, maybe she was just having a tough morning. Whatever it was, he wouldn't get anywhere with her until she'd calmed down.

And, in the meantime, he could try to find some way to keep his own annoyance about that closed door in check.

Seventeen

Lynn knew she'd ticked Mitch off by closing the door in his face, but she'd been in no mood for the conversation that was so obviously on his mind. Nor had she had the time for it.

She finally managed to locate Lexie's hair dryer, which her daughter had a habit of using wherever she felt like it and then leaving it there. Lynn's resulting style wasn't perfect, but at least she didn't look like a drowned rat. She gave up on finding hose, slipped on a pair of sandals and was about to run out the door when the phone rang.

"Mrs. Morrow, this is Lucille at the bank," a subdued voice said when she answered.

"Hi, Lucille. How are you?"

"Fine, and you?"

"Fine," Lynn said, then waited, her heart pounding. Surely this couldn't be some kind of bad news. Last time she'd checked, her account had still been okay.

"I'm sorry to call you about this, but there's a bit of a problem with your checking account."

Lynn sat down hard. "I don't understand. What sort of problem? I went through the statement a week ago, and everything looked to be in order."

"Unfortunately, there have been several overdrafts since then," Lucille said. "I know you have protection for that, but we like to alert customers when this sort of problem arises, especially when there are so many payments involved."

"Now I really don't understand," Lynn said, her temper stirring. "I balanced my checkbook when the statement came. There was still plenty of money to cover the checks I wrote."

"Possibly so," Lucille conceded. "But Mr. Morrow wrote a check for a rather large amount. It wiped out that balance, and it cleared before these other checks started turning up."

The anger that surged through Lynn nearly took her breath away. "You have to be kidding me. Ed's not supposed to be writing checks on that account." Or had she just assumed he wouldn't? Obviously that was a mistake.

"His name is still on the account," Lucille said. "We had no choice but to honor the check he wrote."

"To whom was that check made out?" Lynn asked, her tone icy. "And for how much?"

"To cash. It was for five thousand dollars. That left only a few dollars in the account. Seventeen dollars and thirty-seven cents, to be exact."

Lynn felt sick to her stomach. Helen had probably told her to do some kind of paperwork, but she'd trusted Ed to be an honorable man. Worst of all, he'd taken not only the money he'd paid her for support, but the money she'd deposited from her own paltry paychecks.

"Thanks for letting me know, Lucille. I'll take care of this before the end of the day."

Dazed, she hung up the phone, glanced at the clock and realized she had only minutes to get to the boutique. She grabbed her purse, the money for the register and made the walk to Main Street in record time.

As soon as she'd turned on the lights and put the money into the cash register, she called Helen.

After describing the call from Lucille and listening to a few blistering words about Ed from her attorney, she asked, "Helen, what am I supposed to do? That was every bit of money I had."

"I'll deal with it," Helen promised. "Are you at the boutique?"

"Yes."

"Give me an hour. I'll either call or stop by."

"Thanks, Helen. Should I call Ed?"

"Absolutely not. Let me deal with Ed," Helen said. "I imagine this is going to be the final straw with Hal Cantor. I think I can persuade him to hold an emergency hearing by tomorrow."

"And in the meantime?"

"I'll get that money replaced one way or another, Lynn. I promise you that."

Lynn hung up, relieved to leave everything in Helen's capable hands, but shaking with fury just the same. Even though Helen had sternly advised against it, she dialed Ed's private line at work.

"How could you?" she demanded when he answered. "What kind of man virtually bankrupts his wife and children?"

"Stop exaggerating," he said, though he sounded shaken by her outrage. "You're hardly bankrupt."

"Seventeen dollars, Ed. That's what you left in that account. You not only took the support money. You stole *my* money, too."

"Stole?"

"Yes," she said flatly. "That was money I'd worked for. Every single check I wrote to pay our bills could have been returned, but thank heavens we'd put overdraft protection on the account. How I'm supposed to cover them, though, is beyond me."

"Look, it was a short-term bind. I'll put the money back into the account."

"When? By noon would be good."

"Not possible," he said. "But soon."

"Not good enough," she declared. "I doubt the judge is going to look favorably on this. And don't even think about trying this again. I'll be opening a new account at the bank, and your name will not be attached to it. In fact, since your name is still on this account, I imagine Helen could make a pretty good case that you're the one responsible for all these bad checks. We'll just add that to your list of sins when we go back to court."

He was still trying to protest that when she slammed the phone down.

What on earth was going on with him? she wondered when she'd finally calmed down enough to think rationally.

Fortunately, before she could break down and indulge in the tears that were threatening, several customers came in. She made a couple of decent sales that improved her mood by the time Raylene arrived.

"Everything okay?" Raylene asked, studying her worriedly. "You look awfully pale."

"Just a frustrating morning," Lynn said, unwilling to disclose the depths to which her husband had sunk. She knew Raylene would keep whatever Lynn said to herself, would even offer sympathy. She was afraid, though, that at the first hint of pity, she'd start crying and wouldn't be able to stop.

* * *

Mitch wasn't sure how Lynn pulled it off, but she managed to avoid being alone with him for a second. While she took his calls, she always got off the line immediately with one excuse or another. When he stopped by, she was out.

"She picked up a few extra hours at the boutique," Lexie explained, though even she seemed to think there was more to Lynn's increasingly frequent absences.

"Thanks," Mitch said. "You doing okay? I haven't seen you next door much lately."

Lexie shrugged. "I have a lot of midterms, so I'm studying."

"Jeremy, too? He hasn't been over to help out."

Lexie shrugged. "Who knows what he's doing?" she said, as if her brother were a complete mystery and one she wasn't especially interested in solving.

Mitch forced a smile. "Just tell your mom I stopped by, okay?"

"Sure. Anything else?" she asked hopefully.

Nothing he intended to relay through her daughter, he thought as he shook his head.

"See you soon," he told Lexie, intending to make sure of it. "We'll go out for pizza one night."

Lexie's expression brightened. "That would be awesome."

It was the first hint of animation he'd seen on her face since he'd arrived. "Then it's a plan," he said. "Take care, kiddo."

"You, too, Mitch."

He walked slowly back to Raylene's. The crew had gone, and there was nothing left to be done that couldn't wait until morning. Instead of going into the addition, he headed for the kitchen. As he'd expected, he found Raylene in front of the stove. She smiled at him.

"You staying for dinner tonight?" she asked at once. "Roasted chicken with mashed potatoes and gravy."

"Put some information on the menu and I might," he responded.

She gave him a curious look. "What kind of information?"

"What's going on with Lynn? She seems determined to avoid me. Lexie says she's picked up some extra hours working for you at the boutique."

Raylene's hand stilled over the gravy she'd been stirring.

"I honestly don't know what's going on," she told him. "She asked for the extra hours, and I've tried to accommodate her." She turned to him. "There was something in her eyes that really worried me, Mitch."

"What?" Mitch asked.

"Real desperation," she said. "She didn't open up about anything and I didn't want to pry. I just knew I had to do whatever I could to help. Extra hours was all she asked for, so that's what I gave her. I've been coming up with excuses to be away from the boutique to justify it."

Mitch slammed his fist onto the table, wishing he could have taken aim at Ed's face instead. "It's that jerk of a husband again," he said grimly. "I'd put money on it."

Raylene nodded. "I think so, too. I've invited her over here with the kids a couple of times, but she has so much pride. Not only has she refused, but now Lexie and Jeremy are steering clear, as well. Mandy's upset. She knows something's wrong, but Lexie won't say a word, either."

"Yeah, she pretty much stonewalled me just now, too," Mitch said. "How are we supposed to help, if we don't know what's going on?"

Raylene shrugged helplessly. "The only thing I can think of is to take our cues from Lynn. We need to let her know we're here for her, for whatever she needs." She met his gaze. "I'll be honest, though, the situation scares me a little. I have nightmares that they're over there with not enough food on the table, just like before. I can't very well go barging over there with covered dishes, though. She'd be humiliated."

Mitch muttered a heartfelt expletive in frustration. "If the situation is as bad as you're thinking, I'm surprised we haven't heard some gossip around town. Grace usually has something to say about everything, but she's been real quiet on the subject of Lynn and her divorce."

"I know. I haven't heard a peep out of anyone, either," Raylene said.

Mitch stood up. "Well, we need to get to the bottom of this," he said decisively. No woman he cared about was going to suffer on his watch, not if he could help it.

"Where are you going?" Raylene asked, looking alarmed. "You're not going to see Ed, are you?"

"No," he said. "Lexie said Lynn's working. I assume at the boutique, unless she's picked up some other part-time job."

Raylene shook her head. "The boutique closed an hour ago. If she's at work, it has to be someplace else."

"Where else would she be working at this hour?" Mitch asked. "Waiting tables someplace?"

"At some mini-mart or one of the big-box stores?" Raylene suggested.

Mitch thought of the day he'd found Lynne in the parking lot of a mini-mart in the worst area of town. "Let's hope it's in one of the big-box stores," he said grimly.

"But her car's in the driveway," Raylene pointed out. "How would she get there?"

A temporary wave of relief washed over Mitch. If she couldn't drive to the box stores, she couldn't get to that mini-mart, either. That was the good news. The bad news was, he had no idea where else to look.

Two days later, at loose ends and still thoroughly frustrated by his inability to catch up with Lynn, he found himself walking into the town's favorite watering hole, a place with decent hamburgers and a variety of beer on tap. The place had provided a little too much solace during that rough patch after Amy's death.

Tonight he settled in a booth, avoiding the temptation of sitting at the bar. He glanced at the menu, then looked up and straight into Lynn's horrified face.

"Here?" he said incredulously. "You're waiting tables in here?"

Her cheeks flushed bright pink, either with humiliation or indignation, he couldn't be quite sure.

"It's a perfectly respectable place," she told him tightly. "You should know. I gather you used to be a regular."

The low blow was a surprise, but he knew she'd delivered it to get herself off the hook.

"I was," he said mildly. "That's not the point."

"Then what is?" she asked with a touch of defiance. "It's none of your business where I work."

Mitch bit back the retort that was on the tip of his tongue. "Why, Lynnie? Why are you working a third job? What's Ed done now?"

For a minute, he thought she might actually answer the question, but then some sort of resolve seemed to settle over her. "Did you want to order?" she asked. "Or do you need a minute?"

"I need answers," he said, barely containing his exasperation.

"Not here," she replied.

He nodded. "Fair enough. What time do you get off?"

"Not tonight, Mitch. I need to get home to the kids. I don't like them to be in the house alone so late."

"What time, Lynnie?" he said, refusing to back down. "I'll drive you home. You'll get there that much quicker."

She looked everywhere except directly at him. "I need to get a check to that table over there," she said. "And my drink order's ready for the booth in the back."

She darted off before he could argue. He sighed as he watched her go.

One good thing, though: he could be patient when he needed to be. She was bound to get off sooner or later, and he would be sitting right here whenever that happened to be.

The second she'd spotted Mitch, Lynn couldn't help wishing the floor of the bar would open up and swallow her. After all his declarations about not drinking, she'd thought this was the last place he'd ever wander into again.

It wasn't that she thought there was anything at all wrong with good honest work. It was knowing he'd guess that she was desperate for money again. And he had. In less than a heartbeat, he'd jumped to the conclusion that Ed was responsible for her needing a third job.

She'd gone looking for additional work as soon as she'd spoken to Helen the same evening she'd discovered Ed's latest financial betrayal. Helen had warned her that it was going to take longer than anticipated to straighten out the mess Ed had made of things.

"It's worse than we thought," Helen had reluctantly acknowledged.

"How can it possibly be worse?"

"Did you know that Ed had taken out an equity line of credit against the house several months ago?"

"What?" Lynn had been incredulous. "Absolutely not. Wouldn't I have needed to sign off on that?"

"Theoretically, yes. But we're talking Ed and his old cronies at the local bank," Helen said with disgust. "A line of credit for a good old boy? No big deal. Of course, that was before he missed those payments. Now I doubt he'd get it. The bottom line, though, is that the bank is muttering once more about foreclosure."

Lynn had listened to the news with a sense of being caught up in an unending nightmare. She'd made up her mind by the end of the call to never allow herself to be in this position again. She'd spoken to Raylene about extra hours and gone looking for another part-time job the next day. Thankfully, the bar had an opening. It wouldn't have been her first choice, but the hours were manageable with her other work.

She picked up her order for the customers in the back booth, dropped off a check at one of her tables, took their credit card to the bar, then returned for a signature. She stopped to check on refills for another group before finally acknowledging that she couldn't put off returning to Mitch's table forever.

"Decided yet?" she inquired.

"The cheeseburger, medium, with fries," he said, snapping the menu shut and putting it back between the condiment bottles on the table.

"Anything to drink?" she inquired, a challenging note in her voice, despite her attempt to mask it.

"Large Coke," he said, looking directly into her eyes as if he'd grasped the intent behind what should have been an innocent question.

She nodded, oddly relieved by his response. "I'll be right back."

Other than delivering his meal, Lynn managed to avoid Mitch for most of the evening, though she could feel him watching her as she worked. It was evident that he had no intention of leaving until she did. He ordered repeated re-fills on his Coke, nursing the drinks as if he was ready to wait all night if need be.

"This is crazy," she muttered at one point. "You don't need to wait for me."

"Sorry. I think I do," he said, his gaze steady and un-relenting.

It was after eleven and nearly her quitting time when Ed walked in. Lynn stared at her husband in shock. He never came here. In fact, other than Sullivan's with its high-powered regional reputation, he rarely went into any of the restaurants in town. He didn't like being seen any-place he considered low-class. The country club was his hangout of choice.

To Lynn's further shock, just after he entered, Jimmy Bob joined him.

Reluctantly, Lynn walked over to their table. "What can I get you?" she asked, every polite word tasting bit-ter on her tongue.

"Why are you working here?" Ed demanded. "Is this meant to be more humiliation for me?"

Lynn stared at him, openmouthed with astonishment. "You really do not want to ask me that," she said in an undertone. "Because, believe me, once I get started, you're going to get another earful."

"Leave it be, Ed," Jimmy Bob ordered at the same time.

Just then, Mitch stood up and headed their way. Lynn gave him a warning look, but he kept right on coming.

"Problems?" Mitch asked, his tone deceptively mild. Lynn saw the coiled tension in his body.

Ed rose halfway out of his seat, but a hissed order from Jimmy Bob had him sitting right back down again.

"I'll send over another waitress," Lynn said, walking away before the scene could escalate.

Thankfully, Mitch returned to his own booth, apparently satisfied that she was going to keep her distance and that Ed wasn't going to start anything with her.

"Betty Lou, could you handle table nine for me?" Lynn asked her coworker.

Betty Lou nodded in immediate understanding. "Got it, hon. Why don't you head on out? I'll pass along your tips tomorrow."

Lynn regarded her gratefully. "Thank you. You're an angel."

The older woman chuckled. "Hardly that, but I know trouble when I see it."

Lynn spoke to their boss, who readily agreed, then grabbed her purse from the back room.

She walked outside, drew in a deep breath of fresh air and counted herself lucky that things hadn't been worse.

"You okay?" Mitch asked, pulling away from the wall where he'd been leaning.

Lynn jumped. "You just about scared me to death."

"I figured you'd be expecting me to be waiting out here."

"Well, I wasn't."

"I'll let that little white lie pass," he said. "My truck's just down the block."

"I don't want to take you out of your way. I can walk," she insisted, making one last attempt to put off this conversation.

"I don't think so," he said evenly.

She gave him an exasperated look. "Lordy, but you're stubborn."

He grinned then. "You'd be wise to remember that."

He held the door to his truck open and put a hand under her elbow to help her up. Lynn had to admit that sitting down and sinking into the comfortable leather seat felt good. She still wasn't used to being on her feet all day long, first at the boutique and then here.

"You look worn-out," Mitch said, glancing over at her.

"How flattering," she murmured.

"If you're looking for flattery, I can list all the ways I find you beautiful, but I thought maybe you'd like an honest observation."

"I didn't need one, thank you," she said wryly. "I *am* worn-out. I can hardly pretend otherwise."

"Then why are you doing this, or do I even need to ask? You need money."

"Why else does anyone work three mundane jobs?" she said angrily, then realized that one of those mundane jobs was his. "Sorry, no offense."

"None taken," he assured her.

"I just meant that if I was working purely for professional satisfaction, I'd be hunting for a different career, something interesting and challenging."

"I know." He paused before asking. "What's Ed done now?"

She looked away from the compassion she saw in his

eyes. "I can't talk about it," she told him. "I'm too exhausted to have this conversation now, Mitch. Besides, it's humiliating."

"We're friends, Lynnie. And a lot more, I thought. There's no such thing as humiliating between us."

There was so much gentle sincerity behind his words, it brought tears to her eyes. She looked away. Here was this wonderful man, willing to do anything he could to help, and she was such a mess that all she wanted was to go home and hide under the covers and nurse her wounds…alone.

"Humiliation goes hand in hand with having to admit how stupid I was to fall in love with that man or to trust him for a single second." She turned back to him and asked with genuine bewilderment, "How could my judgment possibly be that misguided?"

"Love and good judgment don't always go together," he said simply. He waited, but when she offered no details, he shrugged. "Okay, if you don't want to tell me what Ed did this time, how about this? Tell me what I can do to help."

She immediately shook her head. "You've already done more than enough."

"Obviously not, if you're working three jobs just to get by."

"This isn't to get by," she said, then added, "This is to dig myself out of a hole so deep the whole blasted town could be buried in it." She knew the bitterness in her voice would set Mitch off again, but she couldn't hide it. It came over her in waves.

As expected, Mitch regarded her with genuine shock. "It's that bad?"

She nodded, her ever-present tears welling up and spilling down her cheeks. "It's that bad."

"Then I'll ask again. What can I do to help?"

She let his offer hang in the air, absorbing the kindness behind it like a sponge in need of water. "Just your wanting to help is enough for now."

He pulled into her driveway, shut off the truck's engine, then turned to face her. There was a quick flash of anger in his eyes when he saw her tears.

"Not if you're crying, it's not," he said gently. "It's not nearly enough. Come here."

He pulled her into his arms and let her cry herself out, all the tears of anger and frustration and panic that she'd been holding back for days.

When she was finally done, she managed a wobbly laugh. "I've drenched your shirt. I'm sorry."

"Don't be," he said gruffly, rubbing the dampness from her cheeks with the pad of his thumb. "You're killing me, Lynnie. I want to help, but I have no idea what to do. I have a feeling that if I offer you money, even as a loan, you'll turn me down flat."

She smiled. "You know me too well."

"Just know the offer is there. You need cash, it's yours. You need me to pummel some sense into Ed, consider that done, too."

She smiled a little at that, then drew in a deep breath and allowed herself to sink once more into the comfort of his arms. "Just this," she told him. "For now, this is more than enough."

With his strong arms around her and the steady beating of his heart against her cheek, she felt secure for the first time in days.

As terrifying as her current financial crisis was, it was dealing with it all on her own, trying to keep her panic from the kids, that had taken the heaviest toll. Knowing that she had Mitch in her corner as backup…well, it meant the absolute world to her.

Even if she knew she'd never allow herself to take advantage of him like that.

Eighteen

Donnie worked with the volunteer rescue squad, so he kept a police scanner in the house. Ever since she'd moved in two days ago, Flo found herself listening to it whenever she was in the house alone.

While she was ironing a blouse to wear to the senior center, she was reminiscing about how many blouses she must have ironed over the years for other people. Suddenly the mention of a familiar address caught her attention. Panicked, she listened more closely. Something about a fire. Possible injuries.

"Please don't let it be Frances," she prayed as she unplugged her iron, grabbed her purse and cell phone and ran to her car. She called Liz en route and told her what she'd heard.

"Want me to pick you up?" she asked. "I'm already on my way."

"No. Travis is home," Liz said, sounding every bit as shaken as Flo. "I'll have him drive me straight over there. You'll be there quicker if you don't have to detour to get me."

"Okay, then. I'll see you there."

Five minutes later, Flo squealed to a stop a block away

from Frances's apartment building, unable to go any farther because of the fire trucks and emergency vehicles in the road. She barely remembered to cut the engine before getting out and running.

A neighbor and former colleague of Frances's at the school spotted Flo. "She's over there with the EMTs," Naomi said quietly. "She's shaken up, but basically okay, I think."

"What happened?"

"I'm not really sure. I smelled smoke, opened my door, and the smoke was pouring from her apartment into the hallway. I called the fire department, while I was pounding on her door. Thank goodness she'd given me a key. One of the volunteer firefighters arrived ahead of the trucks, and he went inside and got her out."

Flo gave the retired teacher a fierce hug. "Thank God you were home and reacted so quickly. I need to go check on her."

Naomi laid a restraining hand on Flo's arm. "Wait one sec," she said, looking Flo in the eye. "She's getting worse, hon. I know you and Liz must see that, too."

Flo drew in a deep breath and reluctantly nodded. It was time to call Frances's kids, if Frances wouldn't do it herself. Time, more than likely, for assisted living, too. Just thinking of it brought tears to Flo's eyes.

On her way to the ambulance, Flo stopped and composed herself, dabbing at her cheeks and praying that her eyes weren't red-rimmed from crying. Thankfully, she spotted Liz and Travis arriving just then.

Travis helped Liz up the street. She looked as if she'd aged just since Flo's call.

"She's okay?" Liz asked, looking around at the scene with a terrified expression.

"With the EMTs, I'm told. I haven't seen her yet."

"Was the fire in her unit?" Travis asked.

Flo nodded. "I'm not sure how it started, though."

"It hardly matters, does it?" Liz said wearily. "We have to do something."

"I know," Flo said, dabbing at her eyes again.

"You two go to her," Travis said gently. "I'm going to call Karen and Elliott Cruz. They're like family to her. Maybe she can stay with them until someone gets in touch with her kids."

Flo nodded. "Thanks, Travis."

When she took Liz's arm, Flo realized that Liz was trembling. Her complexion was ashen, too. She and Frances shared a lot of history. This had to be even harder on her than it was on Flo.

Flo studied her with concern. "Liz, are you okay? Maybe you need to sit down a minute."

"After we've seen Frances," Liz said with determination. "I'll be fine once I've seen for myself that she's all right."

"She's not, you know," Flo said with regret. "The fire may not have caused any injuries, but she's not fine."

Liz's eyes filled with sorrow. "I know. We knew this day would come."

Flo nodded. "I just hoped it wouldn't be quite so soon."

"Me, too," Liz said, then drew herself up. "Okay, I'm ready."

They found Frances sitting on a stretcher in the street behind an ambulance, holding an oxygen mask over her nose. She blinked when she saw them, then removed the mask.

"What are you doing here?" she asked as if this were some casual drop-in visit.

"I heard about the fire on the scanner at Donnie's," Flo

said. "That thing is better than going to Wharton's for finding out what's going on around town."

Frances rolled her eyes. "I think Grace concentrates on secrets, not emergencies."

Liz sat down on the stretcher beside her. "Well, you sound feisty enough," she said, her own color finally improving. "What on earth happened?"

"I put the teakettle on," Frances said with a shrug. "I decided to rest my eyes a little while the water came to a boil. I knew the whistle would alert me when it was ready. Apparently, I fell back asleep and never heard it. The whole apartment was filled with smoke before I woke up. The firemen say there was a bit of smoke damage and that the stove may have to be replaced, but otherwise I should be back in there in a couple of days."

Flo glanced at Liz, who nodded. It was Liz who took the initiative.

"Frances, I think this is it," Liz said gently.

Frances looked disconcerted. "What are you talking about? It was a foolish accident. It could have happened to either one of you, and no one would think a thing of it."

"Maybe so," Flo said. "But it happened to you. It goes along with other things that individually might not mean much. Added together, though, at the least it's time for you to call your family and tell them what's going on. Then you can decide together what you want to do next."

"What I want is to stay right here in my own apartment," Frances said firmly, though tears were gathering in her eyes as she apparently grasped the unlikelihood of that happening.

"You promised us," Liz reminded her. "It's time. You said when we told you that, you'd make the call."

Frances's glance went from Liz to Flo and back again.

"I suppose you'll make that call if I don't," she said, sounding resigned.

"We'd have no choice," Flo confirmed, hating that the time had arrived for this next step.

Just then Elliott and Karen arrived together, looking shaken. Karen sat on Frances's other side and held her in a tight embrace.

"You scared us to death," she told the woman that Flo knew Karen thought of as a mother figure. Tears were streaming down Karen's cheeks.

Elliott pulled Flo aside. "Is she really okay?"

"Physically she seems fine, but Liz and I just told her she needs to explain what's been going on to her children. Even her neighbor seems to think we can't put that off any longer."

"I was afraid of this," Elliott said. "It's going to break Karen's heart. That woman has played such a huge role in my wife's life. She was there as the only support Karen had when her life was spinning out of control after her divorce."

"Frances has always stepped in whenever she saw a need," Flo said, regarding her friend with admiration.

Elliott nodded. "I told Karen that Frances could come and live with us, but I honestly don't know if that's a good idea. It would be tricky with the kids. I wouldn't feel comfortable leaving her alone with Daisy and Mack, even though they're getting old enough to look after themselves to some degree. And with Karen pregnant…"

"You can't take the chance," Flo said for him.

Elliott nodded, his expression sad.

Flo walked back toward Frances with him and heard Karen arguing with her.

"You're going to stay with us until this is all sorted out," Karen insisted. "That's that, right, Elliott?"

He grinned at Frances. "Don't you know by now that there's no point arguing with my wife once she's made up her mind?"

Frances gave him a considering look, as if trying to gauge whether he really was in agreement with his wife or had reservations. "If you're both sure," she said at last, "then I'd love spending a day or two with you."

"We're sure," Karen confirmed. "And I'll help you make those calls to your family, so they'll know what's going on. Invite them this weekend. We'll have a big Sunday dinner for them. I'll talk to Dana Sue and make sure I'm off so I can cook."

Flo caught her eye and mouthed a silent, "Thank you."

Liz stood up then. "Why don't you two take Frances on out to your house to get settled?" she suggested. "Flo and I will pack up a few of her things if the firemen say it's safe for us to go inside. If they don't want us in there yet, we'll run to the store and pick up a few necessities until we can go in." She turned to Travis. "Could you check with the firemen and see what they think?"

"Will do," Travis said.

Elliott spoke to the EMT, who confirmed that Frances was well enough to leave the scene.

"We'll see you at Karen and Elliott's," Flo said, giving her friend a hug. "We won't be long."

"Just one thing," Frances called after her. "If you have to go shopping, Liz, I want you to promise me that you'll choose my lingerie. Flo will just bring me a bunch of that lacy stuff that's way too sexy for a woman my age."

"Just imagine what a few sexy undergarments might do for your social life," Flo taunted. "They certainly seem to be keeping Donnie's interest alive."

"Flo Decatur, you're outrageous!" Frances said, but there was a welcome twinkle in her eyes when she said it.

As terrible as the morning had been, Flo thought maybe Frances had come through it better than any of them had imagined possible, with her good spirits and spunk firmly intact. Too bad there was so little hope for her ever truly being her old self.

Mitch was going over his final punch list for Raylene's addition, making sure that every last detail had been completed. The cleaning crew he'd hired had vacuumed up all the drywall dust and debris, the floors had been polished, the windows left spotless.

He was about to go into the kitchen to get her when Raylene walked into the expansive room.

She stood on the step, looking across the room, first toward the fireplace, then to the gleaming windows that soared from the floor to the vaulted ceiling.

"Mitch, I think this may be the most beautiful room I've ever seen. We may have to have you remodel the entire house now to live up to the standards you've set in here. Everything else is suddenly looking awfully dated."

He beamed at her reaction. "You have my number. Call whenever you're ready."

She crossed the room to join him. "It really is finished, isn't it? I can't believe how perfect it is, just the way I envisioned it."

He smiled at her enthusiasm. "I'm glad you're pleased."

"Pleased doesn't even begin to describe it. I can't wait till Carter gets home tonight to see it now that it's all spiffed up and ready for furniture." She grinned, a wicked glint in her eyes. "Come to think of it, I wonder if he can take an extended lunch break."

Mitch held up his hands. "I really do not need to know about any plans you have for your husband that put such a sparkle in your eyes."

Raylene laughed. "You're actually blushing."

He winced. "It's a curse. Comes with the red hair."

Raylene linked an arm through his and held his gaze. "You are not to be a stranger around here, you understand? Just because the addition is finished doesn't mean we don't expect you here for dinner at least once a week."

"I won't say no to that," he agreed readily.

Her expression turned more serious. "Now, are you rushing off or do you have a minute? I came looking for you to talk to you about something."

"Sure, I can always spare some time for my favorite client."

In the kitchen, she automatically poured a cup of coffee for him. "I've been thinking a lot about Lynn since the last time we talked," she said. "How about you?"

"Loaded question," he responded wryly.

"Okay, you think about her all the time. I get it," she said, grinning. "I was thinking more in terms of her situation. Working three jobs isn't going to solve her problem, and it's wearing her out."

"No question about that," Mitch said at once.

"And she won't accept help," Raylene added.

"Not a chance."

"What she needs is a business of her own," Raylene said. "I know because opening the boutique was the perfect fit for me. It was exactly the fresh start I needed, something all my own that would be an exciting challenge."

Mitch stared at her incredulously. "Raylene, I know your heart's in the right place, but opening a business requires capital. Lynn can barely pay for groceries, as near as I can tell."

"True," Raylene said, then added excitedly, "but there are small-business loans to be had, especially for women. Or there can be investors. None of that would require her to come up with a lot of cash up front."

Mitch still had his doubts. "But she would need to have her personal finances in order," he said. "I don't think that's the case."

Raylene clearly wasn't daunted by the obstacles he saw. "Not if the investors were people who knew the situation and knew what an excellent risk she would be," she said.

"You're talking about people like you and me," Mitch concluded.

"And a few of the other Sweet Magnolias who are in a position to help," Raylene said. "I think I can convince her that this is what we do—help our friends when they need it, no matter what it is that they need. It's what Helen and Dana Sue did to help Maddie out by opening The Corner Spa as a joint venture. A bunch of the guys were backing Elliott as a partner in Fit for Anything, too."

"But Lynn's never expressed the slightest interest in opening any kind of business," Mitch said, even though the idea was slowly starting to grow on him. "What would she do?"

Raylene stood up, grabbed a pad of paper from the counter and sat back down. "I was hoping you'd at least be intrigued enough to ask. Sarah, Annie and I did a little brainstorming a few nights ago."

"Over margaritas?" he asked skeptically. "Can you trust anything you come up with while you're drinking those things?"

"We were perfectly sober," Raylene informed him

haughtily. "All three of us are trying to get pregnant, so we've been behaving."

He felt heat in his cheeks again. "There you go with too much information," he told her.

She merely laughed. "The point is," she said, tapping the notepad, "we came up with a list of businesses the town needs. Sarah stopped by Tom McDonald's office to discuss the suggestions with him. As town manager, it's been his biggest priority to get more businesses into downtown Serenity. He thinks we have some terrific ideas here."

"Such as?"

"An ice cream shop," she began.

Mitch frowned. "Competition for Wharton's?"

"Ice cream is the least of what Grace serves. I think she'd be fine if she didn't have to bother with it."

"Maybe so," he conceded, thinking of how packed the place was for breakfast and lunch, to say nothing of the teens who swarmed in for burgers on date nights. "What else?"

"A bookstore, a bakery, a yarn shop, a quilt shop—"

Mitch cut her off. "Hold on a minute. You mentioned a bakery. Have you eaten Lynn's pies or cakes? They're out of this world—every bit as good as Erik's over at Sullivan's, not that I'd ever say that to him."

Raylene's eyes lit up. "I thought a bakery was the real winner, too. It just felt right the minute we discussed it." She grinned. "And the space right next door to my shop is available. It's been sitting there empty for a couple of years now. I'm not sure how smart it is to have people eating all those baked goods right before they shop for clothes, but, then again, if they put on a few pounds, they'll need a whole new wardrobe. Or the reverse could be true, too. They get worn-out from shopping for clothes and stop next door to recharge their batteries. Either way, it could be a win-win."

Mitch couldn't help being impressed by the way her mind worked. "You really have put some thought into this, haven't you?"

She nodded. "We all got excited about it. I think it's the perfect solution for her. Cupcakes are really in right now. People always need special birthday cakes. And, as you said, her seasonal pies with all the local fresh fruits are amazing." She searched his face. "Agreed?"

Mitch nodded slowly. "But we're going to have to be very cautious about how we approach her about this. Lynn could well think it's charity or something and turn you down flat."

"Oh, I can be sneaky when it's called for," Raylene said proudly. "In fact, I already have one idea."

"What's that?" he asked cautiously, not sure how he felt about the twinkle in her eyes.

"I was thinking maybe I could buy that space and that maybe someone I know could do the renovations, all on our own. Kind of get the ball rolling, if you know what I mean. In the meantime, I'd start laying the groundwork with Lynn, talk about how badly the town could use a great bakery, have some of the others mention the same thing, then bingo! A lightbulb goes off and we ask her why she doesn't do it."

Mitch chuckled at her naive belief that she could pull that off without Lynn guessing what she was up to. "She's a smart woman. She'll see right through you," he warned.

Raylene shrugged. "Maybe so, but what's the worst thing that could happen? Lynn will balk, and you and I will have created a ready-to-go space on Main Street we can rent or flip."

Mitch had to admit he was intrigued by the idea. There were other empty spaces on Main Street in dire need of the same sort of renovation. He'd been so busy for the past few years with other people's jobs, it had never crossed his mind to buy a few places as investment properties for himself, then fix them up for resale or make them available as rentals for the new businesses Tom was encouraging to locate in Serenity. A lot, he imagined, were put off by the sorry state of the current properties. Turnkey spaces could be a real selling point for Tom.

With Tom aggressively going after new business, the timing for this struck Mitch as exactly right.

"There are a couple of other spaces on Main Street on the market, too," he said thoughtfully. "Maybe we're thinking too small."

Now it was Raylene's turn to look surprised. It was evident he'd managed to kick her excitement level up another notch.

"I was just thinking about pulling this off for Lynn, but you're right," she said. "We could do even more. That way it wouldn't be all about Lynn."

"Interested in a partnership?" he asked. "We pick three or four of the most attractive locations, talk to Mary Vaughn Lewis about a package deal for buying them, and go from there. I can come up with some cash."

"So can I," Raylene said. "I have some money from my ex-husband that I've never wanted to touch because it makes me sick just thinking about him. Investing in Serenity would be a fantastic way to make something good out of something horrible."

Mitch nodded. "Why don't I make an appointment for us with Mary Vaughn? After that, if we decide we want to proceed, you set something up with Helen so we can work out the legalities. And then you can speak to Lynn. Let's see where it takes us."

He'd barely stood up when, before he could guess her intentions, Raylene threw her arms around him.

"I knew this idea had potential," she said. "I am so excited, Mitch. This is going to work. It really is."

He nodded. It was easy to believe that the overall project had huge potential. It was a lot harder to envision Lynn falling for their scheme quite so readily.

Lynn had grown used to Mitch popping into the bar at the end of her shift. Conveniently, he was always there just in time to drive her home. On occasion, he even convinced her to sit down and have something to eat before they left. She'd become addicted to Monty's hamburgers and fries. It probably had something to do with the open-flame grill he had in the kitchen.

"For an itty-bitty thing, you sure do have an appetite," Mitch teased one night when she'd finished every morsel of food on her plate.

"I think it's finally come back," she responded. "For a long time, I was so worried about making sure the kids had enough to eat, I barely touched anything at home. Thank goodness for those meals at Raylene's and the leftovers she insisted on sending home. I think they saved me."

Mitch looked angered by her comment for some reason. "Ed ought to be strung up," he muttered.

"I won't argue," Lynn said. "Sooner or later things will settle down, or at least Helen promises me they will."

"Do you have a final court date?"

"A couple of weeks. Helen hasn't been pushing because she's wanted her financial investigator to have plenty of time to find out what Ed's been up to. We should know something next week. For now, thanks to you, Raylene and this job here, we're getting by."

"Then what, Lynn? You may be juggling all those balls just fine in the short-term, but you can't do it indefinitely. And you told me yourself, you're doing this for the paycheck, not because you're passionate about any of it."

"True," she said. "Passion doesn't enter into it."

He leaned back in the booth. "What are you passionate about?" he asked, a gleam in his eyes she wasn't sure how to interpret.

"I have to say you've caught my fancy," she teased, mostly because talk of the future seemed pointless when she was doing the best she could just to get through each day.

"Good to know," he said, chuckling. "But I was thinking more in terms of a job you might be passionate about. Or do you think your settlement will keep you and the kids comfortable?"

She immediately shook her head. "No, I've learned my lesson. I'll never be so reliant on a man for anything again. Not only is it foolish, but it sets a terrible example for Lexie. I want her to know how to be an independent woman. This whole situation would have been far less scary if I'd learned that lesson at her age."

Mitch nodded, looking oddly pleased by her response.

"Any dream jobs in mind?" he asked. "What are you happiest doing?"

"I'm happiest in my kitchen," she admitted. "But opening a restaurant's out of the question. There's no way I'd want to compete with what's already here, and it would be much too demanding while the kids are still at home, anyway. I know how hard Dana Sue works."

"You make a terrific pie," he commented in a casual

way that suggested he was trying to make a point. "Your cakes and cookies are real good, too."

Lynn studied him suspiciously. "You know, Raylene said something very similar to me just recently. Have you two been talking?"

"Sure we have," he said innocently. "We just went through the final punch list for the addition a week or so ago."

She frowned at him. "I meant about me."

He shrugged. "I imagine your name came up. It usually does. You know how she is. She's no better than Grace when it comes to matchmaking."

"I don't believe you," she said, and saw the immediate rise of color in his cheeks that told her she was exactly right to be skeptical.

He held up his hands. "Hey, I'm an honest guy. Have you ever known me to lie to you?"

"No, but that doesn't mean you're incapable of it."

"Let's forget about me and get back to your future," he suggested. "Have you ever thought about baking as a career?"

Lynn decided to let him get away with the evasive maneuver. Mitch wasn't a complicated man. Sooner or later whatever was really on his mind would be revealed. She shook her head. "I don't have any professional training."

"You have a few recipes, don't you?"

She laughed at that. "Mitch, I have recipes going back to my great-grandmother. Every woman in my family baked all the traditional Southern pies, cakes, cookies and even doughnuts."

"Well, then, it sounds to me as if you'd have everything you need to open a bakery, at least if it were something that held an interest for you," he said. "Ever thought about it?"

"Not really, at least not until recently."

"Well, I know I'd be a regular for a morning cup of coffee and that pecan cake thing you've made me a time or two."

Ever since Raylene had planted the seeds several days ago, Lynn had been giving the idea of a bakery more consideration. She had to admit that she liked the thought of being able to share all those old family recipes with everyone in town. Could she run a business like that, though? Where on earth would she get enough money to start it? She certainly wasn't in very good standing at the bank these days.

Wearily, she shook her head. "It's crazy," she told Mitch. "There's no way I can start any kind of business. If we had a bakery, I'd probably enjoy working there, but we don't."

"I thought you wanted to set a good example for Lexie," Mitch chided.

Lynn frowned. "Of course I do."

"Then do you want her to hear you sounding defeated before you've even tried?"

"I'm being realistic," Lynn argued.

"Without exploring a single option? Sweetheart, that's not being realistic. That's self-destructive. You'll never succeed in this world if you don't believe in yourself. Do you think people in town would buy your baked goods?"

She nodded. "I always sell out first at the school bake sales."

He smiled. "Well, there you go. You're already a success. You have a reputation to build on."

"And not one cent to my name to invest in this business," she reminded him, trying not to let herself get carried away by the excitement he'd stirred in her. She was in no position to latch onto crazy dreams at this point.

"What would you call your business?" he prodded, ignoring her doubts.

"Sweet Things," she said at once. "It's simple. It's clear. And it sounds like one of those Southern endearments— you sweet thing, you." She regarded him hesitantly. "What do you think?"

"Sign me up for coffee at eight," he said. "You'd have tables and chairs, right?"

"A few," she said, reluctantly allowing herself to dream. "And blue-checked café curtains on the windows and flowers on the tables. I think the tables and chairs should be mismatched old kitchen sets painted in pretty colors, too. I'd like pictures on the walls."

"What sort of pictures?" he asked, clearly encouraging her.

"Paula Vreeland's botanical prints if I could afford them," she said readily. "They're beautiful."

"I imagine she'd make you a deal," Mitch said.

Lynn sighed. It was such a lovely daydream, but it was time to get back to reality. "Enough of this pie-in-the-sky stuff," she said. "No pun intended. I should get home. Lexie was hanging out over at Mandy's tonight since it's not a school night. I trust her, but I don't want her to be wearing out her welcome over there."

"Where's Jeremy?"

"With his dad." She shrugged at Mitch's surprised look. "It's taking everything in me to try not to interfere in that relationship. Jeremy doesn't know about all the things Ed's done. I'd like to keep it that way."

"Does Lexie know?"

"When she's asked me directly about something, I haven't lied to her, but I try really hard not to scare her or to make her think any less of her dad than she already does. He's her father. They should have some kind of relationship, but she's not interested. I've tried to intercede on Ed's behalf, but I won't force her to spend time with him."

"That seems reasonable to me," Mitch said.

"I wish Ed thought so," she said. "He blames me for her attitude. He just can't see that she's too smart to be fooled by his pretenses of caring when his actions have clearly shown otherwise."

"I imagine that's one more regret he'll be able to add to his list if he ever starts thinking clearly again," Mitch said. "Okay, let's get you home."

A few minutes later, parked in her driveway, he turned to her, his hands gripping the steering wheel. "One of these days," he said, his eyes locked with hers, "both of your kids are going to be on sleepovers and I'm not going to be saying good-night in your driveway."

She smiled at the intensity in his voice. "Looking forward to it," she said, her heart thundering in her chest. She'd forgotten what it was like to feel this kind of anticipation.

Still gripping the steering wheel as if to prevent himself from doing anything out of line, he leaned over and touched his lips to hers. Lynn leaned into the kiss, prayed he'd deepen it, but he demonstrated remarkable restraint. Darn him!

"Good night, sweet thing," he said with an exaggerated drawl and a wink as he walked her to the door. "See you tomorrow."

Lynn watched him leave, then sighed. Once in a while old doubts surfaced. She caught herself worrying about whether he was truly over his drinking and how she'd react if she discovered he wasn't, but more and more she felt herself falling head over heels in love with the kindest, sexiest man she'd ever run across.

Nineteen

Even before Lynn walked over to Raylene's on Memorial Day, she could smell the scents of hamburgers and hot dogs on the grill and hear the laughter of the younger kids as they raced around the big backyard. The littlest ones were splashing happily in a wading pool with a couple of the teens watching them.

Music was pouring out of the windows of the new addition. Good Jimmy Buffett party music from what she could tell. This holiday was the one time they tended to veer away from country music. Buffett was the perfect complement to a summer kickoff party.

Mitch came around the fence just as she was coming out her back door with the assortment of pies she'd baked for the occasion. He saw the picnic hamper and sniffed appreciatively.

"Apple, blueberry," he said, his eyes closed as he apparently considered the aromas. "What else? Cherry, maybe?"

"And strawberry rhubarb," she told him, smiling at his reaction. "And you can stop swooning over them. I get it. You and Raylene want me to open a bakery. A couple of days ago even Helen dropped a hint. I'd have to be dumb as dirt not to get the message."

"And?" he asked. "Are you listening to us?"

"I'm considering the possibility," she said. "I might even be thinking about it seriously, but the postponement in court last week came as another shock. I certainly can't do anything until the divorce is resolved and I know where I stand financially."

"Fair enough," he said, trying to take the heavy picnic hamper from her.

She held it away from him. "I'm not sure I can trust you to get these next door without sneaking samples."

"Then I guess you'll have to stick close and guard them from me," he teased, managing to take the basket.

For once when Lynn walked into the party, she felt like less of an outsider. She'd grown closer to all these women over the winter and spring months. And, to be honest, she felt more comfortable because Mitch was by her side. Unlike Ed, who would have thought the whole backyard celebration to be too much of a cliché compared to some stiff, formal event at the club, Mitch clearly fit right in here, and happily so.

Lynn directed Mitch to take the pies into the house, then followed him inside. Not a single one of the women gathered there were even a tiny bit subtle with their speculative looks when Lynn and Mitch walked in together.

"Your duty's done," she told him, flushing under all that scrutiny. "I'm sure you don't want to hang out in here with the women."

He leaned down. "I'd like to be hanging out with one woman," he whispered in her ear, then winked. "But I can wait till later."

As soon as he'd left, Dana Sue picked up a dish towel

and fanned herself with it. "That man is so hot for you," she said. "It reminds me of the good old days when Ronnie was trying to win me back. He looked at me just like that."

"Ronnie *still* looks at you like that," Maddie reminded her. "Do you have any idea how many times I've wanted to tell the two of you to get a room?"

"And you think that's not how Cal behaves around you?" Helen teased. "Every time I see the two of you together, I have to go racing straight home to my husband. He's gotten lucky on more than one occasion, thanks to you and Cal and those vibes you send out."

"Okay, enough," Raylene declared. "We're embarrassing Lynn. Let's talk about these pies of hers, instead. Don't they smell amazing? And look at the crusts. They're a perfect golden brown. Have you ever seen anything prettier?"

Lynn shook her head. "Not even close to subtle, Raylene. I know what you're up to."

Maddie looked from Raylene to Lynn. "What's she up to?"

"I want her to open a bakery on Main Street," Raylene said at once. "In the space next to my boutique."

"What a fantastic idea!" Dana Sue said at once.

Though her surprise seemed feigned, her enthusiasm at least sounded genuine. Lynn wanted to be sure, though. If she moved forward with this business, she didn't want to tread on the toes of any of the existing business owners.

"You'd be okay with that?" she pressed Dana Sue.

"Why wouldn't I be?" Dana Sue responded readily. "Erik makes amazingly decadent desserts, but we don't usually sell them to anyone other than people dining at Sullivan's. A lot of folks want a whole pie or cake to take home or maybe just a cupcake with a cup of coffee in the afternoon after shopping." Her expression brightened.

"Which is why you want it next door to your boutique, isn't it, Raylene?"

"Precisely," Raylene said.

"Are you really considering it?" Maddie asked eagerly. "I could help you put a business plan together. I did the one for The Corner Spa and helped the guys with the one for their gym."

"She helped me out with mine, too," Raylene said. "Maddie's got this knack with numbers and knowing how to put something together that will make sense to the bank or investors."

Lynn turned to Maddie. "Seriously? You'd do that?"

"Sure. It would be fun. The spa's practically running itself these days. This would give me a new challenge."

"If you want a silent partner, I'm in," Dana Sue said.

Jeanette McDonald walked into the kitchen just in time to overhear. "Somebody's starting a new business? Count me in. Filling up all those vacant storefronts on Main Street makes my husband very happy. If I can help do that, I want to."

Lynn looked around the room. "Did you all plan this?"

"Plan what?" Maddie inquired innocently.

"All this unexpected and unsolicited support," Lynn said.

"Absolutely not," Dana Sue said. "This is the first I've heard about the possibility of your opening a bakery. It's a great idea. If I can help, I'd like to. Anything that's good for Serenity is good for my business, too."

Raylene draped an arm over Lynn's shoulders. "I told you it was an amazing idea, didn't I? Just listen to them. They're all smart businesswomen in their own right."

Though she had her suspicions about being set up by these sneaky Sweet Magnolia women, Lynn couldn't help the surge of anticipation that made her want to run home and start writing up that business plan for Maddie to peruse. Not that she had the first clue about what her starting point ought to be.

"I'll think about all this," she promised. "And, Maddie, maybe I will give you a call, if you don't mind."

"Anytime," Maddie said. "It really will be fun to help you plan this."

"And I can show you that property tomorrow," Raylene said.

Lynn's suspicions rebounded. "You can?"

Raylene shrugged. "Actually, I bought the space. There are renovations already under way. I can promise you a really good deal on rent."

Lynn shook her head incredulously. "I can't decide if you're crazy or just incredibly confident in your powers of persuasion."

"Both," Sarah chimed in as she joined them. "The men are getting restless, by the way. Erik said the burgers and hot dogs are almost ready. He's wondering what happened to the rest of the food."

"We don't want to tick off the self-appointed chef of the day," Raylene said. "Let's get all these salads on the table. If everybody grabs something, maybe we can do this in one trip. Helen, there are pitchers of tea and lemonade in the refrigerator for the kids. Soft drinks are in a cooler outside. This year I remembered to put it far, far away from the beer cooler. We had a few too many close calls with the kids grabbing the wrong drinks last year."

Outside, the heat of the day had cooled to a few degrees above simmering, but a breeze kept it from being too oppressive. The kids were served first and sent off to find places on the blankets that had been spread around the yard.

Lynn filled her plate, then headed for a lounge chair on the deck. She wasn't a bit surprised when Mitch took the chair next to her, balancing a plate in one hand and carrying two beers in the other. She stiffened at the sight of them.

"Having fun?" he asked as he settled beside her. He held out one of the beers for her. "They're ice-cold. Perfect for this weather."

When she didn't immediately reach out to take the one he was offering, he regarded her curiously. "You don't want one?"

She shook her head. "I have iced tea."

He studied her intently. "And you disapprove of me having the beer," he concluded.

"It's not up to me to approve or disapprove. I just thought you'd…" She shrugged. "Never mind."

"Say it, Lynnie. You thought I'd stopped drinking."

She nodded, her expression challenging his. "That is what you told me."

"One beer isn't going to turn me into a drunk," he said defensively. "I told you that even when things were bad and I was grieving, I recognized when it might be problematic and stopped."

"But obviously not permanently," she said, fighting tears. "Do you have a drinking problem or not, Mitch?"

He frowned at her. "Look, I get why it would matter to you if I had a problem with alcohol."

"No, you don't. You can't possibly know why," she told him.

"Then I think you'd better explain it to me," he said.

"I grew up with an alcoholic, Mitch. I lived every second with uncertainty, not knowing what sort of mood my dad would be in when he got home or even if he *would* get home." She gave him a defiant look. "I won't do that again. Not to myself, and certainly not to my kids."

Mitch looked taken aback by the vehemence in her voice, or maybe it was simply the revelation that threw him. Either way, he seemed shaken. "I had no idea."

"Of course you didn't. Nobody here knows. I never invited anyone to my house after we moved here. I can promise you, though, that I live with the scars every day of my life."

"Okay, I understand what you're saying. Does it bother you that just about everyone else here is drinking tonight?"

"Not really," she responded, aware that he was trying to make a point.

"And those Sweet Magnolias parties—people drink margaritas at those. That doesn't freak you out?"

She shook her head. "I know what they can handle. I've never seen one of them falling-down drunk. And don't think you're the only person with whom I've reacted this way. Until I know how someone handles their liquor, I always have a knot in my stomach around them when they're drinking, if that's what you're getting at."

"Have you ever seen me falling-down drunk? For that matter, until tonight had you ever even seen me with a drink?"

"No, but that's what scares me. I heard about your drinking back after Amy died. Then you even admitted you had a problem. Raylene mentioned recently that all you guys were going out for beers after playing basketball. I'll admit that set off an alarm. Just now, seeing you with that beer terrified me. Alcoholics can't have just one, no matter how hard they try to delude themselves that they can."

"I honestly don't think I'm even close to being an alcoholic," Mitch said. "I relied on drinking to dull the pain after Amy died, realized it was a bad way to handle things and stopped. I never overindulged before that and I haven't since." He looked her in the eye. "But if it scares you this much to see me with a drink in my hand, it's gone, okay? I'd choose you over a beer or a whole truckload of beers any day."

He stood up, walked to the edge of the deck and after glancing below poured both beers out. "That's it. They're gone."

He gave her a smile. "Of course, now you're going to have to share your tea with me."

Lynn laughed, breaking the tension. "I'll get you your own pitcher," she offered.

Mitch smiled. "That's better. I hate seeing you upset, and I don't ever want to be the one responsible for it."

"I'm sorry for overreacting."

"I don't think you were," he said. "I think you were bringing a very bad past experience into the middle of our relationship. Now that I know about that, I can deal with it."

"I wasn't exactly being fair to you, though. You were honest with me from the beginning, and you've never done anything to cause me not to trust you."

"I'd say right now you have plenty of trust issues on your plate. I may not be responsible for any of them, but I can take it if they spill over in my direction. You *can* trust me, Lynnie, but I'm not going anywhere while you work on accepting that."

There it was again, that steadiness she'd been craving, that unwavering commitment. She wanted to reach out and hold on to it for dear life, but even now she was still shaken by the one instant of doubt when she'd seen those beers in his hand. One instant, weighed against everything else, shouldn't matter, she knew.

But it did.

Mitch had finally convinced Lynn to join some of the other couples who were dancing on the deck after dinner, when he glanced across the yard and spotted Luke standing there, slack-jawed with shock. His heart stilled at his son's obvious dismay.

"Lynn, I need to go," he said, stepping away from her.

She regarded him with surprise, her expression vaguely dazed. As soon as she got a good look at his expression, though, she clearly understood that something was wrong.

"What is it?" she asked.

He nodded toward where he'd last seen his son. "Luke just showed up."

"And saw me in your arms," she concluded. "Oh, Mitch, go find him."

"You'll be okay?"

"Of course."

"I'll be back or I'll call you later if I can't get back," he promised.

"Whatever. Just go."

Mitch searched the yard, cursing himself as he went for being so careless. He'd left a note at the house for Luke, telling him to stop by the party, but the truth was, he hadn't really expected him to show up. He certainly hadn't envisioned the consequences of Luke's seeing another woman in his dad's arms.

"Have you seen Luke?" he asked Maddie's son, Kyle Townsend, who was about the same age and had been in school with Luke.

"He was here for a couple of minutes, but he took off," Kyle said. "Did something happen? He looked upset."

"My fault," Mitch said. "Thanks, Kyle."

He jumped in his truck and headed for home, praying that Luke had gone straight there rather than cruising around town. He had no business being behind the wheel when he was hurt and probably angry.

As he turned the corner, he spotted his son's small Mini-Cooper in the driveway and breathed a sigh of relief. After cutting the truck's engine, he drew in a deep breath and tried to figure out what on earth he was going to say to him to make this right.

He found Luke in the kitchen, an unopened beer on the counter, as he slapped some lunch meat between two slices of bread on which he'd slathered enough mayonnaise to make potato salad for twenty. He barely looked up as Mitch entered, but there was no mistaking the deepening scowl on his face.

"I'm sorry," Mitch said succinctly.

Luke did glance up at that. "For what? Cheating on Mom?"

Mitch held his gaze until his son finally blinked, then sighed.

"Okay, I know that was a low blow," Luke said, his expression miserable. "I just wasn't expecting it."

"I know," Mitch said quietly. "I should have prepared you."

"You'd only need to prepare me if this is serious," Luke said. "Is it, Dad? Are you really involved with Mrs. Morrow? That's who it was, right?"

Mitch nodded. "Lynn and I went to school together. We've known each other forever."

"I thought she was married to that hotshot insurance guy."

"She was. They're getting a divorce."

Luke frowned. "Because of you?"

"No, the divorce was already well under way before I walked into the picture. She lives next door to Raylene and Carter Rollins."

"Where you were tonight," Luke said, putting it together. "So she was handy."

Mitch didn't much like the tone in his son's voice, but he gave him a temporary pass. "It wasn't like that at all," he corrected mildly. "We reconnected, just a couple of old friends going through a tough time."

"Dad, I may not be a genius, but I'm not exactly brain-dead. What I saw tonight wasn't some platonic thing between a couple of old friends."

Mitch nodded. "Fair enough. It is more than that, but her life is still pretty complicated. We're moving slowly." He pointedly held his son's gaze. "Glacier-slow, in fact."

"Given that heat I saw, the whole glacier thing must be in danger," Luke said.

Mitch chuckled. "Every minute I spend with her."

"Then it is serious?" Luke repeated.

"Getting there, if I have my way," Mitch responded candidly.

Luke put away his unopened beer, then took his time pouring himself a glass of iced tea, his expression thoughtful as he apparently tried to absorb what he'd learned. Mitch waited him out.

"Why didn't you tell Nate and me?" Luke asked eventually.

"Because I knew it might be hard for you, and I wasn't sure there was anything to tell," Mitch said.

"Oh, there's something to tell," Luke said wryly. "And don't worry about Nate finding out. I've already called him. He'll be home in the morning."

Mitch regarded him incredulously. "To do what? Lock me in my room?"

Luke grinned. "You and Mom did that to us a time or two when you thought we were acting crazy," he reminded Mitch.

"You were kids. Last I checked, I'm still your parent."

Luke shrugged. "Maybe for a minute there tonight, I overreacted," he said sheepishly. "I thought you might be acting like an out-of-control teenager."

"Thanks for having such a high opinion of my judgment," Mitch said, but he couldn't help laughing. "You really called your brother home to lecture me?"

"Pretty much."

Mitch picked his son up in a bear hug. "Do you have even half a clue how much I love you guys?"

"Yeah, yeah, yeah," Luke said, breaking free. "Don't go getting all mushy on me."

He finished putting his thick sandwich together, eyed it longingly, then held the plate out to Mitch. "Want one?"

Mitch wasn't the least bit hungry, but he accepted the peace offering. "Thanks."

Luke made himself another sandwich, this one twice as thick, then regarded Mitch thoughtfully. "So when do Nate and I get a closer look at this woman? If this is getting serious, you need our stamp of approval."

"I don't *need* it," Mitch corrected. "But I sure am hoping you'll give it to me."

"Then tomorrow would be good," Luke said. "No point in letting Nate waste a trip home."

Mitch wanted to defer, to give Lynn time to adjust to the

idea of meeting his sons, to let them absorb the fact that he was dating, but the unyielding look in Luke's eye suggested that he'd be wasting his breath by suggesting a delay.

"I'll see what I can work out," he said eventually.

Luke grinned, apparently recognizing his discomfort. "Looking forward to it," he said, a glint of amusement in his eyes.

Mitch hesitated, then asked, "You're really okay with this?"

Luke's expression turned thoughtful. "With your dating? I guess so. Nate and I talked about it. We knew you'd eventually want someone new in your life. As for Mrs. Morrow, I guess I'll have to reserve judgment till we spend more time with her."

"You're going to like her," Mitch predicted.

For the first time, a flash of sorrow darted across his son's face. "Is she anything like Mom?" he asked.

"She's sweet and strong like your mother," Mitch said. "But she's not an exact replica, no. Nobody could replace your mom, Luke."

He spotted the faint sheen of tears in his son's eyes as Luke said, "She was one of a kind, wasn't she?"

Mitch nodded. "She was one of a kind," he confirmed.

And she'd given him two remarkable sons. It was unlikely he'd ever forget all she'd brought to his life.

But now there was Lynn, and a whole new phase of his life unfolding. He'd never been more certain that there were seasons to a person's life, each one meant to be lived to the fullest.

Twenty

It was nearly eleven when Lynn's bedside phone rang. "Mitch?" she asked anxiously. Ever since Mitch had left Raylene's, she'd been thinking about him and about his son's reaction to seeing the two of them together. Poor Luke! It must have come as such a shock to see his father with someone else for the first time since his mother's death.

"I'm sorry it's so late," he apologized. "This took a little longer than I'd planned."

"Is Luke okay?"

"He wasn't at first," Mitch told her. "But I'm telling you, Lynn, sometimes even I'm amazed by his maturity."

"Why? He is your son, after all."

"I can't take the credit for this. This was all Amy. Despite his initial shock, he was able to look at this from my perspective and keep an open mind."

He chuckled, though Lynn thought she heard a hint of nervousness beneath the humor. "What?" she asked.

"Unfortunately, it remains to be seen how Nate has taken the news that I'm moving on," he explained.

"Nate knows, too?" Lynn asked, surprised. "Did you call him?"

"No way. We can thank Luke for spreading the word. I gather he was on his cell phone to his brother before he ever left Raylene's. Nate will be home in the morning," he added, a rueful note in his voice.

"Oh, my," she said, joining in his amusement despite the seriousness of the situation. "Tell me, is Dad in trouble?"

"Hard to say just yet," he said. "A lot depends on your willingness to step up."

Lynn stilled. "Step up how?" she inquired cautiously.

"Luke thinks a family gathering is in order, an inspection, so to speak."

Lynn's stomach fell. "You're kidding! And you're going along with it?"

"I didn't feel I had much choice. I want them to be as crazy about you as I am." He hesitated. "So, will you do it? I know it's asking a lot, but will you join us for lunch or dinner tomorrow? I'd even suggest breakfast since it's a lot more casual and you could win them both over with that pecan coffee cake, but I'm not sure what time Nate's likely to roll in."

"Tomorrow's a workday, remember? I'm at the boutique all morning and early afternoon, then I have to go straight to the bar. Monty needs me early tomorrow. It's a chance to put in a full shift for a change."

"Then we'll have dinner there," Mitch decided. "You can join us whenever you get a break. That way it won't be quite so formal, anyway."

"Do you really want the first time I see your sons to be while I'm waiting tables in a bar?" She couldn't imagine it would be a terrific first impression.

"As you informed me very clearly, it's honest work,"

Mitch said. "I'll fill them in on why you're doing it, if you're worried about what they'll think. Not that I can imagine them disapproving of you for any reason. You're going to win them over, Lynn. There's not a doubt in my mind about that."

"Do they need to be won over?" she asked worriedly. "Was Luke more upset than you told me just now?"

"No, I swear, he came around as soon as we talked."

"But you're not so sure about Nate, are you?"

"I suppose that depends on how worked up Luke got him when he called Nate on his way home from Raylene's," Mitch said. "Luke wasn't thinking quite so rationally then. Both boys were close to Amy, but I think her death hit Nate even harder than it did Luke. For a long time he just couldn't accept that she wasn't going to make it after the accident. I swear to God, it was the longest week of my life sitting in that hospital room, knowing things weren't going to change but trying to let Nate adjust to the truth."

"How perfectly awful for all of you!" Lynn said, her heart aching. "I hadn't realized that she didn't die instantly in the crash."

Mitch sighed. "In some ways it might have been easier if she had. At least that's what I think now, but at the time I was grateful for that little bit of time to get used to the idea of losing her."

"Mitch, don't you think maybe it's too soon to be introducing me to your sons?" she asked, wanting to postpone an encounter that was likely to be hard for all of them.

"Sorry, sweetheart, that ship has sailed. Luke wants this to happen and, to be honest, so do I."

Lynn resigned herself to a few awkward moments, maybe more if Nate proved to be difficult. "If this is what you want, then," she said. "Mitch, I know on some level you're envisioning a big, happy family gathering, but I don't want Lexie and Jeremy involved in this. There's bound to be a lot of tension, at least at first."

"I agree," he said readily. "I think they can skip this."

Lynn still thought the whole thing was a lousy idea. "Mitch, isn't there some way we could put this off?" she asked one more time. "Shouldn't you and I know where we're headed before you introduce me to your sons?"

"I know where we're headed," he said confidently. "I think you do, too. You're just having a little more trouble accepting the idea than I am."

"You know it's not that simple," she said.

"Simple never entered into it, Lynnie. As for postponing, believe me, the thought crossed my mind, too. But with Nate already planning to come home in the morning and Luke gung-ho for getting together, I don't see how we can wait, not without making this more complicated than it should be. I don't want either one of them getting the idea that we have anything to hide."

"Okay, then, but I'm trusting you to lay the groundwork for this so I don't come off like some low-class barmaid who's out to trap their successful daddy."

Mitch had the audacity to laugh at that. "Lynnie, you couldn't come across as low-class in a million years. I think you can cross that worry right off your list. We'll see you tomorrow around seven, how's that? You usually get a break around seven-thirty, right?"

"I'll make it work," she agreed reluctantly. "If I didn't like you so much, Mitch Franklin, I think I could hate you right now for putting me in this position."

"Sweetheart, hormones put us in this position. If I hadn't been longing to be close to you and holding on so tight when we were dancing, Luke wouldn't have freaked out in the first place, and we wouldn't be having to explain ourselves like a couple of horny teenagers."

She laughed at the image, relaxing for the first time since he'd called. "Too bad you couldn't stick around long enough to make out in the shadows," she said daringly.

He sucked in a sharp breath at the taunt. "Definitely too bad," he said. "But that day will come, Lynnie. I'm counting on it."

Truthfully, most of the time, so was she.

In movie parlance, it had to be some sort of *Freaky Friday* take on *Meet the Parents,* Mitch thought as he walked into the bar with his sons in tow. Rather than either Nate or Luke bringing home a girl, he and Lynn were the ones on display, seeking approval. Judging from Nate's negative attitude all afternoon, it wasn't going to come easily.

Just inside the door, Mitch latched onto his older son's arm. "Behave," he ordered. "Do not embarrass me or yourself. Understood? Your mother raised you better than that."

His reference to Amy drew a glare.

"Don't drag Mom into this," Nate said. "This is all on you."

"Chill," Luke ordered his big brother. "If I'd known you were going to go nuts, I'd never have called you."

"*You* were nuts when you called me," Nate reminded him.

"But I actually listened to what Dad said. All you've done is overreact and keep throwing Mom in his face as if he's betraying her."

"Well, he is," Nate insisted.

"Okay, that's it," Mitch declared, ready to drag the two of them right back out the door. "Let's go."

Nate's scowl deepened. "We're already here. We might as well eat."

"And you'll keep a civil tongue in your head?" Mitch asked.

"I'll see to it, Dad," Luke promised, shooting a warning look at his brother.

"Okay, then," Mitch agreed, reluctantly leading the way to a booth toward the back. At least if there were fireworks, they wouldn't be in plain view of the other customers.

To his surprise, it was Betty Lou who came over to wait on them. She winked at Mitch. "Thought this might be best," she said, her voice low as she leaned in close. "She'll be over on her break."

She straightened up and smiled. "What can I bring you gentlemen to drink?"

When Nate ordered a beer, Mitch regretted that he couldn't join him. Instead, he, like Luke, settled for a Coke.

"I'll have those for you in a sec," she promised.

"So where is she?" Nate asked, looking around. "Hiding out in the kitchen, I'll bet."

Just then, Lynn did emerge from the kitchen, laden down with a heavy tray filled with plates. She kept her gaze averted as she passed by.

"That's her," Luke said, nudging Nate, obviously recognizing her from the glimpse he'd caught at Raylene's.

Mitch saw the surprise in Nate's eyes. "Not the floozy you were envisioning, is she?" he asked quietly.

Nate winced. "Sorry. When you said she worked here, I didn't know what to think. Monty's isn't exactly a dive, but it's a long way from Sullivan's." He shrugged. "Besides, I couldn't remember her all that clearly from before. Even now, I don't recognize her. Doesn't seem as if I ever saw her around town."

"Maybe not," Mitch told him. "She and I are the same age, but her kids are younger than you two. We don't go to the same church or live in the same neighborhood. I doubt she and your mom were in any of the same activities."

"She doesn't look like Mom," Nate observed as Lynn hurried past, heading back into the kitchen.

"Not a bit," Mitch agreed.

"But she is pretty," Luke said, trying to intercede. "She looks a little tired, though."

"Three jobs," Mitch said succinctly.

Even Nate's skeptical expression changed then. Looked to Mitch as if she might have climbed a notch in his son's estimation.

"She's really working three jobs?" Nate asked.

"Long story," Mitch said. "Her divorce isn't going smoothly."

"But she's married to Ed Morrow," Nate said. "Isn't he loaded?"

"I honestly don't know the details of what's gone wrong, but I do know he hasn't been doing right by her," Mitch said, heat in his voice. "Enough said about that. I'm not going to spread gossip or share my opinion. Besides, here she comes." He gave each of them a pointed look. "Be nice."

"Hi," Lynn said, sliding into the booth in the space Mitch had left for her next to him. She managed a wan smile. "I can't stay but a second right now. For some reason we're swamped tonight. I thought everyone would be staying home after the holiday, but obviously not."

"Lynn, these are my sons, Luke over there and that's Nate next to him."

"I'm so glad to meet you both," she said, her well-honed Southern manners not quite enough to cover her nervousness. "Your dad has told me so much about you and about your mom. I wish I'd had the chance to know her."

Mitch bit back a smile at the look on Nate's face when she brought Amy openly into the conversation.

"Mom was incredible," Luke said.

"And from everything your dad has said, she's the one responsible for you both being amazing young men. I hope I do half as well with my kids."

"How many do you have?" Nate asked.

His tone was stiffly polite, but at least he was making an effort, Mitch thought, proud of him for trying.

"A boy, Jeremy, who's ten, and a daughter. Lexie's fourteen."

"I can vouch for them being pretty incredible," Mitch said. "I think Jeremy's destined to be a contractor or an architect. I've never had a kid ask me so many questions."

Luke looked startled. "That's the kid Terry's been talking about, isn't it? The one who was following you around over at Carter and Raylene's place?"

Mitch laughed. "That's the one."

"Your dad has been very patient with him," Lynn said, slipping out of the booth. "Sorry. I need to check on my tables. I'll be back when I can."

After she'd gone, Mitch glanced at Nate. "Well?"

"She's not at all what I expected," he admitted.

"She seems nice," Luke added. "I liked that she talked about Mom. Not everybody does. They avoid mentioning her. I know they do it so we won't be sad, but we are sad. And not talking about her makes it feel as if she never existed or something."

Nate nodded. "I liked that, too. I liked that she acknowledged how important Mom was to us."

"Because there's no denying that," Mitch told him.

"None of us are ever going to forget your mother, Nate. Lynn gets that. She's never going to try to compete with our memories of her. That's not the kind of woman she is. She has a warm, generous heart, just like your mom did."

Luke glanced in her direction as she went past with another order and shook his head. "Every time I see her with one of those trays, I want to rush over and take it from her. Those things must weigh a ton."

"Yeah, she brings out the protective instincts in me, too," Mitch said, "but trust me, she'd slap you silly if you tried."

"I know you said you didn't need my blessing, Dad, but you've got it," Luke said.

"Thanks, Luke." Mitch looked at Nate. "How about you?"

Nate looked uncomfortable. "I'm not quite ready to jump on the bandwagon, especially if you're going to rush into something. I think it's way too soon." He held Mitch's gaze. "But I will reserve judgment, Dad. If she makes you happy, I promise to give her a chance."

Mitch nodded. "That's all I ask, son."

And, after the way Nate had reacted earlier in the day, it was a lot more than he'd had any reason to hope for.

By the time Lynn was finally able to take a real break, Mitch and his sons had finished their meal. In a way it was a relief not to have to sit there and try to swallow food around the knot that had formed in her throat as she'd endured their frank scrutiny. She'd been able to tell that Nate wasn't even remotely resigned to having her in his father's life.

As she slid into the booth again, she noted three beer bottles lined up on the table between Mitch and Nate. Since she hadn't paid attention to who'd been drinking them, her heart did yet another nosedive.

Apparently, Mitch saw her expression and interpreted it correctly. He pointedly tapped on his own glass of soda. Even though she was relieved, her unease didn't entirely disappear. Her first reaction told her it was going to be a long time before she believed his drinking days were truly behind him.

"Dad says you're working three jobs," Luke said. "How are you able to juggle them all? I can barely handle one."

"I imagine your work for your dad is a lot more physically demanding than my jobs," Lynn told him.

"Are you kidding me?" Luke said. "Those trays you carry can't be light."

She laughed. "No, they took a little getting used to," she agreed. "The first two days, I was terrified I was going to dump every single plate into some customer's lap." She grinned. "I'm proud to say I haven't done it yet."

"Where else are you working?" Luke asked.

"I work part-time for Raylene in her boutique and part-time for your dad."

Nate immediately sat up straighter. "Dad's paying you? To do what?" he asked suspiciously.

Mitch immediately scowled at him. "Watch your tone, son."

"I'm just asking what kind of work she's doing for you," Nate said, refusing to back down. "I doubt she's hanging drywall."

"I'm handling billing and payroll," she said, determined not to take offense.

"But Dad always—" Nate began, only to yelp and shoot a confused look at his father. "What?"

"I can't keep up with it in the spring and summer when I have too many crews working," Mitch said.

Nate didn't look convinced, but he fell silent. Lynn had gotten the message, though. Hiring someone to do those tasks wasn't something Mitch always did. He'd obviously done it as a way of helping her out. She resolved to straighten that out the first chance she got.

"I'd better get back to work," she said, standing. "I'm so glad I had a chance to meet you both. I'm sure I'll see you again."

She left the table without waiting for either of the young men to respond. She was well aware that the evening hadn't gone well. She was sorry about that for Mitch's sake, because he'd obviously been counting on her winning over his sons. Judging from Nate's reaction especially, that approval wasn't likely to come anytime soon.

Not for the first time, she wondered if she and Mitch weren't deluding themselves that this relationship had even a slim chance of succeeding. Her life at the moment was way too complicated for her to spend a lot of time worrying about the future when she couldn't even be sure what the rest of the day might bring. Maybe it was time to pull back, give them both some breathing room.

But even as she resolved to do just that, she recalled Mitch's confidence that what they had was important and real. She had a feeling that he wasn't going to let go easily.

Mitch knew the dinner with his sons had been as close to a disaster as anything he'd done recently, even though there'd been no overt fireworks. Combined with Lynn's doubts about his drinking, he knew he had a lot of work left to do before their relationship could move forward. He just hadn't expected Lynn to go into a complete tailspin and do everything in her power to avoid him.

In the past week alone, she'd balked at every dinner invitation he'd issued. When she refused a fourth invitation, he called her on it.

"What's going on, Lynn? It's just dinner. Is this about what happened at the barbecue on Memorial Day? I thought we'd settled the whole drinking issue. Is it about Luke and Nate? Are you worried about coming between us? That's not going to happen."

She sighed, her cheeks coloring. "Look, doubts don't fade away just because we might want them to. As for your sons, they're not happy about us. That's real. We need to face it. Nate especially might never accept what's going on."

"Nate will come around," he said, determined to be optimistic. "And Luke has already given me his blessing. He liked you, Lynn. He told me so."

"I'm surprised," she said, looking pleased. "And you obviously know Nate better than I do, so if you say he'll adjust to seeing us together, I have to accept that. But those aren't our only obstacles, Mitch. I just think we need to take a step back."

"Okay," he said slowly. "But before I agree, I could use a little more clarity than that."

She looked taken aback that he'd challenged her, but eventually she nodded. "Okay, then, here it is. My life is a complicated mess right now. I love your company, probably a little too much. I'm attracted to you, and believe me when I say I wasn't expecting that to happen to me for a long, long time."

"So far I'm not getting the problem. That all sounds positive to me."

"Because you're a man," she said wryly. "If sex or the prospect of sex seems to be in the equation, all's right with the world."

Mitch frowned at her comment. "And you think that's how I am? You're selling me short, don't you think? I've only kissed you a couple of times. I've held off out of respect for your situation. I've wanted to do a lot more than that, but I'm being as patient and understanding as I can possibly be because of the circumstances."

There was real misery in her eyes as he spoke. "I know all that," she said softly.

"Then you're making excuses, Lynn. What's really spooked you?"

"It's all the uncertainty, I guess."

"Uncertainty? About us?"

A smile came and went. "No, you've been clear enough. But I have no idea when my divorce is ever going to be final and, let's face it, no matter what you want to believe, you're still getting over Amy's death. We're like two lonely souls who're adrift. The timing is lousy for us to even consider getting involved."

He understood what she was saying. Some of her words were actually amazingly encouraging. Her conclusion, however, was not.

"As I said, sweetheart, it's just dinner."

She frowned at that. "I think we both know better, unless something's changed for you."

Mitch laughed. "My testosterone is perfectly fine, thank you, so nothing's changed. I definitely want a whole lot more than dinner. I want you in my bed, Lynn." He determinedly held her gaze. "Is that plain enough for you? I want you in my life long-term."

He smiled at her. "That said, I'm also a patient man and,

as you just noted, I have baggage of my own. Rushing into bed held a lot of appeal way back when. Now I understand the value and rewards of extensive foreplay."

She seemed startled by his comment, but then she chuckled. "Extensive foreplay, huh?"

He nodded. "It works for me. Care to risk that much at least? It'll give you time to decide if I can be trusted or not." He dared a grin. "And you can enjoy knowing that being around you and being on my best behavior is pure torture for me. Cold showers and sleepless nights have become a regular part of my routine."

He could tell that she was weighing the taunting offer from every angle, probably trying to decide if she dared to take him up on it or even if she trusted herself to stick to the rules. Finally, a smile broke across her face, one that spoke volumes about her own feelings.

"So we're really going to go public?" she asked, looking more intrigued than he'd expected, given the doubts she'd expressed.

"That's the plan," he confirmed. "Unless you think being seen around town with me is going to get Ed all worked up again. You want to run that by Helen? The last thing I want to do is cause trouble for you."

She hesitated, then shook her head. "No need," she said firmly. "It's my decision, not Helen's or Ed's." She held out her hand. "Okay, deal."

He allowed himself a full-blown smile then. "Oh, no you don't, Lynnie. Any deal this important deserves to be sealed with a kiss."

"But you said—"

The protest died on her lips as he covered her mouth for just an instant, long enough to determine yet again that one kiss would never be enough. To his relief, as a soft moan escaped her lips and she clung to him, it seemed fairly evident that it wasn't going to be enough for her, either.

Twenty-One

The tension inside Karen Cruz's home was thick enough to cut, Flo thought as she and Liz arrived to join Frances and her family for the dinner that had been arranged to discuss what Frances's future living arrangements ought to be.

Frances was sitting all alone in a big overstuffed chair, her expression stone-faced as the conversation swirled around her. She looked a little lost and way too sad. Instinctively, Flo and Liz went over to perch on the arms of the chair, each of them taking a hand and giving it an encouraging squeeze.

"You doing okay?" Liz asked worriedly.

"No, I'm not okay," Frances snapped. "They're all acting as if my brain's already gone, talking around me and about me. Not one of them has looked me in the eye and asked what I wanted."

Flo felt for her friend, but she also felt terrible for her son and daughter and the spouses who were caught up in this unexpected situation. She, Liz and Frances had had time to adjust to the news of Frances's deteriorating health. It was all very new to her family. Not only were they grappling with their own distress, but they were trying to fig-

ure out a solution to one of the more difficult problems
any family could face: how best to help an aging parent.

Flo looked at Frances's daughter. Jennifer was in her
late forties. She and her husband were both teachers and
with two daughters of their own in college and another one
about to enter in the fall, Jennifer was obviously stressed
to the brink over finances.

Jeff, Frances's son, had a wife who'd never been particularly interested in his family. She'd been tied by the
apron strings to her own mother and sisters and had remained aloof from Frances over the years. Flo had a feeling
she was unhappy even to be in the room for this difficult
conversation.

"Obviously, Mother can't go on living alone," Jeff declared. "I suppose she could stay with us some of the time
and with you the rest of the time, Jen."

Martha, Jeff's wife, looked horrified by the suggestion.
So, for that matter, did Jennifer.

"That will never work," Martha said, giving her husband
a defiant look. "We simply don't have the room."

Dave, Jen's husband, frowned at his sister-in-law and
even at his wife. "We could make it work," he said. "The
girls are away at school most of the time, anyway."

"But we both have jobs," Jennifer protested. "Someone
would have to stay home or we'd have to bring in help."

Flo had heard enough. She glanced at Liz, who nodded.
They'd talked about stepping in, but only if the conversation seemed to be deteriorating. They didn't want Frances
to sit here listening to her children implying that she was
little more than a burden to them.

"May I say something?" Flo said, giving Frances's hand
another squeeze. "Liz and I have spent more time around
your mother than any of you have recently." When Jen

started to protest, Flo held up a hand. "I was not saying that to be judgmental. It's just the way it is. While it's true that there have been a few more incidents recently, I'm not sure a decision has to be made today. I also know your mother well enough to understand that the last thing she wants is to impose on any of you."

"Well, what other choice is there?" Jeff asked with evident frustration. "She can't continue to live alone in that apartment. The landlord called us after the fire. He wants her out."

Though the news annoyed the daylights out of her, Flo understood that Ned Kildare probably felt he had an obligation to the safety of his other tenants, as well as to Frances herself.

"We understand that," Liz said. "But we've talked all along about looking for a senior community where the three of us might be comfortable, one that has various levels of care, independent living for as long as we're able, assisted living for when the time comes that we need it. Flo's circumstances have changed recently and so have mine, but I still think this is a viable solution."

"Mom can't afford some expensive retirement community," Jeff said. "And at the least she should be living close to one of us."

"Do you really want to uproot her from the community where she's spent her entire life?" Flo asked. She turned to Frances. "Hon, I don't want to speak out of turn here. This is up to you. Why don't you tell us what you want?"

Tears glistened in Frances's eyes. "I want to stay at home with Lester," she said in a whisper that could barely be heard around the room.

At that, Jennifer burst into tears and crossed the room, pulling her mother into her arms. "Mom, you know

Daddy's been gone for a long, long time," she said, her voice thick.

Frances blinked. "Lester's gone?"

Jen wiped away her mother's tears. "Yes, Mom, he's gone. And you sold the house a couple of years after that. You've been living in an apartment, remember?"

Frances frowned, then seemed to come back from whatever moment in time she'd been in. "Well, of course, I remember," she said irritably. "And I know I should have looked for a retirement place back when I was first diagnosed, but I guess I've been living in denial, thinking that I'd be one of the lucky ones who'd never progress beyond having a mild cognitive disorder. There's no fool quite like an old fool, is there?"

"Mom, you've never been foolish," Jeff said. "And it doesn't matter if you've been in denial. We're all facing this now and we're doing it together." He gave his wife a defiant look as he said it.

Karen, who'd been silent until now, crossed the room and knelt beside Frances. "Whatever you decide, you know that Elliott and I want you to stay right here until you find exactly the right situation. There's no rush, okay?" She shot a disappointed look at Jeff and Jennifer. "Daisy, Mack and Elliott and I love having you here. You were always there for me, and I'm more than happy to do whatever I can for you now."

Jen looked vaguely chagrined to have this younger woman who had no family ties to Frances step up in a way she hadn't. Even so, she seized on the apparent lifeline.

"Karen, are you sure you're up to this?" Jen asked. "You have a baby on the way, a job to consider."

"We want to do it," Karen insisted. "Elliott would be here to tell you that himself, but we decided it was best to take the kids over to his mom's for dinner so you all could discuss this in peace."

"It would only be until we could find a place where Mom will be comfortable," Jeff said, looking relieved. "I'd insist she come with me, but I know how much she adores Daisy and Mack and this town. She'll be much happier here with you and with her friends close by."

"And we'll take her to visit all the retirement homes in the region," Flo offered. "When we've narrowed it down, we can let you know and you can look over the ones your mother likes best."

Jen looked around the room gratefully. "You have no idea how much it means to me knowing that Mom is surrounded by so many people who care about her."

"More than my own children do from what I can see," Frances said, her expression sad. She stood up. "I think I'll go to my room and rest."

She walked out with Liz at her side.

Flo glanced at Jen and saw tears streaming down her cheeks.

"She's right," Jen said. "You're the ones who've stepped up. All I could think about was how on earth we'd manage."

"It would have been hard," Jeff said, looking directly at his wife when he spoke. "But we could have made it work. Still, I am grateful that there's an alternative."

"And you've no need to feel guilty about that," Flo told him.

Though she was disappointed that Frances's family hadn't reacted differently, she understood from her own time living with Helen, Erik and Sarah Beth while her broken hip healed that it was often difficult having three generations under one roof. To have to make such an adjustment on the spur of the moment would be incredibly difficult.

"And try not to let what your mother said upset you too much," Flo advised them. "She's under a terrible strain trying to accept that she needs help from anyone. She's a proud woman, and she's been able to live independently for years. This is going to be a big change for her. She's entitled to lash out from time to time."

Jen managed a wobbly smile. "Given some of the tongue lashings she gave me as a teenager, I think we got off easy today. And despite what I know you must think of us right now, we will step up and be there for her. I promise you that."

Karen gave Jen a fierce hug. "You were so lucky to have had her as a mother. I've only had her in my life for a few years. Maybe it'll help to know how very much I love her, too. She's not going to face any of this alone."

"No, she's not," Flo said just as emphatically. Heck, maybe in another year or two she and Donnie would be ready for the right retirement home, too. Especially if there were regular dances!

"Why are we here?" Lynn asked, when she met Helen outside the courtroom just two weeks after that uncomfortable evening with Mitch's sons. "Is the judge finally ruling on the divorce settlement today?"

Helen shook her head. "Apparently, Jimmy Bob has filed some kind of new motion, and Hal wants to have a full hearing before he takes it into account."

"A motion? And you haven't seen it?"

Helen rolled her eyes. "Jimmy Bob is particularly fond of blindsiding the opposing attorney," she said, clearly disgusted with his tactics. "The court frowns on it, and it means there can't possibly be any kind of ruling because we haven't had time to respond, but it's all a big game to him. I'm surprised the bar association hasn't sanctioned him for pulling this stunt too many times."

Helen studied her. "Do you have any idea what this could be about? Has Ed said anything recently that might give you a clue?"

Lynn shook her head. "He's been giving me a wide berth lately. He doesn't want to hear any more of my rants about his failure to make the payments he's supposed to be making. Thank God I'm bringing in enough money now for us to get by, at least for food and utilities. I'm still scared, though, that we'll wind up losing the house."

Helen smiled. "I don't think that's likely, despite the way he's systematically removed the equity from it. I think we're going to be able to make a very good case to have that situation rectified."

"You've heard from the investigator?"

Helen nodded, looking pleased. "Those Cayman Islands accounts do exist. I can't prove how much is in them because the secrecy walls are a mile high, but their mere existence is going to infuriate Hal. He'll garnishee every penny of Ed's he can to make sure you get what you deserve once he knows about those."

Lynn shook her head. "Has his father acknowledged that he was taking money from the business, too?"

"Not to me," Helen said. "As you anticipated, he's protecting Ed till the bitter end. Once I can call him to the stand and have him declared a hostile witness, I imagine we can wrest out enough damning information to make Hal sit up and take notice."

"Do you think we're talking about a lot of money?" Lynn asked.

"He wouldn't be setting up secret, offshore accounts if it weren't," Helen said.

"But why?" Lynn asked, still perplexed. "Is he just greedy?"

"That could explain some of it, but I have two different theories," Helen said.

"Really?"

"First, it's possible he's been gambling and suffered some losses."

Lynn was shocked. "I can't imagine that," she said. "He never even wanted to play poker or blackjack when the club had Vegas nights. It just didn't interest him. What's your other theory?"

"That he's being blackmailed."

Lynn's mouth dropped open. "Blackmailed? No way. By whom? Why?"

"You have no ideas?"

"Not a one. I'd be stunned if he'd ever done anything at all that someone could use against him."

"You mean other than stealing from you and the business?" Helen said wryly.

"Yeah, those are shockers, too. I guess you never really know anyone quite as well as you think you do." She regarded Helen with bewilderment. "But if he has all that going on, why isn't he more anxious to get this divorce behind him? He could just settle this and focus on all the other craziness."

"Maybe there's no money left for a settlement," Helen said. "Or maybe this motion he's filed is some last-ditch effort to keep the court from granting you anything."

Lynn regarded her worriedly. "Is that possible?"

"Anything's possible," Helen said. "He can certainly

try, but he won't get away with it, Lynn. You don't need to worry about that."

"I still wish I knew what he was up to. I don't like going in there without a clue."

"And you can't think of a single thing?" Helen pressed again.

Lynn thought about the last conversations she'd had with Ed. They'd mostly been brief and contentious. She hadn't wanted to dwell on any of them. "I do think he's had some pressure from his folks about the kids. Could that be it?"

"What sort of pressure?"

"They want guaranteed visitation. They've been livid because Lexie won't go over there. Of course, they blame me, even though it was some comments Wilma made that upset Lexie in the first place."

Helen nodded. "That could be it. Let's hope so. We should be able to get that resolved fairly quickly. The kids are old enough to have some say in how much time they care to spend with their grandparents, and if we can document that Wilma has been bad-mouthing you in front of them, it'll definitely weaken their case."

Lynn regarded her with alarm. "Does that mean Lexie would have to testify? I don't want to drag her into the middle of this."

"Let's not get ahead of ourselves," Helen said. "It may not be about that at all. Let's just go in there and see how this plays out."

Lynn nodded and followed her inside the courtroom. Ed was already seated with Jimmy Bob. She noted that he didn't even glance at her as she took her seat. That couldn't be good. And his parents were seated right behind him, their expressions smug.

Once Hal Cantor had been seated behind the bench,

Jimmy Bob stood. "Your honor, we've filed a motion to amend the shared custody agreement we were originally seeking."

Lynn stared at him in shock, then turned to Helen. "Can they do that?"

Helen patted her hand. "Don't worry. Let's just see where this is going."

Jimmy Bob's expression turned almost as smug as Wilma Morrow's as he announced, "Ed would like to request full custody of Alexis and Jeremy."

At that, even as Lynn's head reeled, Helen was on her feet. "That's absurd. On what grounds?" she demanded.

"It's all in the motion," Jimmy Bob said.

"Which, amazingly, has not yet been delivered to my office," Helen said, skewering him with a scowl. "Your honor, this is outrageous, even for Mr. West. I request an immediate postponement and an order that a copy of the motion be in my hands within the hour."

"Granted," Judge Cantor said, regarding Jimmy Bob with disdain. "You know better, counsel."

"This is an emergency, your honor," Jimmy Bob insisted. "I'm sure the courier has already made his delivery by now."

The judge didn't look impressed. "If I had my copy yesterday in order to schedule this so-called emergency, then Ms. Decatur-Whitney should have had it yesterday, as well. I can only assume it was a deliberate oversight on your part." He skewered Jimmy Bob with a look. "Not on my watch, Mr. West."

Ed's parents looked vaguely shaken by the judge's unmistakable fury. Clearly, they'd come expecting to leave the courtroom today victorious.

"Helen, we have to know what this is about," Lynn said urgently. "I need to understand this now."

Helen nodded. "Your honor, before we go, perhaps Mr. West would like to summarize the grounds for this emergency change in the previously approved shared-custody arrangement."

Jimmy Bob jumped up eagerly. "We have just learned that Mrs. Morrow is now working in a bar and is involved with an alcoholic. With both children at such an impressionable age, this is no longer the appropriate environment for them. Mr. Morrow, whose parents are more than eager to help out with their care, is requesting full custody, with only supervised visitation by Mrs. Morrow to be permitted. I think there's little question that the Morrows are respectable, God-fearing individuals who will provide a safe environment for Alexis and Jeremy."

Lynn heard his words with mounting shock and anger. She was on her feet before Helen could restrain her. "Are you crazy?" she demanded, her heated gaze going from Ed to the sanctimonious Morrows. "This is the most outrageous claim I've ever heard in my life. You're going to regret it, Ed. You can count on that." She turned to Helen. "Let's get out of here. The smell is making me sick to my stomach."

Helen gave her a commiserating look. "Hold on a sec. Give the judge a chance to leave," she murmured. "Hal's looking a little ill himself."

"Court's dismissed," the bailiff said when Hal had left the room.

Lynn headed for the door with Helen right on her heels. She couldn't even bear to look at Ed as she went. When this had started, she'd vowed to do everything in her power to keep it civil for the sake of the kids. Allowing Ed to malign a man like Mitch in order to gain custody of their kids—not because it was right, not even because he really wanted it, but to satisfy his parents—was beyond the pale. That he would dare to attack her for taking a job that he'd made a necessity by his own irresponsible behavior was even worse.

She turned to Helen. "All bets are off," she said tightly. "Get that investigator to dig in every nook and cranny until we know exactly what Ed's been up to. If there are skeletons, drag 'em out of the closet. My children will not live with a man who'd resort to something like this."

"It could get really ugly," Helen cautioned. "If I'm right, either about the gambling or, worse, about Ed being blackmailed, there won't be any holding it back. The kids are bound to find out, especially if there's anything illegal going on."

The warning gave Lynn pause. She wanted to do everything possible to protect her children, but the best way to do that, she felt certain, would be to keep them away from the man and his parents who would put her in this position in the first place.

"I don't care about ugly," Lynn said wearily. "I just want my kids safe from the likes of those people. It will be a very cold day in hell before Wilma Morrow gets her hands on my children."

Mitch's head was spinning as Lynn paced around her kitchen, clearly furious, but so far not saying a word that made a lot of sense. He'd stopped by soon after she'd returned from the courthouse to see what had happened and had found her in this state.

He stood up, put his hands on her shoulders and commanded, "Stop. Let me fix you some iced tea. You're obviously upset. Once you're calmer, you can tell me what on earth went on in court today."

"I don't think I can sit down. The only thing keeping me from screaming is pacing."

He held up his hands in surrender. "Then pace away. I think I'll pour that tea, anyway. Anything else I can get you? Are you hungry? I'm mostly hopeless in the kitchen, but I could probably whip up an omelet."

To his shock when she faced him, there were tears in her eyes.

"Here I am, acting like I've lost my mind, and you're being so sweet," she said, the tears tracking down her cheeks. "You don't deserve this mess I've dragged you into."

"What mess? And how am I in the middle of it?" he asked. "Are you talking about the divorce?"

She nodded, suddenly starting to sob.

Mitch gathered her close, carried her into the living room and sat on the sofa with her in his arms. He'd been envisioning a moment like this for a long time now, but it certainly had been under different circumstances. For one thing she wouldn't have been sobbing as if her heart were breaking.

"Tell me," he said gently. "What's Ed done?"

"He's filed..." The rest of her words were lost to sobs.

"What's he filed for, sweetheart? Tell me and we'll sort it out. I promise."

She swallowed hard, took the tissues he'd grabbed from a box on the table and dabbed at her eyes. "He wants full custody of Lexie and Jeremy," she finally managed to reveal.

Mitch stared at her, stunned by this latest evidence of Ed's cruelty. "He'll never get it," he said confidently.

"You're an incredible mother. No judge would ever take those children away from you."

"Thanks," she murmured, sniffing.

"What's his reasoning?"

"He says it's because I'm working in a bar," she began, then regarded him miserably, "and because I'm seeing you."

Mitch hadn't expected that. He'd known Ed didn't like him hanging around with Lynn or the kids, but for him to use their relationship to try to take her kids from her was far beyond anything he could have possibly anticipated.

"He won't get away with it," he said tightly.

"I know that. Helen says so, too, but now you're smack in the middle of this. I am so, so sorry."

"Did he say what his big objection to me is?" Mitch asked, as much out of curiosity as anything. Whatever it was, maybe he could fix it.

"He says you're an alcoholic," she confessed in a whisper. "Added to me working in a bar, he thinks that's grounds for the kids to be with him and his parents."

Mitch closed his eyes against the wave of pain that washed through him at Lynn's words. There might not be a bit of truth to Ed's claim, but added to Lynn's own fears about his drinking, this could be the end for them. If there was even the tiniest possibility that associating with him could cost her Lexie and Jeremy, he needed to walk away, no matter what it cost him to do it. This was not a battle she should have to fight.

He cupped her face in his hands and waited until she looked at him. She was obviously embarrassed by having to admit what had been in those court documents.

"Listen to me, Lynnie. I will not be responsible for you losing your children."

"This is about Ed and his sick, twisted mind," she insisted. "It shouldn't be about you."

"He's made it about me," he argued. "Now, I may think he'll have an incredibly difficult time trying to prove I'm an alcoholic, but it would be a lot smarter to take me out of the equation entirely."

She blinked, her expression dismayed. "What are you saying?"

"That I'm going to walk away," he said, every word like a knife to his heart. "It's the only thing I know to do to make sure that he can't use me against you."

"But that's so unfair," she objected. "You haven't done anything wrong. Neither have I, for that matter. Mitch, Helen is going to fix this."

"Nobody has more faith in Helen than I do," he said, "but I'm going to make it easier for her." He touched her cheek, stroked a finger over the silken curve of it, wondering if he'd ever be able to be this close to her again. "I want it to be easier for you."

He stood up, set her gently back onto the sofa, then bent down and kissed her quickly.

"Mitch, please don't go," she called after him. "Not like this."

Filled with an unimaginable sorrow, he faced her one last time. "It won't be forever," he promised. "If you need me, you call me."

"I need you now," she said.

He absorbed the sweet admission, but managed to make himself shake his head. "Right now, the best thing I can do for you is to walk out of here." He held her gaze. "Let me do it, Lynnie."

Once more tears spilled down her cheeks, but slowly

she nodded. "Thank you for being stronger than I am," she whispered.

He smiled at that. "No one is stronger than you are. No one."

Certainly not him, he thought as he fought his own tears as he walked out of the house and away from the woman who'd come to mean more to him than life itself. He'd wanted to give her his heart. How ironic to discover that the best gift he could give her for now was her freedom!

Twenty-Two

Lynn had been in a daze for what felt like an eternity, but in fact had been less than a week. Between Ed's courtroom stunt and Mitch walking out of her life, the stability she'd only recently thought within reach was suddenly shattered in unexpected ways.

She spent almost every night lying awake, which meant she looked exhausted most of the time and felt wretched all the time.

She told Helen what Mitch had done, taking himself out of the equation in an attempt to protect her. She'd expected Helen to be as distressed by that as she had been.

"Sadly, he's probably right," Helen said, regarding her sympathetically. "If Ed's going to be unreasonable, it'll help to have one less thing to fight about when we go back to court next week."

"But Mitch isn't an alcoholic," Lynn said, surprised to discover as the emphatic defense left her mouth that she honestly believed what she was saying. There was no doubt he'd had a drinking problem for a time, just as he'd admitted, but she'd brought her own history to bear on the situation, reacting out of fear, even when all the evidence favored Mitch. He simply wasn't her father. She had absolutely no reason at all to believe he'd follow the same drunken path her father had.

She gave Helen an indignant look. "I don't even know where Ed came up with such a crazy idea."

Helen smiled wearily. "Probably the same sort of gossip we heard from people who saw him in Monty's after Amy died."

"But he hasn't hung out there in months," Lynn said.

"Until you started working there," Helen reminded her. She held up her hand when Lynn started to jump once more to his defense. "Look, I know why he's there, and I've spoken to Monty, who's willing to testify that he hasn't had a drop to drink on any of those occasions, but frankly, it'll be easier if this is one less battle for us to fight."

"It's just wrong," Lynn said, totally frustrated by the injustice of it.

"I agree, but staying apart doesn't have to last forever, Lynn. Once this custody motion is resolved, if you and Mitch want to see each other, there will be nothing to stop you."

"You don't think Ed will go running right back to the judge if he finds out Mitch and I have reconciled?" Lynn asked doubtfully. "Come on, Helen, this might never be over. Ed could keep our lives in turmoil out of spite."

"I think you're wrong. Frankly, I think this was a very carefully devised tactical maneuver to throw some mud in your direction and keep us so busy that we wouldn't have time to dig for whatever real dirt Ed's trying to hide."

Lynn thought about that. At one time, she would never have imagined that her husband could be that devious, but recently? She simply didn't know him anymore. "Maybe so," she conceded. "Do we have that dirt yet?"

Helen smiled. "We're getting very close. The investigator has found a trail of credit card receipts that don't make a lick of sense."

"What do you mean? Personal credit cards?"

"Personal. Company." Helen shrugged. "Ed apparently used them indiscriminately."

"For all those golf trips he's been taking?" Lynn wondered.

"Smoke screen," Helen said succinctly.

Lynn stared at her. "I don't understand."

"Ed may have been doing a lot of playing on those trips of his, but it wasn't golf," she said. "I'm just about a hundred percent sure of that."

"What then?"

"Give me another day," Helen said. "I don't want to speak out of turn. I may not much like your husband these days, but I don't want to do my own share of mudslinging without facts to back it up."

Lynn had never seen Helen look quite so somber. "You're not really loving this, are you? You usually look happier when you have something that can win a case."

"I don't mean to play some cat-and-mouse game with you, Lynn," Helen said apologetically. "I really do want to be sure before I say anything more, okay? It's just not the sort of thing I could wipe out of your mind if I've made an unfair accusation."

Lynn regarded her with dismay. "It's that damaging?"

Helen nodded, her expression weary. "I'm afraid so. Can you trust me just a little longer? Once I have solid proof, assuming it exists, I won't hold back. I promise you that. You'll know everything I know."

"I've trusted you so far," Lynn said. "I see no reason for that to change now."

"It won't be long. As soon as I have something concrete to share with you, we'll talk and decide how you want to handle it from then on."

Lynn frowned at something she heard in her tone. "This really is going to be a shocker, isn't it?"

Helen nodded, her expression somber. "You have no idea."

The back door to the house crashed open, scaring Lynn half to death. She ran in from the living room, only to find Ed standing there in the kitchen looking thoroughly furious. To her surprise, there was none of her usual cowering response to his anger.

She stood her ground and leveled a look at him that would have withered anyone else. "Next time knock," she said quietly, regretting for once that she hadn't been more cautious about locking that blasted door, as Mitch had begged her to. "You don't have any right to walk in here anymore. I thought we'd established that weeks ago."

"I do as long as I'm paying the mortgage," he blustered.

"But according to the bank, not only haven't you been paying the mortgage, you've been taking equity out of the house behind my back," she retorted furiously. "Thanks for that, by the way. Not only are you seriously endangering the roof over your children's heads, but ruining my credit rating in the process."

He waved off her claim as if it were unimportant. "And you're about to destroy my reputation. Watch how fast the gravy train dries up, if you accomplish that," he threatened. "I know what you and that barracuda attorney of yours have been up to."

"You mean the whole fighting fire with fire thing?" she asked. "You started it, Ed, the day you came after my kids and used my job and Mitch to do it. Until that moment, we still had a chance to settle this like civilized adults."

He looked only vaguely chagrined by her charge. "The man has a drinking problem. Ask anyone."

"He had a drinking problem right after his wife died," she said. "He was grieving. I doubt you'll find anyone who's hit an emotional rough patch and hasn't resorted to some sort of bad behavior they come to regret. If I hadn't grown up around a drunk, I might be drinking right now myself."

"Of course you'd defend him," Ed said sarcastically.

She looked him squarely in the eye. "Of course I would," she said quietly. "Especially when there's an unjust charge leveled against him. Of all the people you know, don't you think I'd recognize an alcoholic if there were one in my life?"

Ed flinched at that. He knew more than most what living with her father had been like for her. "Maybe so," he conceded.

"And, while we're on the subject of crummy allegations, do you honestly think I'd be working at Monty's if I didn't need the work because of your outrageous behavior toward your family? Not that I need to defend myself in the first place, because it's a perfectly respectable bar. It's not some low-life dive the way you tried to imply in your motion. Don't you think Hal Cantor knows that, too? He eats in there at least once a week with some of the other judges from the area. I assume you know that, since he was there when you and Jimmy Bob were in there spying on me. That is why you came in that night, right? It's certainly not your usual style."

"Okay, yes, I wanted to see for myself how low you'd sunk."

She merely lifted a brow at that. Ed raked a hand through his hair, then dragged out a kitchen chair and sat down, looking defeated.

He gave her a pleading look. "Lynn, we need to stop this before it spins out of control."

She heard something new in his voice then, a genuine edge of desperation.

"I'm all for that," she said cautiously. "Why this sudden change of heart? Exactly what has Helen discovered that's made you so nervous? What have you done, Ed?"

He regarded her with unmistakable misery. "It's not what I've done, at least not exactly."

"You're not making a lot of sense," she told him, arms folded across her chest as she stood there waiting.

"Could you please sit down? This is hard enough as it is without your just standing over me, waiting for me to trip up or something."

She sat down gingerly on the edge of a chair on the opposite side of the table. "What's going on, Ed? Is it someone else? Is that what this has been about from the beginning? Were you cheating on me and got caught?"

The question hung in the air for a very long time before he finally nodded. "You're not going to believe this. Hell, there are days I don't even believe it myself."

Lynn waited him out. Over all these years, she'd thought she knew and understood everything there was to know about her husband, but she'd never seen him like this. Whatever he was trying to say was clearly costing him. There had been a time when she'd have felt so sorry for him, she'd have let him off the hook, but not now.

"Lots of people have affairs, Ed," she said, trying to give him an opening. "I never thought you'd be one of them, since you weren't exactly passionate when it came to me. I always felt like sex was some kind of chore for you. I was young and naive when we got married, so I didn't know any better, but I understand now that wasn't exactly normal. Was it because there was someone else all along?"

He smiled weakly at that. "You'd probably even forgive me if I said that's all it was, wouldn't you?"

She'd wondered about that way back when Helen had first asked if he'd been sleeping with someone else. Would she be able to forgive him and move on for the sake of their marriage, their children? At one time the answer had probably been yes. She'd learned to live without passion, accepted that as a trade-off for the tranquility she'd found in her marriage.

Now, though, having fallen for a man like Mitch who was willing to give her up rather than hurt her, she wasn't so sure she could ever go back to the selfish, passionless brand of love Ed had shown her.

"No," she said softly. "Maybe once upon a time, but not now, Ed. I have more self-respect these days."

"Good for you," he said. Surprisingly, he sounded as if he really meant it. "I was never the right man for you. I knew that almost from the beginning, but I tried to be, Lynn." His plaintive expression begged her to believe him. "I swear to you that I really wanted our marriage to work. It was just never meant to be."

Now he had shocked her. "Because there was always someone else?"

He nodded.

Lynn waited...and waited some more.

"It's Jimmy Bob," he said eventually.

Lynn heard the words, but they made no sense to her. "What does Jimmy Bob have to do with anything?"

"He and I..." That was as much as he seemed capable of saying.

"You and he," she repeated, even as her mouth dropped open in shock. "You and *Jimmy Bob?*"

"At least he was honest enough never to marry, never to drag someone else into the middle of things, but me, I didn't want to let down my parents. You were right there, loving me, willing to take whatever scraps I handed you. I deluded myself into thinking we could make it work, that no one would ever have to be the wiser. Jimmy Bob wasn't exactly thrilled, but he went along with it because he knew as well as I did how conservative this town can be. We both had big ambitions back then."

"All these years?" Lynn said, unable to grasp it. "And no one guessed?" She certainly hadn't, and she'd been living with the man.

"We were careful. We never spent time together around here. In fact, a lot of people thought there was bad blood between us. There was never a hint of suspicion around town, at least not until someone who recognized Jimmy Bob saw the two of us on a trip out of town."

"And that person is blackmailing you," she guessed, reeling. Suddenly so many things were making sense to her. "My God, Ed, how could you do this? All these years of lies and deceptions? The pretense of loving me? Of not being true to yourself? How could you even look at yourself in the mirror?"

He looked at her sorrowfully. "Because I'm weak. I wanted what I had, what we had. I wanted my parents to go on respecting me. I wanted to be the man people would trust just the way they had my father. I wanted you, at least in my own selfish way, and our kids. You know how it would have been if I'd come out and announced that I was gay. There are not a lot of folks in Serenity who would have coped well with that, even in some superficial way, much less trusted me with their insurance needs." He took a breath. "So I lied, to you, to myself, to everyone."

"Except Jimmy Bob," she said wearily.

He nodded. "I even kept him at arm's length in the beginning, trying to maintain the charade, but it got to be too much. And he was getting tired of it. I could hardly blame him for that. I had a decision to make and I did. I chose him. I swear to you, though, before that he and I weren't, well, we weren't *together* together, if you know what I mean. I insisted on that."

If she hadn't been so stunned, Lynn might have been amused by his odd code of honor.

"We went away after I'd asked for the divorce," he told her. "That very first trip, that's when someone saw us and somehow put the pieces together. That's when the blackmail began and everything started to unravel."

"Why was Jimmy Bob setting up those offshore accounts for you?" she asked. "So you could run?"

"Yes. Once the divorce was final, we planned to leave, get away from the blackmail, all of it. I was tired of hiding. I knew once everything came out, I'd never be able to face anyone here, least of all my parents."

"I see," she said.

"I'm sorry, Lynn. You'll never know how sorry I am for using you like this. I think one reason I've lashed out at Mitch the way I have is because he's the man I wish I could have been for you. I saw the way he looked at you and knew that never, not even once, had I been able to look at you with that much passion."

Lynn had never felt so emotionally exhausted in her life. "I need time, Ed. I need to think about all this."

"Can we work something out?" he asked. "I know I have no right to ask, but I'd like to keep this quiet. It's not something I want the kids to know. I don't want to shatter whatever shred of respect they might still have for me."

Lynn gave him a pitying look. "Ed, don't you know by now that your kids won't love you any less for being gay? The only way you'd lose them is by treating them and me badly."

"There's that Pollyanna side of you," he teased, though his tone was more weary than amused. "You're living in a dream world, if you believe that, Lynn. If all this comes out, I will lose them."

"Don't you think it's going to come out if you take off with Jimmy Bob?" she asked incredulously. "You're not going to be able to have it both ways, Ed. You can continue trying to live a lie, or you can tell the world and live with the consequences. I don't think you'll ever be truly happy unless you choose the latter."

"You're probably right," he agreed. "I'm just not sure I'm that courageous. This is going to kill my mother. And Dad's not going to be all that happy when he figures out how I've damaged the business, what I've stolen from it and from you."

"They're your parents, Ed. They love you. Once they get over the shock, they'll be in your corner. Tell them now, before they find out some other way."

"How?" he asked. "How do you tell your parents something like this?"

"You told me, didn't you?"

"Only because you had my back to the wall," he said. He studied her. "Will you use what I've told you?"

She heard the real fear in his voice. The skepticism she'd been developing about him recently made her wonder if all this hadn't been a huge ploy on his part. If he'd been capable of such a depth of duplicity all these years, why not one more grand act now, one designed to have her call off Helen?

"Do you plan to change your tactics and drop that ridiculous custody suit?" she asked.

"Done," he said at once.

"Then I'll speak to Helen. I think she'll want to have all of us sit down and mediate this before our next scheduled court date."

"Whatever you need," he said at once.

"How do you intend to resolve the blackmail, Ed? You can't live with that hanging over your head. And if you go to the police, it will all come out, anyway," she said, almost feeling sorry for the dilemma he'd found himself in. Sure, it was of his own making, but on some level she could understand the choices he'd made. She might not be ready to forgive him for them, but she could understand them. He'd always craved the respect that the town had bestowed on his father. In marrying her, he'd simply been living up to expectations, or trying to.

He gave her a sad look. "Thus the Cayman Islands," he said ruefully. "Once again, I was planning to take the easy way out."

"Let me ask you one thing, then. If you'd won this custody suit, would you have tried to take Lexie and Jeremy with you?"

"I honestly hadn't thought that far ahead," he said. "Jimmy Bob thought it was a tactic that might scare you into doing whatever it took to put an end to your demands and just cut me loose."

She regarded him sorrowfully. "That's a real pattern

with you these days, isn't it? Not thinking things through, letting someone else influence the choices you make."

"Yeah, that's one of those life lessons I'm going to be spending a lot of time working on," he said.

He stood up then, took a step toward her, then seemed to think better of it and stepped back. "I'm sorry, Lynn, not just for what I've put you through lately, but all of it. You'll never know how sorry. You're a wonderful woman, and you didn't deserve any of this."

"I'm sorry, too," she said.

Not for anything she'd done, but for not understanding sooner, for not seeing how much pain her husband was in, living a lie. She'd loved him blindly for so very, very long. She'd never thought there could be such a thing as too much love, but maybe she'd been wrong. Over the years she'd written off too many things, made too many excuses for him, accepted too much of the blame for the flaws in their marriage.

As he approached the door, he turned back and asked, "How are the kids?"

"Unhappy," she said. "Scared. They miss their father, or at least they miss believing that you might actually care about them."

"I've made such a mess of this," he said, his voice filled with regret. "I will find a way to make things right, I promise." He hesitated, took a step back into the room. "I was going to take off, let you think about all this, but I wonder, would you mind if I stick around till the kids get home from school?"

Lynn thought about the request. She knew it wasn't too much to ask. "You'll keep what we've talked about to yourself?"

"Of course," he said at once. "If we decide to tell them any of this, we'll do it together."

She nodded then. "Okay, then, stay. In fact, why don't you spend the evening with them, too? I have somewhere I need to be, someone I need to see."

He gave her an oddly sad look. "Mitch?"

She regarded him with surprise. "Why would you assume I'd go running to him?"

"Oh, please, Lynn, you've been wearing your heart on your sleeve for a while now. Why do you think I attacked him in court? It's the hottest topic at Wharton's these days. Everybody loves a story about a guy who once never stood a chance finally getting the girl."

She smiled at the description. "Believe me, I'm the one who's finally gotten lucky."

There were probably a thousand things yet to be resolved, and more difficult moments ahead than she could possibly imagine. Even so, she left the house without a backward glance, her heart lighter than it had been for months.

Lynn made a brief stop at Helen's to fill her in on Ed's stunning revelations. "He says he wants to mediate an immediate settlement, that he'll drop the whole custody suit," she told her. "Can we still do that?"

"If that's what you want to do, absolutely," Helen said.

"This is what you were trying so hard not to tell me, isn't it?" she asked.

Helen nodded. "I just hadn't gotten the kind of proof I wanted before saying anything."

"I appreciate your caution. I'm not sure I would have believed it without hearing it straight from Ed. I'm still shocked that I could have gone so long thinking we had a halfway decent marriage."

Helen smiled. "Halfway decent isn't expecting a lot. You deserve more."

Lynn thought of Mitch and smiled back at her. "I think I'm finally figuring that out. I need to find Mitch."

"Will you tell him?" Helen asked.

"Only that it finally looks as if this will be over soon. The rest..." She shrugged. "It's up to Ed to tell people, or not. Personally, I hope he'll get it all out in the open. I think he'll be surprised by how many people might stand by him. I think this town has a generosity of spirit he's underestimated."

Helen looked doubtful. "Maybe, if he'd been honest from the beginning," she cautioned. "But now, after all he's put you through? I just don't know, Lynn. It could be too late. It's not about him being gay. It's about all the rest—what he's done to cover it up, the pain he's caused you and his children."

"I still believe people will find a way to forgive him, especially if I show them the way."

"You can do that, even now?" Helen asked, clearly surprised.

Lynn gave it some thought before answering, then nodded. "I want him to be here for Lexie and Jeremy. And I want them to learn about forgiveness and letting go of anger, not for Ed's sake, but for theirs. It's funny how I held on to my anger toward my parents for so long, and only now can see that the only one I've been hurting all these years is myself. I don't want that for them. We all need to move forward."

"Okay, then. I'll schedule that mediation session for tomorrow. There's no time to waste. I imagine that for once in his life, Jimmy Bob will be wholeheartedly cooperative."

Lynn's laugh was only a little strained. "You'd think so, wouldn't you?"

"You look as if the weight of the world has been lifted from your shoulders," Helen observed.

"That's exactly how I feel. You have no idea what a relief it is to know finally that none of this was my fault, that I didn't somehow fail as a wife. I couldn't have saved my marriage no matter how hard I tried."

Helen waved her toward the door. "Go. You look as if you're going to burst if you don't see Mitch soon."

"I just might," Lynn agreed, grinning.

The paperwork might not be final, the details of the settlement might not be nailed down, but it was over, and she was free to move on, emotionally if not quite legally.

And this time, there wasn't a doubt in her mind that she'd found a man trustworthy enough to treat the love she had to give with the tenderness and respect she deserved.

Twenty-Three

Flo stood outside the assisted-living facility where Frances had finally been settled just this morning, tears streaming down her face. Donnie immediately wrapped his arms around her.

"She'll be okay," he murmured soothingly. "You know she will. This is where she needs to be, and it's a real nice place. You were lucky to find it right off, and even luckier that they had an opening."

"But she looks so sad and lost," Flo said. "I think she's gotten worse just since she moved in."

"I imagine she'll be a little disoriented at first, but she'll find her way around. You and Liz can come over here every day to visit, take her over to the senior center, play cards with her, go out to lunch. You can even take her to those Sweet Magnolias margarita nights, if she's feeling up to it. Isn't that the advantage of finding a good place so close by?"

Flo gave him a sad smile. "Donnie Leighton, do you know how much I love you for trying to make me feel better about this?"

"I'm always going to be around to try to cheer you up," he promised.

"Thank you for coming with me tonight. When Liz said she didn't feel up to it, I was dreading coming by myself. I knew I'd spend the whole time imagining that day when I'd have to make the same decision Frances and her family just made."

"You're a long way from needing a place like this," Donnie scoffed. "Besides, you have me. I'll take care of you."

She smiled at the way he said it without hesitation. "I've been thinking about that lately," she admitted.

"My taking care of you?" He frowned. "You're not going to start carrying on about me being younger, are you?"

"No." She put her hands on his arms and looked him in the eye. "What I was going to say is that I've been reconsidering something."

Unmistakable hope flared in his eyes. "Such as?" he prodded.

"The whole marriage thing," she said, then quickly added, "Now, personally, I don't need it. I'm happy enough just the way things are, but I'm wondering if maybe I've been a little too stubborn for my own good and maybe even thinking too much about myself and not even a tiny bit about you."

"You stubborn? Imagine that!" he said, a glint of amusement in his eyes.

She scowled at him. "Are you going to let me get this out, or do you intend to mock me?"

"Since it's starting to sound as if listening might be in my own best interest, I'll be quiet as a church mouse from here on out," he promised.

Flo gave a little huff. "Then, as I was saying, I've been thinking maybe I should reconsider, possibly even say yes to your proposal." A smidgen of uncertainty crept into her voice, which ticked her off. "That is, if the offer's still on the table."

The smile that spread across Donnie's face was answer enough. "How soon?" he demanded, grinning.

"I imagine we could go down to the courthouse tomorrow, get this done pretty quickly."

"Oh, no, you don't, Flo Decatur. You marry me, we're going to make a fuss about it. We don't have to get married at church, but we will have a fancy ceremony and a reception with all our friends. I imagine Helen's going to want to make sure the knot is tied nice and tight."

Flo laughed and threw herself into his arms. "Yes, I imagine she will."

"Of course, that said, I don't want to take any chances you'll think it over and change your mind again, so let's say a week from Saturday. Would that suit you?"

Flo's heart skipped a beat or two, but she figured it was a good thing under the circumstances. "A week from Saturday would suit me just fine."

He kissed her to seal the deal, then looked into her eyes. "Want to go back inside and share the news with Frances?"

And that, she thought, was why she'd finally said yes, because this man knew her as no one else ever had.

"You read my mind," she said, holding his hand as they walked back inside to share the news with one of her very best friends.

Lynn had to search all over town before she finally found Mitch working in one of the downtown buildings he and Raylene were renovating for new businesses. After spotting his truck at the curb, she parked next to it, walked through the door and grabbed a hard hat. She could hear hammering coming from the back room.

When she saw him, she took a minute to drink in the sight of this man who'd been so kind, so patient, so loving, without asking for a thing in return. Thank heavens he was alone, because what she had in mind didn't need witnesses.

He finished driving nails into a piece of drywall, then leaned over a table to study some plans, giving her an excellent view of that denim-clad backside of his. When he finally looked up and turned her way, a smile broke across his face.

"This is a surprise," he said, just as she reached him, stood on tiptoe and sealed her lips over his. When she finally broke away, his smile widened. "And *that* was an even better surprise. What's going on, Lynn? We agreed—"

"I've come to my senses," she said, interrupting him.

"I didn't know there was ever any question that you weren't in full possession of them," he said.

"I've allowed you to back off, haven't I?"

She started to reach for him again, but he put his hands on her waist and held her carefully in place while he searched her face. "Not that I'm not thrilled to pieces if you've had a change of heart about the game plan, but do you mind filling me in on why? All the reasons I walked away are still valid, aren't they?"

"Not so much."

"I'm going to need more than that."

"I just had a long conversation with Ed," she said, as if that were explanation enough.

"And I look fantastic by comparison?" he inquired, his tone wry.

"You do, but that's not it," she said, grinning because he was so darn good at making her smile. "I realized that thanks mostly to you, I've let it all go—all the anger, all the bitterness, all the self-derision for allowing my marriage to fail. It's gone. All I felt when he was there baring his soul to me was relief. We're going to mediate a settlement, probably tomorrow. The fighting is over, Mitch. It's really and truly over. In a few days or whatever it takes to get it filed and approved by the court, I can truly put my marriage behind me and look toward the future."

There was relief in Mitch's eyes, but an unmistakable hint of caution in his voice. "You sound awfully sure for a woman who's been put through the wringer for months now."

"It's over," she said emphatically. "You'll just have to trust me on that for now." She looked into his eyes. "Can you do that?"

"Trusting you has always come easy to me," he said. He led her to a sawhorse in the middle of the room. He sat down on that and pulled her onto his lap. "Tell me how I fit in."

"Any way you want to," she said. "But I was thinking we could start by getting out of here and going to your place or the Serenity Inn or wherever else you'd like to go for some privacy."

His eyes lit up at the suggestion. "And the kids?"

"Ed's with them." She gave him a hopeful look. "I could probably persuade him to take them home with him for the night, if you think it's a good idea."

"I think it's an outstanding idea, if you're sure."

"I haven't been sure of a lot for a very long time, but I am a hundred percent sure about this."

"And after?" he asked. "What do you envision happening next?"

She hesitated. "I haven't thought any further than what I want tonight, to be in your arms."

"Well, I have." He drew in a deep breath. "I need to say this first. I want you to know that I loved my wife. Amy was my world."

"I know that," she said, scared of where this might be going. Was he going to say this was it, an affair and no more?

"Then you also need to know that a tiny part of my heart must have been held in reserve for you all that time, because when this thing started between us, it felt right from the very beginning. It felt as if we were destined to find each other at just this time in our lives. So for me, this won't be some one-night stand or a fling. If that's what you have in mind, Lynn, count me out. I want the real deal."

Breathless, she looked into his eyes. "The real deal?"

"Marriage, forever, all of it. I want you to marry me. I want to be a stepdad to your kids. I want to be there when Lexie gets her heart broken so I can help you wipe away her tears." He shrugged. "Or make the life of the kid who hurt her miserable."

She smiled through a few tears of her own. "She'd like that."

"And I want to keep teaching Jeremy what I know about construction. Maybe it'll be his calling. Maybe not, but I like the idea of passing it along. My own boys weren't interested." His gaze held hers. "And I want to make you happy. I want to make sure you spend the rest of your life with no cares in the world."

"I doubt you can ensure that," she said, "but I love you for wanting to try."

"So?" he asked. "What do you say? What do *you* want?"

She drew in a deep breath. Just coming after him this

afternoon had been a risk. The next step seemed astonishingly risk-free. "I want to spend the rest of my life with you," she said softly. "I don't think I realized how much I wanted that until just this minute."

Mitch stood up, still holding her tight, and spun her around until she was a little dizzy. Then he studied her intently. "That was a yes, right?"

She laughed. "It was definitely, absolutely yes."

"It'll be sunset soon," he pointed out. "Should we toast our future at my place with a glass of lemonade?"

"Isn't Luke around?"

Mitch muttered a frustrated curse under his breath that had her smiling.

"You know there's a big tradition in this town for romances getting started at the Serenity Inn," she told him. She touched a hand to his cheek, felt the heat rise. "From what I've seen those romances tend to last."

Mitch shook his head. "Darlin', I want more for us."

"And we'll have it," she promised. "We'll have a whole lifetime of more and better and the very best, but for now I just want you to love me."

"Would a fancy dinner after be in order?" he teased.

She smiled. "Let's see how it goes," she said. "We might not be out of bed by dinnertime."

His booming laugh filled the room...and her heart.

Mitch leaned on an elbow and studied the woman stretched out beside him. They were in this forever now. Even if making love to Lynnie hadn't cinched the deal for him, the gossip that was bound to be making its way straight to Wharton's by now would demand it. The Serenity Inn might have sheltered many a romantic tryst over the years, but Maybelle wasn't known for keeping the word of those trysts to herself.

Lynn sighed next to him, then stretched, showing off that gorgeous body of hers and distracting him from his best intentions to take her out to celebrate.

"You're awake," she murmured in surprise. "Why didn't you wake me up?"

"I was content just looking at you," he said. "This has been a long time coming. I wanted to savor every second."

She smiled at him. "In case I haven't mentioned it, you've made me feel like a new woman." She paused then added, "*Your* woman. And this may not make a lot of sense to you, so you'll have to trust me, but I have never been loved like this, Mitch. Never."

Mitch smiled. "That was the goal. I love you, Lynnie." He studied her, his expression sobering. There was something he needed to know. "What brought this on? I mean I know we were destined to get here, but today? What happened?"

"You seduced me," she said, her tone a little too flip.

"I think I could make a strong case that this was on your mind when you found me working on those renovations downtown."

"Yeah, it kinda was," she said. "I thought we'd waited way too long."

"You're not going to tell me what Ed said or did that brought on your change of heart, are you?"

She shook her head. "I can't, Mitch. Can you accept that I might never be able to tell you everything?"

Mitch thought about that. Secrets were no way to start a relationship, but something told him this would be an exception he'd have to learn to live with. "Because you made a promise?" he asked.

She nodded.

"Then I'll have to honor that," he said. "But no more secrets, okay? They're death to a marriage."

Her lips curved into a smile filled with irony. "No one knows that better than I do," she said. "Believe me."

He reached over, stroked a hand along the curve of her hip, felt her skin blaze beneath his touch. "So, do you want to go out for dinner?"

She shook her head. "I want to stay here and talk about the future."

"Our future?"

"Yes. Is that presumptuous of me?"

"Hardly. As Helen would say, I think that question's been asked and answered. We will get married."

"I'm not a hundred percent sure I recall a proposal," she teased.

"Really? Well, let me correct that right now. Will you do me the honor of marrying me, Lynnie? I promise to love and cherish you all the days of our lives. I'll support whatever you decide you want to do, though personally I'm really counting on your moving forward with that bakery idea."

"Even though you could have me as your own personal baker all the time?"

"Even then," he said. "I want you to do whatever will fulfill you. I want you to be your own woman, so you'll never be scared again. Doesn't matter if it's the bakery or something else. Your choice."

"I think I really, really want to open the bakery," she finally dared to admit.

He chuckled. "Good thing, because I've been looking at fancy professional ovens and have a few things on hold."

She slapped at him. "You were that sure of yourself?"

"I was that sure of you."

"Then you probably know what I'm going to say to your marriage proposal, don't you?"

"I hope I do, but I can't wait to hear it from your lips."

"Yes," she said softly. "Yes, I'll marry you, Mitch. Just as soon as all this messiness with Ed is behind me, I will marry you."

"Think Lexie and Jeremy will be okay with it?"

"I think they'll be over the moon. What about Nate and Luke?"

"Luke will be onboard. Nate will come around."

"I don't want to come between you and your son, Mitch."

"I won't let that happen," he assured her.

Because this was too important not to get it right. By the time they walked down the aisle as man and wife, there would be no shadows to darken the way. He'd make sure of that. He'd been blessed once before by love. Now he could count himself twice-blessed. What man could possibly ask for more than that?

Epilogue

"Why on earth do you want to stop by the bakery at this time of night?" Lynn asked Mitch after their dinner at Rosalina's with the kids. "You can't possibly be hungry."

"I have a craving for one of those red velvet cupcakes of yours," he said. "And I know for a fact there were three left over when you closed up. That's exactly enough for me, Jeremy and Lexie."

"All right!" Jeremy said, giving a fist pump from the backseat. "Now that you've got the bakery, Mom, you never make cupcakes at home."

"Oh, please," Lexie scoffed. "You stop by the bakery every day after school and look pitiful till Mom gives you whatever you want."

Mitch grinned. "Does that mean you don't want your cupcake?" he asked Lexie. "Because I can manage to eat two."

Lexie rolled her eyes dramatically. "Don't even think about it," she warned as Mitch pulled into a parking space in front of the darkened bakery. "That cupcake has my name all over it."

Lynn shook her head at the friendly bickering and

reached into her purse for the key. She held it out to Mitch. "Go ahead. You obviously know where they are."

She thought she detected a flash of alarm on his face, but maybe she'd only imagined it since he immediately shook his head and said, "No way. That alarm system is still a mystery to me."

"Don't blame me. You were the one who insisted I have it installed." She climbed out of his truck, unlocked the bakery door, then quickly punched in the alarm code on the box just inside, only to have all the lights come on and shouts of "Surprise!" echo off the walls.

With her hand on her chest, where her heart seemed to be beating wildly, Lynn looked around and into the faces of her friends. Every single one of the Sweet Magnolias was in the room, along with the three women who thought of themselves as the Senior Magnolias—Flo, Liz and even Frances.

Lexie danced in front of her, delight written all over her face. "Are you really surprised, Mom? You didn't have any idea they were going to throw you a bridal shower?"

"No idea," she managed to whisper, her eyes welling with tears. She turned to Mitch. "You knew?"

"Of course he did," Helen said. "It was up to him and the kids to get you here without letting you get suspicious."

"I had to keep the secret, too," Jeremy said, grinning as he added triumphantly, "And I did it!"

"Yes, you did," Lynn said, giving her son a hug. "I nearly had a heart attack when all the lights came on."

Jeremy looked around at all the women gathered there, then gave her a plaintive look. "But there are cupcakes, right?"

"Of course there are," Raylene assured him. "Grace Wharton put in a huge order yesterday, claiming she wanted to give them a try in the restaurant." She gestured to the counter, which had been set up with a beautiful tiered arrangement of cupcakes, plates of cookies and, of course, margaritas. A huge pile of presents graced the end of the counter.

"I'm afraid the margaritas are nonalcoholic tonight," Helen said with unmistakable regret. "At least three women in this room are pregnant, three have no business drinking," she added with a pointed look at her mother, Liz and Frances, "and the rest of us are making a huge sacrifice to keep Carter from feeling the need to raid the premises."

The tears she'd been fighting spilled down Lynn's cheeks then. It wasn't enough that these friends had supported her in getting Sweet Things opened and had sent more than enough business her way, now they were here to celebrate her upcoming marriage to Mitch, which was less than a week away.

Without their unwavering support, she wondered if they'd have made it this far, especially after the news of Ed's relationship with Jimmy Bob had broken and set the town on its collective backside. She'd needed their help in making Lexie and Jeremy believe that the news wasn't the end of the world, that he was the same dad as before and that nothing could change the fact that their dad loved them to pieces.

She had no idea how Helen, Raylene and the others had accomplished it, but she'd not heard of a single cutting remark being made in the presence of her children, not even at school, where old lessons about bullying had apparently had a lasting effect. Even their grandmother's tart tongue had finally been silenced, though if there had been a way to blame this turn of events on Lynn, she was sure her mother-in-law would have found it.

"Okay, Mitch, you can go now," Raylene said, urging him toward the door. "You, too, Jeremy."

"Hey, I'm the groom," Mitch protested halfheartedly. "Shouldn't I get to stay?"

"You'll see these presents soon enough," Raylene told him with a spark of mischief in her eyes. "And, trust me, you're going to want privacy when that time comes."

Lynn felt a blush steal into her cheeks, even as Mitch's face turned an even deeper shade of red. He nodded toward the pile of presents. "Lingerie?"

"You bet," Helen said.

He winked at Lynn then. "In that case, I'll see you at home later."

"But there's an embargo on the lingerie till the honeymoon," Helen said with mock severity. "Understood?"

Mitch planted a kiss on Helen's cheek. "Counselor, correct me if I'm wrong, but I don't think there's a law on the books that would prevent Lynn from giving me a private showing tonight. I'm counting on that."

Jeremy went with him without protest, two cupcakes in hand. Mitch had stolen a couple, as well.

"I thought they'd never go," Maddie grumbled with a grin. "Now let's get this party started. Hon, you have a lot to celebrate."

Once again, tears welled up in Lynn's eyes. "I sure do," she whispered. "And you guys are right at the top of the list."

"Higher than Mitch?" Helen challenged, though there was a spark of amusement in her eyes.

"No one's higher than Mitch or my kids," Lynn said, drawing Lexie close. "But you all are right up there. I never knew how much it meant to have friends like you, the kind who are there at a moment's notice, who listen without making judgments, who'll whip up a margarita at the first sign of a crisis. You're the best."

"To the Sweet Magnolias!" Dana Sue said, lifting her glass.

"To the Sweet Magnolias!" the others chimed in.

"What about me?" Lexie asked. "Mandy and I want to be Sweet Magnolias, too. So do Carrie and Katie and Misty."

The three original Sweet Magnolias—Helen, Maddie and Dana Sue—exchanged a look. "Your day will come, I imagine," Maddie promised. "You already have exactly what it takes."

"What's that?" Lexie asked.

"You understand the meaning of real friendship," Helen explained. "You've all proven that at one time or another. So has every woman in this room."

Maddie linked arms with Helen and Dana Sue, then said quietly, "To lifelong friends!"

"And to those we've come to know," Dana Sue added. "Love you guys."

Once Lynn would have felt like an outsider, but now she basked in the knowledge that she was one of them. And when she walked down the aisle to marry Mitch, they'd be there cheering her on. She'd wanted at least one of them to stand up for her at the ceremony, but it had been impossible to choose. Instead, Lexie would be at her side, and her friends would be in the pews reserved for family. Exactly where they belonged.

* * * * *

Don't miss the next book in the Sweet Magnolias series
Keep reading for a sneak peek of Swan Point
by #1 New York Times *bestselling author Sherryl Woods.*

One

Adelia watched with her heart in her throat as the moving van pulled away from the crumbling curb in Swan Point, one of the oldest and, at one time, finest neighborhoods in Serenity, South Carolina. With moss-draped oaks in perfectly maintained yards backing up to a small, man-made lake, which was home to several swans, the houses had been large and stately by early standards.

Now, though, most of the homes, like this one, were showing signs of age. She found something fitting about the prospect of filling this historic old house with laughter and giving it a new lease on life. It would be as if the house and her family were moving into the future together.

Letting go of the old life, however, was proving more difficult than she'd anticipated. Drawing in a deep breath, she turned to deal with the accusing looks of her four children, who weren't nearly as convinced as she was that they were about to have an exciting fresh start.

Her youngest, Tomas, named for his grandfather on her ex-husband's side of the family, turned to her with tears streaming down his cheeks. "Mommy, I don't like it here.

I want to go home. This house is old. It smells funny. And there's no pool."

She knelt down in front of the eight-year-old and gathered him close, gathered all of them close, even her oldest, Selena.

It was Selena who understood better than any of them why this move had been necessary. While they all knew that Adelia and their father had divorced, Selena had seen Ernesto more than once with one of his mistresses. In a move that defied logic or compassion, he'd even had the audacity to introduce the most recent woman to Selena while he and Adelia were still making a pretense at least of trying to keep their marriage intact. His action had devastated Selena and it had been the final straw for Adelia. She'd seen at last that tolerating such disrespect was the wrong example to set for her three girls and even for her son.

"I know you'd rather be in our old house," she comforted them with a hitch in her voice. "But it's just not possible. This is home now. I really think you're going to love it once we get settled in."

She ruffled Tomas's hair. "And don't worry about the funny smell. It's just been shut up for a few months. It'll smell fine once we air it out and put fresh paint on the walls." She injected a deliberately cheerful note into her voice. "We can all sit down and decide how we want to fix it up. Then you can go with me to the hardware store to pick out the paint colors for your rooms."

The girls expressed enthusiasm for the idea, but Tomas remained visibly skeptical.

"What about the pool?" he asked sullenly.

"We can use the town pool," Selena said staunchly, even though there were tears in her eyes, too. "It's even bigger than the one at home, and our friends will be there. And since we're living so close to downtown now, we can walk to the bakery after school for cupcakes, then stop in and see Mom at work. Or go across the green to Wharton's for ice cream."

Natalia sniffed, but Adelia saw a spark of interest in her eyes.

"I like ice cream," eleven-year-old Natalia whispered, then nudged Tomas. "You do, too."

"Me, too," Juanita chimed in. Until the divorce Adelia's nine-year-old had been boundlessly enthusiastic about everything, but this was the first sign in weeks that her high spirits were returning.

Tomas continued to look unconvinced. "Will *Abuela* be able to find us here?" he asked doubtfully.

"Of course," Adelia assured him. Tomas adored her mother, who'd been babysitting him practically from infancy because of all the school committees on which Adelia had found herself and, more recently, because she was working at a boutique on Main Street. "She helped me to find this house."

Amazingly, for once, her mother had kept her lectures on divorce to herself and professed to see all the positives in the new life Adelia was fashioning for her children. She'd told stories about the days when the elite in town had lived in Swan Point. There had been lavish parties in this very house, she'd reported to Adelia. She'd stuck to focusing on the possibilities in the house and the quiet, tree-shaded neighborhood, not the negatives.

Her mother's support had actually given Adelia the courage to move forward. To her surprise, Adelia had recognized that even in her thirties, she still craved her mother's approval. It was one of the many reasons she'd waited so long to end her travesty of a marriage.

"Can we still go to *Abuela*'s house for cookies?" her son pressed.

"Absolutely," Adelia said. "You can go every day after school if you like, the same as always."

Though he was starting to look relieved, a sudden frown crossed his face. "What about Papa? Is he going to live here, too? He won't like it, I'll bet. He likes our real house, same as me."

Selena whirled on him. "You know perfectly well he doesn't live with us anymore. He's not coming here. Not ever! He's going to live in our old house with somebody else."

Adelia winced at the disdain and hurt in her oldest's voice. Ever since she'd realized that her father had been openly cheating on Adelia, Selena had claimed she wanted no part of him. Her attitude had hardened even more when she'd overheard Ernesto describing her as her mother's child in a tone that made clear he wasn't complimenting either one of them.

Adelia had even spoken to a psychologist about this rift between father and daughter, but the woman had assured her that it wasn't unusual for an impressionable teenager— Selena had just turned thirteen—to react so strongly to a divorce, especially when Ernesto's cheating had been so public and when he'd shown no remorse at all once he'd been caught. In fact, he'd remained defiant to the bitter end, so much so that even the judge had lost patience with him.

At Selena's angry words, Tomas's eyes once again filled with tears.

"Enough," Adelia warned her daughter. To Tomas and

the younger girls, she said, "You'll still be able to see your father whenever you want to." Like Tomas, Natalia and Juanita looked relieved, though they carefully avoided looking at their big sister, clearly fearing her disapproval. That was yet another rift she'd have to work on healing, Adelia concluded with a sigh. Ernesto certainly wouldn't make any effort to do it.

As hurt as she'd been and as much as she'd wanted to banish Ernesto from her life forever, she'd accepted that her kids deserved to have a relationship with their dad. It would be selfish of her to deny them that.

Besides, she'd had enough explaining to do to the rest of her rigidly Catholic family when she'd opted for divorce. Then, to top it off, she'd insisted on moving out of the huge house on the outskirts of town that Ernesto had apparently thought was reasonable compensation for his infidelity. Her sisters had been appalled by all of it—the scandal of Ernesto's cheating, the divorce and the move. Keeping her children away from their father—however distasteful his behavior—would have caused even more of an uproar.

Not that Adelia cared what any of them thought at this point. She'd made the only decision she could make. Her only goal now was to make this transition as easy for the children as possible. She'd do it with as much cheerfulness as she could possibly muster. She might not even have to fake it, since on some level she was actually eager for this fresh start.

For now, though, she forced a smile and looked each of them in the eye. "I have an idea," she announced, hoping to turn this difficult day around.

"What?" Tomas asked suspiciously.

"I think we all deserve a treat after such a long day."

"Pizza?" Natalia asked hopefully.

Adelia laughed. Natalia would eat pizza three times a day if she were allowed to.

"Yes, pizza," she confirmed.

"Not here, though," Tomas pleaded, wrinkling his nose in distaste.

"No, not here. The dishes aren't unpacked," she said. "We'll go to Rosalina's. I'll call your uncle Elliott and see if he and Aunt Karen would like to join us with Daisy, Mack and the baby."

This last was offered especially for Selena, who adored her uncle and who'd become especially close to his adopted daughter, Daisy. Adelia might not intend to keep Ernesto away from his children, but Elliott was the male role model she really wanted in their lives. Her younger brother was loving, rock solid and dependable. She'd be proud to see Tomas grow up to be just like him. And she desperately hoped her girls would eventually find men like him, too.

Once the decision to divorce had been made, Elliott had overcome all his own strong objections to offer her the support she'd desperately needed. She owed Karen for bringing him—and even her mother—around. Her own sisters continued to treat her as if she'd committed a mortal sin.

The prospect of pizza at Rosalina's with Uncle Elliott and his family wiped away the last of the tears, and Adelia took a truly relieved breath for what seemed like the first time all day. Her family was going to be all right. There might be a few bumps along the way, thanks to her determination to shed any of her own ties to Ernesto, but they would settle into this new house.

And, she concluded with new resolve, they would turn

it into a real home, one filled with love and respect, something that had been in short supply with her ex-husband.

Gabe Franklin had claimed a booth in the back corner of Rosalina's for the fourth night in a row. Back in Serenity for less than a week and living at the Serenity Inn, he'd figured this was better than the bar across town for a man who'd determined to sober up and live life on the straight and narrow. That was the whole point of coming home, after all, to prove he'd changed and deserved a second chance. Once he'd accomplished that and made peace with his past, well, he'd decide whether to move on yet again. He wasn't sure he was the kind of man who'd ever put down roots.

Thank heaven for his cousin, Mitch Franklin, who'd offered him a job starting on Monday without a moment's hesitation. Recently remarried, Mitch claimed he needed a partner who knew construction so he could focus on his new family. He'd taken on a second family just as he'd started developing a series of dilapidated properties on Main Street in an attempt to revitalize downtown Serenity.

Gabe had listened in astonishment to Mitch's ambitious plans as he'd laid them out. Despite his cousin's enthusiasm, Gabe wasn't convinced revitalization was possible in an economy still struggling to rebound, but he was more than willing to jump in and give it a shot. Maybe there would be something cathartic about giving those old storefronts the same kind of second chance he was hoping to grab for himself.

"You're turning into a real regular in here," his waitress, a middle-aged woman who'd introduced herself a few nights ago as Debbie, said. "Are you new in town?"

"Not exactly," he said, returning her smile but adding no details. "I'll have—"

"A large diet soda and a large pepperoni pizza," she filled in before he could complete his order.

Gabe winced. "I'm obviously in a rut."

"That's okay. Most of our regulars order the same thing every time," she said. "And I pay attention. Friendly service and a good memory get me bigger tips."

"I'll remember that," he said, then sat back and looked around the restaurant while waiting for his food.

Suddenly he sat up a little straighter as a dark-haired woman came in with four children. Even though she looked a little harried and a whole lot weary, she was stunning with her olive complexion and high cheekbones. She was also vaguely familiar, though he couldn't put a name to the face.

There hadn't been a lot of Mexican-American families in Serenity back when he'd lived here as a kid, though there had been plenty of transient farmworkers during the summer months. For a minute he cursed the way he'd blown off school way more often than he should have. Surely if he'd gone regularly, this woman would have been on his radar. If there had been declared majors in high school, his would have been girls. He'd studied them the way the academic overachievers had absorbed the information in textbooks.

Instead, he'd been kicked out midway through his junior year for one too many fights, every one of them justified to his juvenile way of thinking. He'd eventually wised up and gotten his GED. He'd even attended college for a couple of years, but that had been later, when he'd stopped hating the world for the way it had treated his troubled single mom and started putting the pieces of his life back together.

He watched now as the intriguing woman asked for several tables to be pushed together. He noted with disappointment when a man with two children came in to join them. So, he thought, she was married with six kids. An unfamiliar twinge of envy left him feeling vaguely unsettled. Since when had he been interested in having a family of any size? Still, he couldn't seem to tear his gaze away from the picture of domestic bliss they presented. The teasing and laughter seemed to settle in his heart and make it just a little lighter.

When his waitress returned with his drink, he nodded in the woman's direction. "Quite a family," he commented. "I can't imagine having six kids. They look like quite a handful."

Debbie laughed. "Oh, they're a handful, all right, but they're not all Adelia's. That's her brother, Elliott Cruz, who just came in with two of his. He has a baby, too, but I guess she was getting a cold, so his wife stayed home with her."

Gabe hid a grin. Thank heaven for chatty waitresses and a town known for gossiping. It hadn't been so great when he was a boy and his promiscuous mother had been the talk of the town, but now he could appreciate it.

"Where's her husband?"

The waitress leaned down and confided, "Sadly, not in hell where he belongs. The man cheated on her repeatedly and the whole town knew about it. She finally kicked his sorry butt to the curb. Too bad the whole town couldn't follow suit and divorce him." She flushed, and her expression immediately filled with guilt. "Sorry. I shouldn't have said that, but Adelia's a great woman and she didn't deserve the way Ernesto Hernandez treated her."

Gabe nodded. "Sounds like a real gem," he said.

In fact, he sounded like a lot of the men who'd passed through his mom's life over the years. Gabe felt a sudden surge of empathy for Adelia. And he liked the fact that his waitress was firmly in her corner. He suspected the rest of the town was, too, just the way they'd always stood up for the wronged wives when his mom had been the other woman in way too many relationships.

Funny what a few years could do to give a man a new perspective. Back then all he'd cared about was the gossip, the taunts he'd suffered at school and his mom's tears each time the relationships inevitably ended. He'd witnessed her hope whenever a new man came into her life and then the slow realization that this time would be no different. His heart had broken almost as many times as hers.

Still, he couldn't help thinking about all the complications that came with a woman in Adelia's situation. He had enough on his own plate without getting mixed up in her drama. Much as he might enjoy sitting right here and staring, it would be far better to slip away right now and avoid the powerful temptation to reach out to her. Heaven knew, he had nothing to offer a woman, not yet, anyway.

"Darlin', could you make that pizza of mine to go?" he asked his waitress.

"Sure thing," Debbie said readily.

She brought it out within minutes. As Gabe paid the check, she grinned. "I imagine I'll see you again tomorrow. Maybe you'll try something different."

"Maybe so," he agreed, then winked. "But don't count on it. I'm comfortable in this rut I'm in."

She shook her head, then glanced pointedly in Adelia's

direction. "Seems to me that's just when you need to shake things up."

Gabe followed the direction of her gaze and found the very woman in question glancing his way. His heart, which hadn't been engaged in much more than keeping him alive these past few years, did a fascinating little stutter step.

No way, he told himself determinedly as he headed for the door and the safety of his comfortable, if uninviting, room at the Serenity Inn. He'd never been much good at multitasking. Right now his only goal was to prove himself to Mitch and to himself. Complications were out of the question. And the beautiful Adelia Hernandez and her four kids had complication written all over them.

"Looks as if somebody has an admirer," Elliott commented to Adelia. Though his tone was light, there was a frown on his face as he watched the stranger leaving Rosalina's.

"Hush!" Adelia said, though she was blushing. She leaned closer to her brother. "That is not the sort of thing you should be saying in front of the kids. The ink's barely dry on my divorce papers."

Elliott laughed. "The kids are clear across the restaurant playing video games. You're only flustered because you know I'm right. That guy was attracted to you, Adelia. I recognize that thunderstruck expression on a man's face. I wore it a lot when I first met Karen. I saw it in the mirror when I shaved. It happened every time she crossed my mind."

Adelia smiled at the memory of her little brother falling hard for a woman no one in the family had approved of at first simply because she'd divorced a deadbeat husband. Elliott had fought hard to ensure that they all came to accept Karen and her kids and love them as much as he did. After her own marital troubles, Adelia had come to admire her sister-in-law's strength.

"You were a goner from the moment you laid eyes on her, weren't you?" she said.

"No question about it," he said. "I still am, and I don't see that ever changing. I want that happily-ever-after kind of love for you."

"Maybe someday," she said, not really able to imagine a time when she'd be willing to risk her heart again.

Elliott nodded in the direction of the door. "So, any idea who your admirer is?"

"Stop calling him that," she ordered, blushing again.

"Just calling it like I see it," he teased. "And it's nice to see some color in your cheeks."

She gave him a mock frown. "Don't make me sorry I called you tonight," she scolded. "There are some aggravations I can't avoid, but you're not one of them."

He grinned. "You needed me here to help you corral those kids. And don't even try to pretend that you didn't enjoy the way that man was looking at you. You're not just a mom. You're a woman. You've seen far too little of that sort of appreciation in recent years."

"That may be so, but I'm not even remotely interested in dating anytime soon," she repeated emphatically, though she knew she was wasting her breath. Her brother loved getting under her skin and he'd just found a new way to do exactly that.

"You didn't recognize him?" he persisted, proving her point that he didn't intend to let this drop. "You work right downtown. You're involved in every activity in the school system. You see people all day long."

She shook her head. "I've never seen him before. He must be new in town."

"And Grace Wharton hasn't sent out a news bulletin?" he asked, only partially in jest. Grace, who ran the soda fountain at the local drugstore, prided herself on knowing all the comings and goings in town and being the first to spread the word. "Or are you just pretending that you missed the latest edition?"

Adelia tried a stern look that on rare occasions worked with her kids. "Drop this, please. There's been enough turmoil in my life these past months to last a lifetime. These days I'm a mom first and foremost. I need to get the kids settled in our new house and on an emotional even keel. That's my only focus for now."

"You're still a vibrant, attractive woman," Elliott reminded her, clearly undeterred by her expression or her words. "You deserve to find a man, the right man, who'll appreciate and respect you in a way that Ernesto never did." His expression darkened. "I still wish you'd let me teach him a lesson about mistreating my big sister."

She almost smiled at his zealous desire to stand up for her but didn't because she didn't want to encourage him. "I dealt with Ernesto. Thanks to Helen Decatur-Whitney, he'll be paying for his misdeeds with those generous support payments for the kids for years to come. Every penny is going in the bank. They'll have enough money tucked away to attend any college they choose when the time comes."

"I still don't get why you refused any alimony," Elliott told her, his frustration plain. "The man owed you, Adelia. You have a business degree, but you never used it so you could concentrate on being the perfect wife and mother. Who knows what you might have achieved by now if you'd started a career after college?"

"Being a wife and mother was the career I chose," she told him. "I don't regret that for a second. Now that I'm a single mom, I'll put just as much energy into working and being a good parent. Being independent is important to me, Elliott. I need to know I'm in control of my life."

"I'm just saying that Ernesto's money might have made it easier," he argued.

"Don't forget that Helen got enough money in a lump sum to pay for the new house and to keep our heads above water for a year, longer if I'm careful. I'm making decent money at the boutique, especially since Raylene made me the manager. I want to show my girls they can grow up to take care of themselves."

"I guess that's an admirable goal," he said, though his tone was doubtful.

She smiled at him. "Isn't that what your wife did after her husband left her with a mountain of debt? Karen made a life for herself and her kids. It was a struggle, but she persevered. That's one of the reasons you fell for her, because she was strong in the face of adversity."

"I suppose." He grinned. "But then she found me and now it's my mission to take care of her and our family."

"Funny," she said. "Karen seems to think you have a partnership."

Her brother winced at the reminder. "Sorry. Apparently the Cruz macho tendencies die hard."

"As long as they die," she told him. "But I'll leave it to Karen to teach you that lesson."

Elliott frowned. "How did we get off track and start

talking about my marriage? We were talking about you and that man who just walked out of here after giving you a thorough once-over."

"While the idea of any man staring at me appreciatively is a welcome change," she conceded, "I'm not looking for a relationship now. Maybe never. How many times do I need to say that before you believe me?"

Elliott looked dismayed rather than convinced by her response. "Don't let what Ernesto did shape the rest of your life, Adelia," he said fiercely. "Not all men are like that."

"You're certainly not," she agreed. "And for that I am eternally grateful." She touched his cheek. "I imagine Karen feels the same way. She must count her blessings every night."

"*Most* nights," her brother corrected with a grin. "At least when she's not exasperated with me for one thing or another, like forgetting about that whole partnership thing, for instance."

"Yes, I can see how you might test a woman's patience," she told him. "As a boy you were certainly a pest."

"Gee, thanks."

She patted his cheek again. "Don't fret, *mi hermano*. We all wind up loving you just the same. Even though this conversation is making me a little crazy, I know you mean well and I love you for caring."

Elliott's expression suddenly sobered. "Adelia, promise me something, okay?"

"Anything."

"If a man comes along, you'll leave yourself open to the possibilities. I'm not talking about the man who just left here, but any man."

"Any man?" she echoed, amused.

"After I've checked him out thoroughly," he amended.

"Now *that* sounds much more like the overly protective brother I know and love," Adelia said.

"Promise," he repeated.

Though she couldn't imagine it would be a promise she'd have to keep, at least not anytime soon, Adelia nodded. "Promise."

Just then the pizza and the kids arrived at the table simultaneously and, thankfully, further conversation was impossible.

Time and time again, though, she found herself glancing toward the door and thinking about the man who'd cast a lingering look in her direction. Whether it was the openly appreciative way he'd studied her or her brother's teasing, she felt the oddest sensation stirring deep inside. It was a sensation she hadn't anticipated and didn't especially want, but it felt a whole lot as if she might be coming alive again.

Don't miss Swan Point
A Sweet Magnolias novel
Available wherever MIRA books are sold!

Catch up with all things Sweet Magnolias from
#1 *New York Times* bestselling author

SHERRYL WOODS

Read the books that inspired the hit Netflix series!

  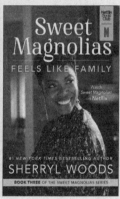

MSW8630MAX

Raise a glass and treat yourself to the official cookbook of the Sweet Magnolias, with original recipes celebrating the flavor and fragrance of the South.